Island Tales

Volume 1

Waiting for a Prince

&

September's Tide

K.C. Wells

Island Tales Volume 1

Copyright © 2014 by K.C. Wells

Edited by S.A. Laybourn

Cover Art by AJ Corza

From K.C. Wells

The Personal Series
Making it Personal
Personal Changes
More than Personal
Personal Secrets

Une Affaire Personnelle
(Making it Personal - French Edition)

Island Tales
Waiting for a Prince
September's Tide

Learning to Love
Michael & Sean
Evan & Daniel
Josh & Chris

Collars & Cuffs
An Unlocked Heart
Trusting Thomas
Someone to Keep Me (with Parker Williams)

Fifty Gays of Shade (anthology)
Winning Will's Heart

Burning First Kiss (anthology)
Back from the Edge

Island Tale #1

Waiting for a Prince

Dedication

For Mark Reed

Thank you for that moment of inspiration
when I glimpsed you in the mirror.

Chapter One

"I really feel sorry for that poor bloke."

Mark paused momentarily in his task of dyeing the new hair extension pieces. "Which bloke?" He was engrossed. Marie had already given him the evil eye twice that morning, and if he didn't get this finished, there was every possibility that she'd start with the *'there are loads of wannabe hairdressers out there just clamoring to get into your shoes'* talk—again. He gave a cursory glance around the salon. "What are you talking about?" he muttered under his breath to Wendy. "We haven't got any male customers in here at the moment." He went back to his task, irritated that she'd spoiled his concentration. Hopefully she'd take the hint and leave him to it.

No such luck. Wendy huffed. "He's not a customer, silly." She nudged his arm and almost sent the bowl containing the hair dye into a dive over the unit. She made a noise of insincere apology. Mark scowled and ignored her as he carefully sponged the dye over each tress, taking extra pains to ensure it got even coverage.

"Look over there," she hissed. "On the couch in the window."

Oh, for God's sake, woman, leave me alone. Mark dropped the sponge into the bowl and straightened, about to tell Wendy where to go, when he felt the hairs stand up on the back of his neck. He twisted around. Yeah, Marie was there all right, her gaze boring into him.

Oh hell, that was all he needed.

He winced, preparing himself for the inevitable request for '*a word, please, Mark.*' Christ, he was hearing that more and more these days.

"Mark, can you come over here a minute please, sweetie?"

Sonia's melodic voice carried above the chatter and the low, unobtrusive music playing in the background. Mark could have kissed her, except for the fact that she had totally the wrong equipment. Avoiding Marie's steely gaze, he hung up the hairpiece and crossed the salon floor to where Sonia had just finished speaking with her customer.

"Mark, would you make my lady a cup of tea, please?" Sonia's eyes twinkled. Yeah, she knew exactly what she was doing. It was sweet of her, stepping into the fray like that, but Mark knew Marie would still have her pound of flesh at the end of the day. Sonia leaned lower to speak to her customer. "Milk and sugar?"

The woman in the chair gave a bored nod. "Just milk, please." Mark met her gaze in the mirror and smiled politely. She rolled her eyes and gave her attention to the celebrity magazine on her lap while Sonia readied the shiny strips of foil required for the hair color.

Mark studied the woman, who seemed to be in her early twenties. He estimated that she would have been quite pretty, but for the hard lines around her mouth and that crease between her eyes. Her lips were thin, not a sign of a happy person in Mark's experience.

He couldn't tell what she was wearing due to the black salon cape which pretty much covered her entirely.

He glanced down at her feet. Expensive-looking shoes. *A*ha. *Comes from money and treats everyone like they're a turd she's just stepped in.* Mark didn't recall seeing her in the salon before. Most of Hair Today's clientele were down-to-earth ladies who always had a kind word and a smile for the staff. And they certainly didn't come with a ton of attitude like this one.

Sonia moved to the red leather sofa which sat in the window. Mark followed her movement and his heart gave a jolt. *Oh yeah, baby...* The man reclining there somewhat awkwardly was tall, maybe over six feet, which was just *perfect*, thank you very much. Mark bit his lip as he took in the earrings, diamond studs and a gold ring. His gaze traveled lower and he caught his breath at the sight of the man's nipple rings, pressed against his white long-sleeved shirt. Not to mention the dark swirls of a tattoo hidden from view, but visible nonetheless. Mark's dick stiffened. *Oh honey, you are my idea of heaven.* Tending toward the skinny side of lean, with short brown hair, just how Mark liked them.

"Would you like a cup of tea?" Sonia offered, kindly. "While you're waiting?"

Mark's future husband opened his mouth to speak but the woman cut him off.

"He doesn't want a drink." The harsh quality of her voice made Mark wince. She swiveled in her chair. "Do you, Sam?" That crease deepened as she glared at the man. *God, she could give Marie a run for her money in the bitch stakes.*

He watched as Sam sagged even lower into the couch.

"In fact, I'm not even sure why you're still here."

Her eyes narrowed. "Surely you have something else you can be doing." She looked down her sharp little nose at him.

Sam dropped his gaze to the floor. Mark could understand that reaction. "No, everything's done for the day." God, even his *voice* was dreamy. "I'll just sit here, if that's okay, and wait till you're done." A pair of blue eyes came into view and Mark felt his knees go weak. "But actually, I *would* like a cup of tea, if it's no trouble. Milk with two sugars."

It took a second or two for it to register that Sam was addressing Mark. Flustered, Mark gave a quick nod, knowing full well his cheeks were already heating up. Why the hell did he always have to blush so easily? He escaped thankfully into the little room behind the reception desk and set about making two cups of tea. While he waited for the kettle to boil, he had a surreptitious glance through the open door at the gorgeous specimen. *Christ, he has long legs.* They were encased in a sinfully tight pair of fashionably worn jeans. Mark couldn't help taking a sneaky peek at Sam's package. He let out a quiet whimper. *And he's hung.* For a moment Mark allowed himself the luxury of imagining those long, lean legs wrapped around his waist as he fucked Sam through the mattress, those blue eyes staring wildly up at him as Mark nailed him repeatedly, that sexy voice begging Mark not to stop, to fuck him deeper. Then reality bit hard. *It's not gonna happen, babe. One, the guy is straight, and two, even if he* were *gay by some miracle, Please God, no* way *would* that *Adonis be a bottom.* Mark shook his head. Reality really sucked.

Mark placed a cup in front of the woman, noting her studious avoidance of making eye contact with him, and then returned to the kitchen to pick up Sam's cup. He placed it on the low table in front of the couch. Sam glanced up at him and gave a brief tight smile. God, those eyes were even more heavenly up close. "Thanks." The word was almost a whisper.

Mark flashed a quick smile. "No problem, hon." His cheeks flamed as Sam arched his eyebrows. He scooted out of there as fast as his legs could carry him back to the sanctuary of the tiny kitchen. Unseen by anyone, Mark leaned against the wall, expelling the air from his lungs in a long, shaky breath. *Way to go, Mark. Could you have* seemed *any more gay*? He gave himself a mental kick up the backside, his cheeks finally cooling.

"Why are you hiding in here?"

Mark almost hit the ceiling. "Fuck, Sonia, don't *do* that!" She grinned. "I've warned you about sneaking up on me like that." He clutched his chest and Sonia rolled her eyes.

"Get over it, drama queen," she snickered. She poked a slim finger at his chest. "You hiding from Marie or what?" That grin was pure evil.

Mark shook his head. "Not exactly." He peered around her to see if Sam was looking his way. OMG, he was staring toward the kitchen. Mark ducked his head back in. Sonia's eyes danced with amusement. She peered into the salon. "Son! Don't look!" he implored her.

Sonia's face lit up. "Ah, it's like *that*, is it?" There was that evil grin again. "Does he push your buttons, sweetie?"

Mark groaned. "Every single fucking one of them. What could only make him more perfect would be if he happened to be gay." Thank God he had Sonia to talk to at work. The fact that Mark was gay was no big deal to her and he always felt totally at ease around her. The rest of the girls made all the right noises, but Mark could tell when someone was genuinely comfortable being around him. And as for Marie… The fewer dealings Mark had with her, the better. Too bad she was his boss.

"You can't hide out in here all the while she's having her hair done," Sonia reasoned. "If Marie catches on…"

She didn't have to say another word. "Okay, okay, I'm going," he grumbled. Back to his hairpieces. He trudged out of the kitchen and back to the center unit, keeping his eyes away from the ex-future husband who sat drinking tea. Mark caught Sonia's sympathetic expression as she returned to her client and he shrugged.

For the next hour Mark struggled to keep his mind on the job. It was as though invisible strings kept tugging at his head to turn it toward the window, no matter how hard he fought to concentrate on his mundane task. Each time Marie passed by, however, Mark kept his head down, fervently hoping she saw how caught up he was in his work. But once she'd gone, there was that urge to look at the perfect straight guy just one more time.

"He your type then?"

Mark looked up to find April standing next to him, her arms loaded down with clean towels, her jaw in constant motion as she worked on yet another stick of chewing gum. Mark feigned puzzlement.

April flicked her head toward Sam. "The tall drink of water on the couch." It was evident she was asking to be sociable. April rarely bothered to speak to him. She was usually more interested in what color she could dye her hair next. Today's choice was purple, and together with the purple sparkly eye shadow and lips the color and size of ripe, swollen grapes, she was getting a few glances—and not for the right reasons. Mark was amazed Marie hadn't said anything yet. He glanced at his watch. The day was still young, though.

Mark gave a non-committal shrug. "Not really," he said, lying through his teeth. "I'm not sure I have a type, in any case." Like he'd discuss it with *her*. April gave a bored nod and went on her way, taking with her the odor of spearmint which seemed to surround her all the time. Mark glanced wearily at his watch yet again and gave a sigh. Only six more hours to go. And time for his break. *Yes*!

He nipped into the kitchen and put the kettle on, before dropping a teabag into his mug. He couldn't resist one more glance. He peered out and then froze.

Sam was stony-faced, his gaze fixed on the woman as she glared at him yet again.

"What do you mean, you didn't book the restaurant?" Her voice grated. Mark shivered to see that gimlet-eyed stare.

"Becky, you—"

She cut him off. "I *told* you not to call me that," she gritted out vehemently. "My name is *Rebecca*."

Sam got to his feet and reached for his black leather jacket, which was draped over the back of the couch.

"Well, *Rebecca*, maybe *you've* forgotten that you said you'd changed your mind and you didn't want to go tonight, but *I* haven't suddenly developed amnesia." He slung the jacket over his shoulder. "So I'll talk to you when you've finished here and you've decided to be civil." He squared his shoulders and met her furious gaze. Mark noted the quick swallow as Sam's Adam's apple bobbed, the slight tremor that rippled through his lean body. Sam's brave stance was clearly a smokescreen. The guy was nervous.

"Where the *hell* do you think *you're* going?" Rebecca shrieked as Sam turned and strolled out of the salon onto the bright sunlit street. Mark watched him walk slowly past the window and head toward Union Street, head down. Mark glanced to see how Rebecca was faring. Her cheeks were mottled purple, her eyes almost bulging from their sockets. Sonia was making soothing noises, but Mark could've told her the attempts to placate Rebecca didn't even register on the woman's spectrum. Sonia didn't exist, as far as she was concerned. The shocked stares of the three clients in the salon served only to infuriate her further. Her lips a narrow slash of bright red, she swiveled in her seat to stare at her reflection, silently fuming. Mark wouldn't have been surprised to see steam coming out of her ears. *Wow… lady has a temper.*

Shaking his head, Mark retreated into the kitchen and poured boiling water onto the tea bag. He stood there, eyes closed, fists clenched. Mark hated scenes like this, so reminiscent of his childhood. Christ, Sam could have been his father, only the man had never once stood up to his wife—like Sam had just now—in all their sixteen years of marriage.

Mark fought to maintain his composure. *Don't think about that now. Dad's out of it, thank God.*

The sound of someone clearing their throat had Mark opening his eyes in a hurry, and then sighing with relief when he saw that it was Sonia. She was regarding him anxiously.

"You all right, sweetie?" Her soft voice was like music. Sonia's family came from Portugal, but her accent seemed to be a hybrid of different nationalities. She always spoke kindly to everyone, and give them their due, no one had a bad word to say about the woman. She laid a gentle hand on his arm.

"Has she gone?" Mark asked. The salon was quiet once more, save for the music and the soft murmurs between the stylists and their clients. Sonia nodded and Mark let the breath he'd been holding escape in a long exhale.

"Anything you want to tell me about, Mark?" That hand squeezed his arm.

Mark shook his head, although he was genuinely touched. "Nothing you could help with, Son." He leaned across and kissed her cheek and she blushed "But thank you." She patted his arm and withdrew, leaving him to sip his tea in silence. Unfortunately, a sip or two was all he had time for. Marie stuck her head around the door and tapped her watch.

"But this is my bre—" That was as far as he got before Marie's eyes bulged.

"The salon is a mess, Mark. That's your responsibility, isn't it? That's what I *pay* you for, isn't it?" There was no humor in her thin smile.

Mark gave up. No use arguing with the bitch when she'd plainly had it in for him since the minute he'd walked through the door that morning. "Yes, Marie," he intoned, the words disturbing the air in front of his face, nothing more. With a final glare she withdrew and Mark poured away the tea with a heavy sigh. Back to work.

Five o'clock and Mark was itching to be out of there. The salon was spotless. The center unit was spic and span, not a single stray hair remained on the laminated floor and to the rear of the salon, the second waiting area with its comfy purple leather couch and silk flower arrangements was immaculate. *Let her find fault with* that.

All the girls waited by the door as Marie gave the salon a final check. April and Wendy were already on their phones, no doubt texting their friends as to where they would all meet up. Mark had gone along with them on a couple of occasions, but he hadn't done that for a while now. He'd grown bored of being required to give his opinion of every guy who walked through the main door of the pub. Apparently, being gay meant he fancied every bloke on the Isle of Wight. *Yeah, right.* Carol, the receptionist was talking animatedly with Deb and Janine about a party that she was giving the following month, to which they had all been invited. Sonia was on her phone, talking to her husband Dave. She caught sight of Mark and smiled.

"All done, ladies—and Mark," Marie announced at last, reserving another thin-lipped smile for Mark. "Have a good weekend, and see you next week."

With smiles and polite phrases the staff filed out of the salon, Mark trailing behind. He avoided making eye contact with Marie as he slipped past her, and was relieved to see Sonia waiting for him. The rest of the girls had already dispersed, most of them in the direction of Wetherspoons for a drink or three.

Sonia's eyes sparkled with good humor. "Want to walk with me down Union Street? I'm parked at the bottom today. There were no spaces near here this morning."

Mark nodded. They were going the same way anyway. They turned the corner and began the trek down the steep hill which was the main street in Ryde. Sonia linked her arm through his and they walked down the street in silence for a minute or two.

"What was going on earlier, sweetie?"

Mark's brow furrowed. "When?" The whole day had been shit from beginning to end.

"When I found you in the kitchen. You were looking stressed out."

Mark thought back. "Oh, it was just that woman treating her husband or boyfriend, whatever, like crap."

"Sure that was all?" He could hear the concern. *Bless her*.

Mark squeezed her hand reassuringly. "Yeah, I'm sure. Besides, day over, right?"

She gave an exaggerated sigh. "Hoo, yeah. Dave says he has a delicious dinner waiting for me."

Mark grinned. "Lucky girl." She beamed. She and Dave seemed to be a match made in heaven. The thought sobered him momentarily.

The Isle of Wight wasn't exactly brimming over with gay men. In fact, the pickings were slim.

Sonia squeezed his arm. "You'll find someone, sweetie." He couldn't help but smile. *How does she do that?* Sonia had a touch of the psychic about her sometimes. She gestured with a wide sweep of her arm. "Somewhere out there is the perfect guy for you."

Mark followed the direction of her arm. "Yeah, exactly—over the Solent in Portsmouth." They both laughed.

They reached the foot of the hill and crossed the road to enter the main car park, which was virtually empty. Sonia stopped by her little VW Polo and pulled Mark into a fierce hug.

"You try and relax this weekend, hon," she admonished. "Enjoy your day off. Maybe go across to the mainland tonight? You never know. Your Prince might be waiting for you in some gay bar as we speak." She winked.

Mark kissed her cheek. "Sorry, Son, but I don't think that's gonna happen. You have *your* fairy tale guy, but they'd run out by the time I came along. Go home to your man and have a nice weekend." Her face fell and Mark felt like shit for passing his negativity onto her. He kissed her again. "Don't mind me. Get a few beers down me and I'll feel much better."

Appearing only slightly reassured, Sonia bobbed her head and climbed into her car. She waved cheerily to him as she headed out of the car park. Mark walked slowly over to his aging Ford Fiesta and got in. Instead of turning the ignition, he stared out through the windscreen at the horizon, where the Spinnaker Tower rose above the Portsmouth landscape across the water.

He could hear the hovercraft revving up, ready to speed its occupants over to the mainland where home awaited some of them, a night of fun for others. He wasn't in the mood.

For some reason his thoughts turned to the couple in the salon. He could still see that beautiful guy—Sam, that was it—and his harridan of a partner. Why anyone would put up with such vitriol was beyond him. He closed his eyes as he recalled a conversation with his father some years before.

"I shouldn't have put up with it for so long, Mark."

Mark clutched his father's hand. "Then why did you?" He had to know.

Fred Horrocks had looked so small and frail, lying there in that hospital bed. There seemed to be tubes everywhere, but the steady beep of the heart monitor comforted the fifteen year old Mark, reassuring him that his father would recover.

"I thought it would get better," his dad said at last. "I thought, 'there has to be an end to all this anger, doesn't there?' I mean, she can't have an infinite supply, can she?" He attempted to smile, but his face suddenly contorted in a grimace as the steady beep changed to a more erratic rhythm. Mark looked around in desperation for someone, anyone, to help his father, and was then pushed hastily aside as the doctors and nurses fought to revive him, leaving the teenager standing beyond the curtain, listening to the last breaths that his father gasped on this Earth. The cardiac arrest which had struck without warning three hours previously had apparently not given up, and his father's damaged heart evidently saw the futility in fighting a losing battle.

Tears streaked down his face as he watched the shadow-play on the curtain surrounding his father, as figures slowly retreated, pulling back in defeat.

"Mark?"

He stiffened at the sound of his mother's voice as she came up behind him. He didn't turn. He couldn't bear to look at her right now.

"You're too late. He's gone."

Mark shook himself, pushing down the painful memory that had only lost a little of its intensity during the last five years. He hoped to God Sam had more strength of will than his father. *No one* should have to put up with so much anger. He prayed Sam had the good sense to walk away while there was still time.

Chapter Two

Mark loved Mondays. Okay, so Sundays were pretty cool too, but that was usually when there were more people out and about over the island, as virtually all the shops closed but the attractions, such as they were, remained open. Sunday was Mark's day to clean his small flat, get the weekly shopping in, and generally work through his To Do list, crossing off each item with relish. Unfortunately, it was also the day his mother usually chose to make her weekly phone call.

Monday was his day off. And summer Mondays were the best.

Mark parked the car at Yaverland car park, and after paying for his parking ticket, he headed down to the beach to go for a walk along the shore. It was a glorious August morning. The temperature was already pleasant, considering the fact that it was eight o'clock, and there were only a few people dotted over the beach. A few lone dog walkers were the norm at this hour. Mark loved coming here at this time, before all the tourists arrived with their kids, windbreaks and other beach paraphernalia. Come midday, this section of the beach would be knee-deep in children and dogs. Not that Mark had anything against children and dogs—it just turned a simple walk along a beach into an obstacle course.

His rucksack nestled easily between his shoulder blades, Mark walked along the shoreline, his bare feet leaving indentations in the moist sand.

The tide was out and the sun sparkled on the sea. The only sounds were the waves rolling over the pebbles and the cries of seagulls as they rode the currents of air along the cliffs. Dressed in a T-shirt, a pair of shorts, his flip-flops shoved into a side pocket of the rucksack, Mark felt the heat on his skin and let out a happy sigh. He loved living on the Isle of Wight, always had. While most people his age couldn't wait to get off the island, Mark had no such yearnings. He loved the place all year round. Yeah, so it was tough living in a tourist spot where the population doubled in the summer, but that was only a small percentage of the year. Mark hated those BMWs—Bitchers, Moaners and Whiners—who were forever complaining about how the level of traffic on the eastern side of the island was a bitch in summer time, how difficult it was to get around with all the tourists everywhere, blah blah blah. *If you don't like living here, the ferry's thattaway…*

Mark headed for the far end of the beach where the crumbling red rock gave way to white chalk cliffs, a leisurely twenty minute stroll away from the car park. It was an unofficial nudist beach and Mark's guilty little secret. Even in the height of summer, few tourists ventured this far along the shore, preferring to stay closer to the car park with its cute, environmentally-friendly sanitation block, complete with wind turbine to generate its required electricity, and the café with outdoor seating, hot and cold food and beach supplies. At this hour, there was no one this far along, which suited Mark just fine.

Scratch that last thought. Mark spotted a solitary figure sitting on the rocks at the base of the cliffs.

From this distance he could see it was a guy, sporting long beach shorts and a hoodie. Mark kept his eyes on him as he drew closer. All he could discern at this point was that the guy had long, tanned legs. *Yum.* Mark was a sucker for tall guys. He found himself thinking about the hunk in the salon on Saturday. What was his name? Yeah, Sam. Now that had been one hot as fuck guy. Too bad he didn't like dick.

As he got closer, the seated figure glanced in Mark's direction and then stared out to sea once more. Mark caught his breath. What were the fucking odds…? It was Mr Gorgeous himself. No.Way. Mark thought quickly. What the hell was Sam doing sitting alone on Yaverland beach at this hour of the morning? *Should I acknowledge him? Say something*? Mark was not a gregarious kind of guy. He kept to himself at work, save for the odd chat with Sonia when the opportunity presented itself. There was a reason his cheeks flamed bright red as often as they did. Mark was very shy. And as for his social life, well, that was…. crap, basically.

He kept his eyes fixed on the white cliffs up ahead, making up his mind not to let on to Sam. He felt guilty about it. He knew how much he liked it when he was walking around the island and fellow walkers, complete strangers to him, would greet him with a brisk nod and cheery hello. Mark always responded with a smile and a similar greeting. He'd never do that himself: the most he'd do was greet everyone with a polite smile. And he hated it when some sullen bastard would stare back coldly at him. Civility didn't cost anything, did it?

As he drew nearer, Mark took a good look at Sam.

He sat on a towel, knees bent, leaning back on his hands and looking out to sea. The light early morning breeze played with his hair. What struck Mark most was Sam's expression. Despite the loveliness of his surroundings, he looked sad. Mark got to within a few feet before Sam became aware of him. He gave a brief nod toward Mark.

"Morning."

Mark gave Sam a nod and a smile, then continued on his way. *Does he recognize me?* He waited for Sam to say something else as he passed by, but there was silence. Mark pushed out a breath and forged ahead up the beach. He wasn't sure why, but the thought of talking to Sam made him nervous. He deliberately kept his eyes forward, unwilling to draw attention to himself. And he was definitely *not* thinking about that gorgeous face he'd just left behind. Face? *Everything* about Sam ticked Mark's boxes. The guy was his fantasy brought to life. Yet a part of him wondered what on earth would make the guy so sad in the midst of such natural beauty.

The nudist beach was empty, so Mark had his pick of where to lay his towel. There were flat sandy areas up on the ledge at the base of the cliff, or he could choose to lie in one of the pebbled dunes below the shelf which marked high tide.

After a second or two of deliberation, he chose a wide sandy spot, sheltered from the breeze and a good vantage point from which to spot any visitors who approached. Mark remembered all too clearly the time when he'd been freaked out by a guy who strolled up the beach, gawking first at Mark, and then at a woman who'd been there on her own.

He'd watched as Creepy Guy walked up to the huge rocks at the end of the beach, did a 180 degree turn and walked back, pausing to gawk once again. When he did yet *another* turn, Mark could tell that the woman was getting seriously pissed off by the unwelcome attention. He'd been about to say something when she had got up and had words with Creepy Guy herself, sending him off with a flea in his ear. Mark had given her the thumbs up and she'd grinned at him.

Mark set his rucksack down on the sand and took out his large beach towel. He spread it out, first pulling it flat and then weighting it down with a few of the larger pebbles. Next came a bottle of water and his sunscreen, and finally, his Kindle. With one last look around, Mark stripped off his T-shirt and shorts and folded them into a small bundle on which to rest his head. He stretched his arms up into the air, loving the feel of the sun on his nude body. He thought briefly about going for a dip in the sea, but on reflection decided that he'd wait until it had had a chance to warm up a little.

He knelt on the towel and applied the sunscreen liberally, making sure it covered as much skin as he could reach, before spreading himself out on his back, legs parted slightly. *God, that feels good.* He closed his eyes and listened to the sound of the incoming waves as they crashed over the pebbles. Hearing it made Mark yearn once more to have a home right on a beach.

His idea of heaven would be to open the windows of his house and be able to hear the sea. It was a sound he never grew tired of hearing.

The crashing waves provided an almost hypnotic soundtrack, lulling him into an extremely relaxed state where it was easy to slip in and out of a doze.

When he opened his eyes and glanced at his watch, Mark realized that he'd been asleep in the sun for an hour. Time to turn over. He rolled onto his belly, wriggling contentedly as he got comfortable, and reached for his Kindle. He searched for the book he'd been reading on Sunday night before going to sleep. It was a great story, despite containing one of the tropes which most aggravated him—gay-for-you—and he soon became lost in the tale once more. His annoyance with the plot was overlooked, however, once the main characters began fucking. God, the sex was hot! Mark found himself humping the towel as he read the graphic scene. The way things were going, this was as close as Mark was going to get to experiencing hot sex. Not that he was a virgin—he'd lost his virginity at the age of seventeen—but opportunities for hooking up were few and far between on the island. The boy who'd taken his virginity hadn't even been gay. He'd been the eager recipient of a blow-job who Mark had finally talked into fucking him in Mark's bed when his mother had gone out one cold winter's afternoon.

As far as first times went, Mark's had been painful and thankfully over fairly quickly. Once was enough: Mark resolved never to bottom again. There was no way, however, that his reluctant fuck-buddy would take a cock up his ass, so that was that. Mark had to content himself with brief encounters in the bathrooms of gay bars, furtive blow-jobs and lightning quick fucks in grubby little toilet stalls.

And never on the island, always on the mainland. It was far from ideal, but it was the best he could do. It didn't stop him from thinking every time, as he shot his load into yet another willing hole, that there had to be something better for him than this.

He slipped his hand under his body and gave his hardened cock a quick tug. Then it was back to the story. His hips rocked as he slid his dick against the towel, becoming immersed in the scene which was unfolding on his Kindle. Mark's imagination took over. Sam lay spread out beneath him, face down, arse tilted, and he was sliding into Sam's tight virgin hole, Sam mewling and moaning as Mark pushed his fat dick into him until he was balls deep. *Oh yeah, baby, ride my cock…*

The sound of feet on pebbles froze him. Someone cleared their throat.

Mark twisted to look over his shoulder, squinting into the sun. A tall figure stood a few feet away, just below the pebbled shelf, the sun back-lighting him so brilliantly that Mark couldn't make out his features, in spite of his sunglasses. Without thinking, he scrambled to stand up. His dick jutted out, twitching with a life of its own and Mark groaned inwardly. *Well, this is fucking embarrassing.*

"I'm sorry to disturb you."

That voice. Mark shielded his eyes from the sun and sure enough, it was Sam, his cheeks flushed. The hoodie was now tied around his waist and his shades were balanced on top of his head. He gave Mark a nervous half-smile, his eyes flicking only once below Mark's waist.

"You're the guy from the salon, right?"

Mark hadn't got a clue how to proceed. Should he get dressed or what? He couldn't very well ignore the man, that was for certain. *Oh well….*

"Yeah, that's right. The name's Mark Horrocks." He held out his hand and Sam stumbled up over the pebbles to shake it. The whole situation felt so surreal.

"I know."

That stopped him dead in his tracks. How in the hell could Sam know his name?

Sam's smile widened. "You don't remember me, do you?"

Oh, trust me, hon, there's no way I'd forget meeting you. The words flitted through his brain but Mark had the sense to keep his lips zipped. He tilted his head. "I'm sorry, I think you might have me confused with someone else. I don't think we've ever met." He was desperately trying to ignore the fact that his dick was waving in the morning breeze. Apparently, it wanted to shake Sam's hand, too.

Sam's expression grew more confident. "Okay, yeah, strictly speaking? We've never spoken. But I remember you. Ryde High School. You were in Year 10 when I was in Year 13."

No. Fucking. Way. "Really?" Mark racked his brains. "I don't remember, sorry." He rubbed at his jaw, his nudity momentarily forgotten.

Sam shrugged. "No reason why you should." He cleared his throat again. "Look, would it be all right if I joined you? I could use the company right now." There was a flash of that earlier expression which had struck Mark so forcefully. That look of sadness tugged at him. Mark came to a quick decision.

"Sure."

Sam beamed and clambered up onto the sandy shelf. He spread out his towel and dropped his backpack onto it. He hesitated. "Er, this is my first time on a nudist beach. Do I have to take my clothes off, too?"

Mark couldn't resist. "Oh, I'm afraid so," he said solemnly, his face straight. "It's kind of a rule." And then he grinned.

Sam's grin mirrored his. "Oh, well, I wouldn't want to break the rules." He pulled at his T-shirt, lifting it up and off, and then undid his shorts, sliding them down over his hips, wriggling out of them. Mark tried hard not to look, but *oh my God*, the man was freaking gorgeous.

Silver rings glinted in the sun where they hung from Sam's tight little nipples. His chest was smooth: Mark liked that. Dark, chaotic swirls adorned his upper arms, spreading out over his torso, thinning out until they reached his groin where they coiled delicately around the base of his cock. And then Mark had to stare. Sam had a Prince Albert. Just looking at the thick ring with its little ball made Mark's mouth water. Sam was cut, and from the look of him, he was a nice size. Perfect, in fact. Mark drank in the lean, ripped body and came to the conclusion that somewhere, God was having a really good chuckle. *Would it have been* so *bad to make him gay, huh?*

"Do you like tats?" Sam asked.

*Yeah, tats, riiiiight…..*Mark dragged his thoughts away from the man's droolworthy body. "Yeah, I do. I've done a design and there's a tattoo place in Shanklin that's going to do it for me, probably in the next month or so."

"Sweet." Sam sat down on his towel and reclined back on his elbows, those long legs stretched out. He turned his face up toward the sun and expelled a sigh. "This is nice. Do you do this often?"

"Not as often as I'd like," Mark admitted. "I only have Sundays and Mondays off, but Sundays tend to get full up with necessary but boring shit. When the weather's like this, though, yeah, I love coming down here." He gave Sam a speculative glance, trying not to stare at the man's bod. "I'm trying to figure out why I don't recall you from school. There weren't *that* many kids in your year."

"Ah." Sam blushed. "I looked a bit different then. My hair was longer, for one, typical island surfer boy hair, long and curly. And I used to wear glasses. God, I was glad to swap the specs for contact lenses."

Mark stared, trying to picture Sam. And then it hit him. His eyes widened.

"Oh my God. Sam Prince." His mouth fell open.

Sam grimaced. "Oh shit. *Now* you remember me. And I can guess why."

Mark was nodding enthusiastically. "Man, you were a legend! You got suspended for—"

Sam held up his hand to interrupt him. "For watching porn in a computer science lesson, yeah, I know." He frowned. "I'm never going to live that down, am I? I keep forgetting what a small island this is."

Mark chuckled. "Well, duh." Sam regarded him for a moment and then smirked.

Mark was nodding, recalling how he and his mates had talked of nothing else for weeks. "I remember now. It was all round the school, how this kid had managed to get through all the protocols and watch porn on the school computer network. Man, we were all jealous as hell."

"You wouldn't have been if you'd heard what my parents said when they found out," groused Sam. "Talk about an ear-bashing. I got grounded for two months, they took my laptop away from me, and if I wanted to use the computer for school stuff, I had to use my Dad's… only I had to do it with him looking over my shoulder the whole time." He winked. "It made watching porn rather difficult."

Mark winced. "Ooh, that sucks. I couldn't have survived high school without porn." The two men snickered. *Yeah*, Mark thought, *but my porn was probably very different to what* you *were watching.* He'd spent ages searching for free porn on the Internet from the age of sixteen, when he'd first realized he was gay. And once he'd found it, there was no keeping him off it. He tilted his head. "Wasn't it Mr. Edwards who reported you to the Head Teacher?" Mr. Edwards had been the head of the ICT faculty.

Sam nodded. "Yeah, but he was also the one who went to bat for me when they were going to ban me from taking my exams. I needed those grades to get onto my university course."

"That was decent of him, I suppose," Mark admitted grudgingly. "By the way, what did you end up studying at uni?"

Sam sighed. "Computer programing." There was a second or two's delay before both young men cracked up laughing.

They spent the next hour or two reminiscing about teachers they'd had in common and relating tales about all the things they'd got up to. It was the most relaxed conversation Mark could remember having in a long, long while. Sam didn't seem in the least bit concerned to be sitting in the nude with him, which Mark found rather endearing. Sam was easy-going and funny, yet Mark got the impression of an undercurrent of…something. In spite of this, he found himself warming to the guy. Time seemed to pass quickly, so much so that Mark had a shock when he glanced up and saw the tide coming in.

"If we don't get a move on, we're going to get trapped by the tide," he advised. Sam followed his gaze and nodded. They packed up their towels. Mark let out a gloomy sigh. "And now for the worst bit." When Sam cocked his head, looking puzzled, Mark gestured toward their nude bodies. "We have to put the clothes back on."

"You know the weird thing?" Sam said as he pulled on his shorts and T-shirt. "It felt so natural being naked, I'd almost forgotten about having to get dressed." He snickered. "Mind you, think of the consternation I would have caused if I'd strolled up to the car park like that." Both men laughed as they began their trek back to the far end of the beach, taking their time. They walked in bare feet along the shoreline, the lacy waves frothing around their ankles as the tide crawled its way up the beach, clawing at the pebbles. The sand was warm between Mark's toes and the sun beat down on his bare shoulders. They didn't talk as they traipsed along. Sam seemed in a world of his own.

Mark saw the slipway which marked the end of the beach. The morning had been very pleasant and he was reluctant for it to come to an end. He liked Sam. During their time together, he'd come to see him less as an object of lust and more as a warm, personable young man who was easy to get along with.

At last they reached the car park. Mark turned to Sam and held out his hand.

"I suppose this is goodbye," he said somewhat reluctantly. Sam took his hand and held it for a moment, looking thoughtful.

"Does it have to be?" he said, a hopeful expression etched across his face.

Mark stilled. "What do you mean?"

Sam flicked his head toward the far end of the car park. "It's nearly lunchtime. Would...would you like to join me for a bite to eat?" His cheeks were suddenly tinged with pink. "It's just, I've had a really great morning talking with you, and to be honest, I don't have anywhere else to be right now." He peered anxiously at Mark. "We could go to Driftwood or one of the hotels on the sea front, if you like." Driftwood was a bar on the beach which served food.

Mark was taken aback. It was gratifying that Sam obviously felt the same way about their time together. He considered the proposition, which he had to admit was a tempting one.

"Please?" That hopeful light in Sam's eyes was hard to resist. That did it. "I'd love to."

Sam's beam of delight made the decision an easy one. And after all, since when was it a hardship to sit in the sunshine and have lunch with a new friend?

Chapter Three

Mark leaned back into his seat and relaxed, loving the warmth of the sun on his bare shoulders. They sat in the far corner of the beach bar, arms resting lightly on the wooden poles that ran around the perimeter. Fortunately there'd been an empty table. Mark knew how busy this place could get. Sam faced him, sipping a Coke. Mark studied the young man in front of him. Mark was twenty, so that made Sam approximately twenty-three. He'd got it right on Saturday: those blue eyes were stunning. But now that Mark had the opportunity to really look at him, there was a vulnerability in Sam's expression that he hadn't spotted previously. *What goes on in that head of yours, hon?*

The server arrived with their lunch and all such thoughts were forgotten as Mark dug in enthusiastically. The sea air always made him hungry. Sam ate at a more sedate pace, looking out to sea at the sailboats and yachts which were making their way slowly around the eastern coast of the island. There were always more boats around the island during Cowes week, when it seemed like half the world's yachting fraternity descended on the island for the boat races and speed trials. Most of the Cowes week activities were confined to the northern shores. The races were exciting enough, but Mark couldn't stand to be among the yachties, with their designer clothes and inane chatter.

Now the Friday night fireworks, *that* was another matter entirely. Live bands, lots of beer and a truly spectacular display to mark the end of the festivities—Mark was looking forward to it.

The edge of his hunger somewhat dulled, Mark nibbled at the ham and cheese sandwich and picked at the side salad. He was amused to watch Sam carefully pushing the pickles to one side.

"I take it you don't like them." Sam jerked his head up and Mark gave a nod toward his plate. "Pickles."

Sam pulled a face. "Can't stand them."

Mark laughed and reaching across with his fork, he stabbed into a particularly fat one. The prongs of the fork skittered over its slippery surface, sending the pickle shooting off the plate and under the pole to land on the sand. "Oops. Slippery little sucker." He winked at Sam, who shook his head. Sam picked up his plate and pushed the remaining pickles onto Mark's plate.

"Next time, just ask." He grinned. "Er, do you want that coleslaw?" Sam pointed at Mark's plate, a hopeful gleam in his eye.

Mark let out an exaggerated sigh as he pushed the coleslaw onto Sam's plate. "Anything else you want while we're at it? The rest of my sandwich, perhaps? My crisps?" Sam gave him a wicked smile and leaned across to snaffle one of Mark's crisps but Mark smacked his hand away before he could reach. "Touch them and die." He squinted at Sam who held up his hands and backed away, smirking. "You don't go around touching a man's crisps."

Sam snickered. "Is this some social etiquette rule I wasn't aware of? 'Do not handle another man's crisps'?"

The two men chuckled.

Sam took another drink of his Coke and then regarded Mark keenly. "So, how long have you been working at Hair Today?"

"About six months." Mark stretched his back and then resettled into his seat. "Mind you, that was after nearly eighteen months of job-hunting. There were no positions anywhere on the island." He stared gloomily at his plate. No wonder loads of young people wanted to move away. Job prospects were thin on the ground. There was always lots of seasonal work, but he hadn't wanted that.

"Did you train at the college?" Sam inquired, referring to the Island's further education center. Mark nodded. Sam tilted his head. "How many blokes were on the course?"

Mark scowled. "Just me that year. I tell you, the amount of ribbing I took from those catty bitches was nobody's business."

Sam winced. "I can imagine. And I'll bet you had to put up with a load of digs about how you must be gay to be doing a beauty therapy course."

Mark stared. Was he trying to be funny? And then he realized. Oh *hell*....

"Sam, I *am* gay." He watched as Sam paled. Mark became very still. *Oh,* please *don't be one of these homophobic fuckers that I seem to be continually running into...*

"Oh God, Mark, I'm sorry, I didn't realize. God, you must think me so rude." Sam looked horrified, but Mark quickly surmised that he was appalled to have made such a gaffe.

Mark gave him an easy smile. "Hey, it's fine, you didn't know." He quirked his eyebrows. "Although I was sure me calling you 'hon' on Saturday was a bit of a giveaway." He smirked.

Sam's brow furrowed. "You did? I don't remember." He took several gulps of his Coke. "So, do you have a boyfriend? Partner?" He seemed flustered all of a sudden. It was actually quite sweet.

Mark shook his head. "Nope." He felt awkward discussing this. Maybe it had something to do with him feeling guilty about lusting after the guy earlier. It was true Mark found him attractive—okay, maybe that was a gross understatement, the man was drop-dead *gorgeous*—but the more they'd chatted on the beach and before lunch arrived, the more Mark started to see the real Sam, whose good looks were simply another part of the whole. Mark was ashamed to have been so shallow. And maybe it was time to change the subject. "So, how long have you and…" he struggled to recall the woman's name. "Becky? Rebecca? How long have you two been together?"

Sam shifted in his seat and looked out toward the sea. He slipped his hands into his pockets. "About a month or so. Not long, to be honest." His expression grew apologetic. "Look, about Saturday, I'm really sorry if we caused a scene." His face fell. "She was in a right mood."

Mark waved a hand. "Hey, don't worry about it. All couples have fallouts now and again."

Sam grimaced. "Now and again, I could put up with." The words were muttered under his breath. Suddenly his face cleared. "Enough of our other halves—or the lack of them. Do you like working there?" It was clear Mark wasn't the only one who wanted to change the subject.

Mark expelled a breath.

"It's not what I imagined, that's for sure. I thought they were going to have me trailing one of the senior stylists at first, you know, finding my feet. But it's been a case of '*clean up the salon, Mark. Make tea, Mark. Sweep the floor, Mark.*' He mimicked Marie's nasal voice and Sam chortled. "I swear my boss hates me." He stared resignedly at the remains of his sandwich. "Maybe it will be better with time." He glanced up at Sam. "Okay, I know you did a degree in Computer programming. What did you end up doing with it?"

It was Sam's turn to look disgruntled. "Working for my dad." Mark cocked his head to one side and Sam explained further. "Dad has a software company based in London. He's got me working on designing some of their new programs. The good thing about it is that I can live where I want, as I work from home. Though Dad keeps harping on about me moving to London."

Mark laughed. "God, Sam, most of our classmates would *dream* of living in London."

Sam scowled. "They can keep it. Loud, dirty place. I much prefer life over here."

"Me too," Mark agreed. "Although…." His words trailed off and his cheeks heated up.

"What?" Sam looked intrigued. Mark gave a quick shake of his head, unwilling to say anything more, but it seemed Sam wasn't about to let go. "Aw, now come on, spill."

Mark cleared his throat. "It's just…" He picked up his Coke and drained the glass. Sam hadn't broken eye contact. *Oh, what the hell…*

"Let's just say if I lived in London, my sex life would be a whole lot more interesting than it is right now. In fact, scratch that last part. At least I'd *have* a sex life."

He watched as a flush spread up from Sam's chest, up his neck, staining his cheeks and finally turning his ears bright red. *Man, that's cute.* Sam composed himself.

"Things a bit too quiet for you on the island?" That gleam was back.

Mark snorted. "Quiet? Try dead." Sam's expression was sympathetic and Mark relaxed slightly. "I'm not kidding, there's not a single gay club on the island."

"So what do you do for… entertainment?"

God, he's sweet when he's embarrassed. Mark snickered. "I don't stay here, that's for certain. I go to Portsmouth or Southampton. There are a few decent clubs over there. Great for one night stands. Not so great places for finding Mr. Right, though." He clamped his mouth shut. He hadn't meant to come out with that last bit.

Sam's expression softened. "So you *are* looking for a Mr. Right, then?"

Mark swallowed. "Aren't we all?" Sam arched his brows and Mark hastily continued. "Looking for that special someone, I mean."

Sam looked at him thoughtfully. "Yeah, I suppose we are." He glanced down at his watch. "And now it's time for me to go, I'm afraid." He got to his feet and held out his hand. Mark clasped it firmly. Sam coughed.

"Look, can I have your number? I've really enjoyed today. Maybe we could meet up again. Go out for a drink in Ryde. Anything."

There was a look on his face that Mark couldn't place for a moment, and then it occurred to him that Sam was lonely.

"Sure," Mark said, pulling his phone from the pocket of his shorts. He opened 'contacts' and handed the phone to Sam. "Put your number in there. Maybe we could do something next weekend."

Sam nodded as he punched in his details. "That'd be great." He handed the phone back and picked up his backpack. "Thanks for a great morning, Mark." With a final warm smile, he turned and made his way out of the bar. Mark watched him walk along the promenade in the direction of the town, waving as Sam turned once to look for him. After picking up his rucksack, Mark left the bar and started the trek back to his car in the opposite direction. The day seemed to have gone so slowly. It was only one o'clock, but it felt as though it should have been much later. He walked along the prom, listening to the waves below as they crashed onto the sea wall. The tide was in, and the waves sprayed over onto the pavements, which dried almost instantly in the heat of the sun. The droplets spattered over his bare arms, cooling him. Mark couldn't hold back his sappy grin. *What a great morning.*

On impulse he pulled out his phone and sent a text to Sam. *Great talking to you. Let's do it again. Soon.*

The message sent, he slipped the phone back into his pocket and continued on his way to the car park, still armed with the sappy grin.

When his phone chimed for the third time that Tuesday morning, Mark already had a smile on his face. Sam had sent him a couple of jokes earlier that had him spluttering coffee into his cereal. It was now eleven and the salon was quiet, so he was taking advantage of the lull to grab his break. Mark had thrown himself into his tasks as soon as he'd arrived, and Marie had watched him with an expression on her face that he'd never seen there before. Oh yeah— that would be approval. He snickered to himself.

"Mark, you got a minute?"

Sonia stood in the doorway of the little staff room off the back of the salon. Her cheery smile always made him feel good. He drained the last of his tea. "Sure. What can I do for you?"

"I've got an hour or so before my next lady arrives, so I was wondering… Want to cut my hair?"

Mark stared at her in surprise. Marie hadn't let him near a single customer with a pair of scissors since he'd arrived. He'd washed hair, swept up, colored hair extensions and made numerous cups of tea and coffee, but nothing that resembled the stuff he'd been doing at college. He gazed at Sonia hopefully. "Really?"

She nodded, eyes bright. "Come on, you can wash my hair first and then we'll work out what you're going to do with it." She winked. "You're gonna make me look fabulous!"

Mark grinned and followed her to the wash station. After he'd draped and fastened a towel around her, he started to wash her dark red hair.

He remembered to do the head massage that he'd watched Wendy doing so many times. The customers really seemed to like it.

"Hmm, you have a nice touch, Mark." Mark glowed at the words of praise. "So, you going to tell me what's put that smile on your face this morning?" Her eyes widened. "Or is it more a case of *who*? You met someone this weekend, didn't you?" There was a wicked gleam in her eyes. "Come on, spill."

Mark laughed quietly. "No… well, yes….but it's not like you think." Sonia's forehead wrinkled. "Yes, I met someone, but he's not a potential boyfriend—more's the pity. He's more like a potential best friend." That was a fair assessment of Sam, he figured. "And you know him. You met him on Saturday when he was here with his girlfriend."

Sonia's eyes grew large and round. "Mr. Fantabulous? The gorgeous hunk who ticked all your boxes?" She stared up at him. "Oh, you've *got* to tell me how this all happened."

Mark chuckled as he rinsed off the shampoo and applied the conditioner. There were no other customers at the wash station and Marie was nowhere in sight. He lowered his voice and told Sonia all about the morning at the beach. She listened in rapt attention, making the odd little noise here and there. When he'd finished, she gave him a warm smile.

"Sweetie, I'm so glad. I think you needed a friend."

Mark had to agree with her. He had lots of acquaintances—people he knew from school, his neighbors, the girls at the salon—but no real friends. He had no one to blame but himself. Being painfully shy really sucked.

He wrapped a towel around Sonia's head and led her to her own chair. As he looked at her smiling face in the mirror, surrounded by damp, straggly hair, Mark found himself nervously rubbing his hand down his pant leg. *God, don't screw this up…*

Sonia's gaze met his. "You'll be *fine*." Her tone brimmed with confidence. Mark's returning nod was nowhere near as confident.

For the next twenty minutes, Mark clipped, snipped and combed her hair, always conscious of Sonia watching him carefully. There had been the heart stopping moment when Marie had appeared beside him, her eyes wide. She opened her mouth to say something—and judging by the twist of her lips, it wasn't going to be good—but Sonia got in there first.

"I thought it was about time Mark showed us what he's made of," Sonia said brightly, watching Marie. "I know I didn't ask you about doing this, but I figured that as the senior stylist here, it was my decision." Both Sonia and Mark watched for Marie's reaction. Mark held his breath. Marie could make life difficult for Sonia if she wanted to. Sonia had come to the salon about a month after Mark, and Marie had been delighted to steal her from Snippets, the very popular salon at the foot of Union Street. Having Sonia was a real feather in her cap, because Sonia's ladies were a loyal bunch. When she left Snippets, so did they.

Marie pressed her lips together and eyed Sonia's hair with interest. "Well, since he's obviously doing such a good job, we'd better let him finish." She smiled thinly and walked away.

Mark regarded Sonia in the mirror, openmouthed. He bent down and spoke into her ear.

"Did I just imagine that, or did Marie actually say I was doing a good job?"

Sonia clutched her ample chest. "I may faint," she whispered, eyes sparkling mischievously. They both laughed under their breath.

At last Mark was finished. He laid down the hairdryer and gave Sonia's hair a final comb through. He held up the large round mirror to the back so she could see how it looked, and then held his breath as she inspected the finished effect with a critical eye.

"Mark, that's a really nice job."

Mark expelled his breath in one long push of air. "Really?"

Sonia's eyes met his. "Sweetie, I wouldn't lie about something so important. You did well. Now go get your phone and take a picture. One for your portfolio." She beamed. "I can't wait 'til Dave sees this tonight."

Mark's chest swelled with pride. The rest of the morning was very pleasant, as the girls stopped by wherever he was working at the time to comment on Sonia's hair. Even Marie had a smile for him. It was his best day at the salon by far. When Marie finally locked the door at five thirty and everyone drifted off in different directions, it was a very happy Mark who walked home, his heart light.

As he reached the front door of his building, his phone chimed. It was Sam.

Day over?

Beaming, Mark typed a reply. *Best ever.*

Cool.

Yeah, it was, Mark thought as he climbed the stairs to his second floor flat. He'd just got through his front door when the phone rang. Sam. Mark smiled as he connected them.

"So what was so good about today, then?" Sam's cheerful voice filled his ear as he switched on the kettle for a much needed mug of coffee.

"I finally got to cut someone's hair!" he announced triumphantly.

"And I take it she isn't going to sue?" Mark could hear the teasing note in Sam's tone.

"Cheeky sod." Mark dropped a spoonful of instant coffee into the mug and shifted from one foot to the other as he waited for the kettle to boil. "I'll have you know, Sonia looked fantastic. *And* I got compliments." That gleeful grin was back.

Sam laughed. "Okay, I believe you. Sounds like you had a better day than I did."

Mark's grin slipped. "Why? What happened?"

"Oh, not much. I was battling with code all afternoon and it was driving me nuts."

Mark let out a relieved sigh. "Is that all? You had me worried for a sec."

Sam chuckled. "So me struggling with a stupid program isn't worth worrying about? Nice to know where I stand." That teasing tone was still in evidence. "Anyway, I only rang to ask you if you wanted to meet up on Friday night. I'm planning on going to the fireworks. Want to join me for a few beers?"

Sam's invitation was the icing on the cake, as far as Mark was concerned. "Yeah, that sounds good. I was going to catch the bus from Ryde. That way, I can get a few pints down."

"In which case, I'll meet you in front of the Royal Yacht Club at seven. The beer tent will be there, and the marquee with the live music. Should be good. The Hamsters are playing."

Mark couldn't believe it. "You like the Hamsters too? They're great. I've heard them live two or three times now." The Hamsters was a tribute band, specializing in the music of Jimi Hendrix and ZZ Top.

"Yeah? Fantastic." Mark could hear the smile in Sam's voice. "I'll let you get on with your evening, seeing as you've just finished work, and I'll see you Friday."

Mark thanked him and hung up. As he poured boiling water onto the coffee, he smiled to himself. A great day at work—and a great Friday night to come. His life seemed to have taken a sudden turn for the better.

Chapter Four

Cowes was heaving as usual. Most of the time it was a trendy little town with fashionable boutiques which seemed to cater exclusively for the yachting brigade, but that went into overdrive during Cowes week. Anyone who was *anyone* was out and about, watching the races, drinking Pimms from the balcony of the Royal Yacht Club and hanging out on some of the more fabulous-looking boats.

But on the Friday, most of the island turned out to see the fireworks, which were always impressive. The quay was a surging mass of spectators, clutching plastic glasses of beer or wine, everyone eagerly awaiting darkness to fall so the show could begin. The harbor was filled with boats as people tried to get the best vantage point from which to observe the proceedings.

Mark loved the fireworks, but that was because he was basically a big kid. Yeah, he listened to the *oohs* and *ahs* of the people around him with a big grin on his face—but his voice joined theirs readily enough.

He stood near the beer tent, clutching his pint of Wight Gold, an island brewed beer. He scanned the crowd, looking for Sam. It was seven thirty and as yet there was no sign of him. Mark thought briefly about texting him, but he didn't want to bother the man, especially as Sam had let slip in his last phone call the previous night that Rebecca might want to come along.

Mark had been puzzled. For a man whose girlfriend had just told him she might be accompanying him, Sam didn't seem all that happy about the prospect.

Mark had spent the last three days since Sam's call in anticipation of this evening. He knew, if he were being honest, it wasn't the prospect of the fireworks, but that of spending time with Sam which had kindled his enthusiasm. Knowing the girlfriend was going to be there had put a slight dampener on his mood that he couldn't account for. It wasn't a date, for goodness sake. *Hasn't stopped you thinking about him all week, though, has it?* The thought gave him a brief pang of guilt.

The marquee near the Yacht club was packed as the people crowded in to watch the band perform. Mark loved live music. The Hamsters were an eclectic bunch of guys, some sporting long beards like the guys in ZZ Top, but the lead singer resembled nothing more than an aging hippie. But when they sang, the hairs stood up on Mark's arms. Man, they were good. The band launched into a set of Jimi Hendrix numbers. The strains of Purple Haze had the crowd joining in with enthusiasm.

"They're good, aren't they?" A voice yelled near his ear.

Mark turned to find Sam next to him, dressed in a T-shirt with a Union flag emblazoned on the front and a pair of tight jeans. In his hand was a pint of beer. Sam's short brown hair was gelled and spiky. Those brilliant blue eyes regarded him. For a second, Mark went weak at the knees. *God, he looks good. Good? Downright fuckable.* No sooner had the thought occurred to him, he pushed it aside, berating himself.

Stop torturing yourself. It ain't gonna happen. In the past week, he had come to look forward to Sam's texts and calls. Every night there'd been something from him. Mark had to admit it—the man always made him feel good.

Sam's face lit up in a wide grin. "You been here long?" He raised his voice to carry over the sound of the band.

Mark shrugged. "About forty five minutes." He held up his watch and stared pointedly at Sam. *"One* of us was on time." His lips twisted into a smirk.

Sam's face fell. "Yeah, sorry about that. Becky got delayed. She was arranging to meet up with her family. Looks like they're all going to be here, too." He didn't look happy at the idea.

Mark glanced around, curious. "So... where is she?"

Sam's furtive look had him wondering. It was as if he didn't want to see her. "She told me to wait here for her. She'll be here in a minute. Her Dad is a member of the Yacht Club and she's meeting him there."

Mark let out a long whistle. "Yacht Club? Is Daddy loaded, then?"

Sam gave a glum nod. "A fact she reminds me of constantly."

His whole demeanor was puzzling. Did he not *want* to have Becky as a girlfriend? Mark couldn't figure it out. It was on the tip of his tongue to ask his new friend what was going on—until a loud, bored voice broke in.

"Sam, who is this?"

Mark bristled at Becky's tone. It hadn't changed since her appointment nearly a week ago.

He turned to face her, taking in the casual clothes which must have cost her plenty. She looked down her nose at him, making no secret of her disdain.

Sam jumped in hurriedly. "This is Mark. You met him last Saturday when you were having your hair done. Remember?" Sam rubbed the back of his neck with one hand, gripping the plastic pint pot containing his beer with the other.

Becky wrinkled her nose. "Oh yes—the tea boy."

Mark's nostrils flared. He clenched a fist tight, but Sam laid a hand on his arm. Mark could just about make out the almost imperceptible shake of Sam's head. He took a deep, calming breath.

"Sam, Daddy wants us to join him at the club." She barely gave Mark a passing glance. "We don't want to keep him waiting, do we?"

Sam gave Mark an apologetic look, although his words were directed to her. "No, I guess not." He dropped his voice lower. "Sorry, Mark. I... I'll call you tomorrow, all right?"

Mark nodded, giving him a reassuring smile. "Go on, have fun." The expression on Sam's face made that doubtful, however. Becky pulled Sam's arm impatiently as she edged her way through the crowd toward the Yacht Club, Sam glancing back at Mark just once before he disappeared into the throng.

Mark drained the last of his pint and looked at his watch. The fireworks weren't due to start until nine, maybe nine thirty, but for some reason the encounter with Becky had taken the shine off his evening. He wasn't even sure he wanted to stay around to watch the display.

What was foremost in his mind was the look on Sam's face. His friend wasn't happy, that much was clear. Mark wished there was something he could do. And then it hit him. In the space of a week, less even, Sam had gotten under his skin. How the hell had he done that so fast? All Mark knew was, Sam had become important to him. And Mark wanted to help him. He'd just have to figure out how.

"You neglected to mention when you invited me to go bowling, that you were absolutely *fantastic* at it," Mark grumbled. He glanced up at the screen where his pitiful scores glared out for all to see. Pitiful when placed next to Sam's, that is. His was a line of strikes and half-strikes.

Sam smirked. "Are we not having fun?" He adjusted his hold on the sparkly blue bowling ball and peered determinedly at the pins. For one brief moment Mark was tempted to nudge him— accidentally, of *course*—but he couldn't bring himself to do it. And he *was* having fun, despite being on a losing streak. This was their fourth game and Sam showed no signs of giving up his impressive lead.

"Another beer?" Mark suggested hopefully. Maybe alcohol would slow Sam down.

"Ooh, by all means." Sam's white teeth gleamed in the lights of the bowling alley. "I play even better when I've had a few." He laughed as Mark groaned loudly. "You really don't like losing, do you, Mark? And you're not above playing dirty, either." He winked.

Mark pouted. "I don't know what you mean."

But he couldn't keep up the act for long. It had been a long time since Mark had had so enjoyable a night out. Sam's jokes had his sides aching with laughter, and the two had talked about the film festival that one of the island's theme parks—there were only two— was about to put on, a week of open air cinema. When Sam suggested that they went along to a couple of the films, Mark had jumped at the chance. Especially when he learned that one of the films on offer was a Spielberg classic—Jaws. Sam's eyes had lit up at the prospect.

"We can take a cool bag with food and drink, and eat before it starts. I've got a couple of inflatable wedges to lean back on, so we can get comfy while we watch."

Mark liked the sound of that. There was something niggling him, however.

"Won't Becky mind you spending another night with me?" It was Tuesday and normally Mark didn't go out during the week, but Sam's phone call out of the blue as he'd got in from work had been a pleasant surprise. Sam had made no mention of the aborted fireworks evening, but the suggestion of a night of bowling had come across as an apology of sorts, one which Mark was only too ready to accept.

Sam frowned. "She wouldn't come tonight because she hates bowling. She thinks it's common." His face flushed. "And she hates Spielberg, so I can't see her wanting to join us for that, either."

Mark shrugged. Privately he was pleased not to have the woman accompany them.

Based on their two previous meetings, although brief, he didn't think an evening with Becky would be all that enjoyable. He was amazed at how well he and Sam got on. It felt as if they had known each other for years.

But still… "As long as you're sure she's not gonna start telling you that you can't play with that Mark anymore." He chuckled.

Sam guffawed. "How old are you? Six?" He shook his head. "Besides, if I want to spend time with you, it's none of her concern. She has her own life, after all."

"What does she do?" Mark was curious. He couldn't for a minute imagine what Becky's profession might be.

Sam's lips narrowed. "Becky's time is divided between the gym, the pool and going over to the mainland to shop." He grimaced. "If shopping were an Olympic event, we'd be talking gold medal winner here." He shook himself and stepped up to the line, bowling ball at the ready. Surprisingly his attempt ended up in the gutter. Mark raised his eyebrows. It seemed he'd found Sam's Achilles heel. The unhappy expression on Sam's face, however, left Mark unwilling to press his advantage.

"How about we call it a night?" It was already gone ten, and Mark needed his eight hours.

Sam shrugged. "Okay by me." The slump of his shoulders and the sudden break in eye contact told Mark a different story. He hastened to make up for bringing about the abrupt change in mood.

"Then how about coming to Wetherspoons with me on Friday night?" Mark suggested. "You could meet me after work and we could grab a bite to eat there."

Sam's brow cleared. "Yeah, that sounds great." The light was back in his eyes and Mark was relieved to see it. He hated that he'd been the one to bring his friend down. They may only have known each other for a short time, but Sam seemed to have slipped into Mark's life, as if he had always been there.

Sonia threaded her arm through Mark's as they walked down the hill. He didn't have the car today so it was taking him out of his way, but he'd wanted the chance to talk with her all that Saturday. It had been a really busy day for the salon, and the opportunity had never arisen. Busy day? It had been a busy *week*.

"So, do you have plans for tonight?"

Mark shook his head. "Not really. I *had* thought about going over to Portsmouth." He wasn't about to admit how horny he was feeling at that moment. It had been a few weeks since he'd been over there, and Mark was tired of having nothing but his right hand to play with. But part of him wanted to call Sam and maybe meet up with him. A week had gone by since his evening with Sam at the Wetherspoons pub. They had met up on Monday down at Yaverland beach, where they'd had lunch once more at Driftwood. It had been a lovely warm day, and the two had lain stretched out on their towels, reading, the silence occasionally punctuated by brief conversations.

Wednesday night had been the open air cinema at Robin Hill. They'd arrived at six thirty and grabbed a spot with a good view, and then spread out the soft picnic rug that Sam had brought along.

Sam's cool bag was filled with bottles of beer and cold chicken salad. They'd eaten slowly, watching the crowds gather, everyone in similar pursuits. The inflatable wedges had proved very comfortable and the two had reclined on the rug, looking up at the huge screen. Mark felt like such a girl when he jumped as the head rolled out from the boat. No matter how many times he'd seen Jaws, it *always* startled him. Of course, Sam *had* to notice his reaction. The huge smirk on his face told Mark how much he'd enjoyed it. The sky had been a beautiful expanse of purples and darkest blue, the stars scattered across it like dust. There was so little light pollution across the island that the view had been staggering. At one point Mark had forgotten about the film and stared up at the night sky in awe. When a quick sideways glance revealed Sam engaged in the same activity, he'd smiled. Sometimes it was important just to stop and take in what was all around. Beauty was everywhere—a person just had to look for it.

Mark loved spending time with Sam, although he'd noticed that Sam avoided any mention of Becky. Which was fine, in Mark's opinion. But in his quieter moments, he would think back on their conversations. The more he thought about Sam's reticence to talk about his girlfriend, the more he was convinced that something was going on. He recalled that first episode in the salon, Sam's nervous behavior.

"Where are you, Mark? You're miles away."

Sonia's words broke through his internal meanderings. He pulled himself together to find her staring at him in amusement.

"Sorry," he apologized sheepishly. He tightened his arm around hers.

"So how were the Cowes fireworks? As spectacular as ever?" She pulled a face. "I can't believe we haven't had time to chat these last few weeks." The salon had been fully booked, keeping all the staff very busy, Mark included.

Mark gave a shrug. "I wouldn't know. I left before they got going."

Sonia stopped dead, her mouth dropping open. "But you were so looking forward to watching them! What happened, sweetie?" The look of concern in her eyes was touching.

Mark tugged at her arm to keep walking. "Let's just say my plans got changed." He hesitated, wanting to say more. Sonia said nothing but carried on walking. Mark stared out across the Solent toward Portsmouth. *I could be over there within the hour. And ten minutes after* that, *I could have my dick buried in some guy's tight arse.* The thought was tempting. Yet the thought of calling Sam persisted. "God, why am I so fucking stupid?" He groaned quietly.

They reached the car park, but instead of going to her car, Sonia pulled him toward the low wall which ran around the perimeter. She hauled herself up onto it and patted the warm concrete beside her. "Sit. Now." Her tone made it clear that refusal was not an option. Mark stared at her and she returned his stare, unblinking. "I mean it. Dave hasn't cooked dinner, because we're eating with friends tonight and we have plenty of time. So you're not keeping me from anything." That stare wasn't going away.

Mark muttered under his breath as he hopped up onto the wall, swinging his legs around until he sat facing out across the Solent. He took off his shoes and placed them next to him. The evening sun was still warm and he flexed his feet, wiggling his toes. Sonia kept quiet beside him, obviously waiting for him to make the first move. When he couldn't take the silence any more, he told her, slowly at first, about his meeting with Sam and Becky at Cowes. Sonia listened intently. When he'd finished, she cocked her head.

"You really like this guy, don't you?" Her expression was serious.

Mark quietened. He found it difficult to put his feelings into words, but he'd give it a try. "Son, I can't explain it. When I first laid eyes on him, all I saw was this gorgeous specimen that I wanted in my bed." Her rising blush was adorable. "But after that morning on the beach, and then lunch, not to mention the phone calls these last three weeks, the nights out, another day on the beach…" His words trailed off.

"Phone calls? Nights out?" Sonia stared at him with widened eyes. "I had no idea. He's really got to you, hasn't he?"

Mark nodded. "And I don't have a clue why. I only know he's great to be with, to talk to. He's intelligent, warm, funny—not to mention sexy as hell—but undoubtedly straight."

Sonia chuckled. "Mark, you're not my only gay friend, you know. I have a few. And I *do* know from talking with them that most gay guys love the fantasy of turning a straight boy gay." Her eyes twinkled. "So would this be you indulging in that particular fantasy?"

Mark groaned. "Oh God, I don't know! If you'd asked me that first Saturday, that would have been easy—yes! But since then…" He broke off and stared down at the golden sand. "I can't get him out of my mind, Son. I know it can't go anywhere, but that doesn't seem to matter to my stupid brain. Apparently I have a crush on a straight guy." Except he knew, even as he said the words, that a crush didn't come close to how he was feeling.

Unfortunately for him, Sonia's intuition was in fine working order. Her eyes rounded.

"Oh my God." Mark stiffened beside her, awaiting her next words. "Wow, Mark… when you fall, you fall fast, don't you, sweetie?"

"I wouldn't know," he murmured, his eyes locked on the sand. "I've never fallen for anyone before." He heard the hitch in Sonia's breathing. He kept his gaze lowered, unable to look her in the eye. He felt her hand against his. "Am I that pathetic? All it takes it for some guy to pay me some attention and I fall head over heels for him?" He scowled.

"Oh, Mark." The warm tone of her voice was comforting. At last he raised his eyes to look at her. Sonia was gazing at him. "I'm sorry, sweetie. It must be awful, knowing nothing can come of it."

Mark shrugged. "I'll live." It didn't stop his chest from tightening as he thought of Sam. He mentally shook himself. "I just need to get my arse over to the mainland and get laid, that's all." He plastered a bright false smile onto his face.

Sonia regarded him closely. "Sure." She didn't sound convinced.

Mark couldn't blame her. As performances went, it had been pitiful. She glanced at her watch. Mark saw the look and swung his feet around, grabbing his shoes. He slipped down off the wall and extended a hand toward her.

"Come on. It's time you went home to the husband. You're going out tonight—you need time to get yourself even more beautiful than you are normally." He attempted a grin.

Sonia laughed. "Ooh, aren't *you* quite the smooth talker!" She took his hand as he helped her off the wall. She pulled him impulsively into a tight hug. "Be patient, sweetie," she murmured into his ear. "Your Prince will find you one day, I'm certain of it."

Mark put his arms around her and squeezed her lightly. "Thanks, Son."

His phone chimed, and glancing down, he saw Sam's name. He chuckled. Talk of the devil... *You out of jail yet? Wanna chat?*

Sonia saw his reaction and gave him another sympathetic glance. "Sam?" He nodded. "Then I'll let you talk." She kissed his cheek. "I'll see you on Tuesday. Have a lovely two days off, and remember—if you need to talk, about *anything*, you have my number." He gave her a grateful nod and she walked toward her car, pausing to wave at him before she got in and drove out of the car park.

Mark began the slow trek along the coast road which led up to Westhill Road and his flat. He watched the tourists coming off the beach and out of the children's amusement park, no doubt heading back to their holiday accommodation and whatever delights the evening held for them.

He pulled out his phone and after plugging in his earbuds and returning the phone to his pocket, he called Sam. After only two rings, Sam answered. "Hey. Day over?"

"Yep." Mark ignored the momentary surge of pleasure that always occurred on hearing Sam's quiet, deep voice. "Long day."

There was a pause at the other end. "You got a minute?"

"Sure." Mark looked across at the Spinnaker Tower, glinting in the evening sun. Portsmouth beckoned, with its siren call of gay clubs and bars, and the lure of anonymous sex in seedy bathrooms. That last thought brought with it a brief stab of discontent. *Is it too much to hope that I can meet someone who actually wants to take me home to his bed? Or who wants to come home with me?* His heart ached for that.

"How do you feel about meeting up for a drink tonight?"

Mark stopped in his tracks and closed his eyes. *Tell him no. Go to Portsmouth, find a willing guy and fuck him senseless. You'll feel better for it.*

Even as the thought crossed his mind, his traitorous mouth went into action. "Sounds great. Where and when?" He couldn't stop himself.

"Wetherspoons at seven? That too early? If you haven't eaten by then, we could always grab something there." There was something in Sam's voice that he couldn't quite decipher. And in the end, that was what decided it for him.

"Yeah, that's fine. I'll meet you there at seven."

"Fantastic." There was no escaping the note of relief in Sam's voice. "See you then." Sam hung up.

Mark pulled off the earbuds and stuffed them into his pocket. Despite the logical part of his brain yelling at him that this was going nowhere, he couldn't fight off the warm feeling which coursed through him at the thought of seeing Sam.

Fuck, he had it bad.

K.C. WELLS

Chapter Five

Mark was having a good time. Well, he would have been having a *great* time, but for the worrying feeling that had prodded him continually.

Wetherspoons was packed. They'd been able to grab a booth to the rear of the bar, a great vantage point from which to see everything happening. He and Sam chatted about films and music, and it had been great to discover they both loved Steven Spielberg's movies. The conversation was light and amusing, and yet Mark was constantly aware of an undercurrent. He caught it in Sam's facial expressions, his tone of voice—something never fully seen but only glimpsed now and again. But as the evening wore on and Sam made no mention of whatever was on his mind, Mark decided that maybe he'd got it wrong after all. His mind was playing tricks on him.

It wasn't until after Mark had bought the third round that he plucked up the courage to ask the question that had been on the tip of his tongue all night.

"Why do you put up with her?" he blurted out. His heart sank as Sam froze momentarily. *Subtle, Mark, really subtle.* Mark kicked himself.

"I don't know what you're talking about." Sam wouldn't meet his gaze but stared resolutely into his pint glass. Mark wasn't backing down though, not this time. The alcohol might have had something to do with that.

"Sam, mate, it's obvious you're not happy with Becky. So why do you stay with her? You two haven't been going out for that long."

Sam's jaw tightened. "Look, I really don't want to talk about this right now, okay?"

Mark stuck out his chin. "See, you *say* that, but I keep getting this weird feeling that you want to tell me something. And I think it has something to do with Becky." He leveled a forthright stare at Sam. "So tell me I'm wrong."

Sam regarded him with an expression bordering on panic. There was no question of it.

Mark backpedaled quickly. He held up his hands. "All right, all right, I'm sorry. Let's change the subject."

"Good idea," Sam mumbled as he got up from his seat in the corner of the crowded bar. "It's my turn to get the drinks in. Same again?"

Mark nodded and watched as Sam edged his way through the tightly packed crowd which had gathered at the bar. It was warm tonight and the huge front window of the bar had been opened up to let in the night air. Mark stared glumly at the table, where the empty bowl stood from the chips they'd shared earlier. *Way to go, Mark.* He cursed himself for putting his foot in it. *Why couldn't you just leave it alone?* That was it. Once Sam returned to the table, Mark was going to bring the conversation back to lighter topics. He only hoped his outburst hadn't soured the mood for the rest of their evening together.

"So when did you first know you were gay?" Sam's words were less distinct now. That probably had something to do with the amount of beers he'd consumed in the last three hours. He wasn't at the slurring stage yet, but Mark could tell he was trying to speak more deliberately. His earlier mood appeared to have been forgotten, much to Mark's relief.

Mark chortled. "You're pissed." Not that he wasn't in the same state.

Sam's eyebrows shot up. "Am not!" he exclaimed indignantly. He gave Mark a wicked grin that made his knees go weak. "Anyway, answer the question." He leaned forward and put his elbows on the table, resting his chin in his hands, staring at Mark in rapt attention. "I'm all ears." There was that cute grin again.

Mark sighed. "Okay, okay… I was fifteen." His mind went back to what had been, for him, a defining moment. "I thought my lack of interest in girls was due to the fact that the girls in my year at school seemed to be uncommonly ugly." Sam snorted. "Yeah, okay, there were a few lookers, sure, but no one girl who got my heart racing, if you know what I mean."

Sam's eyes gleamed. "But someone else did, I take it?"

Mark stilled as he recalled glancing across the classroom during an English lesson, listening to David Elmwood reading aloud a John Donne poem. For the first time, Mark had heard every word. He hadn't been able to tear his eyes away. He'd been struck by David's clear complexion and startling blue eyes. The way his shiny, short black hair lay in soft layers, framing his heart shaped face. Those rose-colored lips as they'd mouthed the beautiful words.

It hadn't mattered to him that David had a girlfriend. What had shocked Mark to the core was his reaction to his fellow student. Mark got hard.

"I got my first erection from looking at a guy. It was the last thing I expected, and I had to cross my legs to hide it. I was convinced everyone could see it." He chuckled. "I pulled my sweater down really fast to cover up my crotch." And of course, no one had noticed. "But it was so weird. Once I'd noticed David, it seemed that everywhere I looked around school, there were all these cute guys that I'd never noticed before. It was as if I'd been wearing blinkers my whole life, and suddenly, they were taken off."

"Did you have a boyfriend while you were at school?"

Mark guffawed. "Oh, you have *got* to be kidding me! I don't know what the students were like in *your* year, but in mine? If you did something stupid, you were told, 'Oh, that's really *gay*.' It was the standard insult." He shook his head. "No way was I *ever* coming out while I was at school." Sam was nodding in acknowledgment. "Come to think of it, I didn't really come out at college, either. It was difficult enough *talking* to other students, let alone coming on to one of them. It took me another two years to pluck up the courage to offer someone a blow-job. I'd been getting a vibe from this one guy on and off for what seemed like ages, so when I found myself alone with him in the college toilets, I went for it." Mark smiled to himself as he recalled how nervous he'd been. "God, I was shaking the whole time, expecting him to lay into me and beat me up."

"But he didn't, right?" A crease appeared between Sam's eyes. Mark was touched by Sam's apparent concern.

He gave Sam a reassuring smile. "No, he didn't. In fact, he loved it that much, it became a steady thing. Once or twice a week we'd meet up in the toilets. I'd suck him off, or him me. It took me a longer time to get him to fuck me, however." He glanced keenly at Sam. "You sure you're okay with this conversation?" Sam showed no signs that he was about to expire of embarrassment, Mark had to admit. The only reaction was the blush on his cheeks.

"Nah, it's fine," Sam said with a wave of his hand. "I don't shock easily." His eyes sparkled. "So you were—what—seventeen when you lost your virginity?"

Mark nodded. He leaned back into his chair and folded his arms. "Enough about my lamentable sex life. Now it's your turn." He winked—and then caught his breath as Sam's lips pressed together in a slight grimace, that killer smile wavering. Sam's mouth opened and closed and he pulled at his earlobe. "Sam. You okay?"

"Sure," Sam croaked and then he cleared his throat. "Sure. Why wouldn't I be?"

Now *that* was interesting.

"Sam? Something you wanna tell me?" Mark lifted his eyebrows.

Sam took several long swigs of his beer. He put down the glass and swallowed as he raised his eyes to meet Mark's gaze. "Okay, so maybe I shock more easily than I'd thought."

Mark snickered. "Oh, *I* see. It's okay for *me* to bare my soul and share my first pathetic attempts at sex, but *you* get to chicken out." He flapped his arms and made bawk bawk noises.

Sam laughed. "Apparently I need to be more drunk before I reveal the sordid secrets of my sex life." He picked up his glass and drained it. "And it's your turn to get them in." He waved his empty glass at Mark.

Mark grumbled to himself as he stood. "Just when things were getting interesting." He winked at Sam to show he was joking and then headed for the bar. There was only an hour before closing time. The beer had given him a very pleasant buzz, but a couple more pints and he'd be on the way to being drunk. He handed over his money and grabbed the two glasses, walking carefully to their corner table. The level of noise in the bar had increased as its patrons grew more voluble.

Sam was leaning back against the padded back of his seat, fingers laced behind his head. His gaze was on the people around him. He lowered his arms and patted the seat next to him.

"Sit here and people-watch with me for a sec."

Mark shrugged good-naturedly and sprawled out on the seat, glancing around the bar. "So, who exactly are we watching?" He reached for his beer.

Sam indicated a young man who was standing near the door on his own, his eyes on the TV screen which was silently showing Sky news. "Would you do *him*?"

Mark almost choked on his mouthful of beer. "Excuse me?"

Sam grinned. "You heard me. Would you do him?"

Mark gaped. " 'Do' as in 'fuck'?" Sam nodded. "Oh, *fuck*, no."

Sam's eyebrows shot skyward. "What's wrong with him?"

Mark stared incredulously. "Sam, he looks like he's not even old enough to be in this *bar*, let alone my bed." He took another mouthful of beer.

"Okay, then, what about *him*?" Sam indicated another guy seated in a group by the window. Mark gave him a quick glance, taking in the heavyset man in a leather biker jacket, a tattoo rising above the neck of his T-shirt and curling up his neck.

"Not really into bikers, but tats? Now, that's a different matter. Still, he's not my type, to be honest."

Sam's eyes gleamed with interest. "Oh, go on, tell me." Mark cocked his head. "Your dream guy—what would he look like?"

It was Mark's turn to swallow. *Oh hell…*

Sam cocked his eyebrows. "Ooh, now you have me intrigued." He nudged Mark conspiratorially. "C'mon, tell me."

Mark picked up his glass and took several large mouthfuls of beer before placing the glass down on the table. *I can't believe I'm going to do this….* He took a deep breath.

"Good sense of humor."

Sam snorted. "Yeah, right. You're not writing an ad for a lonely hearts column here. What would he *look* like? Details, details…"

Mark closed his eyes, his mind picturing Sam that Monday morning on Yaverland beach. "Tall, over six feet. Skinny, but with nice abs and toned legs and arms. Short, brown hair. Blue eyes. Nipple piercings. Tattoos." He swallowed. "Long, thick cock, pierced. Tight arse."

He heard Sam's breathing catch.

Mark opened his eyes cautiously. Sam was staring at him, eyes wide.

"Oh my God." Mark watched as the color slid from Sam's cheeks. Then those gorgeous blue eyes narrowed. "Well, now it all makes sense." His lips pressed together.

Mark's heart stuttered in his chest. "What?"

Sam's gaze had turned cold. "And here was me, thinking you were concerned about me, worrying that I wasn't happy with Becky. Well, now I know what *that* was all about, don't I?"

"W-what are you talking about?" Mark bit his lip, blinking rapidly.

"Oh, come on, Mark!" Sam said, his voice a deep rumble. "First you try to get me to break up with Becky, and then it all comes out that I'm basically your fantasy guy." Mark was shocked into stillness. He stared at Sam, aghast. Sam speared him with an intense stare. "At least you have the decency not to deny it. That *was* me you just described, wasn't it?" Sam sneered. "Was that the plan, then? I ditch Becky and then you make a play for the straight guy?"

Mark gasped. "Oh God, no, it…it wasn't like that, I swear!" A sudden coldness spread through his body, radiating out from his heart which was pounding so loudly, he swore Sam could hear it.

Sam got to his feet and stared coldly at him. "Well, at least I know where I stand. And here was me thinking you and I were friends." He grabbed his denim jacket from the seat beside him. "Bye, Mark. Thanks for the drinks. It was certainly an informative evening." Sam started to move toward the door, but Mark grabbed his arm.

"Sam, please, you've got this all wrong. I *was* concerned about you, believe me." Mark gazed at Sam imploringly. "Don't go. Please."

Sam shrugged off his arm. "Sorry, but right now I can't stand to be anywhere near you." He swallowed, and just for a second, something flickered in his eyes. Then it was gone. "Bye, Mark." He walked toward the door, wavering slightly on his feet, and out into the street.

Mark stared in disbelief. In less than a minute their pleasant evening together had been shattered. He kicked himself for being such an idiot. Why the hell had he told him?

"Too late now," he muttered under his breath. Sam was gone, and the likelihood of him ever reappearing in Mark's life was looking remote. His heart sank. The last three weeks had given him a taste of what it was like to have a really good friend. He'd genuinely liked Sam. All of a sudden Mark wanted to get out of there. He grabbed his jacket, got to his feet and headed out the door. He glanced anxiously up and down Union Street, but there was no sign of Sam. Head hung in misery, shoulders hunched, Mark crossed the street and started the trek home, trying to ignore the tightness in his chest. *Well, you certainly fucked that up.*

No argument there.

Mark woke up with a start, his head pounding. Something buzzed insistently. He glanced toward his alarm clock. *What the fuck?* It was three in the morning.

Groggily, Mark sat up in bed. There it was again. It was the intercom from the main door at street level. He pushed back the solitary sheet that covered his naked form and staggered out of bed. Suddenly, coming home and drinking two or three glasses of whiskey seemed like a *really* bad idea. Mark groaned as the buzzer sounded once more, this time louder.

"Coming." He clutched his aching head as he leaned against the front door of his flat and pressed the intercom. "Who's it?" The words slid out of his mouth unevenly.

"Mark, it's Sam. Let me in." Sam's speech was slurred.

Mark stared in horror at the intercom. *No fucking way.* How in the hell had Sam found him? He'd never been to the flat. Mark scrubbed a hand across his cheek, the rasp of his stubble all too loud. He pressed the button. "Go away, Sam." The words sounded so weary to his ears.

He stumbled back toward his bedroom, but the buzzer's strident tone stopped him in his tracks. Cursing under his breath, Mark lurched back to the door and depressed the button firmly. "I mean it, Sam. Go the hell away. You said all you needed to in the pub." And there was no way Mark wanted to hear it again.

"Mark, please." Something in Sam's voice tore at him. "Don't turn me away. I need to speak to you." There was a pause. "Please, mate. 'S important."

Mark hesitated, his hand hovering over the intercom. He was in no fit state to have a conversation. But a tiny part of him remained stupidly hopeful. Sighing heavily, he pushed the door release button. "Come on up. Second floor. It's the flat on the right."

"Oh, thank God." Mark couldn't miss the note of relief in Sam's voice. Mark staggered into his bedroom and snatched his robe from its hook on the back of the door. He slipped into it, tugging it around him and tying it tightly. He went to the door, unbolted it and pulled it open. Sam had just reached the top stair. He held onto the rail, panting.

"Get in here, quickly." Mark grabbed hold of Sam's arm and hauled him into the flat. He pushed the door closed as quietly as he could. Ron across the hall worked on the rubbish bins and always got up at the crack of dawn. It wouldn't do to piss off his neighbors. Once Sam was inside, Mark shut and bolted the door as silently as possible. Sam leaned against the wall of the small hallway, as if the wall was propping him up.

"Come into the living room," Mark told him and led him into the long room which contained his living room at one end and kitchen at the other. He pointed toward the long sofa. "Sit." He switched on the small table lamp which stood next to the sofa.

Sam flopped down onto the sofa, his head lolling back against the seat cushions. His eyes closed.

Mark shook him by the arm. When Sam opened his eyes, Mark fixed him with an intense look. "What do you want, Sam?"

Sam stared up at him with such a look of abject misery that Mark caught his breath.

"Need to talk to you," he slurred.

Mark was puzzled. "Did you find somewhere else to drink after you left the pub?" Sam hadn't been *this* drunk. Sam's head bobbed once. "Sam, how did you find me?"

"Waited in a doorway 'til you left," he confessed. "I hid when you came out so's you wouldn't see me. Followed you home. Thought 'bout ringing the bell, but didn't have the nerve." He gulped. "Then I went to the off license and bought a bottle o' Scotch." Sam closed his eyes. "I sat on the beach at the end of your road, drinkin', 'til I couldn't stand it anymore." He choked out the words.

Mark could see Sam was hurting. He longed to touch him, to comfort him, but the memory of Sam's coldly delivered speech was still too raw. "You're in no state to talk," Mark said gently. "I think you should go." He winced as his head throbbed.

"Please!" The word burst from Sam's lips. "Don' make me go!" To Mark's dismay, two fat tears slid from beneath Sam's eyelids, rolling down his cheeks. "I don' wanna go home."

The words tugged at Mark's heart. "Oh, Sam." Those piercing blue eyes regarded him anxiously, shiny with imminent tears. There was no trace of the man who had left him alone in the pub. He came to a decision. "Look, why don't I make us some coffee, and then you can crash on my sofa for what's left of the night. We can talk in the morning when we're both a little less worse for wear."

To his relief, Sam nodded and Mark went to make some coffee, looking around every now and then to keep an eye on his guest. Sam rested his head back against the sofa, staring up at the ceiling, the rise and fall of his chest now more even. Mark left the coffee black and brought the two mugs over to the coffee table. He handed one to Sam and then sat down beside him, gazing at his own mug in silence. There were no sounds at all from the building.

"'M sorry."

Mark gave a slight start. He turned to Sam to find him gazing at him, eyes large and round. Mark didn't know what to say. He struggled to find words. "Let's leave the talking for the morning, all right?" He spoke quietly. Sam bobbed his head once more and sipped his coffee. Mark got up and went into his bathroom to fetch a clean sheet from the airing cupboard above the boiler. Then he went into his bedroom and opened the wardrobe to pull out a spare pillow. When he got back to the living room, Sam's eyes were closed, his breathing even, his mug balanced precariously on his lap. Mark put down the bedding and gently disengaged Sam's hands from around the mug, before setting it on the table. He placed the pillow at one end of the sofa and eased Sam into a horizontal position, his head resting on the pillow. Mark tugged off Sam's trainers and socks, and then spread out the sheet over him.

"Thanks." The whispered word pierced the quietness of the room.

Mark smiled. He looked down at Sam's face, his forehead creased. "Get some sleep." Sam stirred, small noises escaping from his lips. "I'll be across the hall if you need me." Straightening, he went into the kitchen and filled a glass with cold water. He placed it within reach on the coffee table and clicked off the lamp, plunging the room into darkness.

Mark slipped off his robe and slid naked under the cool cotton sheet. He lay on his back and stared up at the ceiling. His thoughts were fixed on the man sleeping in the room across from him.

He didn't understand what was so important that Sam would go to such lengths to find him, especially after the way he'd reacted in the pub. Hopefully, all would become clear in the morning. Mark closed his eyes and tried to ignore the ache across his eyes.

It was a long while before sleep took him.

Chapter Six

Mark cautiously opened his eyes and blinked in the sunlight which poured through his bright yellow curtains. He glanced at the clock beside him and did a double take: it was already nine. *Fuck.* He rarely slept this late. He yawned and stretched his body under the sheet—and froze when he came into contact with a warm, solid body which definitely hadn't been there when he'd fallen asleep. He jerked away, rolling onto his back, and stared in disbelief.

Sam lay beside him in the bed, his head nestled in the pillows, eyes closed. Mark caught his breath. Sam's upper body was bare. Mark lifted the sheet carefully and peered beneath it. Fuck—Sam was nude. Mark's brain went into overdrive. What the hell was Sam doing in his bed, and how long had he been there? Mark sat up, all sleep driven from him.

"Morning."

He jerked in surprise. Sam gazed up at him, his expression watchful. He blinked sleepily.

Mark pulled the sheet up around him, dimly aware of the absurdity of this action. The man had seen him naked on the beach *twice*, for goodness' sake. "What are you doing in my bed, Sam?" He kept his tone even.

Sam's eyes opened wide. "The way you're reacting, anyone would think you'd never had a guy in bed with you before."

Mark stared at him meaningfully.

"That might be because I've never *had* a guy in bed with me before." Inside he cringed. What did that say about his sex life? Then it hit him. "Oh my God. Did I…did I *ask* you to come to bed with me?" The state he'd been in, anything was possible. He remembered getting into bed, but after that? There was no recollection of inviting Sam. And just because he didn't remember saying anything resembling that, didn't mean it hadn't happened.

Sam hastened to reassure him. "God, no! I… I woke up a couple of hours ago and I… I didn't want to be alone." His voice dropped to a whisper. "I'm sorry if I did something wrong. I just assumed…"

Mark stretched out his hand across the sheet and grasped Sam's hand. "Really, it's okay. It was just a bit of a shock, waking up to find I had a bed partner." A bit of a shock was something of an understatement. He tilted his head. "A bed partner who seems remarkably calm about being in bed with a gay guy." That last thought gave him pause. "Anything you want to tell me, Sam?" He kept the tone light, but in his head there was a list of questions which was growing longer by the minute.

Sam paled. "Oh fuck…" he said weakly. His gaze dropped to the sheet which covered him. Mark pulled back his hand and threw off the sheet. He got out of bed and picked up his robe from where he'd dropped it earlier and pulled it on. He stood at the foot of the bed and gazed at Sam.

"I think you and I need to talk, because right now, I'm confused. I'm going to make some coffee." He turned and exited the room.

Inside his head was a mass of tumbling, convoluted thoughts. He thought back to the hurt he'd felt when Sam had accused him of manipulating the situation. Sam had been the epitome of the indignant straight guy. *But a straight guy doesn't climb into bed with his gay friend, does he?* And judging by Sam's reaction just now, there was more to this than not wanting to be alone. He switched on the kettle and dumped coffee into two mugs, his thoughts never straying far from the man in his bed. The one thing that refused to leave him was the thought that Sam had looked damn good in it.

From behind him, he heard movement. He looked over his shoulder to see Sam pulling on his jeans, his face flushed. Mark turned back to his task. When he picked up the two mugs and went toward the sofa. Sam sat on the edge of the seat cushion, his torso and feet bare, elbows resting on his knees, head in hands. Mark set the mug down in front of him and then sat at the opposite end of the sofa. A little distance was required right now.

Mark sipped his coffee, wincing as the hot liquid burnt his lip. The silence spun out between them until it was almost tangible. Sam wouldn't look at him. Finally, Mark couldn't stand it any longer.

"All right, talk to me. That's what you came here for, after all, wasn't it?"

Sam looked at him warily. Mark kept his face neutral.

"I'm sorry about what I said last night," Sam said at last. "I had no right to say those things. I knew as soon as I said them that you wouldn't do something so… so…"

"Underhanded? Mean? Sneaky?" Mark suggested. Sam nodded unhappily. Mark pushed out a long stream of air.

"Then why did you leave like that?"

Sam hung his head. "Because if I'd stayed, I might have told you the truth," he whispered.

Mark stilled. "The truth? So that implies what, that you've been lying to me?" Sam kept silent. Mark put down his mug and moved closer, until he was sitting so close to Sam that he could feel the heat pouring off him. "Come on, Sam, you've gotten this far. Don't stop now." His heart pounding, Mark stretched out a hand and cupped Sam's chin, tilting his head upward. Sam's lovely blue eyes had a tortured expression in them. "It's okay," Mark whispered.

Sam blinked, his Adam's apple bobbing as he swallowed several times. He straightened and looked Mark in the eye. "I'm gay, Mark."

Mark froze, staring at him in confusion. "What?" The words wouldn't register in his brain. "I don't understand."

Sam stared at him miserably. "I'm gay."

"Since when?" Mark demanded. A thought suddenly hammered in his brain. "Oh, God, you're not gonna tell me that *I* have anything to do with this, are you?"

Sam's eyes widened. "Oh, God, no! I've known I was gay since I was in high school."

Mark's mouth fell open. "You what?"

"Remember me telling you that Mr. Edwards was the one who caught me on the computer, watching porn?" Mark nodded. "Well, what he didn't tell anyone was that it was gay porn."

Mark was dumbfounded. "Really?"

"Yeah," Sam admitted quietly. "He said he had to inform the Head, but that the…subject matter would be our secret." He gave a wry smile. "I'd always wondered about him. Well, I stopped wondering after that. He was so cool. We had this long chat one day after class. He was the first person I told. I was just starting to be interested in guys, and it was a really confusing time."

"I still don't understand," Mark persisted. "You're passing yourself off as straight. Hell, you have a *girlfriend*!"

Sam wrung his hands. "Mark, there's no way I can be gay. My dad…. My dad just wouldn't understand."

Mark's heart went out to him. Apparently, that was one thing they had in common. "If that's the case, then okay, I get it. But why not stay single? Why go to the lengths of having a girlfriend?"

Sam stiffened. "I…I don't want to talk about Becky, all right? It's…it's complicated." He gazed at Mark imploringly. "Besides, there's something much more important that I want to discuss."

"What?" Mark's brow wrinkled—and then the breath caught in his throat as Sam leaned forward and kissed him. His lips were soft and warm. Mark let out a soft moan and cupped Sam's head, deepening the kiss, flicking out his tongue to lick the seam of Sam's lips, tasting him. Sam groaned and reached for Mark, his tongue demanding entrance. Mark was lost in the heady moment.

Until reality bit—hard.

Mark pushed at Sam's chest, breaking the kiss.

"Wait a minute!" He struggled to get his breath back. Sam stared at him, wide-eyed, lips parted. His cheeks were flushed.

"What's wrong?" Sam asked, his chest heaving.

Mark gave him an incredulous look. """What—you thought you'd tell me you were gay and that would be it? Next stop, between the sheets?" He shook his head in disbelief. "Sorry, Sam, it doesn't work that way." He shivered. Despite his protestations, the kiss had shaken him to the core.

"But…. But…" Sam's voice quavered. "I kissed you—and you kissed me back. I didn't dream that part, did I? That *was* you moaning just now?"

Mark shifted away from him. "So? I'm attracted to you. Hell, you heard me last night. That wasn't a lie." He softened his voice when he saw the confusion etched across Sam's face. "Yes, you're everything I've ever wanted in a guy. But none of that matters." Mark swallowed. "You have a girlfriend, Sam. And I'm sorry, but I will not be a party to you cheating on Becky." His chest tightened as he said the words.

Sam gazed at him incredulously. "So you're telling me you only have sex with single guys? You check every guy who ever comes onto you to see if he's wearing a wedding ring?" His lips twisted.

Mark met his gaze. "Yes, actually." He picked up his mug and took several mouthfuls of coffee. Sam was staring at him in startled silence. Mark sighed. "Okay, so I have no idea if they're in a relationship or not. They're only there to get blown or fucked. But I *do* look, every time." He fixed Sam with an intense look. "But that's beside the point. I don't know every guy I hook up with—not that there have been *that* many, I hasten to add—whereas I *do* know you. I've met Becky."

He shook his head once more. "I'm sorry, Sam. Much as I would love to take you into my bedroom right now and fuck your brains out,"—Sam jerked his head back in surprise—"I'm not going to."

There was a moment of stunned silence before Sam spoke. "You… want me?"

Mark chuckled. "Oh God, Sam, you have *no* idea how much I want you." He watched Sam's pupils dilate, and that simple physical reaction spoke louder than words ever could. "But we can't," Mark stressed, as gently as he could. Even as he said it, he felt his cock harden, his nipples tighten into hard little nubs. God, he ached. He looked down at his mug of coffee, deliberately avoiding Sam's gaze. He heard the hitch in Sam's breath and waited for his next words.

"You're right." Despite his words, however, there was no mistaking the note of reluctance in Sam's tone.

Mark heaved a sigh of relief. He'd instinctively known that Sam was an honorable guy, but it was good to hear him confirm Mark's faith in him. It didn't stop Mark's heart from sinking, all the same. *Why in God's name do I have to be so principled?*

"Would you mind if we talked some more?" Sam's question was almost shy.

Mark smiled. "Not at all. I have some questions of my own." He watched as Sam nervously gulped down his coffee. Mark had an idea. "How about we go somewhere and have some breakfast? I know somewhere quiet where we could grab a couple of bacon sandwiches and sit and look at the sea. What do you say?"

He mentally crossed his fingers. Anything to get Sam out of his flat and away from the temptation of taking him to bed. Having principles was one thing, but Mark wasn't Superman by any stretch of the imagination. He had no idea how long he could resist the lure of those blue eyes, that tight body. Right now, he was fighting the urge to stretch Sam out on the couch under him and trace every tattoo with his tongue, and play with the silvery rings through his nipples, tugging at them with his teeth.

Thankfully, Sam appeared to like the idea. "That sounds good," he acknowledged. "Can I ask a favor, though?" Mark waited expectantly. "Would it be okay if I grabbed a quick shower? I was sitting on the beach for a good few hours last night, and I feel kind of sandy." He flushed as he looked down at the couch. "I hope I didn't get sand everywhere."

Mark got to his feet and collected Sam's empty mug, along with his own. "Sure. I was going to have a shower myself. You go first. I'll find you a towel." Sam gave him a grateful smile. Mark deposited the mugs in the kitchen sink and went in search of a clean towel.

And while he's showering, I need to steer clear of the bathroom, Mark thought decisively. No, definitely *not* Superman.

"I've never been here before." Sam gazed around at the Beach Shack café as they sat in the sunshine, two cups of coffee in front of them. Mark loved coming down here to the south coast of the island. The café was nestled at one end of Steephill Cove. The quiet little bay comprised a collection of cafés and holiday homes. Below the railing of the café, waves crashed onto the green, algae-covered rocks. The bay was a horseshoe of sand, surrounded by a perimeter of similar rocks over which children and adults alike clambered in search of rock pools. A structure which resembled a lighthouse stood at the other end of the bay. The holiday home wouldn't have looked out of place in New England, its white boards and white picket fence glaringly bright in the morning light.

"I love it down here," Mark breathed. "I think it's the sound of the sea that draws me." He closed his eyes for a moment, focusing on the music made by the waves as they frothed onto the rocks below. Footsteps approaching their table had him opening his eyes. It was Richard, the chief server.

"Two bacon sandwiches," Richard said with a flourish, placing them on the table. "Anything else you want, Mark?"

Mark shook his head. "No, that's all for the moment, thanks, Richard."

"Then I'll be back when you've finished, with your second cup of coffee." Richard grinned at Sam and winked. "Never known Mark to ever stick at one cup of coffee."

Mark chortled. "You know me far too well." He indicated Sam with a nod of his head. "This is my friend Sam. It's his first visit down here."

Richard dipped his chin in acknowledgment.

"How's business?"

"Can't grumble," Richard said with a smile. "Andy's pleased, so it can't be bad." Andy was the owner. "Anyway, I'll leave you to your breakfast." He flashed them another quick smile and walked away, straightening chairs and tables as he headed toward the rear of the café.

"How long have you been coming here?" asked Sam. He took a bite out of the sandwich and moaned. "Oh, that's good."

Mark stifled a groan of his own as the sounds Sam made went straight to his dick. It was no use—as attracted as he was to Sam, it was now clear that nothing was going to happen between them, so he *really* needed to organize a trip across the Solent one day soon. "About three years," Mark replied. "Since Andy took over the place." He bit into his sandwich, savoring the crisp bacon. The taste was divine. In no time at all the sandwiches were demolished.

Mark drained his cup of coffee, knowing that Richard wouldn't be long in bringing another one. He glanced across at Sam who was looking out to sea, a contented expression on his face. Mark could understand that. He knew he wore the same look every time he came here.

"Was that what you wanted to tell me last night?" he prodded gently. "That you were gay?"

Sam nodded. "I felt awful, lying to you for the past three weeks. You were so open with me, and yet there I was, hiding my sexuality. It felt so wrong." The look of contentment was replaced by one of misery.

"There's *nothing* wrong with that," Mark stressed. "It's no shame to be in the closet, especially if coming out would spoil your relationship with your dad." Heaven knew, Mark wished *he'd* stayed in there longer. Coming out had made his already strained relationship with his mother ten times worse.

Sam tensed. "There's more to it than that, but it's not something I can really talk about, okay?" Mark gave him a nod of reassurance and he watched Sam relax into his seat.

"I know you said you and Becky had been together about a month. Was there anyone before that?" Mark itched to know more about what Sam was doing with Becky in the first place, but he didn't push. He figured Sam would tell him when he was ready.

"No, no one." Sam had his eyes fixed on a lone figure out on the water in a canoe. "I went out to a couple of gay clubs when I was in London a few times, but to be honest, I was scared to death. It wasn't like I imagined." He shivered.

"Tell me."

Sam scrubbed his fingers through his short hair. "I don't know, it was just so…. The music was loud and throbbing, the dancers… My God, the dancers were naked!"

Mark chuckled. "Oh, you went to a gay strip club. I've been to one a couple of times." He didn't mention the fact that he'd hooked up with one of the strippers after the show for a lightning-quick fuck in the alley behind the club. Something in Sam's words registered. "Sam… have you…what I mean is…" He cleared his throat. *Oh, for God's sake, just* ask *him*! "Sam, what have you done with a guy?"

A slow tide of red spread upward from Sam's chest, crept up his neck and across his cheeks. The blush was adorable. "I've blown a couple of guys, and been sucked off a few times." He fell silent.

"Have you and Becky had sex?" More silence. Mark waited, and when it became clear that no more would be forthcoming, he sucked in a deep breath. "Sam... are you a virgin?"

Those cheeks were suddenly bright red—and Mark had his answer.

"Sam. You're twenty-three." Mark couldn't imagine getting to that age and not having fucked *someone*, at least once.

"Look, my parents brought me up to see sex as something that happens when you meet someone and fall in love." Mark couldn't miss the defensive note in Sam's voice.

"Wait a minute—you had oral sex." Mark's eyebrows shot up. "So oral sex doesn't count as sex?"

Sam's cheeks were hot. "Sorry. I guess I think of sex as being when someone actually.... *you* know..." The words trailed off.

Mark's cheeks burned and his chin dropped to his chest. His face tingled. "Actually, I think it's great that you waited. Makes me wish I had."

Sam jumped in. "Oh, but being experienced is good, too." His cheeks glowed. "I know I want *my* first time to be with someone who knows what he's doing."

All of a sudden Mark heard his mother's voice in his head, the memory as clear as if it had been yesterday, not five years ago. He snorted. Sam gave him a puzzled glance. Mark explained.

"My mother's idea of the birds and the bees talk? 'Just make sure when you have sex for the first time that it's with someone who has a clue what they're doing. There's nothing more pathetic in this life than the idea of two virgins fumbling around together.'"

Sam's horrified expression said it all. "I… I don't think that's pathetic at all."

Mark looked away, crossing his arms over his chest. A feeling of heaviness settled over him. Things might have been different if his dad had been alive. He was certain his dad wouldn't have reacted to Mark's coming out in the same way as his mother did. A familiar slow tide of rage threatened to surge through him, but he fought against it, determined not to let anything spoil the day and this time he shared with Sam.

He fixed his gaze instead on the figure who was tugging a canoe up onto the beach. He recognized the young man clad in a bright blue wetsuit immediately. Taylor Monroe operated a small business down in the bay, hiring out surf boards, kayaks and wetsuits. Mark had just joined Ryde High School when Taylor had been about to finish his final year there. He'd been a bit of a loner at school, a typical surfer who seemed to spend every spare minute out in the water. Mark envied him his life. Taylor had a house right on the bay, a large white painted edifice with a porch where he would sit throughout the summer. Mark had often imagined living there. To be able to open a window and hear the sea. Heaven.

"Just so you don't feel *too* sorry for me." Sam broke through Mark's reverie. Mark gave him his full attention. "I do have a few toys." Sam grinned.

"Oh really?" Mark arched his eyebrows and Sam's grin widened.

"Yeah, but I have to be careful. I don't want to imagine how Becky would react if she found my Fleshjack." He paused before continuing. "Especially seeing as it's a replica of Brent Corrigan's arse." There was a moment of silence before both men fell about laughing.

Mark chortled. "Yeah, I can see how trying to explain *why* you have a replica of a gay porn star's arsehole might be rather difficult." Sam snickered. Mark looked at the handsome face of the man beside him and was seized by the sudden desire to reveal why Sam's kiss had blown him away.

"Seeing as it's confession time," he began, after drawing in a deep breath, "I want to say thank you." Sam cocked his head, narrowing his eyes. "When you kissed me earlier…." He dried up, ashamed to share the importance of Sam's impulsive action. Sam reached across the table and brushed his fingertips lightly down Mark's forearm. The simple gesture brought him a measure of calm. "You said that experience was good. Well, my experience of sex so far has been confined to furtive hook-ups in club bathrooms. I meant what I said this morning—there has never been another soul in my bed 'til you slid into it in the early hours." His chest tightened. "I've had sex in bathrooms, alleyways, dark corners of the dance floor"— Sam's eyes grew positively huge—"but never in a bed. And until this morning…" He pressed his fingertips against Sam's and then looked into his eyes. "No one had ever kissed me."

Sam caught his breath. "I was your first kiss?" Mark nodded, unable to tear his eyes away from the joyful expression on Sam's face. "Then we shared a first together. You were my first gay kiss, too."

Warmth flooded through Mark. The silence that fell following Sam's words was a comfortable one, broken only by the appearance of Richard with two fresh cups of coffee. Mark gave him a grateful smile as Richard slipped quietly away.

Sam sipped his coffee and gazed out over the bay. Little by little the sandy beach was filling with families: children running around, laughing and shrieking; dogs running into the waves, only to run back to their masters, shaking themselves violently and spraying water everywhere. It was an idyllic scene.

"Are we still okay?" Sam's quietly spoken question broke through his contemplation. Mark gazed at him quizzically. "What I mean is, are we still friends?" Sam twisted his watch around his wrist.

Mark stared at him in surprise. "Of course," he said with some force. "Why would you ask that?"

Sam puffed out a breath. "Because of last night and this morning. What with me treating you badly, and then sneaking into your bed, and then—"

"We're *fine*," Mark stressed. "Honestly." For which he was extremely grateful. Sam's friendship was important to him. "And Sam?" His eyes twinkled. "You're a good kisser."

Sam blushed. "You, too." He looked out to sea once more. "I love it here. This was a great idea."

Sam may be older than I am, Mark thought, *but he needs a keeper. Someone to take care of him.*

Chapter Seven

They walked along the path which led past the lighthouse and around the corner to where a sea wall had been constructed out of heavy boulders, which were held together in metal netting. The waves pounded the rocks on the shore as Mark and Sam headed up the steeply rising coastal path. As they walked, they talked.

Sam had lots of ideas for computer games. He shared these enthusiastically and Mark had to admit they were impressive.

"Will your dad let you design all those?" he asked.

Sam shrugged. "Maybe he'll let me do one and see how it goes. If it works out, he might let me do more of them."

"I love your ideas. It's great to hear original stuff that isn't basically a rehash of some old, tired game done far too many times already." Mark didn't play often on his PS3, but he liked games that made him think. He wasn't into mindless violence or loads of CGI. "And if your dad won't give you a shot, then maybe think about taking your ideas elsewhere. Trust me, *someone* will snap them up."

The path curved up to its highest point where a wooden bench had been placed, right at the cliff edge. Mark sat down, patting the sun-warmed wood beside him. Sam joined him. For several minutes they stared out to sea, the only sounds the waves and the harsh cries of the seagulls as they rose up on the air currents along the cliff.

So many thoughts tumbled through Mark's head, but one prodded him persistently.

He couldn't get over the feeling that Sam was heading for trouble. Before he could say anything, Sam spoke.

"I really am sorry for reacting the way I did in the pub. It was just the last thing I'd expected to hear, that I was basically your walking fantasy. And it was easier to hide behind an angry facade than come out and tell you the truth." His expression was glum. "I should have been honest with you."

Mark cleared his throat. "Look, I know you don't want to talk about what's going on between you and Becky." The words rushed out of him and he could have kicked himself as Sam tensed up yet again. Mark persisted. "And while I can't pretend to understand it, I just want to say one thing. If you ever need to talk, about *anything*, I'm here for you."

Sam's shoulders slumped forward and he pressed his palms to his eyes. "Thank you," he said at last, his voice shaking. "You don't know what it means to me to hear you say that." He lowered his hands and looked Mark in the eye. "I could really use a friend right now." Mark grasped Sam's hand tightly and Sam looked down at their joined hands with a smile. He lifted his chin. "And for the record? I didn't get into bed with you this morning so we could ma—have sex." Those cheeks were pink again. "I just wanted to be near you. But the impulse to kiss you was so strong, I couldn't fight it." He shook his head. "It…it won't happen again." His chin dropped to his chest.

"Sam." Mark freed his hand and cupped Sam's cheek, forcing Sam to look at him. "I won't deny it: if you were single, this morning would have ended *so* differently."

God, yes. Mark forced himself not to imagine Sam in his arms, kissing him, touching him… He inhaled sharply. "But you're not. So yes, I'll be your friend." He gave Sam a wry smile. "I could use a friend right now, too." He extended his hand and after staring at it blankly for a moment, Sam took it. They shook hands, Sam's grasp firm.

"Friends," Sam repeated, more confidently this time.

Mark smiled. "Friends." He was not a mean-spirited person, but in that moment, he found himself wishing fervently that Sam had never laid eyes on Becky.

Because Mark wanted him.

Mark felt the hairs stand up on the back of his neck. "She's behind me, isn't she?"

Sonia smirked. "Uh-uh, but never mind. Concentrate on what you're doing." She handed Mark another foil, her gaze focused on his hands as he applied the hair dye evenly and folded the strands of hair into the foil, crimping the edges securely. "You're doing a great job," she said in a low voice, and then leaned forward to whisper in her customer's ear. "Isn't he, Kathy?"

The lady in the chair giggled. "Mark, you're doing fine."

Mark had to smile at that. He was hyper aware of Marie's presence, which made it that much more difficult to focus, but he took several deep breaths and pressed on. It was his first attempt in the salon at coloring hair.

Sonia had definitely taken on the role of mentor, and despite Marie's obvious initial misgivings, his boss had let Sonia get on with it. What a difference a month had made. It was now late September and Mark was finally beginning to feel comfortable at work. Sonia's decision to let Mark cut her hair had proved the catalyst. A lot of the girls had jumped on the bandwagon at the thought of a free haircut, and Mark had found himself faced with demands that he do their hair too. He had risen to the challenge. When Marie finally offered him some dry words of praise, Mark knew he'd turned a corner. At last.

The last of the foils in place, Mark adjusted the timer and leaned forward with a bright smile to address his customer. "That's going to be about twenty minutes. Now, can I get you a cup of tea or coffee?"

Kathy beamed. "Ooh, a coffee would be nice." Mark gave her a grin. Kathy had been a regular throughout his time at the salon, and it had been Sonia's idea to leave Mark in charge this time. Nevertheless, he'd been grateful for Sonia's reassuring presence throughout. He gave Kathy's shoulder a quick squeeze, and after handing her a selection of magazines, he headed for the kitchen. As he stood waiting for the kettle to boil, his phone chimed in his pocket. He grinned when he saw the screen. Sam.

"I know that smile." Sonia winked at him from the doorway. "What are you two up to this weekend?"

Mark opened the message and frowned. "Nothing, apparently." He puffed out his breath in exasperation. "Becky says she has *plans*."

That would make the third Sunday in a row that Sam had canceled on him, and each time it had been something to do with Becky.

Sonia gave another smirk. "Hasn't she worked out yet that there are *three* people in this relationship? That's very inconsiderate of her." Mark stared at her open-mouthed and she laughed. "Oh, come on, Mark. You and Sam spend time together every Sunday and Monday, not to mention meeting up on weekday evenings occasionally. You're inseparable." She winked. "I think it's kind of cute."

"It's not funny," Mark groused. "She tells him they're going to be doing something, and then changes her mind at the last minute, only by then it's too late for us to do anything." If he didn't know better, Mark would swear it was deliberate on Becky's part. Sam promised him it wasn't. Mark poured boiling water over the instant coffee and stirred it briskly, trying not to let this new development spoil his good mood. "And we were going to go for a walk along the coastal path near Whale Chine," he said gloomily. Sam had suggested packing a picnic lunch if the weather allowed. The western side of the island was less inhabited, and its beaches less frequented. The plan had been to leave the car at the viewpoint above the theme park at Blackgang Chine and walk along the path as far as Brook village, have their lunch on the beach and then walk back. It would have taken up the major part of Sunday.

Sonia came fully into the kitchen and closed the door behind her. "Mark, I've been wanting to say something for a few weeks now, but I've kept putting it off." #

Mark's forehead furrowed.

"Sweetie, are you sure you know what you're doing?"

Mark stiffened and gave her an incredulous stare. "What do you mean?"

Sonia sighed. "The amount of time you two spend together. Now, don't get me wrong," she said, holding up her hands as Mark took a step back. "I think it's great that you have such a good friend." She moved closer and took hold of his hand. "But sweetie, you talk about him *all the time*. You should listen to yourself. It's 'Sam did this' and 'Sam said that,' several times a day." She gazed at him. "If I didn't know any better, I'd swear you were in love with him." She gave Mark a keen glance, finally falling silent.

Mark cringed. *Damn her*. He sucked in a deep breath, saying nothing, not trusting himself.

Sonia placed her hand over her chest. "Oh hell. I hate being right all the time." Her voice was soft.

Mark shrugged. "I don't know what you mean." He ignored the sudden dry mouth and the tingling in his stomach. Sonia leaned forward and grabbed his hands.

"Mark, this is me you're talking to. You know, Sonia, the woman who sees right through you?" Her eyes were kind. "You're in love with him."

Mark closed his eyes. "It doesn't matter whether I am or I'm not. He has Becky." His chest felt as though an iron band had been tightened around it, limiting the flow of air into his lungs. A lump formed in his throat. He felt tears prick his eyelids as Sonia suddenly pulled him to her in a warm hug, her arms tight around him.

"It'll be okay, sweetie," she whispered into his ear. He rested his head against her shoulder, taking comfort from her solid presence. Tears slid down his cheeks and soaked into her pink cotton blouse.

"I'm a fucking mess," Mark whispered back. "I told myself I could do this. I could just be his friend." What he hadn't counted on was Sam. The man was addictive. The more time they spent together, the more strongly Mark felt himself drawn to him. A day didn't go by without some contact with him in one way or another. Phone calls. Facebook. Texts. Skype. Sam was the last thing in his thoughts each night as he drifted off to sleep. He'd wake the following morning to a smiley on his phone and a cheery *Morning*! Certainly nothing earth-shattering, but he looked forward to his morning texts with eagerness.

Sonia cradled him in her arms. "Is it serious, him and Becky? Because I have to ask myself—if it's doing this to *you*, how is Sam coping?"

Mark groaned. "I don't *know*!" And that was the hardest part. He really didn't.

Sonia reached into her pocket and pulled out a crumpled paper tissue. She handed it to him and he wiped his eyes angrily. "You must think I'm such a basket case."

"Oh, sweetie." Sonia pulled away to look him in the eye. "Now, you need to listen. This has to stop. It isn't good for you." Mark drew back from her, swallowing. "You know I'm right. Okay, so Sam's gay, but he's got a girlfriend."

All of a sudden her head tilted and her eyes widened.

"Oh my God—she could just be a beard!" Mark gasped and Sonia's eyes sparkled. "What—you didn't think I knew what a beard is? I told you, I have a few gay friends apart from you." She bit her lower lip. "Do you think Becky knows she's just a cover?"

"I don't give a *fuck* what Becky knows." Mark spat out the words. "I only know she has Sam and I don't, and it's killing me." He hated the plaintive whine in his voice. "God, just *listen* to me. How sad am I—in love with my best friend."

Sonia nodded, her eyes never leaving his. "And that's why you need to pull the plug, sweetie. Before you get in any deeper."

Mark snorted. "I think I'm in as deep as it gets." He gave himself a mental shake. "Anyway, I have to take Kathy her coffee." He reached for the cup but Sonia stopped him, laying a hand on his arm.

"Let me do that. You pull yourself together in here for a sec." She gave him a tight smile and walked out of the kitchen with the coffee. Mark wiped his eyes once more and blew his nose. He knew Sonia was right, of course. This was doing him no good at all. But the thought of walking away from Sam wrenched at his heart. *I don't think I can do it.*

Only thing was, he couldn't see any other way out of this mess. Someone's heart was bound to get broken in the process—and Mark could lay money on it being his.

"God, I need a drink," Mark muttered under his breath as he tidied up the mobile units containing hair curlers and assorted brushes. The salon was looking tidy once more, ready for Monday morning.

"And I think you might have company for that drink," Sonia murmured next to him. Mark gave her a puzzled glance. "Take a look out the window."

He straightened and looked toward the window—and froze. Sam waited across the street, leaning against the whitewashed wall, his eyes trained on the salon. Mark couldn't help his reaction. Warmth radiated throughout his body and he was suddenly conscious of his racing heartbeat. Then he looked more closely. What the hell?

Sam had a blackened right eye.

"Has he been in a fight?" Sonia had obviously noticed, too.

"If he was, he hasn't said." There'd been no mention of it in Sam's earlier texts that day. Mark gave a cursory glance at the wall clock. Five minutes to go. He hurried into the little staff room to collect his jacket, thoughts colliding in his head. Sam hadn't been to the salon since the day Mark had laid eyes on him seven or eight weeks ago. His gaze was drawn continually to the tall, lean figure dressed in a plain sky blue shirt and tight, dark blue jeans.

"Seeing as you seem to have a friend waiting for you, and you've finished your work, you can leave, Mark."

Mark jerked his head back. Marie stood behind him, watching the scene. She smiled.

"Really?" He cursed himself silently for his reaction.

Fortunately for him, Marie appeared to be in a good mood.

"Yes, off you go. I'll see you Tuesday morning."

Mark grinned impulsively. "Thanks, Marie." To his amazement she returned his grin. Mark dashed over to Sonia and gave her a quick impulsive peck on the cheek before diving out the door. He watched Sam's eyes light up when he caught sight of Mark. Sam crossed the narrow street, smiling widely. Mark knew his face wore a sappy grin, but he didn't care.

"I thought, seeing as we can't have our walk tomorrow, you might like to go for a drink," Sam suggested.

Mark snorted. "You are a mind reader. I swear, one minute I'm thinking how much I need a drink and the next? I look up to see you standing there." He grinned. "Lead on." They walked along the street and turned the corner onto Union Street. Wetherspoons stood on the left hand side of the street, and already the seats in the window area were filling up. As they crossed the street, Mark gave Sam a sideways glance. "So you gonna tell me what happened?" He gestured toward Sam's eye.

Sam shrugged. "Got up at some ungodly hour this morning to go to the bathroom and walked into the door." He lifted his hand to touch the area around his eye gingerly, and winced. "Next time, I'll put the light on." He didn't meet Mark's gaze, however. "Anyway, don't you think it makes me look...butch?" He smirked.

Mark guffawed. "That wasn't the *first* word that came to mind, I must admit." They entered the pub and Sam headed straight for the bar. Mark smiled to himself. After all these weeks, he knew Mark's drinking habits.

Mark found the corner booth empty and quickly slid across the bench seat, claiming it. This had become their corner. Sam appeared not long after, clutching two pints of Wight Gold. Mark took several long swallows, trying not to gaze at Sam's throat as his Adam's apple bobbed. God, the man had a lovely neck. Mark shook himself. Enough of the torture. That eye looked sore, but Sam appeared to pay it no mind. "Where's Becky tonight? And why has she let you off the leash?"

As soon as the words escaped his lips, Mark cursed himself. Sam tensed. "She's out with some of her girl friends," he said, his voice tight.

"I'm sorry, Sam." Mark lowered his voice. "That was wrong of me." To his dismay, his apology did nothing to improve the situation. Sam seemed ill at ease all of a sudden. Mark concentrated on his pint, draining it quickly. Sam said nothing but stared sullenly at his pint glass. Mark leaned closer. "I mean it, Sam. Please, forgive me." He bit back a sigh of relief as Sam finally relaxed a little, giving a brisk nod of his head before downing his pint. "Look, do you want to go for a walk on the beach? It's a lovely evening."

He watched as Sam appeared to consider his suggestion. September was still clinging valiantly onto the coattails of summer: the last few days had been warm, the evenings balmy.

"Sure," Sam said at last. "Let's get out of here."

They left the pub and began to walk down Union Street, which fell away steeply as it reached the pier. Automatically Mark headed toward East beach which was at the foot of his road. The early evening sun was still warm on his shoulders.

Beside him, Sam walked in silence, eyes on the ground. As they passed the car park the two men went onto the beach, took off their trainers and carried them, the sand warm under foot as they walked along. The sunlight sparkled on the water, and Mark watched the catamaran as it made its way across the Solent, heading for Portsmouth. Mark fought the urge to reach for Sam's hand. In spite of his earlier acknowledgment that this situation couldn't continue, Mark let himself relax, enjoying Sam's presence beside him. *Just let me enjoy this a little longer*, he pleaded with whoever was listening.

"This is nice," Sam murmured contentedly. "It feels as if we're in a world of our own here." Mark's heart stuttered in his chest. His thoughts exactly. He stopped walking and looked around. The wide beach was deserted, the tide already on its way out. Mark dropped his trainers onto the sand and turned to Sam, his heart pounding. Sam was staring at him, that familiar puzzled crease between his eyes. The sunlight glinted on his hair, and the evening light lit up his face. And suddenly Mark knew exactly what he wanted. He leaned in close and cupped Sam's cheeks with both hands.

"Forgive me," he murmured. Sam's eyes widened. Mark stared at the beautiful face which was always in his thoughts. Sam's breathing speeded up.

"For what?" Sam licked his lower lip.

"For this." Mark's hand slid around to grab Sam's nape as he brought their faces together—and kissed him.

Sam froze, his trainers falling from his hands onto the soft sand, and then let out a soft whimper as he relaxed into the kiss, his tongue sliding deep to explore Mark's mouth hungrily. Mark attacked his mouth, sucking at Sam's tongue, losing himself in the increasingly sensuous kiss. He slid his hand down Sam's back, skating along his spine, coming to rest just above the swell of his buttocks encased in those tight jeans, molded around him like a second skin.

Sam groaned into his mouth, the sound full of urgent need. He clutched at Mark's back. Mark pulled Sam against him, rocking into him, all too aware of Sam's erection against his hip, his own rigid shaft pressing against the zipper of his jeans.

"God, I want you," Mark moaned, reaching with both hands now to cup Sam's arse, pulling him tight against him.

Sam froze and with a low cry he pushed Mark away, eyes suddenly full of misery.

"Why are you doing this?" The cry seemed to be torn from Sam's lips. "And why am I *letting* you? God, we must be mad." Sam ran his fingers through his hair. His eyes locked on Mark, and Mark's heart sank to see the pain reflected in them. "We can't do this, Mark."

"I-I'm sorry." Mark's stomach rolled as Sam reached down and grabbed his trainers. "Sam?" He found it difficult to breathe as Sam backed away from him, visibly trembling. "Please, Sam, don't go." His heart was hammering. "I don't want you to go. Come home with me. Please."

Sam swallowed.

"If you only knew how much I want to do just that." But still Sam backed away across the sand, his expression haunted. "I'm sorry, too." Mark couldn't speak. Fear was thick in his throat. He could only watch in horror as Sam turned and fled, running back to the road and heading toward the pier. At last Mark found his voice.

"SAM!"

Sam didn't turn back. Not once. Mark watched as Sam reached the corner of Union Street and turned, disappearing from sight.

"Sam." The whisper slid out of him. "What the fuck have I done?"

He stood there on the sand, his limbs shaking, his gaze never leaving the corner where Sam had disappeared from view, as if keeping his eyes fixed on that spot would somehow bring Sam back.

It was a long time before he felt the inclination to move.

The blue LED light emanating from his alarm clock cast a ghostly hue over his bedroom. Mark had given up checking the time. He'd come to bed some time after ten, when he realized that he'd been staring at the TV screen for a couple of hours and hadn't registered a single thing that had been on it. It was nearly midnight. Through his open window he could hear the raucous laughter of the nearby pub's patrons who had spilled out onto the streets and were wending their way home, albeit in a noisy fashion.

Sam hadn't answered a single call.

Sam hadn't returned one of his seven or eight texts.

Mark was screwed.

He still couldn't figure out why he'd kissed Sam. He only knew that as Sam had stood there on the sand, looking so heartbreakingly beautiful, Mark had been seized by the urge to hold him in his arms, to kiss those warm lips one more time. And once kissed, he wanted more…

It didn't matter. That look of sorrow on Sam's face was burned into Mark's memory.

The intercom buzzer shattered the silence. Again. And again.

Mark glanced at his clock. Midnight. Hurriedly he hopped out of bed, naked, and ran to the door. He pressed the button. "Hello?"

"Mark, it's Sam. Please, let me in." At least this time he sounded sober.

Chapter Eight

Mark couldn't hold back his groan. "I can't do this again, Sam. Please, go home." His heart almost stopped as he heard the distinctive sound of someone weeping.

"Please, Mark. I...I need you."

Mark jammed his finger against the door release button and then yanked back the bolts. He turned the key and flung open the door. As Sam came into view, Mark gasped.

Sam was bleeding profusely from a cut above his right eye. There were scratches across his cheeks and arms, some of them bleeding.

"Oh my God, what happened?" Mark pulled him into the flat and closed the door. Sam sank to his knees on the hall carpet, as if his legs would no longer bear his weight. Mark dropped to the floor beside him and cradled him in his arms, ignoring the blood which smeared onto his bare skin.

"I can't take it anymore," Sam wailed as Mark held him, Sam's arms hanging limply at his sides. "Please, let me stay."

Mark took a closer look at the cut. It seemed deep. "We need to get this seen to. It looks like it might need stitches." His mind reeled. "Sam." He held Sam's face as carefully as he could, gazing at him anxiously. Sam was still weeping. "Sam." More urgently now. At last Sam met his gaze. "Who did this to you?"

Sam shook his head vehemently, his lips pressed together into a fine line. "Can't...can't."

"Please, babe." The endearment slipped out. "You have to tell me."

Sam stared at him blankly, seeming to almost crumple in front of him. Trembling, he opened his mouth to speak, and the one word that pierced the silence of the hallway shocked Mark into stillness.

"Becky."

It was as if Mark's heart had been plunged into ice.

"Becky? Becky did this?" He stroked the hair away from Sam's forehead, sticky with blood. Sam was shaking, his eyes huge. "Look, we can talk about this later. Right now it's more important to get your head looked at." He slipped his arms under Sam's and helped him up onto his feet. He guided Sam into his bedroom and sat him on the bed. Sam looked so lost and confused. Mark dashed into the bathroom and pulled a small hand towel from the airing cupboard. He held it under the tap and ran cold water over it until it was sodden, then he wrung it out. When he got back to the bed, Sam hadn't moved an inch. He winced as Mark wiped carefully at the blood on his face, Mark patting his cheeks scored with long scratches to try and remove some of the dried blood from them.

One more trip to the bathroom to rinse out the towel, and then Mark folded it and pressed it against Sam's forehead.

"Hold it there, please, and press as hard as you can" he instructed the subdued Sam, who automatically raised his hand and did as he was told, his eyes wide and staring. Mark glanced down at himself.

"I'll put on some clothes and then I'll take you to St. Mary's, okay?" The hospital was only about twenty minutes away.

Sam gave him a dazed look and then nodded. His silence worried Mark. He made sure Sam wasn't about to fall off the bed and then grabbed his jeans and T-shirt. As he squirmed hurriedly into the jeans, he continually glanced over at Sam. He shoved his bare feet into his trainers and then helped Sam to stand. After grabbing his jacket and car keys, Mark led his stunned friend out of the flat and down to the street.

The Fiesta was parked in a parking area behind the flats, surrounded by trees. As they approached the car, the floodlight was activated and bathed the area in bright white light. He opened the passenger door and eased Sam into the seat, watching carefully to ensure he didn't catch his head. From the look of him, Sam was in shock. Mark secured his seatbelt and then got behind the wheel.

Mark drove the car through the quiet streets toward the center of the island to Newport. There was little traffic around and Mark nudged the accelerator impatiently, slowing only when he neared the stretch of road which contained one of the island's only three speed cameras. Sam's head lolled back against the headrest, eyes closed, his hand still holding the damp towel in place. When Mark saw him shiver, he put his foot down, and in no time, the hospital was in view.

Mark pulled into an empty parking space and reluctantly left Sam for a moment while he fumbled in his jeans pocket for change for the parking meter. Once the ticket had been placed on the dash, Mark held out a hand to Sam.

"Come on, babe. Nearly there." Sam opened his eyes and stared at Mark, his eyes clouding. Mark grabbed his hand and helped him to get out of the car. After locking it, he put his arm around Sam's shoulders and guided him to the main door of the hospital. Just inside the main building on the right was the Beacon Center, the out-of-hours clinic. It was still open. They entered through the automatic sliding doors and went to the reception desk. Several people were sitting around, quiet pockets of chatter taking place. Mark saw a couple of lads looking very much the worse for wear: they'd clearly been in a fight.

The nurse behind the desk looked up as Mark and Sam approached. Her gaze took in Sam's head and the spots of blood which had spattered his blue shirt. "What's the name?"

"Sam Prince." Mark spoke for his friend. He had to wonder how much information Sam was capable of giving in his present state. Sam leaned against the desk, his arm resting on the smooth counter top.

"Address?" Mark saw Sam frown as he tried to focus, but he managed to stutter out an address in Sandown. The nurse took down his details. "Okay, you need to take a seat. The doctor will call you."

Mark helped Sam to a seat in a quiet corner, away from the clinic's other occupants. Sam leaned back against the wall, his eyes staring unseeing at the ceiling. The hand containing the towel fell limply into his lap. For several long minutes neither of them spoke. Mark stared down at the floor. There were so many questions going around in his head.

"Do you think we'll have to wait long?"

Mark could have wept with relief to hear Sam speak. "There aren't that many in front of us." He gazed anxiously at Sam. "How are you feeling?"

"Head hurts," he whispered. Sam closed his eyes. Mark yearned to take hold of his hand, but he wasn't sure how Sam would feel about that, given their location. He glanced at the cut: the bleeding seemed to have stopped at least.

"What happened, Sam?" Mark couldn't hold it in any longer.

Sam winced. "Not now. Please." He kept his voice low. He opened his eyes. Mark was jolted by the pain he saw reflected there. "When I'm finished here, can we go back to your flat? I promise, I'll tell you everything." Sam swallowed.

"All right," Mark acquiesced. The look of relief on Sam's face was palpable. "Just close your eyes and rest quietly. It won't be long now." Sam gave him a careful nod and closed his eyes. Mark sat back in his seat, his gaze fixed on the wall clock. He tried to shut down his thoughts but it wasn't happening. All he wanted right now was answers.

Mark opened the front door to his flat and let them in. Sam had been very subdued all the way home. Mark supposed some of that might be due in part to the late hour, not to mention the headache. When the doctor had examined Sam's head and found a lump the size of a golf ball at the back of his head, it had suddenly become clear to Mark why his friend had been so out of it.

"The doctor said you can take two painkillers before you go to bed," he reminded Sam as they walked into the living room. "Do you want them now?"

Sam stared at him uncomprehending. "I... I don't understand."

Mark became still. "You've had a couple of stitches in your head and you've been disoriented since you turned up on my doorstep. You're staying here tonight. No argument." Sam regarded him in silence for a moment and then nodded, once. Mark switched on the lamp beside the sofa and then went to the kitchen cabinet where he kept his first aid box and various medical supplies. He pressed out two paracetamol into his palm and then filled a glass with water. Sam was perched awkwardly on the edge of the seat cushion. Mark put down the glass and tablets, and then grabbed a cushion and placed it at one end of the sofa.

"Okay, take these." He handed the tablets to Sam who swallowed them dry with a grimace, before taking two large gulps of water. "Now lie down, please." Sam looked up at him questioningly, but Mark fixed him with a firm look. Sighing, Sam stretched out on the sofa, and Mark pulled off his trainers. Then Mark sat on the floor beside him, hugging his knees. "So...."

Sam stared up at the ceiling.

"Where do I start?" He spoke in almost a whisper.

"How about telling me what happened tonight?" Mark suggested gently. "We can sit like this, if it makes it easier not to look at me while you talk." He badly wanted to reach out and take Sam's hand. *Let him talk first. This has to come out.*

Sam took a deep breath. "Becky saw us tonight."

Mark's jaw dropped. "Where? When?"

"On the beach. She was across the road at the Ryde Castle hotel in the bar with four or five of her friends." Sam swallowed heavily. "She saw us kissing."

Oh hell..... Mark's heart sank. "Oh God, this is all my fault. Sam, I'm so, so sorry."

Sam rolled onto his side to face Mark, his expression grave. "No, it isn't. That's what I'm trying to tell you." He inhaled deeply. "I'll get to that in a minute. She told me that I wasn't to see you again. And that if I ignored her, there would be… consequences."

Mark's stomach rolled at the thought of losing Sam. "What did you say to her?" His heart fluttered as he waited to hear.

Sam gave him a weak smile. "I told her that she and I were through. I… I stood up to her." He shivered as he gestured toward his face. "You can see how well *that* went down." Sam swallowed. "She… she hit me with a wine bottle first. Then when she really lost it, she threw a wineglass at my head. But when I wouldn't back down, she went at me with her nails—fuck, they're more like talons—and scratched me all to hell."

Mark stared at him incredulously. "And you just *let* her?" Sam flushed.

A sudden coldness spread throughout Mark's body. "This wasn't the first time she'd done this, was it?" Sam shook his head slowly, his eyes full of misery. "The black eye?" Nod. "And before that?" Sam closed his eyes and Mark felt a wave of nausea. "Oh, please tell me why you'd stay with someone who did that to you."

"That's a long story." Sam whispered.

Mark couldn't hold back any longer. He took hold of Sam's hand and clasped it tightly. "We have as long as it takes. I'm not going anywhere." Those gorgeous blue eyes opened wide and Mark was floored by the look of gratitude he saw there. Mark leaned forward and kissed the tip of Sam's nose.

Sam puffed out his breath unsteadily. "Thank you." He reached across and stroked Mark's cheek softly with his fingers before wrapping them around their joined hands. He took a breath. "You already know Becky's dad, Donald, is well off. Well, he and my dad were at school together. They were inseparable, apparently. Both are now very successful business men." Mark nodded. "About three months ago, Dad came over to the island for a week or so and the two of them got together. Dad and I were invited to a big party at Donald's place in Seaview. It was there that they introduced me to Becky." He shivered and Mark tightened his grip. "Dad made some joke about how it would be nice if she and I went out together, sort of keeping it in the family." He laughed bitterly. "There was nothing I could say. He'd already mentioned quite a few times to me on the phone that it was strange I hadn't had a girlfriend yet. The last thing I wanted was Dad becoming suspicious."

"You're sure he'd react badly if you came out?" Mark wanted to know. "Maybe it would be okay. Maybe—"

Sam shook his head. "Trust me, Mark. I know *exactly* how he'd react. He's not reticent on the subject, believe me." Tremors rippled through him, and Mark knelt beside the sofa and stroked his back gently, watching as his shivering eased. "I had no choice but to say yes. And it was okay, for the first few weeks at least. I didn't do anything more than kiss her a couple of times, and I could tell she was surprised that I didn't make an attempt to get her into bed. It wasn't long after that, though, that I started to hear the stories."

"What stories?"

Sam let out a wry chuckle. "You know how things work on the island, Mark. It's a very small place. Everyone knows everyone else. And secrets don't *stay* secret for very long." He winced.

"Is your head okay?" Mark regarded him with concern.

Sam smiled. "You are such a sweet man." He lifted Mark's hand and kissed it tenderly. The gesture warmed Mark inside. "I started to hear rumors that Becky had a temper, and the tales appeared to be emanating from some of her ex-boyfriends. Except that saying she had a temper was apparently putting it mildly. One ex complained that she'd become violent." His gaze clouded over. "I asked her about it. She didn't react well. It seemed her dad had heard the same stories and was trying to get her to attend some anger management course on the mainland."

Mark snorted. "I take it she didn't want to go."

Sam shook his head. "She didn't think she needed anger management, and she thought her dad was over reacting. But when he started making noises about how she had to attend the course or *he'd* start thinking about cutting her allowance, she needed a way to convince him that the boyfriends were lying."

Mark widened his eyes. "Oh, *this* is gonna be good."

Sam's stare became distant. He slumped into the seat cushion. "It was then that she went rooting around in my chest of drawers and found my magazines—and my Fleshjack." He gazed at Mark, eyes full of misery. "And of course she put two and two together."

Mark froze. "What happened?" he whispered.

"I was convinced she'd break it off between us after that, but it seemed Becky had other plans." He gulped. "She told me that we were going to stay together and that I had to somehow convince her dad that there was no truth to the stories—or else she would go straight to *my* dad and tell him his son was gay."

Mark tensed. "That bitch. That blackmailing little *bitch*!"

Sam's chin trembled. "I had no choice, Mark. I had to agree to it. So she began arranging meals out with her family, giving her dad plenty of opportunities to see how *great* we were getting along." He gave a sardonic laugh. "I must be a *really* good actor, because her dad took me aside to tell me how pleased he was that we were together and that I was obviously a good influence on his daughter."

The breath died in Mark's throat at the expression on Sam's face. So much pain...

"Sam, just look in the mirror. This is more than Becky having a temper. Where will it stop?"

Sam's eyes opened wide. "But it *has* stopped. I left her. I couldn't stay with her after this."

"But what about your dad?"

Sam stiffened. "Can't do anything about that now. It's coming. She said as much tonight." He drew a sharp intake of breath. "But I've had three months of this shit. No more. To be honest, it only got bad in the last few weeks, when...." Mark caught his breath, unable to look away. "When I started to realize I had feelings for someone." The words slipped out into the quiet room and Sam met Mark's gaze.

Mark's heart gave a leap in his chest. *Oh God, please.....* "Sam, I..."

"Yes?" There was such a hopeful expression on Sam's face that Mark couldn't breathe. "Mark?"

Mark laid his hand gently on Sam's scratched cheek and leaned in close, their lips meeting at last. Sam's eyes closed and he gave himself up to the sweet, tender kiss. How long they kissed, Mark had no idea. He lost all concept of time, aware of nothing but the silkiness of Sam's lips, his sweet breath, the heat radiating from his body. When at last they parted, Mark let out a contented sigh.

"Oh Sam, I love you."

Sam became still. Those soft lips parted as he stared at Mark, eyes so large and round. That poor, damaged face was never lovelier. "I love you, too. I wanted to tell you how I felt, but—"

Mark laid a finger gently on Sam's lips. "It's okay. I know." His face broke into a smile of sheer joy. "You don't know how happy I am to hear you say those words."

He hadn't removed his hand from Sam's face. He dropped his voice to a whisper. "Say them again."

Sam's face was wreathed in a beautiful smile. "I love you, Mark."

Mark let out his breath in a slow, steady exhale before moving closer once more to take Sam's mouth in a kiss that seemed to spin out into yet another time-stopping moment. Sam sighed into his mouth, the sound swallowed up as Mark kissed him softly.

Reluctantly Mark broke the kiss and pulled away slightly. "I have to tell you, I'm so relieved that you broke up with Becky." He focused on Sam, his eyes narrowing. "But why didn't you tell me what was going on?"

Sam's cheeks burned and he tried to look away, but Mark wouldn't relinquish hold of his face, forcing him to look Mark in the eye. Sam's breath suddenly hitched. "How could I tell you? The idea of telling anyone, even you, that a woman hit me. I mean, women don't hit guys, do they? God, Mark, I was so ashamed."

Mark let out a soft sigh. "Oh, Sam, if you only knew…." The crease between Sam's eyes appeared. Mark let go of him and sat back on the floor, winding his arms around his knees once more. He was aware of Sam watching him, forehead furrowed. *God, this is hard.* Mark swallowed and met Sam's anxious gaze.

"When I was growing up, there was stuff going on at home that I never told a soul about. I couldn't, because I felt too ashamed." He heard Sam's breath catch. "My mum…. My mum has a temper." He hesitated, unable to believe he was finally about to share his painful secret. "And she took it out on my dad."

Sam stared at him wide-eyed. "Oh Mark." He reached for Mark's hand and grasped it tightly. "Was...was it bad?"

Mark snorted. "Bad? How about bad enough that it sent him to an early grave?"

Sam's mouth fell open. "Oh no."

Mark closed his eyes, but it was no use. He could still see his father's haunted expression as he lay in the hospital bed. "He never stood up to her, not once. He just took it all. I used to get so angry, wondering why he didn't just walk out of there." He swallowed several times. "I know now. He told me when he was in the hospital. He didn't want to leave me alone with her. And there was no way he would ever have challenged her for custody. The shame was too great. You were right. What man ever wants to own up to being hit by a woman? " Hot tears pricked his eyelids and he wiped them away with the back of his hand.

Sam sat up and scrambled off the sofa, kneeling beside Mark and wrapping his arms around him, pulling him close. Mark buried his head against Sam's neck, fighting valiantly to hold back the tears which threatened to spill. Sam kissed his head, forehead, cheeks, little murmurs escaping his lips as he comforted Mark.

"It's okay, baby, he's free of it now."

And then the dam burst. Mark sobbed, his tears falling freely onto Sam's blood-spattered shirt. Sam held him close as he cried for his father. All the pain of those years poured out of him, the feelings of impotence as he stood by and watched his mother hurt his father, first with a vicious tongue, and later with her fists and anything else that was at hand.

Mark had never forgiven her. Even though she had never laid a hand on him, he had drawn away from her, from the day of his father's death, right up to the present. He barely said a word when she phoned him once each week, confining his replies to short, clipped sentences or monosyllabic answers. And it would stay that way.

"Thank you for trusting me with this," Sam murmured into his hair. "It means so much to me." He cupped Mark's cheek and gazed into his eyes. "Love you."

Mark's heart soared. "Oh God, Sam, I love you." He curled his hand around Sam's nape and pulled his face closer, their lips meeting once more in a heady kiss. He felt Sam sag against him. Mark broke the kiss and gave Sam a searching glance. "Wonderful though this is, you need some rest. We can talk more in the morning." Mark was already flagging. He got to his feet and held out a hand. Sam looked at it, forehead creased. Mark smiled. "Come to bed. I want you in my arms tonight."

The look on Sam's face made his heart sing. "Oh yes," he breathed, his face alight.

Mark took hold of Sam's hand and led him to the bedroom in silence.

Chapter Nine

The early morning sun spilled through the yellow curtains of his bedroom, bathing the room in a warm light. Mark lay there, his arm around Sam, body curled around his, and just drank in the sensations. He could still detect the medicinal odor of the dressing on Sam's stitches, an unwelcome reminder of the previous day's event. Mark nuzzled his chin into the juncture where Sam's neck met his shoulder, inhaling the aroma that was Sam, familiar and comforting. *That's better*.

He smiled to himself as he recalled them undressing last night. Even after spending a number of Mondays naked on the beach with him, Sam's cheeks had flushed as he'd stepped out of his jeans, leaving his boxers in place. Mark had followed his lead and left his briefs on. At that moment the only thing on his mind was to get Sam into bed and hold him. And the soft murmurs that emanated from Sam when Mark had spooned up around him, told Mark that Sam was more than content to lie in his arms. They'd kissed briefly, but it had soon become clear that both men were badly in need of rest. Once the light was out, Mark had succumbed quickly, drifting off into a deep, velvety sleep.

To awaken and find Sam still in his arms was like a dream.

Mark kissed Sam's shoulder, the skin silky and warm beneath his lips. Part of him still couldn't quite believe that Sam was really there.

He moved slowly across Sam's back, laying a carpet of tender kisses across his shoulder blades, then down his spine, only to drift upward to his shoulders. Mark's hand was pressed against Sam's chest, stroking the smooth skin of his pecs, before moving slowly downward to his abs, trailing fingertips over the contours. Sam stirred slightly, his back stretching as he leaned into Mark's touch.

"Good morning." Mark spoke quietly into Sam's ear before kissing it lightly. Sam shivered.

"Morning." Sam reached back to touch Mark tentatively, the angle awkward. Mark wasn't having that. He shifted his body away from Sam's warmth and pushed Sam onto his back. He pressed his body up against Sam's side. Sleepy blue eyes regarded him, no trace of unease in his expression. Sam reached up to put his arms around Mark, stroking his fingers down Mark's back and over his biceps, finally gliding over his chest. Sam let out little sounds of pure contentment. "Your skin feels good, soft." Sam smiled shyly. "I love touching you."

Mark loved being touched.

"I've never had this before," he murmured. Sam tilted his head. "Someone touching me so…" The word 'lovingly' hovered on his tongue, and in that second he recalled Sam's declaration of several hours ago. It wasn't a dream, was it? All of a sudden, his stomach roiled. He bit his bottom lip, his throat suddenly dry as dust.

"Mark." Sam's voice broke through. Mark gazed down at him, taking in the gentle smile which played around his lips, and the eyes which regarded Mark with warmth—and something resembling amusement.

"Mark, I'm going to have to stop touching you for a sec. I need the bathroom." Yeah, there was definitely a twinkle in those eyes.

Reluctantly Mark pulled away and Sam slid out of the bed. "There are fresh towels in the airing cupboard," Mark said, trying to anticipate Sam's needs. He watched as Sam walked around the bed, Mark's eyes feasting on the lean, tall body, the dark swirl of those tattoos which were *so* sexy. His gaze moved lower to where the tattoo disappeared below the waistband of Sam's boxers. Mark swallowed, instantly picturing the delicate swirls which he knew lay coiled around the root of Sam's cock—and then he forgot to breathe as he took in the sight of Sam's erection which had already tented the fabric of his boxers.

Mark was aware that Sam's breathing had changed. He lifted his eyes to find Sam staring at him, cheeks flushed, obviously conscious of Mark's focus.

"And what if I need something other than a towel?" Sam asked breathlessly. His pupils dilated.

Oh fuck. "There…there's a new toothbrush under the wash basin and toothpaste in the wall cabinet."

Sam blinked and cleared his throat. "And where do you keep your condoms and lube?" His scarlet cheeks betrayed his nervousness. Sam swallowed. "That is, if you want to—"

"Oh God, yes," Mark breathed.

Sam grinned. Mark could almost see the tension slipping from him. "I'll be right back." And then he was gone. Mark lay in bed and listened to the sounds coming from the bathroom, and his pulse started racing.

Swiftly he reached into the drawer of his bedside table and pulled out a strip of condoms. He scrabbled about until he found the bottle of lube. He placed them next to the lamp, an ear cocked toward the door as he listened to Sam's movements in the next room. And then it hit him. It would be Sam's first time. Would Sam expect to top? Would he be prepared to bottom? Mark's anticipation faltered as his breathing accelerated. He only knew he had to make it good for Sam. Memories of Mark's own first time assaulted him and he was determined to give Sam a much better experience.

"Stop thinking so hard."

Mark started. Lost in his thoughts, he hadn't heard the tell-tale signs that Sam had finished in the bathroom. He glanced up—and caught his breath.

Sam stood in the doorway, nude, his hard cock jutting out from his body at a right angle, the thick ring through the end of his dick making Mark's hole clench. Okay, so Mark didn't bottom—but for once he ached to know how that would feel as it slid into his arse and nudged his prostate. Sam stroked his cock lazily, tugging at it, squeezing it, and the sight of pre-come glistening at the tip spoke loudly to Mark. Sam was eager.

"Give me a minute, all right?" Mark pleaded, as he leaped from the bed and pushed past Sam to dart into the bathroom. As he dashed through the fastest wash-up of his life, he could hear Sam's dry chuckle. Mark's teeth and toothbrush came together in a brief but thorough meeting, and then Mark was done.

When he returned to the bedroom, he found Sam lying in the middle of the bed on his back.

He was still playing with his cock while he reached past his balls to play with his hole. Sam already had a finger in his arse, his breath coming out in hoarse pants as he pushed into the tight channel.

"Wanted to get myself ready for you," Sam panted. Mark groaned, now hard as a rock at the thought of sliding into Sam's virgin arse. Sam's eyes pleaded with him. "Come here and kiss me."

Mark needed no second invitation. He clambered onto the bed and knelt beside Sam, bending low to kiss him, their kisses no longer tender but full of urgent need. Sam moaned as Mark plunged his tongue deep into Sam's mouth, exploring him eagerly. Mark reached down and took hold of Sam's hand, forcing him to relinquish his cock as he guided it to his own. Sam's eyes opened wide as he wrapped his hand around Mark's swollen shaft. He broke the kiss, breathing heavily.

"Oh God, Mark. Want you in my mouth."

Mark's breath caught as Sam got up onto his hands and knees and, grasping Mark's cock firmly in one hand, he opened wide and took all of Mark's length into him. Mark shuddered to feel hot, wet heat surrounding his prick, and he resisted the urge to thrust, letting Sam take control, his head bobbing furiously as he sucked Mark deeper.

"Oh my God, you're good at this," Mark gasped out as Sam worked his cock, establishing a steady rhythm which was driving Mark out of his mind. He heard what was undoubtedly a chuckle which vibrated around his dick—and then Sam speeded up.

K.C. WELLS

Mark looked down at his lover as he hungrily sucked Mark's dick, and then his gaze traveled along the lovely line of Sam's spine to his arse, to where two rounded globes lay in wait for him. Mark caressed the length of Sam's back, stretching over Sam to slide a finger along his crease, in search of his prize. Sam shuddered violently as Mark pushed a single finger into Sam's pulsing hole. Sam groaned loudly around his cock, tremors rippling through him.

"You want me inside you?"

Sam nodded eagerly, his head bobbing faster, small whimpers escaping from him almost constantly now. Mark pressed deeper into the tight, hot tunnel that was begging for his cock and Sam moaned around his length. Mark didn't want to wait any longer.

"God, Sam, I need you."

Sam pulled away from his dick with a loud groan and knelt up, wrapping his arms around Mark and kissing him fervently, his cock heavy and hard against Mark's belly, its ring slick with pre-come. Mark reached around him to slide his finger once more into Sam, pressing between his cheeks, seeking that hot little hole. Sam pushed back, clearly desperate for more.

"W-want you, now." Sam's voice quavered. Mark kissed him deeply and then pushed him onto his back in the center of the bed, Sam's head propped up by numerous pillows. Sam regarded him with shining eyes. Mark had never been this hard in his life.

"I want you to grab hold of your legs and pull them back," he instructed, tugging at his shaft which was leaking pre-come furiously.

The breath caught in his throat as Sam obeyed him without hesitation, revealing his tight pucker which quivered. "Oh God, Sam… I need to taste you."

Sam's eyes rolled back in his head as Mark stretched out on his belly between Sam's spread thighs and boldly licked over his hole. He shuddered as Mark pressed his tongue into him. "Oh fuck, Mark, no one's ever…." His words died as Mark tongued around the rim and slid a finger into him at the same time. "M-more," he moaned softly. Shudders coursed through him as Mark lost himself in his task: he wanted Sam to be begging for his cock. And getting Sam there was going to be fun.

Mark loved rimming, but it was a delight he rarely enjoyed. Brief hook-ups in club bathrooms didn't allow for indulging in some hot tongue play, and now that Mark had Sam exactly where he wanted him, he was going to take his time. And he could do this *all day*. Mark worked Sam's hole with tongue and fingers, searching for his prostate. When Sam arched up off the bed, eyes wide, mouth open in a silent scream, Mark knew he'd hit pay-dirt.

"Jackpot," he said softly, and then slid in a second finger, pushing them into Sam slowly and then crooking them to rub over that little knot that had Sam seemingly on the verge of coming. Sam shook, thighs trembling as he succumbed to Mark's eager ministrations.

When Sam began to tremble more violently, Mark ceased his sensual tongue bath and reached for a condom. Sam's eyes never left him as Mark tore open the foil wrapper and slid the latex over his thick shaft.

K.C. WELLS

Mark slicked himself with lube and then pushed two glistening fingers into Sam. Mark knelt at Sam's arse, cock aching to be inside him.

"Ready?" he asked softly.

Sam locked eyes with him, his body rippling with anticipation. "Ready."

"I want you to relax. Breathe. It will make this much easier." Mark held his dick steady at Sam's hole, the swollen head pressed against him, and slowly pushed inside him, noting Sam's immediate grimace. "Breathe, baby." He wrapped his hand around Sam's rigid cock and gently worked it, rubbing his fingers over the thick ring through the head, listening to the changes in Sam's breathing. Sam panted, his face contorted.

"It b-burns."

Mark paused about half way inside him and waited, letting Sam's body adjust to the intrusion. He held himself still and bent low over Sam, kissing him tenderly. He watched as the tremors died away, Sam's face finally relaxing. With a supreme effort, Mark forced himself to keep still, knowing Sam's body would tell him when it was okay to continue. After a few minutes, Sam began to push down on Mark's cock, slowly at first, but then with increasing speed.

"Better?" asked Mark with a grin, already knowing the answer, Sam's body talking to him, louder than words ever could. Sam's eyes opened wide and he nodded.

"Oh God, Mark." Shivers rippled through Sam. "God, it feels good."

Mark let out a low moan as he pushed slowly into Sam until his cock was buried up to the hilt in tight heat, their bodies pressed together.

"Mark, please…. more."

Mark's grin widened as he began to rock into Sam, hips rolling fluidly as he thrust into him repeatedly, Sam no longer lying passively but pushing upward to meet his thrusts.

"You feel so good," Mark murmured as he slid deeply into Sam, loving the low moans that escaped his lover's lips. "You're so tight around my cock. You feel amazing." He rocked faster, hips snapping as he plunged again and again into the furnace of Sam's body. Sam brought his legs up to wrap around Mark's waist, gripping him tightly as Mark slid into him, the head of his cock nudging Sam's gland almost continually.

"Mark, I'm not going to last much longer." Sam's chest was flushed deep red, his balls high and tight.

Mark leaned down and kissed him, sliding smoothly into him, his hand working Sam's cock continually. "It's okay, babe. Come. Come for me." Mark pulled back until only the head of his dick remained inside. His eyes glittered. "We're going to do this again,"—he thrust forcefully into Sam, causing him to cry out—"and again,"—another punishing thrust until he was balls-deep inside his lover—"and again."

Sam howled as his cock erupted into Mark's hand, and as Sam's channel tightened around his dick, Mark groaned. "Oh fuck, you're making me come."

His balls emptied into the latex and he shuddered through his orgasm, head dropping down to Sam's shoulder as he stroked Sam's chest which gleamed with a light sheen of perspiration. Sam let his legs fall back to the bed, his breathing erratic as he came down from his climax, hands reaching for Mark to pull him close, their lips meeting in languid kisses which seemed to go on and on, Mark's cock still deep inside him.

"Love you." Sam's whispered words caused Mark's heart to soar. He gazed in awe at the man in his arms, their bodies still joined.

"Love you, too." Sam's body cradled his as Sam wrapped arms and legs around him once more, locking him into a fierce embrace as they kissed. They were oblivious to all but the beating of their hearts and the whispered words of love which slipped from their lips, between kisses that were so sublime as to almost take their breath away.

"What day is it?"

Sam chuckled. "Is that what good sex does to you? Scrambles your brains?" He winked.

Mark sighed happily. "It feels like we've spent *days* in bed." He knew it was only two days, but it felt longer. Monday night had arrived, and with it the gloomy prospect of going back to work the next morning. "Can't we just stay here?" He whined a little, but his eyes twinkled.

Sam groaned and rolled on top of him, the sheet riding low over the globes of his arse. He kissed Mark enthusiastically and began to roll his hips. Mark let out a low moan as he reached down to cup Sam's cheeks, pulling him tight, their dicks rubbing against each other, both men getting harder by the second. "Want you inside me," Sam whispered, grinning.

Mark's breath hitched. *God, yes.* So far, Sam had bottomed each time they'd made love—and it *had* been making love, so far removed from Mark's previous experiences that there was no comparison—and had seemed very content for it to remain that way. But for the first time since he was seventeen, Mark contemplated bottoming. He hadn't said a word to Sam yet, figuring that they had far more pressing issues to discuss.

"My God, you're insatiable." He let out a contented sigh when Sam giggled. The last two days had been a slice of heaven. Sunday afternoon they had finally got to have their walk along the coastal path, along with their picnic lunch on the beach near Brook. Monday had been a warm enough day to spend it on Yaverland beach, soaking up the last of the sun. Autumn was surely hovering around the corner.

The rest of the two days had been spent making love.

Slow, sweet lovemaking that lasted well into the early hours of Monday. A lightning-quick fuck in the shower that had Mark convinced his neighbors were about to bang on the walls—Mark was been a little loud in his enjoyment of Sam's body, and their orgasms had been nothing short of explosive.

Sam's first experience of public sex when Mark had gotten him on all fours on the beach, facing out to sea, while he plowed into Sam from behind, his hands gripping Sam's hips so tightly that he left finger marks. Sam had been so keyed up by the prospect of being caught that he'd lasted for precisely five thrusts of Mark's cock and had come all over the beach towel with a hoarse cry, Mark climaxing not long after him.

Mark had always known that falling for his best friend in the space of two months was going to be one-sided. Never in his wildest dreams had he expected his feelings to be reciprocated. So to find out that Sam loved him was a moment of sheer joy. But Mark also lived in the real world, and he knew that reality was about to intrude, bringing pain into Sam's life, and thereby, his life also. Sam had said nothing, but Mark knew his lover well enough to see those moments when the thought of what was coming right at them was clearly on Sam's mind.

Sam rocked against him, the slow rolling of his hips by now a tell-tale sign that Sam wanted to make love, but Mark knew he couldn't put off the moment any longer.

"Are you going to tell your dad before Becky does?"

He felt Sam go still on top of him, his body stiffening. Sam's head dropped to his shoulder, burying his face in Mark's pillow. Instinctively, Mark wrapped his arms around his lover, holding him close. He could feel Sam's heart pounding strongly behind his ribs.

"You think I should, don't you?" Sam whispered near his ear.

Mark held onto Sam as he rolled him onto his side, the two men facing each other on the bed.

Sam's eyes were dull, his joyful mood having fled him. Mark kicked himself mentally for putting that look on Sam's face, but he knew they needed to address the issue sooner rather than later.

"Baby, it's up to you. I would never dream of telling you what you should do." Mark swallowed. "But maybe it's something that he needs to hear from his son, rather than from that evil bitch. And once you tell him, no matter what his reaction, her hold over you is lost." He stroked the hair out of Sam's eyes, hating the pain he saw reflected there.

Sam shuddered out a long, shaky breath. "I know you're right, of course. Doesn't mean to say that makes it any easier."

Mark kissed him, letting his lips linger, loving how Sam melted right into it. As he pulled away, he met Sam's gaze. "But I'll give you something else to think about, something much more pleasant." Sam cocked his head. "Whatever he says, whatever happens, good or bad—I don't want to be apart from you a moment longer than I have to." Mark took a deep breath. "Live with me. Either here, your place in Sandown, or somewhere completely different—I don't care where, I just want you with me." Sam's eyes were suddenly so large that Mark had a fluttery feeling in his stomach. He forged ahead. "I know it might seem too soon, after the relatively short time that we've—"

All the breath was stolen from his body as Sam kissed him.

Mark sank into the kiss as Sam pressed up against him, the two men entwining their arms around each other. Sam hooked his leg around him to pull him in still tighter.

When at last Sam broke the kiss, breathless and bright-eyed, Mark could only stare at him in wonder.

"Yes." That was all the response Mark got. Sam's cheeks were flushed, and Mark was shocked to see the glimmer of tears on his cheeks. But the huge smile on Sam's face was what sent waves of warmth radiating throughout Mark's body.

"Yes?" Mark had never felt so alive as in that one glorious moment. *Sam said yes.*

Sam nodded, his eyes never leaving Mark. "If I have you by my side, I can face anything the world cares to throw at me." His expression grew more sober. "And if the worst comes to the worst? We'll deal with it—together."

Mark could live with that. Hell, yes.

Chapter Ten

"Okay, out with it."

Mark gave Sonia a look of wide-eyed innocence. "Out with what?"

Sonia snorted. "Yeah, like I believe *that* look." She fluttered her eyelashes. "Aw, come on, sweetie, you can tell *me*."

Mark guffawed and almost sprayed her with his mouthful of tea. "And don't try those puppy dog eyes on me. You know I can never resist when you do that."

She winked. "That's what I was counting on." Mark continued to meet her gaze with a reasonably straight face, but he burst into laughter as she grew more and more impatient. "You are a pain, do you know that, Mark Horrocks? Now tell me what's going on, because you've had a smile a mile wide plastered across your face all morning." Sonia took a bite out of her sandwich and gazed at him expectantly.

Mark was in a brilliant mood. Being back at work after his two days spent with Sam was a real drag, but he consoled himself with the fact that he'd see Sam after work. They were going to talk seriously about their living arrangements. Waking up that Tuesday morning with Sam in his arms had been sheer heaven. There were definite advantages to sharing his bed. Top of the list would have to be morning cuddles—which had turned swiftly into mutual morning blow-jobs.

Mark smiled to himself as he thought of their shower together, a little awkward as the shower was above the bath. A decent sized shower was going to be on their must-have list for a new place together.

A new place together… Mark still couldn't believe that Sam had agreed to them moving in together. He was pretty sure his face was sporting a sappy grin, but right now, he couldn't give a damn.

Sonia cleared her throat impatiently and Mark was pulled from his delightful thoughts. He grinned sheepishly. "Sorry. I was miles away."

Sonia pouted. "Yeah, but it's where you were that's driving me crazy." Suddenly her eyes opened wide. "This is about Sam, isn't it?"

Mark laughed. "Well, duh! It's taken you all morning to work *that* out? Your psychic powers must be failing." He couldn't hold back the gleeful giggle that burst out of him. *Have I ever felt this happy?* The answer was easy. Hell, no.

"Mark, are you still on your lunch break?" Wendy stuck her head around the staff room door. "'Cause you have a visitor." She retreated.

Mark frowned. No one ever came to see him when he was at work. Sam had gone back to his flat to get some work done. Seems he'd gotten a little behind over the weekend for some reason.

There was that grin again.

Mark hauled himself up off the tiny sofa that he was sharing with Sonia. She demolished what was left of her sandwich in two bites.

"I'd better come, too," she mumbled as she swallowed the last of it. He gathered up the two mugs and hurried out of the small staff room, curious to see who had arrived. To his surprise, Sam stood in the middle of the salon, his face pale and drawn, nervously twisting the denim jacket which he was holding in his hands.

Mark went up to him. "Sam, what's wrong?"

Sam's eyes were red, but it was the dull look in them that grabbed Mark's attention. This was not the same man who'd kissed him goodbye a few hours ago. "Can we go somewhere and talk, please?"

Mark glanced swiftly at the wall clock. He had ten minutes left of his lunch break and Marie was nowhere in sight. "Sure, come with me." He led Sam back into the staff room and pushed the door shut behind him. No sooner had he done that, Sam had his arms around Mark, holding him so tightly that Mark grew concerned. "Babe, what is it? What's wrong?" He could feel Sam shaking. Mark pulled him toward the tiny sofa. "Come on, sit down for a sec."

Sam sat down, seemingly unwilling to let go of him. Mark was shocked to see tears sparkle in his eyes. He pulled Sam to him and held him close, stroking his hair. "I've got you, Sam. Talk to me."

Sam said nothing for a moment, but the shaking eased. He raised eyes full of misery to gaze at Mark. "I rang my dad."

Mark's heart sank. "I take it he didn't react well."

Sam swallowed. "Apparently I have to start looking for a new job, because he isn't prepared to have his *gay* son working in his company." He grimaced. "And that's the polite version."

Mark didn't know what to say.

He'd hoped against hope that Sam had it wrong, that his dad wouldn't prove to be a complete arsehole. But for him to fire his own son…. Mark could only imagine the pain that Sam was going through. A thought occurred to him.

"How did your mum react? Is she like your dad?" He held Sam's hand, stroking it.

Sam shrugged. "I didn't think so, but he wouldn't let me talk to her. I could hear him yelling at her when she wanted to know what was going on." His chin dropped to his chest and he sagged back into the sofa. "This is such a mess."

Mark shifted uncomfortably. "And it's all my fault." His chest felt tight when he thought of the pain he'd brought into Sam's life.

Sam jerked his head up, his eyes blazing. "Don't you *ever* blame yourself for this. I meant what I said last night. We both knew it was never going to end well, but we can deal with it—together." He jutted out his chin. "Understood?" Those beautiful blue eyes gazed intently at him.

Mark leaned toward Sam and kissed him softly on the lips. When they parted, he met Sam's gaze. "Understood."

The door opened suddenly and both men jumped. Sonia came into the room, looking flustered. Her eyes went wide when she saw the two of them sitting so closely together, Sam's hand clasped firmly in Mark's. She gave Sam a quick nod and then turned to Mark.

"I'm sorry to intrude, but I really think you need to get out here now. Sam, too."

Mark's eyebrows shot up.

They got up quickly and walked into the salon. Mark stifled a groan as he saw who was waiting by the reception desk, her fingernails tapping against the counter. Becky stood with her back to them, immaculately dressed in a linen jacket and pants. Even from the rear, her body language was plain. She was clearly not in a good mood. Mark glanced around the salon. There were only a few ladies being seen to. He puffed out a sigh of relief. This was not going to be pretty, and the fewer observers, the better. He walked slowly toward her, Sam behind him.

As they neared her, Becky whirled around, her eyes gleamed malevolently when she caught sight of Mark. When Sam appeared from behind him, she gave him an intense, fevered stare.

"I might have known *you'd* be here," she flung out at him.

Sam opened his mouth to speak but Mark laid a warning hand on his arm. He could already see the expression on Marie's face from the doorway of the kitchen. She stared in astonishment at Becky.

"What do you want, *Becky*?" Mark struggled to keep his tone polite, although his hands itched to slap the bitch when he thought about how she'd treated his Sam.

Becky walked slowly across to Mark, until she was standing so close to him that he let out an involuntary shiver. She leaned closer, her breath puffing into his face. "I've come to warn you to stay away from Sam." Her eyes were cold. "You leave him alone, or else."

Mark held himself straight and looked her in the eye. "Or else what? Is that a threat, Becky?" He kept his voice low. In his peripheral vision he saw Marie moving toward them.

Everyone in the place had their attention focused on them.

"I could make life very difficult for you here," Becky hissed. "You might think differently about being with Sam if you lost your job because of him." Her eyes glittered. "I could make that happen, y'know. I know people on this island."

Mark wanted to laugh at this deluded woman who clearly believed she wielded that much power. Before he could say another word, Sam stepped in.

"Becky, you need to leave now." He spoke quietly, but Mark picked up the slight tremor in his voice. "I've already told you—we're through." The decisive edge to Sam's voice made Mark's chest swell with pride. This was not the same Sam who had sat in the salon all those weeks ago.

Becky's eyes narrowed. "I will talk with you later."

Sam met her gaze head on. "We have nothing to talk about. I made my feelings clear on Saturday night and nothing has changed." He gave her a sad smile. "Except that I have to tell you, I spoke with Dad this morning, so your bargaining chip is useless." Then his face hardened. "I'll be sure to give my regards to Donald when I ring him later today. I'm sure he's going to be very interested in what I have to tell him about his daughter. And show him, of course. The photos we took on Saturday of my face should prove useful when I visit the police station, too."

Becky blanched. Inside Mark was singing. *Oh, you beautiful man…*

"Sam, you wouldn't…." Her words trailed off. She gazed beseechingly at him, all trace of anger melted away.

To Mark's surprise, Sam took hold of her arm and began to lead her away from Mark toward the door of the salon. Mark followed. No way was he letting Sam go through this alone. He glanced across at Marie who was watching the proceedings with a disapproving look. As Sam walked Becky toward the door, Marie's face cleared. She was obviously relieved to see the back of Becky. Mark could understand that. Becky struggled, but Sam held her arm firmly. Mark marveled at this new, stronger Sam.

They got to the door and Sam reached around Becky to open it. He let go of her arm and gestured to the street. "Bye, Becky. I don't expect to see you again, but it's a small island. You never know." Mark watched her stumble into the street. Becky's face was white.

From his vantage point behind Sam, Mark could hear her panicked tone, so different from earlier. "Are you really going to talk to Daddy?"

Sam nodded, his expression grave. "I'm sorry, I have to. You need help." When her eyes widened, he gestured toward his face. "Doesn't *this* tell you something?" Her gaze dropped and she flushed. "You know I'm right." She mumbled under her breath and Mark couldn't catch the words, but her inability to look Sam in the eye told him a lot. Becky pulled her linen jacket tightly around her body. With a final slow nod at her, Sam stepped back into the salon and closed the door. He turned to face Mark, his shoulders sagging. Despite his apparent confidence, the encounter had clearly taken its toll on him.

Mark regarded him with shining eyes. "I am *so* proud of you."

Sam flushed and opened his mouth to speak, but he was interrupted by the sound of Sam's phone ringing. He pulled it from his jean's pocket and looked at the screen, becoming very still. He flipped it open, his hands shaking. "Mum?"

Mark gaped. He watched Sam's face break into a joyful smile as he listened intently to his mother, interjecting now and again. The call only lasted a minute or so, but the change to Sam's expression was enormous. When he'd finished, he put the phone back into his pocket and turned to Mark, his face glowing.

"Mum said, whatever Dad may say, she still loves me."

Mark let out a huge sigh of relief. "Oh, that's great." At least Sam wasn't cut off from his family entirely. "Does she think your dad will come around?"

Sam shrugged. "I don't really know. To be honest, I'd be surprised if he did. He's not one to change his mind once he'd made it up. Knowing that Mum's in my corner makes it more bearable, though."

He stepped closer to Mark, and Mark caught his breath at the look in those eyes. "But having you by my side?" Sam reached out his hand and cupped Mark's cheek tenderly, and Mark couldn't help leaning into that touch. "That makes my life perfect." Before Mark could say a word, Sam drew Mark to him and kissed him. Mark closed his eyes and melted into the kiss, dimly aware of noises from the people around, soft gasps and murmurs of surprise. He couldn't have cared less. Sam was kissing him, not holding back as he deepened the kiss, and the rest of the world simply faded into the background.

Until he heard Sonia's heartfelt exclamation. "Oh my God, that's so *beautiful*."

Mark let out a low murmur as Sam pulled away, a sheepish grin on his face. "I think we're creating a scene," Sam whispered, "so maybe it's time I got out of here."

Mark felt a stab of disappointment. "Do you have to go?" The last thing he wanted to do right now was work. Even as he said the words, however, he knew he was being unreasonable.

Sam chuckled. "Er... yes? I have to start looking for a new job, for one thing. And then start looking for a new place for us." He leaned in and kissed Mark once more, his lips warm and soft. "I have a favor to ask."

"Name it." Mark was in such a good mood, he'd agree to anything right now.

"Would it be all right if I moved in with you 'til then? I don't want to waste another second being apart from you." Those breathtaking eyes pleaded with him.

Mark beamed. "Oh God, yes." The thought of Sam moving in filled him with joy. And then he had an idea. He reached into his jeans pocket and pulled out his key ring. He fiddled with the ring for a moment as he worked two door keys off it. Mark opened Sam's palm and pressed the keys into it. "Key to the main door. Key to my flat. There's a spare set at home."

There was no mistaking the look of joy on Sam's face. He grasped the keys tightly. "Thank you." He leaned in and kissed Mark lightly on the lips. "In which case, I'll be waiting for you when you get home."

He winked. "So hurry home to me, okay? I'll have dinner waiting." He leaned closer to whisper in Mark's ear. "And after dinner, I have something special planned."

Mark's pulse raced as he considered what that might be. Sam's gaze was smoking hot, leaving him in no doubt that whatever he had in mind, Mark was going to enjoy every minute of it. Sam's eyes glittered and Mark's cock hardened. *Oh God.* He went weak at the knees.

And with that, Sam turned to the ladies who were watching and gave them a cheery wave. "Bye, ladies." He grinned as he stepped out of the salon, waving through the window at Mark as he set off down the street. Mark watched him until he was no longer in sight.

Mark felt so light, he could have floated across the salon. The salon. Oh hell—he suddenly remembered where he was. He glanced around at the faces which regarded him, all of them smiling, even Marie. Sonia beamed at him, her eyes sparkling. She winked at the staff.

"Looks like our Mark finally found his Prince Charming after all!" Snickers and chuckles greeted her words.

Mark reddened and then gruffly cleared his throat. "Okay, time I did some work, I think." He glanced up at the clock. Five hours to go until he could go home—to Sam's arms.

"How come you never told me you could cook like that?" Mark pushed away his empty plate with a contented sigh. He'd arrived home to the strange experience of being buzzed into his own flat, since Sam had his keys, only to be greeted by a wonderful aroma as he climbed the stairs to the top floor. Sam was leaning over the bannister, watching his approach, the mouth-watering smell emanating from the open door behind him.

Sam blushed. "I wasn't sure if you'd like it." He'd prepared chicken breasts in a delicate white wine and cream sauce, along with brown rice and broccoli. The flavor had been sublime.

Mark lifted the tray from his lap and placed it on the floor, before leaning across to kiss Sam on the mouth. "I loved it," he murmured as he pulled away from the kiss. "I feel positively spoiled."

Sam winked. "Then you're going to love this." Mark's eyebrows lifted as Sam got up from the couch and went to the fridge. When he pulled out a bottle of champagne, Mark's eyes lit up. Sam flushed. "I thought it would be nice to celebrate us deciding to live together."

"I couldn't agree more," Mark said wholeheartedly. He got up and went to the cupboard where he kept his glasses and withdrew two tumblers. He looked sheepishly at Sam. "Okay, I need to buy some wineglasses, I get it."

Sam snickered. "What does it matter what we drink it out of? It won't change the taste of the champagne, will it?"

Mark's heart swelled with love. His man—eminently practical. *My man.* Damn, that sounded good.

Sam poured the champagne and handed him a tumbler. He brought his glass to Mark's and clinked it lightly.

"To us." The words were uttered softly, Sam's gaze fixed on Mark.

"To us." Mark's reply was equally soft. They drank the bubbling gold liquid, its taste bursting into life on Mark's tongue. He took Sam by the hand and led him to the couch, where they sat and sipped their champagne.

"This is wonderful." Sam leaned back into the couch and sighed happily.

Mark couldn't agree more. "So, what are your plans?"

Sam tilted his head. "Plans?"

"For a job. Moving in here. Stuff like that."

Sam stretched out his long legs. "I rang round a few games design companies this morning and one of them expressed an interest. They want me to interview next week."

"That's great," exclaimed Mark.

Sam waved a finger. "Don't get carried away *just* yet. This isn't a done deal, all right?"

Mark nodded, his eyes shining. "They'll *love* your stuff," he declared emphatically. He paused, unsure of how to phrase his next sentence. "Have you thought… you could take your dad to court, you know. What he's doing in illegal. He's discriminating against you because you're gay."

Sam sighed.

"Yeah, I know, but I'm not about to sue my own father, even if he *is* being an arsehole. I'm just going to find a company who want me and design them the best games I can. I figure success is the best revenge." He gave a sad smile and then sipped more champagne. "I brought enough clothes and stuff from my flat to last until the weekend. Then I figured you could help me move out on Sunday." He quirked an eyebrow. "Does that sound okay?"

Mark stroked his chin. "Well, only if you're going to pay me for my services." He grinned.

Sam stared at him, his pupils large. "What did you have in mind?" His deep voice was suddenly husky.

Mark gazed at Sam's full lower lip, moist from the champagne. Sam's breath hitched as Mark took the glass from his hands and placed it with his own on the coffee table. The air was crackling with sexual tension as Mark slowly leaned in to kiss Sam, taking his time. He ran his tongue lightly across Sam's lips, feeling the shudder that rippled through his lover. To his surprise Sam pushed him flat onto the couch and stretched out on top of him. He rolled his hips, the sensual movement pushing his erection against Mark's. The motion became more urgent as Sam claimed Mark's mouth in a kiss full of need. Mark moaned softly as Sam's weight pressed him into the seat cushions, pushing up his hips to meet the insistent thrusting of Sam's cock.

"Want to be inside you."

Mark froze as Sam's words penetrated his brain. *Oh fuck.*

Sam raised himself on his arms and stared down at Mark, an expression on consternation clearly etched across his face.

"You… do you not want me to….?" His words trailed off. He started to pull away, and Mark groaned inwardly to see the hurt in those eyes. He grabbed Sam and pulled him down onto him.

"*Never* think I don't want you, okay?" His eyes pleaded with Sam. Mark swallowed. "It's just that I… " He took a deep breath. "I've only ever been fucked once. My first time when I was seventeen." He tried not to shiver as he recalled the brief but painful encounter.

Sam stroked his cheek. "But I'm not talking about fucking. I'm talking about making love." He leaned down and kissed Mark softly on the lips. "To the man I love." His eyes were so large and round, the barest sliver of blue around those wide pupils. "Please, Mark, I want to do this. I want to be inside you."

Mark's heart swelled with love. He couldn't deny Sam anything. "Then yes," he whispered. He cupped Sam's nape and pulled him down into a fierce kiss, Sam moaning into his mouth as he got into it. He broke the kiss to meet Sam's urgent gaze. "Make love to me."

Chapter Eleven

No sooner had the words left his lips than Sam got to his feet and held out a hand. "Bedroom." Sam was trembling, but Mark could see the stony outline of his cock. He allowed Sam to lead him into the bedroom, and once there, he began to undress Mark slowly. Mark punctuated each item's removal with a soft kiss, his arousal increasing with every glide of Sam's hands over his bared skin. He reciprocated by taking Sam's clothes off, piece by piece, until at last both stood nude, facing each other. Sam's dick was a rigid column of flesh, and Mark's hole clenched as he looked at the heavy ring through it. The thought of that sliding over his gland sent shivers of anticipation dancing up and down his spine.

Sam pulled back the sheets and climbed onto the bed. He lay on his back and held out his arms. "Come here." Mark got onto the bed and crawled across to where Sam lay. He straddled Sam's hips and leaned down to kiss him, pushing his tongue insistently at the seam of Sam's lips, demanding entrance. Sam opened for him with a low moan as he ran his fingers through Mark's hair, and then slid his hand down Mark's back, the movement raising goosebumps over Mark's skin. Mark shifted position to slide his shaft against Sam's, starting slowly but moving more insistently as small gasps escaped Sam's lips.

Sam startled him as he stretched toward the bedside table and pulled open the drawer hurriedly.

"They're in here, aren't they? Your condoms and lube?"

Mark smiled at the slight edge of panic in Sam's voice. "Here, let me." He climbed off Sam, scooted across the bed to the table and pulled out a condom and a bottle of lube. He handed them to Sam and grinned. "How do you want me?"

The tension on Sam's face melted away. "In my arms." Once more he beckoned to Mark and Mark slid across the bed into his waiting arms. Sam held him close, kissing him softly, the kisses growing in intensity as he moved down Mark's neck, nuzzling him. Mark clung to him, losing himself in the headiness of the moment, until Sam moved his hand lower, stroking down his back until he reached Mark's crease. He caressed the firm globe, squeezing it gently. In a move that had Mark catching his breath, Sam grabbed his leg and lifted it until Mark's knee was almost resting against Sam's shoulder. He heard the click of the bottle and then let out a low gasp as Sam slowly slid a finger into him. Mark rolled his head back, but Sam held him close as he pushed all the way in.

"Oh my God." Sam's eyes were wide. "You're so hot, so tight…"

"More," Mark managed to croak out. Sam claimed his mouth in a searing kiss as he slid a second finger into his hole, and Mark nearly howled when Sam found his prostate. "God, *there*, yes!" Sam plunged his tongue into Mark's mouth, devouring him as he pushed deeper inside him, robbing him of speech.

Mark started to unravel. He whimpered as Sam finger-fucked him, as expertly as if he'd been doing it for years. At this rate, once Sam finally slid into him, Mark wouldn't last long.

"Please, babe, I need you."

Something in his tone must have communicated the urgency of his request. Sam pulled free and eased Mark onto his back, before opening the foil square with trembling fingers. Mark watched him roll the latex over the ring, and for one brief moment he considered how it would feel to have Sam bare inside him. He pushed the thought aside. Time enough for discussions and testing later. Right now, Sam was slicking up his cock.

Sam pulled Mark back into his previous position and held his dick stiffly against Mark's hole. Mark could feel its heat, the head pressing against his entrance. He reached down and placing his hand over Sam's, he guided Sam's cock into his body. Sam groaned loudly as he inched his way into Mark's tight passage. Mark held his breath, trying not to tense up as the thick length eased slowly into him, until finally Sam was seated all the way inside him.

"Are you okay?"

Mark loved the note of concern. The visible effort of holding back was there on Sam's face, yet he was waiting, making sure that Mark was all right. Mark clung to his shoulders and nodded. Sam's gaze never left his face as he rolled his hips and began to move inside him, the motion smooth and unhurried. Sam was taking his time. He cupped Mark's cheek and kissed him tenderly.

"It feels so good inside you," he murmured. "Like you're pulling me into you, as deep as I can go." He rocked up into Mark, his thrusts increasing in speed as he slid his hand around to Mark's back, pulling him tighter. With a groan Mark surrendered to the sensations which exploded within him.

A feeling of being so solidly connected to Sam that it took his breath away.

"Love the way you make me feel," Mark gasped out as Sam pushed all the way into him. His eyes rolled back into his head as the ring in Sam's cock grazed his spot, sending shudders throughout his body, spreading outward like ripples in a pond. He felt the tremors which coursed through Sam as his lover began to speed up his thrusts, the movement of his hips more erratic as he plunged deeper into Mark.

"Oh Mark, so good." Sam gazed down at him, eyes wide, mouth open, his breath coming in short bursts as he buried his dick up to the hilt in Mark's arse. He grabbed hold of Mark and rolled onto his back, Mark straddling his hips. Mark rode that thick cock, his body undulating as he took Sam fully into him over and over again. Sam strained up from the bed, harsh cries escaping as he pushed up with his hips, fucking up into Mark with increasing speed. Mark pressed him back to the mattress, hands on his chest, and began to fuck himself on the rigid length that filled him completely. His dick pointed skyward and he wrapped his hand around it, tugging it. Not that he needed to make himself come like that. Sam was bringing him perilously close—Mark was going to come on his cock.

"God, Sam... never.... never felt..." Words failed him. He watched the rising tide of red that covered Sam's chest and he reached back to cup Sam's balls. Sam groaned, the sound low and urgent, and Mark knew he was close. He bent low and seized Sam's mouth in a hungry kiss, moaning as Sam's hips speeded up.

All too soon Mark felt his orgasm approach. He broke free with a gasp. "Going to come soon." Fuck, he was so close.

Sam reached for Mark's cock and grasped it firmly. His eyes locked onto Mark's. "Want us to come together." He thrust up into Mark, keeping time with his hand as it worked the shaft.

Mark cried out as Sam hammered into him. "Oh God, yes." He couldn't look away from those expressive blue eyes. So much emotion there. "Make me come, baby." Beneath him Sam arched up into him, mouth wide in a hoarse cry, and suddenly Mark could feel the slow throb of his cock inside him as Sam came. "Yes!" Mark froze as his dick began to pump out come over Sam, long threads of white which coated Sam's chest, reaching as far as his chin. Mark's body shook as he gave himself over to his orgasm, letting it roll over him in a relentless tide. He dropped his head down to Sam's shoulder and kissed the warm skin of Sam's neck, before moving upward to meet that beautiful mouth.

Sam responded to his kisses with a feverish intensity as his body jolted through the last of his climax. Mark could feel the tremors that shook him, and he covered Sam with his body, holding him close as they rode out the aftershocks together, Sam's cock still buried inside him.

"Love you," Sam gasped out, his arms coming up to wrap around Mark, clutching at his back. Mark kissed Sam's lips, cheeks, forehead, a carpet of kisses that didn't come close to sharing the enormity of what Mark was going through. He whimpered as Sam's softened cock slipped from his body. Sam's answering low cry was an echo of his own.

Sam pulled the condom from him, tied it and dropped it to the floor, before grabbing Mark in a tight embrace. "That was incredible." He stroked Mark's face with his fingertips. His eyes held an expression of peace that warmed Mark inside.

"I loved it." Mark uttered the words softly. "Having you make love to me was….." He smiled. "I'm sorry. You were right after all. Good sex scrambles my brain. Except *that* was *phenomenal* sex." Sam's blush was adorable. "And we *will* be doing that again."

"We don't have to." Sam looked at him through his eyelashes. "I mean, if you're happy to top, I'm *more* than happy to bottom." His cheeks heated up. "I love having you inside me."

Mark cupped his chin. "Me too. But you just opened a new door for me. I never knew it could feel so good." He kissed Sam tenderly on the lips and snuggled closer. "Thank you."

The soft glow in Sam's eyes said so much. The whispered words that followed said it all.

"I love you, Mark."

"I love you, too."

Mark loved the lassitude which spread through him, a feeling he'd never encountered. It had been more than sex. He couldn't explain it. Words simply weren't enough. He wrapped his arms around Sam and let himself be lulled by the hypnotic sound of his breathing, more even now. He could feel Sam's heart beating strongly.

Mark held his lover close, enjoying the moment. The real world lay beyond his front door, but there was plenty of time to make plans.

Later. Right now he could only think of a lifetime stretched out before him of days and nights with the beautiful man in his arms . He wondered if that would be enough time to show Sam just how much he loved him.

Probably not.

The End

Island Tale #2

September's Tide

Prologue

"If you don't take your finger off the damn buzzer, I'm gonna break it off when I get this door open!" David Hannon yelled as he fumbled with the deadbolts across the front door to his apartment. His head throbbed. Who in the hell was bugging him at this unearthly hour of the morning? The last bolt slid out of the way and David flung open the door, glare already in place. He growled at the sight of Juliet standing in the hallway, sunglasses perched on top of her head holding back her long brown hair, her lips pressed together. "What in God's name are you doing here at this hour?"

Juliet fired a glare back at him. "What are you talking about? It's nine-thirty." Her expression changed when she peered more closely at David. Her eyes narrowed. "You've been drinking again."

"What's it to you, *Mom*?" David ground out sarcastically.

She ignored him and pushed past him into the apartment, her silk scarf trailing behind her. She sniffed the air. "Christ, it reeks in here. When did you last clean this place?" Juliet dumped her capacious bag onto the hall table and headed for the kitchen. "I'll put on some coffee. Looks like you need it."

David stared after her in disbelief. "Did you want breakfast too? Gee, I'm sorry, I'll send out for some, 'cause there's not a damn thing in the refrigerator." He knew sarcasm went right over her head, but he couldn't help himself.

Juliet appeared in the doorway, coffee pot in hand. "And your mother wouldn't be seen dead here, not after the way you spoke to her *last* time." She grimaced.

"God, David, the state of this place. I knew I should have been round here sooner." She disappeared back into the kitchen and soon David heard the welcome gurgle that spoke of imminent coffee. He swiped his hand through his unruly mop of blond curls. Christ, he needed a haircut. As he slid a hand across his cheek and felt three days of growth, he realized that maybe he needed a little more than that. A quick glance in the hall mirror made him wince. He looked every one of his forty-six years—and then some.

"You're a mess."

He turned slowly to face her. He wasn't up to dealing with her shit. Not today. "Juliet, just tell me what was so goddamn important to get you over here for the first time in four months, and then you can go." He was so weary he ached. He wanted to go back to bed, pull his comforter over his head and tell the world to go to hell.

Juliet retreated into the kitchen and poured out two mugs of coffee. She handed one to him and then leaned against the worktop, gazing thoughtfully at him. "How's the book coming along?" The question came out sounding light and inconsequential—David knew it was anything but.

He groaned. "You could have asked me *that* over the goddamn *phone*, woman!" He slurped his coffee noisily, wincing as it burnt his tongue.

Those brown eyes were on him, all her fire gone. "I left you alone for a while, figuring you needed some space. I kept the phone calls to a minimum. I updated your website, your blog, answered your fan mail—and all because I knew *you* wouldn't be doing any of it."

David scowled. "You *know* how I feel about all that shit."

Her face hardened. "Yeah, well, all that *shit* keeps you on the Best Sellers lists week in, week out, so don't knock it." The crease between her eyes deepened. "Do you know how hard it is, inventing this whole other life for you? Everyone wants to know about James Blanchette, the reclusive writer of detective fiction. What he wears, what he likes, where he gets his inspiration...."

David huffed wearily. "I know, I know. Juliet, you do a fantastic job." That much was true. David owed her, big time. She dealt with all of it, leaving him free to concentrate on the writing. *Except that I'm* not *writing, am I?*

And of course, he'd forgotten that his agent was a damn mind reader on occasion. "You didn't answer my question." There was that intuitive look of hers, the one where David swore she could see every single thought in his head.

He turned and walked into the living room, where the late August sun was already trying to claw its way under the blinds that held the room in darkness. He winced once more as Juliet followed him and opened the blinds fully, the light spilling into every crevice of the room. She looked around and tutted.

"You can't live like this, you know." She fixed her eyes immediately on the desk by the large window, where she knew he usually sat when he was writing. The laptop's layer of dust said more than words. When her eyes met his, he was jolted momentarily by the understanding in her expression. "You heard something else about the little shit, didn't you?"

He snorted.

"Seems every day I get to hear some new tale of what he was up to while we were together. What gets me is that no one thought to tell me all of this at the time."

Juliet groaned. "Who was it this time?"

"Remy. He couldn't *wait* to share." Not that he didn't have his suspicions as to why Remy Dumant was bothering to tell him about Clark's indiscretions.

Juliet barked out a harsh laugh. "Yeah, right. Remy was probably more concerned that if you bring out a new book, you'll wipe the floor with him. His last one was total crap and he knows you're overdue for a new one. Little fucker wants to psych you out, put you off your stride." She glanced sadly around the room. "Not that he had to try too hard, did he?"

David followed her gaze, taking in the empty beer bottles that lay strewn around the coffee table, the takeout boxes stacked up against it, the empty bags that had once contained potato chips… Dust lay everywhere, the air thick with neglect. *Christ, this looks bad.*

From her vantage point next to the window, Juliet shook her head. "Okay, this has got to stop." She opened the window and instantly David was assailed by the noise of the traffic. New York wasn't the quietest place to live. Juliet inhaled the morning air before facing him once more. He said nothing, figuring she'd get around to the point of her visit at *some* point.

He watched as she walked over to the bookcase which contained all his books and picked up the photo frame which lay face-down on the shelf.

David drew in a sharp breath. He had no wish to look at Clark's lying, smiling face. Why he hadn't thrown the photo out the window by now was beyond him.

Because you loved him, that's why.

The thought cut him deeply. Even though in the end Clark had proved himself to be a lying little gold-digging bastard, David couldn't escape the fact that they'd been lovers for more than two years—until the day five months ago when David had come home early and found Clark in their bed, with his dick in someone else's ass.

To his relief, Juliet stared at the photo for a minute, not bothering the mask the disgust she plainly felt, and then replaced it on the shelf, exactly as she'd found it. Her gaze met David's.

"You're getting out of here." She set her jaw.

David gave a start. "Excuse me?" Whatever he'd been expecting, this certainly wasn't it. "And where exactly am I going?"

Juliet slipped back into the hallway and grabbed her bag. She reached into it, withdrew a plastic folder and walked over to David. She thrust it at him. "Here." She disappeared briefly into the kitchen, emerging a few seconds later with her coffee mug. She sipped it, her eyes on him.

Frowning, David opened the folder. The first thing he saw was a building that could almost have been a scaled-down version of a lighthouse, complete with small turret and white slats, a white picket fence in front of it.

David's brow furrowed. "I am *not* going to New England. I hate it there."

The house was typical of the holiday homes that littered the coastline of Maine.

Juliet let out a dry chuckle, the first sign of mirth since her arrival. "Well, then it's a good thing I'm not sending you there, isn't it?" She smirked. "Look closer, Sherlock. Read the damn thing."

David held the folder at arms' length, squinting, until at last he gave up and reached into his top pocket for the rimless glasses he hated. He put them on, peered once more and scowled.

"Where the hell is the Isle of Wight?"

The chuckle became a giggle. "England. I'm sending you to England—yeah, baby." Juliet did her best Austin Powers imitation.

David's mouth fell open. "What the fuck?" He stared down at the sheet and read aloud from further down the page. "An island off the south coast of England." He stared incredulously at her. "A fucking island? Why in God's name are you sending me to a *rock* off the coast of England?"

Juliet arched her eyebrows. "The Isle of Wight is not a rock. It's twenty-five miles across and fourteen miles deep. It has one hundred and twenty-five thousand inhabitants, but that just about doubles in summertime."

David almost growled. "Don't give me the goddamn Wikipedia bio on it—tell me why the *fuck* you're sending me there!" His head throbbed again.

Juliet became still. Her expression softened. "David, when was the last time you wrote anything?" He opened his mouth to retort, the lie ready, but she shook her head. "And tell me the truth. You haven't written since you threw him out, have you?"

David closed his eyes. There was a painful tightness in his throat and suddenly it was difficult to draw a breath. He jumped when he felt the tentative touch of Juliet's hand on his arm. He hadn't heard her move closer. He opened his eyes. She stared at him, her expression grave.

"You need some time away. I've booked you into this place—it's called the Lighthouse—for a month. You'll be there for all of September. Your flight leaves JFK tomorrow at nineteen hundred hours."

David stiffened. "A month? Leaving tomorrow? I can't go tomorrow! I...I have commitments!"

"Yeah?" Juliet's eyes glinted. "Name one."

David faltered. "But I—"

Juliet shook her head. "No arguments. I've booked everything—your plane tickets, your travel from Heathrow airport to the coast, even your ferry. And you'll be met when you land." She gave him a gentle smile. "You need this, babe. Use the time to get your head together. Take the laptop. Do some writing. It doesn't even have to be the book. Write anything that comes to mind. Let the place inspire you." She locked eyes on him. "And for God's sake, David—leave Clark behind."

Whatever words David had been about to say died in his throat. He glanced at the white building which was almost blinding in the sunlit photo.

Maybe she's right. Maybe this is just what I need. And then he grimaced. England? Warm beer, bad food, stuck-up people…. This could end up being the vacation from hell.

K.C. WELLS

Chapter One

David leaned against the window and peered out into the Solent as the catamaran bounced over the waves. He was bone-tired. The seven-and-a-half hour flight to Heathrow would have fatigued anyone, but it was only as the plane was about to land that he'd realized just how much traveling there was still to do. He'd landed at six thirty in the morning and queued at the carousel to grab his luggage, the largest suitcase he possessed. Yawning, David had emerged from the baggage hall to be greeted cheerfully by a taxi driver with the obligatory card bearing his name. How anyone could be so goddamn *chirpy* at that hour of the morning was beyond David. Another journey of some fifty minutes where he grunted staccato replies to his driver's well-meant but inane comments as he was whisked across London to Waterloo railway station. Okay, so London was nowhere near as crowded as New York, but he'd been amazed by the hordes of people at the station. It was past nine o'clock and it seemed to David as though *everyone* in London had decided to pass through there.

It hadn't taken him long to find the train heading to Portsmouth Harbour, and he even had time to grab a coffee from a Starbucks stand on the concourse. He gulped it eagerly while he scanned the departures board for his train. Thank God it was on time. He lugged the heavy case along the platform, searching for a less populated carriage. His suitcase safely stowed, David had collapsed into the nearest seat and all but inhaled the rest of his coffee.

He grabbed his backpack and clasped it tightly to him, guarding its precious cargo within—his laptop.

David still couldn't believe he was actually going along with this madness.

"Why there?" he'd demanded with a wild-eyed stare. "Couldn't you have found anywhere a little closer? Say, in the same fucking *country*?"

Juliet had huffed. "I wanted you to go somewhere you'd never been before. I wanted you to step out of your comfort zone and see if it got your creative juices flowing again."

He'd grumbled something about *liking* his comfort zone, thank you very much, but it was clear Juliet wasn't about to listen to him. Besides, it seemed as if she'd considered everything. He'd gaped when he saw the reservation date.

"You booked this three months ago!"

Juliet had merely shrugged. "Okay, so I put off telling you—sue me." A sly look stole over her face. "I knew if I told you about it then, you'd make excuses, you'd have me canceling it, shit like that. Well, it's too late to cancel—so get packing!" That gleeful expression was more than David could stand. He'd all but pushed her out of the apartment before turning his mind to the thorny problem of what to pack.

The train had pulled into the station and Juliet's instructions stated that he was to walk to the far end of the platform, where the 'FastCat' would take him across the Solent to the Island. The catamaran was about half full and David had shoved the case into the central storage area and grabbed a seat by the window.

Not that he could see a whole lot. Spray came up and hit the windows, which weren't exactly clean to begin with. The sunlight on the water was blinding, too. Nevertheless, David was able to catch sight of a land mass up ahead that had to be the island. But the Cat certainly lived up to its name. A mere eighteen minutes later, the catamaran was pulling up alongside the dock, and David had finally arrived at his destination—five hours after landing at the airport.

He lumbered down the gangway, dragging the suitcase behind him, its little wheels struggling, and his backpack slung over his shoulder. Around him milled families with small children, obviously off to spend some holiday time on the island, business men, couples, people of all ages, and all heading into the main building. David watched the man who'd been seated across the aisle from him on the Cat, as he tried to push through the crowds, clearly anxious to get somewhere in a hurry—and then David caught his breath to see him walk up to a young man dressed in white pants and a white T-shirt, who was standing by the Booking office, a red rose clutched in his hand. The two men didn't embrace, but simply looked at each other, the younger man's face alight with joy. He held out the rose to David's fellow traveler who took it, his face wreathed in a wide smile, and then the two walked off together, hand in hand, all haste forgotten, objective achieved.

Nice to see that it does *work out sometimes.* David found himself silently wishing the pair good luck. He was so engrossed in watching their exit that he almost bumped into a tall, slim woman with blonde hair scraped back into a ponytail.

"Sorry," he murmured under his breath, and attempted to edge around her, but she blocked his path.

"Would you be David Hannon?" Her soft, lilting voice made his name sound almost musical.

David started. "Yes. And you are...?"

The woman gave him a warm smile. "Vanessa Dickson. I own the Lighthouse."

David remembered his manners. He grasped her outstretched hand and shook it firmly. "Sorry," he apologized. "It's been a very long journey."

Her expression grew sympathetic. "I can imagine." She glanced down at his case. "Is this all your luggage?" He nodded. "Well, we should be able to fit it into the boot. Might have to put the roof back up, though." She started to lead the way through the hall and down a ramp to the car park.

David struggled to follow the conversation. *Fit it into the boot?* He had to smile as Vanessa stopped next to a little beige gold Nissan, a convertible. Damn, that thing was small but undeniably cute. Vanessa opened the trunk and peered inside. David glanced into the trunk and his eyes widened. The glass roof of the car was folded into it, the whole thing resting on a black canvas that was suspended across the available space. There was room below it, but definitely not enough for his case.

"As I thought," Vanessa mused. "When the roof is down, there isn't a whole lot of space in the boot."

"Oh, *now* I get it." Comprehension dawned. David grinned. "The boot is the trunk," he declared triumphantly."

Vanessa gave him a puzzled look and then her brow cleared.

"Oh, sorry. I forgot you Americans call it a trunk." She smiled.

David waved a hand. "Yeah, well I'm sure there are gonna be a whole lot more words I'll need to learn." He gave her what he hoped was an easy, laid-back smile. "Will the case fit on the back seats?"

Vanessa snickered. "I don't think so. Whoever designed this car may have *intended* it to be for four people, but only if you could fold up the back seat passengers *very* small." She closed the trunk and walked to the side of the car.

He followed her gaze and peered inside. David snorted. "I see what you mean."

Vanessa shrugged and climbed into the driver's seat. She fired up the engine and then pressed a button. The trunk whirred into action, opening itself with a whine. David watched, fascinated, as the roof unfolded itself elegantly, sliding into position and locking into place. He heaved the suitcase into the trunk and closed it. He took one look at the position of the front passenger seat and reached below it, fumbling for the release to move the seat further back. There was no *way* he'd get his long legs into there. The car clearly wasn't built for guys who were six feet tall.

Once that was done, David got in and sat with his knees bent. Vanessa gave him a sideways glance. "Your agent made no mention of your height when she asked me to arrange a hire car for you for your stay." She clicked her tongue. "This might require a rethink."

David gave another start. "This is for me?" Vanessa nodded. David's face creased into a slow smile. Okay, so it would be a snug fit, but he liked the little car. "No, leave it. This will be fine."

Vanessa arched his eyebrows and David chuckled. "Yeah, so I'm a masochist. Seriously, don't change it. I like the idea of driving this little baby over the island."

"Well, if you're sure." She sounded doubtful. David was sure. He was already anticipating driving along country roads, the wind stirring his hair, the sound of birdsong loud as he sped through tiny hamlets and along the coast roads. Then he grinned to himself. He had no idea if the island was anything like the idyllic picture he'd just painted—but he sure hoped so.

As the car turned out of the parking area, David was stunned to see that they were at the end of a long wooden pier. They drove along it at ten miles per hour, the town looming larger as they neared the end. Two church spires rose majestically above the roofs.

"Do you like the Beatles?" Vanessa asked as they passed through the barrier and onto the main road. Puzzled by the question, David replied in the affirmative. Vanessa smiled. "This is Ryde, so if you think about it, you had a ticket to Ryde."

David thought for a moment and then guffawed. "Damn, that's funny. Maybe the Beatles wrote the song during a visit to the Island," he offered as a joke.

Vanessa's smile widened. "Oh, don't laugh, there's a story around here that says they did just that." David stared incredulously. "Seriously."

He shook his head as he watched the passing scenery. He hadn't been sure what to expect, but so far the island seemed no different to the areas he'd passed through on the train.

There were lots of houses, traffic… and then after about fifteen minutes they passed through an area of little cottages with thatched roofs, images he'd long associated with an England of long ago. David's jaw dropped.

"Are there many places like this?" he wanted to know, his gaze drinking in the quaint old houses with their country gardens.

Vanessa chuckled. "If you like this, you'll *love* Godshill. It's a little village that looks like it belongs on the lid of a box of chocolates, or an old-fashioned jigsaw puzzle. We get tourists flocking there all through the season, usually in coaches that block the roads and get the locals complaining bitterly."

"Are you a local?"

She beamed. "Born and bred. My family date from way back. Proper caulkheads."

David frowned. "Corkheads?" He struggled to get his tongue around the word.

"That's what we call people who were born on the island. Those who move here from the mainland are called overners."

David was fascinated, even though jet lag was seriously kicking his ass. Once they had left the pretty houses behind, the road wound through an area of green fields and hills, where David could glimpse the sea beyond. As they rounded a corner he gazed to his left, and the view almost took his breath away. In the distance a bay curved round to end in white cliffs. The sea was so calm that the cliffs were reflected in its still waters.

"This is a beautiful place," he murmured.

The sunlight sparkled on the water, and David could make out sailboats, their sails brilliant splashes of white in the afternoon sun. The road dipped and twisted, and it seemed to David that around every corner there was something to draw the eye.

"We think so," Vanessa said quietly. David could hear the pride in her voice. It was certainly not misplaced. They passed through a little town that seemed more run down than the previous ones. "This is your nearest town, Ventnor. It has everything you need—a couple of supermarkets, two chemists, a couple of pubs, even a Chinese restaurant."

David nodded as he picked out the supermarket on the corner. "Great. How far are we from the house?"

"About five minutes by car, but you could walk it, if you felt so inclined."

And now the houses changed. Gone were the smaller semidetached houses that were so abundant nearer to Ryde. Instead, these were larger, with huge, elaborate gardens and long driveways, giving a much more affluent feel to the neighborhood. Everywhere there was green. Compared to the built-up area of central New York where his apartment building was located, this was heaven.

Vanessa turned left into a little road. David chortled when he saw the name of it.

"Love Lane? Really?" To the right he could see an expanse of green, dotted with men in white pants and sweaters, playing cricket. People lazed on the slopes of the cricket ground, applauding lazily. This was just so surreal. The road narrowed to a single lane.

At the end of the lane Vanessa drove the little car into a parking space and turned off the engine.

"Here we are."

David looked around. All he could see was the back of some houses, and a hedgerow. As he climbed out of the car, he picked up a sound, low and persistent, which reminded him of the wind through trees. Then it hit him. It was the sound of the sea. Vanessa opened the trunk and he lugged out his case, the backpack already over his shoulder. "Where now?"

"This is as close as you can get by car," Vanessa explained as she locked the car and handed David the keys. "The owner's manual is in the glove box, along with the rental agreement, and it's keyless entry. All you do is depress the clutch and the brake as you turn that knob." She pointed to a small black knob to the right of the steering wheel. "You've seen how to open and close the roof. And to lock it, just press the tiny button below the door handles." David tried to follow every word, but a huge yawn cut out her words. Vanessa regarded him with amusement. "I think you need to put your head down and get some rest." She led him towards three steps that merged onto a path.

"You might find it tricky getting down the steps with that suitcase." She pointed to her left. "These steps are quite steep and lead straight to the end of the bay where the Lighthouse is situated. But that way"—she indicated the path to her right—"is a more gradual slope with a steep bit at the end. That brings you out at the other end of the bay, near the Beach Shack café." She eyed the suitcase speculatively. "I'd say we take the sloping path."

David bobbed his head in acknowledgment and followed her lead, pulling the case behind him. The path was steep to begin with but evened out after a little while. But the last part David had to go very carefully until at last he stood on level ground. To his right was a white brick café, but dead ahead was the sea, the waves rolling in to crash onto the rocks just beyond the café.

Vanessa went off to the left and David followed, his sneakers crunching on a path of sand and pebbles. He could see the little bay to his right, a horseshoe of sand surrounded by huge rocks, the tide high and breaking over them dramatically. All he could hear was the sea. Then he yawned. The sightseeing could wait another day. His ass was really dragging.

Vanessa pointed to a white painted house on the left, Cove Cottage. "That's my house. So if you need anything, I'm not far away."

David nodded absently. His attention was claimed by the building at the end of the bay that he recognized from his folder. He followed Vanessa along the path, hardly noticing the rest of the scenery as he focused on the house. She opened the gate in the white picket fence and led him onto the decking and up to the front door.

"The house actually sleeps six, so you'll have plenty of room. There's a bedroom with bunkbeds, a double room and an master bedroom up in the turret." She unlocked the door and they stepped across the threshold into a small hallway. David was struck immediately by the light in the place. White walls, lots of windows... it gave the building a feeling of space.

The hall led into a large room which contained a kitchen area with a large oval dining table to the left, and a living room area to the right. Arched glass doors opened from the kitchen onto the deck, where David could see a table and four chairs set out. A patio door led from the living room to the deck. A large corner sofa looked out onto the deck.

"This is great," David murmured. He could already see himself being very comfortable here.

"Let me give you a quick rundown of the place, then I'll leave you to grab some rest. You must be really tired by now."

Vanessa showed him through the door beyond the living room into the two bedrooms, and then opened a door at the rear to reveal a bathroom containing toilet, bath and shower. The kitchen looked like it had everything he'd need, including a dishwasher and washing machine— *handy*. To the left of the front door a staircase curved up into the master bedroom.

David gasped. The room filled the turret, with windows virtually all the way around. There was a shower room and a huge wardrobe, but the room was dominated by the large bed—and the view. All he could see was the sky, so breathtakingly blue that it hurt the eye. Vanessa opened one of the windows and the room was filled with the sound of the sea as the waves crashed onto the rocks which surrounded the spit of land on which the house was situated. David imagined going to sleep with the gentle sound of the waves below his window.

He turned to Vanessa. "This is perfect."

Her smile widened.

"I'm glad you like it." She handed him the keys. "Because for the next month, it's all yours."

David grinned as he took them. He glanced at the view. The whole bay stretched out before him, with its dramatic backdrop of trees covering the cliffs which rose up above the bay. He looked toward the beach where numerous families played on the sand. Little kids clambered over the rocks, nets in hand, obviously searching for rock pools and their inhabitants. His eye was drawn to a lone figure swimming out in the bay. He could just about make out that it was a man in a wetsuit, wearing a snorkeling mask. David watched as the man dived beneath the waves, only to resurface moments later. He seemed to be at one with the water, his movements graceful and fluid.

"Christ, is that guy half seal, or what?" David muttered. Behind him, he heard Vanessa cross the wooden floor to stand beside him and peer out.

She chuckled. "You're not far off, actually. That's Taylor Monroe. He owns Cove Kayaks here in the bay. He hires out canoes, boards, wetsuits, stuff like that." She shook her head. "I think that boy's spent most of his life in the water."

David watched for a few moments longer as the young man dived and swam. David envied him. He loved swimming but never seemed to find the time or the inclination to make it as far as his nearest pool. He took the occasional dip at his gym, but the pool there was small and David was more concerned with the weights room.

Vanessa headed down the stairs and David dragged himself away from the view to follow her. She gave the place one last look and then held out her hand. David shook it firmly.

"Thank you. If I have any difficulties, I'll be sure to let you know."

Vanessa bobbed her head in acknowledgment. "You'll find my number in a folder in the kitchen. Don't hesitate to call if you need me"—she grinned—"although you may find it easier to simply come over to the house. Phones don't work too well down here, and as for the Internet…"

David let her words sink in. No phone. No Internet. No contact with the world he'd left behind. A slow smile creased his face.

"That's the best news I've had all day."

Juliet was a goddamn genius.

Chapter Two

Why is it so goddamn difficult to get to sleep?

David rolled over to look yet again at the alarm clock next to his bed. Twelve-thirty in the a.m. *I knew I shouldn't have had that nap when I got here.* He'd only slept for a couple of hours before getting around to unpacking, but he'd felt so much better for it. Once all his stuff had been safely stowed away, David had ventured out in the car, although he only went as far as Ventnor. Driving in itself had been quite the adventure. For a start, he had to remember to drive on the wrong side of the road. Fortunately the road led straight into the town, which made things a lot easier.

Once he'd found the parking lot, the supermarket had been just across the road from it. David had bought enough groceries to last him about a week. Luckily the store had a good selection of local beers which had delighted him. There was a decent choice of wines, too. David ignored Juliet's voice in his head—he swore he could hear her tut-tutting at him all the way from New York. Okay, so he'd been drinking a fair bit in the last few months. It wasn't like he was an alcoholic, though. All the same, maybe it was a good idea to use this time to cut down on the alcohol.

Dinner had been some prepared pasta with a tomato and basil sauce, accompanied by a glass or two of a pretty decent rosé. That should have guaranteed him some sleep, but for some reason, he couldn't shut his brain down. Thoughts of Clark plagued him, only this time he remembered the good stuff. Their holiday in Cancun, where they'd divided their time between the pool and their bed.

Hot nights filled with even hotter fucking. God, Clark certainly knew how to push David's buttons when it came to sex. And then a rush of cold washed over and through him as he recalled that fateful afternoon. Opening the apartment door to hear Clark's grunts and another guy's harsh cries as they fucked in David and Clark's bed. Standing in the bedroom doorway, open-mouthed in horror as he watched Clark thrusting deep into a complete stranger's ass—only he clearly wasn't a stranger to Clark, judging by the dirty talk which flowed back and forth between the two men. David's cry which had disturbed the lovers, shortly before David had turned and fled the apartment.

David shook himself. *Not going to go there.* He threw back the sheet and climbed out of bed to walk to the window. The moon was almost full, and the waves sparkled in its ethereal light. There was no sign of life, not even a single light from any of the properties which made up the small bay. In fact, there was no light to be seen, period. No street lighting, nothing. David had never been in a place with a complete absence of light pollution. He peered at the clear sky. David was amazed to see the sheer amount of stars that were visible. He wanted to see more. He pulled on his jeans and a T-shirt, grabbed his sandals and went downstairs and out the door. He walked along the path that led to the boat ramp which went down to the beach. On impulse, he took off his sandals. The sand was cool beneath his feet. It was a warm night with little breeze.

He looked up into the night sky and the breath caught in his throat. *God, the stars….* The velvet blackness above him was sprinkled with so many stars, they resembled dust.

And right above him, something he had only ever seen in books or on TV—the Milky Way. David craned his neck to stare in amazement at the band of stars which snaked across the sky. It was truly impressive. David couldn't have said how long he stood there, humbled by the majesty of it all. In the end he chose a huge rock by the entrance to the beach and lay back on it, staring up at the sky, the sight filling his vision.

A sound disturbed his contemplation. David sat up abruptly, just in time to see a figure emerging from the water. Someone had been swimming? He peered out into the bay and watched as a tall slim figure walked toward him over the sand. Moonlight gleamed on bare, wet skin and David realized with a shock that the figure, a young man, was nude. There was just enough light for David to see he was lean, smooth-skinned, with a little neat patch of pubic hair just above….

David swallowed. The boy had an absolutely beautiful uncut cock. In fact, the whole package was stunning. Dark wavy hair, he couldn't tell in this light whether it was dark brown or black. He estimated his height at around five ten, maybe a hundred and forty pounds. David caught a glimpse of three different tattoos. God, he was simply beautiful.

The boy came to a stop in front of him. He didn't seem in the slightest bit perturbed to find David sitting there. He looked David up and down with a wry smile on his face.

"Well, judging from the way you're looking at me, I'm going to hazard a guess that you're not exactly straight."

His voice was soft, with that same lilting quality that David had noticed about Vanessa. Obviously an island boy.

David found his voice. He cleared his throat. "Got it in one." The words came out more of a croak than he'd intended.

The smile widened. "Cool." The young man extended his hand. "Taylor Monroe." David shook it, Taylor's skin still damp. "You're the American who's hired Vanessa's place, right?"

David was stunned. He'd only been here half a day.

Taylor laughed. "You're going to learn, it's a small island, and things get around fast." He nodded toward the shore. "I live just over there. I was going to go home and make some hot chocolate. You want to join me?" The way he was studying David made him think that maybe hot chocolate might not have been the only thing on offer. And fuck, that was a tempting thought. He hadn't gotten laid since…

And just like that, it was as if ice water was poured over his loins.

"Actually, I think I'll pass, though I'm grateful for the offer. And it's David, David Hannon."

Taylor nodded. "Okay, David, another time maybe?" His eyes gleamed in the moonlight. "Nice meeting you." That easy smile was so sexy. "Any time you want to come over, feel free. If I'm around, of course." And with that Taylor walked past David up the boat ramp and across the path to a large white house with canoes and kayaks piled up in front of it. David watched him let himself into the house, turning once to wave at David before disappearing.

Talk about a surreal situation.

188

David stared at the sand where Taylor's feet had left light indentations. Had he imagined it? Had he read too much into the bold way in which Taylor had looked him up and down? Somehow, David didn't think so. It was kind of flattering—the boy had to be at least, fifteen, maybe twenty years younger. Perhaps Taylor had a thing for older men. David liked the way he'd seemed totally unfazed at being nude with David. Definitely an interesting young man.

He yawned. Maybe all this fresh sea air was finally getting to him. When another yawn stretched his jaw, David decided to head back to the house and hit the sack. He gave Taylor's house a final, lingering glance. Another time…

Juliet was a total bitch.

David stared morosely at the rain which had been hitting the windows pretty solidly for the past two days and cursed his agent. Why the fuck was he here? Goddamn crappy British weather. She could at least have sent him to some place where the climate wasn't so changeable. The words of a song came to mind. *Four seasons in one day.* Yeah, that pretty much described it.

The laptop sat forlornly on the coffee table. David had put it there in the hopes that it might stir him to actually write something, but the voices in his head were silent. It seemed none of his characters were talking to him. And they'd been that way for months.

David would never have admitted it to Juliet, but he was panicking. He hadn't gone this long without writing in quite a while.

His first book, 'Tell Me The Truth', had been released over ten years ago to public acclaim. Up until that point he'd been a teacher of English in a mediocre high school in Manhattan. It had been soul-destroying. Kids who didn't want to learn, staff who didn't want to be there... After eleven years of teaching, David had been tearing his hair out. When his job reached an all-time low, David knew he had to find a way to break the cycle. His doctor had suggested he find an outlet, something creative to counterbalance the negativity and stress of his life in the classroom. And then came the fateful morning when he'd awoken at stupid o'clock, just because there was this guy in his head, telling him he was a detective called Ed Manning.

The book had simply flowed out of him. He hadn't been able stop it. In just over six weeks he'd written eighty thousand words, and it hadn't stopped there. Once he'd typed those wonderful words, The End, he'd racked his brains who to send it to. 'Cause there was no *way* he was gonna send it to a publisher without *someone* casting an eye over it. He finally got up the nerve to approach a friend, Ann Fredericks, and begged her to read it and give him an honest opinion. Emailing it to Ann had been torture. The cursor had hovered over the *Send* button for so long, as indecision plagued him. In the end, he'd thought *fuck it* and hit send. There followed a few days anxiously waiting to hear her reaction. When she called him at two in the morning, having spent the whole day unable to put it down, his heart soared with sheer relief. She loved it.

David knew enough to expect lots of rejection slips, so he hadn't been prepared for the email twelve weeks later from the first publishing company on his list, Phantom Press, telling him they would be delighted to publish his book. And so James Blanchette, writer of detective novels, was born. It had been a heady experience. The book had rocketed up the Bestseller's list—and stayed there. When the publishing company started making demands about public appearances, blog tours, promo, David knew he needed help. Into his life walked Juliet Summerville, a literary agent and publicist who was worth every cent he paid her, even though he bitched at her enough times to make her consider leaving him on a regular basis. Juliet had just started out as an agent and things had progressed so swiftly that she only had one client—David. She dealt with the countless emails from fans, prepared all his PR shit, and basically made sure he wasn't touched by that side of things.

The books had given him a good life so far. Money in the bank, a great apartment in New York city, regular holidays all around the world… James Blanchette was a single straight guy with simple tastes. No tattoos. No piercings. No vices. To his friends, David Hannon was a gay guy who liked a lot of sex, had a few piercings and a kick ass tattoo—and who secretly wanted nothing more than to find one guy to settle down with. And up until five months ago, he thought he'd done just that…

The sound of the rain was depressing. At least he didn't have to go out to shop. *When is this fucking rain gonna stop?* He pulled his phone from his pocket to check it for the fifth time that morning.

Vanessa hadn't been kidding when she'd spoken about the poor signal down there. He went up into the bedroom and peered through the rain-streaked windows at the bay. God, there were actually people out walking in the rain, kitted out in raincoats. *These Brits are crazy*! He glanced at Taylor's house, but there was no sign of the young man. Perhaps that was a good thing. Seeing him the other night had stirred up all kinds of thoughts. He'd gotten into bed, tugged the sheet over him and closed his eyes, determined to sleep, only to have his mind pull up an image of Taylor, skin glistening in the moonlight, that gorgeous cock rising to greet him. It was enough to give him an instant hard on. David had slipped his hand under the sheet to palm his dick and it was only a few moments later that he'd come, his breath escaping in short bursts as he jetted come over his abs, barely pushing the sheet out of the way in time. A quick clean up in the en suite and then he'd climbed back into bed, finally succumbing to sleep within minutes.

A glance across the bay showed there were customers in the café, despite the inclement weather. Now *there* was an idea. After two days holed up in the house, David was going stir crazy. He went downstairs, grabbed his jacket and sandals, and left the house. He shivered as the cool rain met his skin. He hurried along the path to the cafe, shoulders hunched as the drops of rain dripped under the collar of his jacket. Once at the café, he shook the rain from his hair and then looked around. A serving hatch with a counter was on his right, where a tall man was taking orders. There was a line of tables which each seated four people along the edge of the café, looking out over the sea and the rocks beneath.

The end of the café opened out into a wider section arranged with tables and chairs, but this was deserted due to the weather. Facing the serving hatch was an area with high stools, with enough space for about four people. There were only five or six people in the café.

"Afternoon." The man behind the hatch gave David a warm smile. "What can I get you?"

There was a menu on the counter, David glanced at it and his eyes lit up when he saw the different varieties of coffee served there. "An Americano, please." His gaze went beyond his handsome server to a covered tray which contained different kinds of cake. His mouth watered. "And what kind of cake do you have there?"

Without turning, the server counted off on his fingers. "Carrot cake, bread pudding, chocolate brownie, rock cakes." He winked. "I can recommend the carrot cake."

David grinned. "You've sold me. A piece of carrot cake, too."

"Excellent!" The server totted up the total and David paid him. He looked with amusement as he was handed a rounded pebble, painted with a number seven. "If you take a seat, it'll be brought to you."

The grin didn't leave his face as David picked up his pebble and walked along past the tables until he reached the end. Around the corner was a covered area with bench seating all the way around it. There was no one there so he took a seat. From his vantage point he was able to look out at the waves which rolled in, crashing over the rocks. Spray flew up and soaked the tables nearest to the railing.

The sound was incredible. It had only been two days but already David loved that sound. He'd fallen asleep for the last two nights with the window open, the hypnotic noise filling the turret room.

He was so engrossed in his sea gazing that he didn't notice the approach of his server, bearing a tray with his large mug of coffee, a little jug of hot milk and a plate with his cake.

"That was fast," David exclaimed.

The server grinned. "We aim to please." He cocked his head. "You're Vanessa's American, right? Staying at the Lighthouse?"

Jeez, Taylor hadn't been kidding about it being a small island. "Yeah, guilty as charged."

The server gave him another warm smile. "Then we might get to see quite a bit of you." He held out his hand. "I'm Richard." David shook it. "Andy runs this place. You'll probably meet him sooner or later. You can't miss him—he'll be the one with the hat." There was that wink again.

David liked Richard's expressive brown eyes. The man appeared confident and David found himself warming to the friendly Brit. "Pleased to meet you, Richard. And I dare say I'll be seeing you again." He returned Richard's smile.

Richard gave him a brief nod and disappeared in the direction of the kitchen. David took a cautious sip from his cup. Oh, thank God—they knew how to make decent coffee. It seemed the horror stories he'd heard tell about the UK weren't true after all. He forked off a piece of carrot cake and tasted it, and then fought back to urge to let out a moan as the subtle flavors burst upon his tongue.

Man, that was good.

His phone vibrated in his jeans pocket. Surprised, he withdrew it and smiled as he saw the caller ID—Michael.

"Michael, how are you? To what do I owe this pleasure?"

"Oh, thank God." He could hear the relief in Michael's voice. "Okay, bitch, why aren't you answering your phone? I've been calling the apartment for two days solid. And this is the first time I've been able to get through on your cell."

David chuckled. "There's virtually no signal where I am for the cell. And it would be rather difficult to answer the phone in the apartment, seeing as I am on a different continent."

There was silence at the other end for a moment. "Right, spill it. Where in the hell are you, exactly?"

"The ass end of nowhere," David grumbled.

"Huh?"

David quickly explained where Juliet had sent him, and why. "Apparently you can Google this place. Look for the Lighthouse, Steephill Cove, on the Isle of Wight. There's a virtual tour, so my hostess tells me. You can see exactly where I'm staying."

At that moment the heavens opened and the rain hit the plastic sheeting above David's head with an almighty crash, sounding like dried peas being poured onto a drum from a great height.

"What in the hell was that?" Michael sounded shocked.

"That would be rain," David said gloomily. "The same rain that's been pouring down for the last two goddamn days." He glanced out to sea at the heavy sky and the sea the color of molten lead. "I can't believe she sent me here."

K.C. WELLS

Any pleasure he'd derived from his initial impressions of the bay had long since dissipated. The weather had seen to that.

"Hold on a minute." David heard Michael's fingers tapping away on his keyboard. After a moment, he spoke. "Hang tight, babe. The weather's due to change by tomorrow, according to the forecast I'm reading."

"Really?" David looked doubtfully at the view before him.

"Uh-huh. And when it does, I advise you to make the most of it. You needed a break."

David let out a tired sigh. "And just what do you suggest I do while I'm here? 'Cause the writing certainly seems to have dried up." That feeling of panic resurfaced, tightening his chest. His throat closed up. *I am not gonna let this get to me.* David took a deep breath, trying to force more air into his lungs.

"Go exploring," suggested Michael. "It looks like it's a beautiful place. See as much of it as you can. Get drunk." There was the minutest pause. "Get laid." He could hear Michael's snicker. "Unless English guys are too fugly for ya?"

David snorted. "Getting laid is the last thing on my mind." *'Cept that's not strictly true, is it?* "Besides, it's too soon after...." His voice faltered. He couldn't bring himself to say the name. Clark had been on his mind a lot in the last two days. David blamed Taylor. It was all the fault of the hot boy who'd got him all riled up. Well, he had to blame it on someone.

"David?" He could hear the note of hesitation in Michael's voice. "Do... do you think you made the right decision throwing Clark out?"

David stared at the phone in silence, too shocked to say a word. "David?"

At last David found his voice. "How can you even ask me that?" He spoke in a low tone. "You know what he did. Hell, you've been hearing the same stories I have, for Christ's sake!"

"Sure, but how do you know the stories were true?"

David grimaced. "When everyone starts telling me the same thing, I kinda got the picture. Besides, coming home and finding him in bed with that Miguel guy was pretty unequivocal."

Michael wasn't giving up. "We all make mistakes, David. I know I've made a few doozies in the past. But I've talked with Clark. He says he tried to talk to you, to apologize, but you threw him out."

David was incensed.

"What the fuck did you *expect* me to do? He was dicking that guy in *our* fucking bed!" He was shaking. He looked around quickly, checking that no one had heard his outburst.

"Yeah, but it was the first time he'd ever cheated on you," Michael persisted.

David almost growled at his friend. "Yeah? Is *that* what he told you?"

"Okay, okay, take it easy." Michael's voice took on a soothing quality. "I just thought maybe you acted a little hastily, that's all, and that you might have reconsidered, *you* know, maybe thought you'd made a mistake."

David didn't believe what he was hearing.

"Since when did *you* become Clark's number one fan? I seem to recall *you* advising me to dump the bastard, along with the rest of them." He bristled. The *nerve* of the man. "Sorry, Michael, but I've just about had it with this conversation. Congratulations. I didn't think I could feel any more pissed off than I already did, but fuck me, you just pushed it to a whole new level." He took a deep breath. "Do me a favor. Don't ring me again, all right? For the rest of September. It's gonna take me that long to calm down from this." And with that he disconnected the call.

He dropped the phone onto the table and stared at it in amazement. His whole body was tensed up and flushed with heat. His jaw ached and he briefly wondered why—until he realized he was grinding his teeth. How in the hell could Michael take Clark's side? And more importantly, why would he—unless Clark was fucking him. David pushed the thought aside. Surely even Michael wouldn't betray him like that.

He drank his coffee automatically, hardly tasting it. The rest of the carrot cake sat untouched. And as he sat there, his anger gave way to another emotion. Had he been too hasty? Too quick to throw Clark out? The last five months had been damn lonely. David had shut himself off from the world, hardly venturing out of the apartment. Had loneliness somehow altered his perception of events?

He thought back on what his friends had told him, second guessing their motives for doing so, and finally questioning his own actions. His mind was in a whirl as he went over everything again and again, until his head was pounding.

You're gonna drive yourself mad at this rate. For God's sake, let it go. You made your decision, and it was the right one.

He listened to the calm voice of reason in his head. Yeah, of course he'd made the right decision.

Hadn't he?

.

Chapter Three

The following morning, David awoke bright and early, beating his alarm clock by half an hour. He blinked in the strong sunlight which streamed through the windows. Wait a minute—*sunlight*?

David sat up in bed and stared in astonishment at unbroken blue sky. Not a cloud in sight. He pushed back the sheet and went to the nearest window. It was a gloriously beautiful morning. The tide was in and the waves lapped gently at the rocks around the spit of land. It was as if the rain had never been there. With a much lighter heart, David went downstairs to have some breakfast.

Breakfast done, a cup of coffee in hand, David stood on the deck and breathed in the fresh morning air. Now *this* was more like it. The temperature was very pleasant. Maybe the UK got Indian summers too. He decided to make the most of the day and go out for a drive around the island, maybe finding a pretty spot to have lunch. Michael's comments still rankled, but David was doing his damnedest to push them aside. Nothing should be allowed to spoil such a beautiful day.

By nine thirty he was in the car and pulling out of Love Lane, the car roof folded into the trunk. Vanessa had thoughtfully left a map of the island in the house and David had sort of worked out a route. He'd already seen the eastern side of the island the day he'd arrived, so he figured he'd head west. The road took him through an area densely populated with trees, which led ultimately to a quaint little village, Niton. From there on the scenery changed dramatically.

David drove along a road which according to the map, ran the length of the western side of the island as far as Freshwater. What a difference. Fields, where cattle grazed or crops grew, stood on either side of the road with a few houses dotted here and there. A couple of older holiday camps sat beside the sea, with camping grounds and chalets. A vast expanse of blue sea stretched away to his left, and white chalk cliffs rose in the distance. At the end of the road, David could see the white cliffs of Tennyson Down, the farthest western point of the island. He imagined that the view from up there would be spectacular. Maybe one day if the weather was good, he'd go walking up over the tops.

David spotted a parking lot coming up on the left and on impulse he swung the little Nissan into it. He switched off the engine and got out. A pebbled path led down to the beach, and the light breeze which blew up from there carried with it the smell of the sea.

David crunched along the path, breathing deeply. The air was invigorating. At the foot of the path he turned right and walked along the sandy beach. There were groups of children with their teacher, and from what David could make out, they were fossil hunting. He had to hold back his laughter when one little blond haired boy, trembling with excitement, handed his teacher his find, wanting to know if it was a dinosaur bone.

The teacher regarded his prize in all seriousness, before telling the youngster he'd actually found a coprolite. The little boy looked puzzled, and then highly amused, when he was informed that a coprolite was 'fossilized dinosaur poo'.

The boy burst into a peal of delighted laughter and hurried off to tell his classmates, holding the coprolite aloft, his face wreathed in a proud smile.

Shaking his head, David continued his walk along the beach. The sun was climbing higher into the sky and the morning was warming up nicely. He felt good, the misery of the last two days obliterated in the sunshine and heat of the day. *Maybe Juliet didn't do so badly after all.*

David strolled along the shore for about forty minutes and then turned to head back to the parking lot. The salty breeze played with his hair and the deep lungfuls of air were starting to make him hungry. By the time he got back to the car he was ravenous. He got behind the wheel and steered the car out of its space. As he edged carefully back onto the main road, he spotted a sign for Brighstone. Another impulse seized him and he followed the sign, driving along twisting country lanes with those cute thatched houses here and there, until at last he came into another little village. On the corner of the lane was a pub, the Three Bishops.

David sat in the beer garden to the rear of the pub, digging into a 'ploughman's lunch', which was a large salad with cheese, sliced ham, pickles and delicious crusty bread which smelled divine. The temptation to sample the beer was tremendous, but that was one rule David never broke—drinking and driving just *did not mix*. The meal was tasty and the ginger beer was zingy, but his surroundings were perfect. David had rarely felt so content.

He spent the rest of the afternoon driving over the island, with stops here and there where David got out to admire the view.

A ridge of hills went right the way across the island like a backbone, from which it was possible to see both the southern side and the mainland across the Solent. There were plenty of sail boats to be seen, their spinnakers either white or vivid flashes of color, as they glided in the channel between the mainland and the island. Add to that the experience of driving with the roof down, the wind in his hair, the sun shining down, and David was having a wonderful day. By the time he parked the car at the bottom of Love Lane, it was already six in the evening, the sun was getting lower in the sky—and David was officially in love with the Isle of Wight.

He clambered down the steep steps to the left of the path and emerged very close to the Lighthouse. There were still a few families on the beach, but they were in the process of packing up their belongings, no doubt heading back to their accommodation in time for their evening meal. The tide was coming in, and as David gazed out into the bay, he saw a familiar figure emerge from the sea and walk toward him through the frothing waves. Taylor wore a dark blue wetsuit and carried a spear gun and what looked like a catch of fish. He moved sinuously, every line of his body flowing. David stood and admired the view. Goddamn, did that boy have to make him hard every single time he saw him?

As Taylor neared the pebbled path he caught sight of David and grinned. "Hello again."

David raised his hand in a lazy wave. "Looks like you've been busy."

Taylor held up his catch and smiled. "Yeah, three sea bass— good sized ones, too."

The fish glistened in the early evening light. Taylor cocked his head. "Hey, why don't you join me for dinner? There's more than enough fish to go around, and I'm doing new potatoes and salad to go with them."

David almost salivated on the spot. He'd done no real cooking since he'd arrived, only heating up ready meals, and the thought of a proper, home-cooked meal was sorely tempting. Still, he held back out of politeness. "Thanks for the offer. It's really kind of you, but—"

"Oh please, don't say no." Taylor interjected. "I rarely have company for dinner, and you must be fed up of looking at the same four walls after all that rain." He gave David a lopsided grin. "If it makes you feel better, you can bring the wine." He gazed at him imploringly.

David laughed. "All right then, you've twisted my arm."

Taylor beamed. "Okay, give me time to clean these and then come over to the house about seven. That sound okay?" David nodded. "Great. I'll see you then." Taylor gave him one last warm smile and then headed up the boat ramp which led up to his front porch. David watched him enter the house and then looked down at himself. Time for a shower and a change of clothing. The thought of spending an evening with the young man sent a shiver of anticipation down his spine. *Down, boy,* he told himself firmly. No matter what David thought he'd sensed that first night, he wasn't going round there with any expectations. But company would be good.

David sat back into the comfortable couch and sipped his wine. He'd offered to do the dishes but had been firmly rebuffed as his host informed that guests didn't do 'the washing up.' God, he loved the way they talked over here. He'd met a few people today with the same musical quality to their voices that Vanessa and Taylor possessed, but there had also been a few people with London accents.

"That was delicious, by the way," David called to Taylor. He could hear him moving about in the kitchen. The fish had been grilled, cooked to perfection, and had certainly tasted nothing like fish bought in the stores back home. The flavor had been superb.

"Make yourself comfortable while I put on the coffee." Taylor's voice wafted back.

David took the opportunity to look around. The living room was large, with a huge window overlooking the bay. The furniture comprised of a large couch and two overstuffed armchairs, a thick rug in shades of reds and browns on the floor in front of the fireplace—a *real* fireplace, and one that was obviously used when the weather required it. David could picture himself living in this house. There was a nice feel to the place. David knew he was susceptible to atmospheres in places he visited. He often picked up on vibes and at times it made him uncomfortable to the point where he couldn't wait to get out of there. But in Taylor's home, he felt relaxed. That meant a lot.

One thing he did notice was the large amount of books. Taylor was clearly a voracious reader. David got up from the sofa to wander across to the bookcases which filled the wall space on either side of the chimney breast. He couldn't help but notice the wide array of travel books. *So Taylor likes to travel, huh*? The books covered just about every continent. There was a huge choice of fiction, and…

David stared in astonishment. One shelf contained nothing but James Blanchette novels, starting with *Tell Me The Truth*. He pulled it from the shelf. It was a dog-eared copy, creased and clearly well-read. David smiled to himself. Taylor was a James Blanchette fan. He'd never actually spoken with a real-life fan before, in spite of his ten years of writing. He had no wish to interact with the public, especially people who might be inclined to gush. That's what he paid Juliet for.

"Do you like him too?"

David turned to see Taylor standing in the doorway holding two coffee mugs. The aroma of the coffee drifted across the room. Taylor walked over and handed him a mug.

David gave a noncommittal shrug. "He's okay." There was no way he was about to reveal himself. He didn't know Taylor well enough for that. He sniffed the coffee appreciatively.

"I love his stories," Taylor continued. "He has this detective, Ed Manning, who's really cool. I always try to figure out who the bad guy is, but he always keeps me guessing." Taylor flopped onto the couch after putting down his coffee mug on the low table which sat on top of the rug. David said nothing but came to sit next to him.

Taylor rested his head back on the seat cushion and regarded David speculatively. "So, David, tell me about yourself. What brings you to the island?" He winked. "It's a long way from the States, that's for sure."

David had already considered how much information he was prepared to give out. "Actually, I'm a writer too. Nothing like James Blanchette—I'm only just starting out, for one thing—but I seem to have hit a brick wall lately. Someone suggested I get away from it all and they came up with this place." He gestured toward the window. "And I have to say, it's a beautiful place to live. I envy you."

Taylor beamed. "It is, isn't it?" He obviously loved his home. His eyes widened. "You write, too? Wow. Would I have read anything of yours? What genre do you write?"

David shook his head. "Nah, you won't have read my stuff. Like I said, I'm just starting out. But right now I have a serious case of writer's block."

Taylor gave him a sympathetic look. "Oh, I'm sorry. That must be such a pain."

You have no *idea*, David thought. "Let's change the subject," he said abruptly. "Tell me about Taylor Monroe."

Taylor stretched out his long, toned legs, the skin tanned and smooth below the hem of his denim shorts. "Well, I was born on the island, and I have a huge family—two brothers, two sisters, loads of cousins, aunts, uncles… Every Sunday it's pretty much an open door policy at my parents' house. Everyone who still lives on the island piles over there and mum cooks up a storm."

"That sounds great," David murmured.

Taylor nodded. "My grandmother lives with them—she's getting on a bit, she's ninety and she's looks like this frail little old lady." He grinned. "But she has the sharpest tongue."

"It must be cool to have a big family," David remarked wistfully. He was an only child, and his father had walked out on his mother when David was just four. Life had been hard for her, bringing up a little boy on her own.

Taylor grimaced. "The downside is everyone is always sticking their nose in everybody else's business." He finished his coffee and glanced at David's nearly empty wineglass. "There's more wine, if you want some."

Dave thought about it. He'd been pretty good the last few days. "Yeah, go on, let's live a little."

Taylor snickered. "It's not like you have far to go to get home, is it?"

There was that. Taylor went into the kitchen and returned with a freshly opened bottle of white wine. He poured out two generous glasses and then sat back down.

"So how long have you had the kayak rental business? It must pay well to provide you with this place." David sipped the chilled wine.

Taylor snorted. "The business would never have paid for this. The house belongs to my parents. They rent it out sometimes in the summer. But I get to live here rent free."

"Sweet." David cocked his head. "So is business not good?"

Taylor shrugged.

"I rent out the kayaks, canoes and boards for about six months of the year. The rest of the time I do whatever work I can get. I have friends who have their own businesses—gardening, construction—and I do work for them. For two summers I worked in a water sports center, but that was an exception. I rarely do the same job twice. And I save every penny to be able to go traveling."

David smiled. "I did notice all the travel guides. Where have you been?"

Taylor suddenly had a faraway look in his eye. "Oh wow, I've been to Thailand, Indonesia, Australia, Singapore....The next trip I'd like to do is to Japan." He took a long drink of his wine. "Have you traveled much?"

"A fair bit," David admitted. "Not as much as I'd like to." He loved the sound of Taylor's life. It seemed as laid-back as the young man himself.

They spent the next hour or so drinking wine and talking about their likes in music and movies. David learned that Taylor was a classic rock fan, but when he was cooking, he preferred blues or jazz, something mellow and sexy that he could lose himself in. They both liked action movies, although Taylor had blushed when admitting to secretly liking all things Disney.

David had snorted. "God, you're such a man-child." Taylor giggled but didn't bother to deny it. David was completely chilled out, and although he put it down to the alcohol, a tiny part of him had to admit that maybe it was partly due to Taylor. The boy was easy to talk to. And that gleam in his eye from the first night was back. Definite interest there.

They'd demolished nearly two thirds of the bottle, and Taylor had edged closer to David, trailing his fingers softly along David's denim-clad thigh. David wasn't even sure Taylor knew he was doing it—until Taylor leaned in close and kissed him.

God, it's been so long.... David responded automatically, cupping Taylor's head and pulling him closer, deepening the kiss. He darted his tongue between silky soft lips and Taylor opened for him with a low noise, the kiss moving from sensual to scorching in seconds. When Taylor slid his hand across to stroke David's burgeoning erection, David couldn't control the whimper that escaped him, and he fumbled with the button, desperate to feel Taylor's hand on his shaft. Taylor smiled against his lips as he slipped his hand into David's briefs and wrapped it around his hot cock.

"God, yes," David murmured fervently as Taylor pulled his length free and broke their kiss to bend over the rigid cock. The breath died in David's throat as Taylor's hot, wet mouth engulfed him, his head bobbing furiously as he worked the shaft, his lips tight around it, the suction just about perfect. When Taylor began to bob faster, David felt his balls ride up. "Fuck, Taylor, you're gonna make me come."

Taylor pulled free of his dick and David groaned. Taylor peered up at him. "Can you come twice in one night?"

David almost growled. "How old do you think I am, boy?" Taylor snickered. "Yes, I can get it up twice in one night—though it might take me about twenty minutes." He had to be honest. After all, he was no spring chicken anymore.

Taylor's grin widened. "Then I'm going to suck you off 'til you come, and then you're going to come upstairs to my bed and fuck me." He leered. "You approve of that plan?"

By way of an answer, David put both hands on Taylor's head and pushed him insistently back down to his cock which was pointing straight up. Christ, he couldn't remember the last time he'd been this hard. The thought of sliding his cock into Taylor's tight little ass had him almost coming on the spot. He breathed deeply, desperate to stave off the urge to come. Taylor chuckled around his shaft as he resumed his sucking, and David groaned loudly as Taylor worked with renewed vigor. "God, you're good at this." He grasped Taylor's hair in his fist and held on tight. "You're quite the talented little cocksucker, aren't you, boy?"

Taylor's low moan was music to David's ears. He wondered briefly if his young host had a bit of the submissive in him. Christ, he hoped so. His breath quickened as Taylor sucked him deeper, and suddenly he came, pumping his seed down Taylor's throat, Taylor struggling to swallow his load.

"That's it, boy. Swallow every last drop. Then clean my cock with your tongue." The words were gasped out as his body jolted its way through his orgasm. The feel of Taylor's tongue licking him with enthusiasm was just heavenly. Taylor looked up at him through dark lashes and licked his lips. His gaze smoldered.

"Now take me to bed and fuck me." His voice was hoarse with arousal. "Now."

David wasn't about to be told twice.

Chapter Four

David opened his eyes and stared at an unfamiliar window. Sunlight poured in and reflected off light cream walls. For a moment his tired brain couldn't compute. Then he remembered. *Taylor.*

"Morning," a sleep-heavy voice rumbled from behind him.

He rolled onto his back to be confronted by two sleepy green eyes and an unruly mop of wavy dark brown hair. Taylor looked adorable when he first woke up. "Good morning." David's voice cracked a little. "What time is it?"

"A little after seven." Taylor yawned widely, stretching his arms up into the air, giving David a lovely view of that chest with a sun tattooed onto it over his sternum. There was also the snake on the inside of his left wrist, and the words 'Take Me As I Am' tattooed onto his inside right bicep. David loved ink on a guy. David recalled Taylor's wide eyes the previous night when David's shirt had finally come off—who was he kidding? Taylor had all but *ripped* it off him in his eagerness to get David inside him—and Taylor had caught sight of the rampant dragon in shades of green and gold spread out over his back, its forked tale pointing toward his hole. And David vividly recalled achieving almost instantaneous hardness when Taylor had insisted on sliding his tongue over the tattoo, licking and sucking his way lower, lower, until at last he was lapping at David's hole, eating his ass with fervor.

David shuddered as the memories of their night together assailed him. The boy was so responsive, and the noises he made… David's dick hardened at the thought.

"I'll make us some coffee." Taylor slipped from the bed. He grinned at David. "You stay here and I'll bring it up. You must be knackered after last night." He strolled naked out of the bedroom, that tight little ass looking downright delectable.

David stared up at the ceiling. Oh fuck. Much as he'd loved every single minute, in the cold light of day he was already beginning to have second thoughts. Yeah, the boy was hot, but he was so fucking *young.* David hadn't even asked Taylor's age. He was almost scared of hearing the reply. *And what happens now? Is he gonna see sex as some sort of commitment?* The thoughts bounced around David's brain until he was dizzy. He'd never fucked anyone so many years his junior and he had no idea what to expect.

"I can hear the cogs from here."

David looked up as Taylor brought over two mugs of coffee, handed him one, put his own on the bedside table and then climbed back into bed.

"Cogs?" David hadn't a clue what that meant.

"The cogs in your brain. Stop thinking so much." Taylor gave him that lazy, sexy smile. "Because I'm pretty sure I know what's going on in that head of yours right now."

David doubted it.

Taylor moved closer and stroked his hand over David's chest. "Last night was incredible. I have to tell you, I have this thing for older men, but you're the first guy I've been with who was over twenty-five." His eyes sparkled. "I know I probably should've asked this earlier, but just how old are you?"

David let out a sigh. *Too goddamn old to be fucking you.*

"Forty-six."

Taylor's eyes lit up. "Cool." He slid his hand lower, edging toward David's dick which was already tenting the cotton sheet. David grabbed it around the wrist and held on tight.

"And while we're on the subject, how old are *you*?"

"Twenty-six." That easy grin again. "Want to tell me why you don't seem to want me near that magnificent cock of yours?" He licked his lips and suddenly David could think of nothing but that sweet mouth on him.

For fuck's sake, stop thinking with your dick for one goddamn minute, will you?

He hesitated, unsure of how to begin. Taylor had this intuitive look that was somehow reminiscent of Juliet.

"David, it was just sex, okay?" He locked eyes with David. "No strings, no promises, just great sex." He tilted his head. "Is that okay?"

David heaved an internal sigh of relief. It was more than okay. "Yeah, that's fine."

Taylor pulled his hand free of David's grasp, sat up in bed and reached for his coffee. After taking a long drink, he studied David for a minute or two. David sipped his drink, inhaling the wonderful aroma. The boy made great coffee.

"Look, I'm going to say something here. You don't have to agree, it's just an idea."

David was intrigued. He sat up and looked expectantly at Taylor. "Go on."

Taylor drank a little more.

"You're going to be here for how long?"

"Until the end of September."

Taylor nodded. "Okay, then how about we make this a regular thing?"

Well, he hadn't expected *that*. "Say what?"

Taylor's cheeks heated up. "Look, there's something you have to know about me. There aren't that many opportunities over here for hooking up with guys. I've never been in a steady relationship. My experiences have so far been limited to one-offs where I could get them—and usually with straight guys." David's eyes widened. Taylor snickered. "Yeah, seems there's no *end* of bi-curious men out there, wanting to fuck a guy. I've had quickies, married guys, an occasional fuck buddy, but nothing permanent. And you know how tedious it can get with just your hand to play with."

Oh, David knew that only too well. He snorted. "Tell me about it."

Taylor appeared more confident. "Right, so I'm suggesting that while you're here, you and I make the most of it. No strings attached." He winked. "Though I have to warn you. I love sex, the more the better. And I've been starving lately." His eyes glittered. "So, what do you think?"

David considered the proposal. His dick certainly liked the idea. And he knew from past experience that he wrote better when he was getting laid regularly. Good sex always seemed to get his creative juices flowing. Okay, so it was a selfish way to look at it, but hell, they would both be getting their itches scratched.

"You've got a deal."

Taylor beamed at him. "Excellent!" He glanced down at the sheet where David's cock was almost vertical beneath it. "It would be a shame to waste this," he added slyly, as he slid his hand under the sheet and grasped David's shaft around the base, gently working it along its length. David let out a low moan and Taylor grinned.

Game over. "Then what are you waiting for, boy? Get down there."

Taylor licked his lips. "Yes *sir*. It will be a pleasure." And he dived under the sheet.

Oh fuck. There was a possibility that David might not survive nearly a month of Taylor. But he sure was gonna have fun trying.

David sat in the 'cave' at the Beach Shack café. This was the shady spot under the willow-strewn roof where he'd sat that rainy Wednesday. What a contrast. It was a warm, sunny Saturday, and David had ventured out, laptop bag in hand, to have a coffee and greet some of the locals. Okay, so far he hadn't written a word, but at least he was reading through the first three chapters, which was as far as he'd gotten with *Lies and More Lies* before....

David gave himself a mental shake. *Nope. Not gonna go there.* It had been a few days since thoughts of Clark had pushed their way into his mind, and David wanted it to stay like that. He hadn't seen Taylor for two nights, which was actually a good thing. For one, he needed time to recover. Taylor wore him out, but in a *really* good way.

David had worried that he'd find the boy constantly on his doorstep, demanding to be satisfied, but so far that hadn't been the case. *Maybe this will work out after all.*

"David, you staying with us for lunch?"

Richard peered around the corner, a menu in hand. David glanced at his watch. Hell, he'd been sitting there contemplating for the last hour, and it was already one.

"What do you recommend?"

Richard pursed his lips. "We have salads, sandwiches, crab tart and two kinds of soup. Today it's fresh mushroom or crab. Andy makes them, by the way."

The idea of crab soup had David trying hard not to drool. "Crab soup, please." Richard smiled and gave him a brief nod before disappearing. This was David's third visit to the café, but already he was starting to feel at home. He'd met Andy, the owner and his wife Cho. There were also two perfectly adorable little kids. David had yet to see Andy without his leather, wide-brimmed hat as he dashed around the place, greeting new and regular customers in the same friendly manner. Yet another place where the atmosphere made David feel good.

He looked at the screen. Already he could spot places where the manuscript needed tweaking and tightening. Having all that time away from it had been a good thing after all. Before he could get down it, however, his lunch arrived. David dug in. The sea air was doing wonders for his appetite. That first spoonful of soup was a revelation. Delicately spiced with peppers, velvety texture… The freshly baked bread was sublime with butter, too.

He forgot about the book and concentrated on enjoying his delicious meal.

Not a smear of soup remained. If he could have licked the bowl clean without drawing attention to himself, he would have. He caught sight of Richard smirking at him as he walked by. Yeah, it was pretty obvious he'd liked it. He pushed the empty bowl to one side and opened up the laptop. He went to the first chapter and began work.

"David. *David.*"

The insistent voice finally broke through. David looked up with a scowl. Andy was standing in front of his table, grinning. "David, we're about to close."

David flicked his eyes to the time on his computer screen. It was four thirty. He knew the café closed at four. "Oh, I'm really sorry. Were you guys waiting for me?"

Andy laughed. "You've been on another planet this afternoon. We didn't want to disturb you, especially when you seemed so into it. But we're about to shut up now." His expression was suddenly apologetic.

David quickly saved his work and closed the laptop. "Thanks, Andy. Today was a really good day."

The genuine smile on Andy's face was a delight to see. "Oh, that's good." He stood to one side to let David slide out from behind his table. "Will we see you tomorrow?"

"Possibly." David liked it there. The sound of the waves hitting the rocks was almost hypnotic and he couldn't complain about the service. And as for the staff, they were a friendly bunch.

He shook Andy's hand and walked toward the little gate which Richard unlocked for him.

"See you again," Richard said with a grin. David thanked him and started along the path past the houses, small café and the little shop that sold coffees and ice creams. He glanced up at West View, Taylor's house. Taylor was pulling a canoe up onto the boat ramp. When he saw David he smiled broadly.

"Hi there. You had a good day?"

David returned his smile. "Yeah, I actually managed to work on my book. I've not written anything new, but I was able to improve what was already written."

Taylor beamed. "Hey, that's fantastic!" There was no mistaking the look of delight on his face. David was touched. "Maybe your writer's block is crumbling at last." He winked. God, David certainly hoped so. Taylor finished tying up the canoes and straightened. "Listen, I'm going out for a dive tomorrow morning. Would you like to join me? I've got a wetsuit that will fit you, mask, snorkel… what do you say?"

Now that *really* pressed David's buttons. "Oh wow. That sounds great. I've love to."

"Cool." Taylor said. "How about you come over here eight-ish for a light breakfast, and then we'll get out there ASAP. If there's enough light, I have a camera that I can take underwater shots with. I can take a photo of you while you're down there."

David liked that idea. "Okay." He looked Taylor up and down, taking in the firm biceps, his tattoo rippling as he lifted the board which displayed his prices.

And just as quickly he dismissed the idea of getting together with Taylor that evening. He wanted to be alert for their swim in the morning, and a night spent fucking Taylor wasn't exactly conducive to waking up fresh as a daisy. Ironically, he watched Taylor's gaze travel the length of his body. Yeah, Taylor had clearly been having the same thoughts.

"Another night," David murmured quietly. Taylor's expression of disappointment was adorable. He opened his mouth to retort but then closed it abruptly.

"Yeah, you're right, I suppose." Taylor's eyes danced with mischief. "But tomorrow night? That's a different story."

David laughed and waved a hand at him as he walked toward the house. Tomorrow night that cute little ass would be all his.

Taylor looked at his watch in exasperation. It was already nine thirty and still there was no sign of David. Even though he'd known him a relatively short time, Taylor didn't think it was like the man to be this late. He didn't have David's mobile number—not that it would have done him much good, signal being what it was—so phoning him was out of the question. He picked up the James Blanchette novel he'd been reading last night and tried to focus on the page, but it wasn't happening. His mind kept straying to the lighthouse and its American occupant.

Taylor liked David. He would have liked him solely based on their evening together, but the sex was the cherry on top. God, the man had a great cock and he knew how to use it.

After so many encounters with straight guys, it was wonderful to be with a gay man who knew what he liked in bed and went for it. Taylor was versatile, but he'd been mostly a bottom with his casual fucks. That was the way they wanted it. And the two times he and David had fucked, Taylor had bottomed. He wondered if David had ever bottomed in his life. Taylor thought not. There was something about David Hannon that screamed Top with a capital T. *Yeah, but imagine sliding into that arse.* A smile played around Taylor's lips as he indulged in a fantasy of fucking David, bringing him to the point where he was begging Taylor to fuck him harder.

A child outside squealed with excitement, shattering Taylor's reverie. He looked at the clock on the mantelpiece. It was nearly ten. David clearly wasn't coming. For a second or two Taylor was ready to shrug off his annoyance and just get on with his day, but something niggled away at him. *Maybe something is wrong.*

That did it. Taylor grabbed his keys and was out the door in a flash.

The bay wasn't crowded yet. There were a couple of families setting themselves up on the beach with towels, beach tent and all the rest of their paraphernalia. The tide was on the way out, the tips of the rocks by the café just starting to emerge. Taylor strode along the path toward the lighthouse where there was no sign of life. He went through the little gate and up onto the deck and peered in through the window. No David. On impulse he walked around the back to the door and tested the handle. Not locked. *Now what do I do?* Stupid question. Taylor opened the door quietly and went inside.

The house was silent. Taylor looked around with interest.

He'd only seen the interior on the photos that Vanessa used in her posters advertising the place. From what he could see, David was a fairly tidy man. When he spied a packet of tablets in the kitchen, its contents strewn over the worktop, he took a closer look. Oh fuck. Painkillers. He went back to the door and crept quietly up the wooden staircase.

David was in bed, a pillow wrapped around his head. An empty glass stood on the bedside table. All that was visible of David was his back with that stunning tattoo, and the muscled arm that held the pillow in place. The sheet just about covered that beautiful arse. The sight had Taylor's cock stiffening. Taylor gave himself a mental kick. David obviously wasn't well and here *he* was, perving over the man's arse. He approached the bed, unsure if David was sleeping.

David stirred slightly. "Whaaaa?" The sound was muffled by the pillow.

Taylor sat on the bed and reached across to gently stroke David's back. "David, it's Taylor." He kept his voice low.

David moved his arm and the pillow immediately fell away, revealing his face. David squinted in the bright light. "Taylor? What are you doing here?" The words were almost a whisper. "What time is it?"

"I got worried when you didn't turn up for breakfast. And it's ten now. What's wrong?"

David closed his eyes. "Woke up at six with a blinding headache. I got up and took some pills, but they took a while to work. Guess I must have fallen asleep."

"Do you still have the pain?" Taylor wanted to know.

David became still, almost as if he were assessing the state of play in his head.

A slow smile crawled across his face. "It's gone." The look of relief was so obvious that Taylor had to smile with him. "Sorry about our dive." Taylor could hear the apologetic tone.

"Forget about that," Taylor admonished. "It's more important that you're feeling better. What you could do with is some fresh air." And then he had a marvelous idea. "David, do you get sea sick?"

David raised his eyebrows. "Er, no. Why?" The vaguest suspicion of a smile played about his lips.

Taylor plowed ahead. "I have a mate, Eric, who has a boat. He asked if I wanted to go out on it this afternoon. Just out into the Channel, maybe do a spot of fishing. Want to join us?"

David sat up and scrubbed a hand across his chin. "Thanks, but I wouldn't want to impose."

Taylor chuckled. "Trust me, you wouldn't be. He does this a lot."

David tilted his head. "Look, just how big a boat are we talking about here? I mean, it could be a row boat with oars and everything. Or are we talking bigger than that?"

Taylor winked. "Oh, I'd definitely think bigger if I were you. Eric comes from money. The boat is a thirty-five foot yacht."

David's eyes widened. "Really?" Taylor could tell he was wavering. "And you're sure he wouldn't mind?" There was a wistful expression on his face.

That decided it. "David, you're coming along. You'll love it. The fresh sea breeze will blow all your cobwebs away."

David chortled. "Just as long as it doesn't blow me overboard." He glanced down. "In that case, maybe I need to think about getting a shower and then eating something." A second later his stomach growled. He grinned sheepishly.

Taylor had another idea. "I tell you what, you climb into the shower and I'll go downstairs, see what you have in the fridge and make you something. What do you say?"

David stared at him in surprise. "You don't have to go to all that trouble."

Taylor shrugged. "It's no bother. You've had a crap start to your day. You're bound to be feeling a little fragile. I wasn't going to be working today anyway, so I might as well make sure you're fed before I drag you out on Eric's boat."

"Then yes, thank you. That would be great." David threw back the sheet and got out of bed, giving Taylor a fantastic view of that hot naked body. David clearly took care of himself. Taylor particularly liked his arms which had great muscle tone. He remembered how good they'd felt wrapped around him as he and David had lain on their sides, David sliding into him from behind with ease.

A cough broke through his reminiscences. Taylor found David staring at him, head tilted to one side, an amused expression on his face. "I'd love to know what you were thinking about just now," David said, eyes sparkling. "Whatever it was, it made you smile."

Taylor felt the blush rise in his cheeks. He wasn't about to share. "Never mind," he muttered and got up from the bed. He fled downstairs before David could say anything else.

He could hear him chuckling.

He looked inside the fridge. David had eggs, cheese, tomatoes, and some ham. Taylor gave a satisfied smile as he pulled out the ingredients for an omelet, nothing too heavy for David's stomach. He searched through the cabinets until he located a bowl and a chopping board, and then he set to work. By the time he heard the shower click off upstairs, he was almost ready. He had a plate sitting in hot water in the sink to warm it, and when he heard David's feet on the stairs, he drained the water and dried the plate.

David came into the kitchen as he was tipping the frying pan to slide the omelet out. David's eyes grew wide. "Oh wow. And here was me thinking you'd make me a sandwich or something." He looked so pleased that Taylor had to look away. He didn't want David to see him blush *again* like some schoolboy. Taylor fished out some cutlery and placed the plate on the table. David looked overwhelmed as he sat down, his gaze on his meal.

"Okay." Taylor cleared his throat. "I'm going to go now and let you eat in peace." When David looked up in surprise and opened his mouth to retort, Taylor held up his hand to stop him. "No, really. I want to put some lunch together to take with us, plus I need to ring Eric and tell him we're coming." He glanced at the clock on the wall. "I'll do that now, and then I'll let you know what the plan is."

David nodded as he lifted a forkful of omelet to his mouth. Taylor watched a blissful expression spread across his face. David grinned. "Damn, boy, you sure can cook. You'll make someone a wonderful wife." He winked.

Taylor guffawed and then batted his eyelashes.

"Why, Mr. Hannon, is that a proposal?" David cracked up laughing. Taylor chose that moment to exit. *Always leave 'em laughing*.

Chapter Five

David watched the rigid inflatable boat bounce across the waves as it came into the bay, steered by a young man in sunglasses with tanned skin and hair so blond, it was almost white. David and Taylor stood on the sand, Taylor's cooler at their feet.

"This is where we get our footsies wet," Taylor said with a smile as he took off his flip-flops. David copied him. Farther out in the bay, Eric's boat gleamed in the midday sun, a beautiful vessel, mostly white with sleek black flashes on the hull. The billowing sail rippled in the breeze.

The RIB got within a few feet of them. "All board, gents." Eric's smile revealed perfect teeth. *Something else they got wrong about the British*, David thought. It was something of an urban myth in the States that British dentistry was not at the top of its game. *Wait 'til I get home. I'll put 'em right*. He and Taylor waded out to the RIB, the water frothing around his ankles. Eric helped him clamber in, Taylor following.

David took the cooler from him and grunted. "Good God, Taylor, what in the hell have you got in here? Just how many people are you feeding?"

Taylor winked. "You've never seen Eric eat."

Eric huffed. "Just for that, you may *accidentally* go for an unscheduled swim this afternoon." He gazed at Taylor over the rim of his shades. "You *did* bring your swim shorts, didn't you, boys?" He winked at David.

Taylor snorted. "Yeah, right."

He turned to David. "We usually go for a swim while we're out there, but swim shorts? Give me a break. We go skinny-dipping as you Yanks say." David laughed. If this was the norm, then he liked the laid-back attitude of Taylor and his friends already. And he certainly had no problem stripping off. Shy wasn't in his vocabulary.

The RIB swung around in a wide arc and headed toward the boat. Taylor squinted into the sun. "Did you say Jason was coming?" The boat bounced along, the breeze ruffling David's hair. It promised to be a beautiful warm afternoon.

Eric nodded, his gaze focused on the boat out in the bay. "Yep, and Shane and Mark." He smirked. "Mark seems to have brought along the contents of a brewery."

David was surprised. "Do you drink when you're on the boat?"

Eric steered the RIB alongside the stern and a young man with jet black hair and piercing blue eyes threw him a line. "Not me. This lot, however… that's a different story." He tied up the RIB and then caught hold of the metal ladder to climb aboard. David followed after handing Eric the cooler. "God, he's right, Taylor. This thing weighs a ton."

"Any more comments like that and you won't get any of Andy's crab tart," warned Taylor as he stepped into the boat. Four heads swiveled in his direction. There was an immediate chorus of approval.

"Andy's crab tart? Good man!"

"Nice one!"

Taylor caught David's eye. "This lot are real easy to please. Feed them and they're like putty in my hands."

He gave a wicked cackle. David grinned. He gave his surroundings a quick glance. The deck of the boat had seating all the way around and four young men, roughly the same age as Taylor, were sprawled on the varnished wooden seating. There was a covered cabin which contained the wheel and equipment, and in the center of the boat was a raised section with steps leading down.

"What's below?" David asked as he took a seat and Eric prepared to raise the anchor. Taylor sat next to him.

"There's a cabin with bench seating at one end, a mini kitchen in the middle and bedroom and shower room in the hull," the black-haired young man said. David caught that lilting accent that he loved hearing. "I'm Jason, by the way." He cast a withering glance in Taylor's direction. "Seeing as *someone* hasn't seen fit to introduce any of us." He winked at David, who couldn't help warming to him.

Taylor spluttered. "Give me a break, you sod. We've only just this second got on board."

A young man to David's left with red, curly hair and a spattering of freckles across his nose and cheeks chuckled. "God, Taylor, it's so easy to take the piss out of you." He leaned across and held out his hand. "I'm Shane, and the guy facing you is my twin brother Mark." David shook it and gave Mark a nod of acknowledgment. Now that he looked, the resemblance was obvious. Something Shane had said caused him some confusion, however.

"I have to ask. What does that mean, 'to take the piss out of Taylor'? 'Cause I gotta tell you, guys, that sounds nasty." He wrinkled his brow and they laughed.

"It means to make fun of him," Mark explained patiently.

David's brow cleared. He was learning new stuff every day. Maybe at some point in the future he'd have to write an English guy into a story. He'd certainly have enough material to work with, *that* was for sure.

Eric steered the yacht carefully out of the bay. Taylor had told David that there was a natural channel at Steephill, and that boats needed to be careful not to hit the reef. Eric obviously knew what he was doing. The man exuded confidence.

David leaned back against the boat, the sun warm on his face. "How do you all know each other?" He tilted his face upward, closing his eyes and listening to the waves as the boat cut cleanly through them. This was heaven. He'd always wanted to go out on a boat and Eric's was a beauty.

"We all went to school together," explained Jason. "And we stayed in touch once school was over."

Shane grinned at Taylor. "We were Taylor's best mates at school."

Mark chuckled. "Yeah, *someone* had to save him from getting beaten up once they found out he was a friend of Dorothy's." His eyes danced with amusement.

David snorted. "God, you have that saying over here too?" The young men laughed.

"I take it you bat for the same team?" said Jason with a wide grin. David nodded and Jason merely bobbed his head in acknowledgment. "I figured as much."

David was pleasantly surprised at their easy-going attitude. "Are you all straight, then?"

Everyone nodded apart from Eric, who was concentrating on steering.

"I take it you two have been engaging in some horizontal dancing," Shane said, winking at David, who had to bite back his laughter. Oh, he *really* liked Taylor's friends.

"*Shane!*" Taylor sounded appalled. "For God's sake! The first time I bring someone along and *this* is how you act? I'm certainly going to think twice before I do *this* again." He turned to David, his expression apologetic. "I'm sorry, David."

David couldn't hold in his reaction any longer. He took one look at Taylor's earnest, anxious expression and burst out laughing. "Hell no, don't apologize. I think your friends are really cool." Taylor seemed slightly mollified. David turned to Shane. "I love the euphemism, by the way." Shane gave a half-bow. "But you got me curious. How in the hell did you know Taylor and I had fucked?" He felt comfortable enough in their company to be blunt, and he was too long in the tooth to deal in flowery language.

Shane snickered. "Just a hunch. Our boy here seems awfully relaxed around you. And besides, I know Taylor. He's a real… what's that expression you have over the pond? A horn-dog?"

David guffawed. Taylor's cheeks were bright red. It was adorable. "Aw, come on, you know they're right," he said to Taylor. "You said as much yourself the other night. And let's face it, the night we met when you were coming out of the sea—you weren't *really* inviting me back to your place for just *hot chocolate*, were you?" He cocked his head. "Or was I imagining that look in your eye?" He grinned wickedly.

Taylor stared at him in stunned silence for a moment—and then his lips twitched, followed a second or two later by peals of laughter. Everyone joined in, David included.

"I like him, Taylor," said Jason, wiping his eyes. "He can come out with us again before he goes back to the US." David's chest swelled to hear this seal of approval.

"Here's a nice spot, guys," Eric called back. "Anyone for a swim?" David could hear the low whine as the anchor dropped and then the engine switched off. The young men reacted with appreciative noises and everyone started to strip off their clothing. David wriggled out of his shorts and tugged off his polo shirt. Taylor's cheeks had cooled by the look of them. He got undressed next to David, shucking off his shorts and T-shirt.

"Ever done this before?" he asked David. He shook his head. David loved the feel of the sea air on his nude body, his dick half hard in the stiff breeze. Taylor looked positively beautiful, his tanned skin glowing warmly in the sunlight, hardly a tan line in sight. David guessed he did this regularly. He watched as Taylor climbed up onto the side and dived neatly into the water, only to emerge a few feet away, shaking the water from his wavy hair. He beckoned to David. "Come on in. It's great!"

David needed no second invitation. He jumped into the water, landing with a huge splash. God, the water was cold. Sunlight filtered through the water as he pushed upward, bursting into the light with a loud exhale. He hadn't felt this alive in years. Taylor swam to him with clean, easy strokes. David admired the way he seemed so at ease in the water.

David wasn't sure what it was about the whole situation—the water, the guys' attitudes, the warmth of the sun—but *God*, he was horny. He grabbed at Taylor and pulled him close, the water swirling around them.

"These guys gonna bat an eyelid if I kiss you?" he wanted to know. Hell, he wanted to do more than kiss him, but even he had limits in polite company.

Taylor clung to his shoulders and stared at him, eyes wide. On a whim, David slid his hand below the surface of the water to where Taylor's cock rose to meet it, despite the cool water. Oh, Taylor was turned on, too.

"Go for it," Taylor gasped back. David didn't waste a second. Their lips met in a kiss that began with no hesitation, both of them clearly into it. He fondled Taylor's dick as they kissed, tongues sliding together in an erotic ballet. Taylor moaned into his mouth, oblivious to the shouts of the others as they jumped into the water.

David broke the kiss and brought his mouth close to Taylor's ear as they treaded water. "Gotta tell you. If we were alone right now, I would be balls-deep inside you as soon as was humanly possible."

Taylor's pupils were so large. "God, yes," he breathed, the water lapping around his shoulders. "Later?" David nodded, his hand continuing to stroke Taylor's cock gently under the water. Taylor shuddered against him.

Suddenly they were splashed from all directions, water drenching them completely. David spluttered and coughed, Taylor along with him.

He looked around to see the others regarding them both with expressions of amusement as they treaded water.

"If you two want, we can all stay out here for a swim while you get back on board to fuck in the cabin," Eric suggested, his eyes gleaming. He grinned. "Sorry about the splashing. But we thought you needed cooling off a bit."

"Sorry," Taylor apologized sheepishly. His eyes caught David's. "We'll behave." He moved away from David and swam a short distance away. David felt a brief pang of disappointment. Taylor had felt damn good in his arms.

"Oh hell, don't apologize," said Shane. "I've never seen you kiss a guy before, and I have to say, even for a straight like me, that was fucking hot." He leered at Taylor. "Not that I have any intention of joining the dark side, you understand."

Taylor guffawed. David thought it such a surreal conversation to be having in the middle of the English Channel, the sun hot on his shoulders, the water not feeling so cold now. They swam for about fifteen minutes. David laughed as Shane and Mark tossed Eric into the air in a back flip. They all seemed so at home in the water. *Guess that's what comes from growing up on an island.* He swam at a leisurely pace, loving the feel of the water on his body. Taylor caught up with him and they swam together, matching stroke for stroke. David turned onto his back and sculled, looking up at the brilliantly blue sky. He kicked lazily. This was heaven.

Taylor swam up to him and caught hold of him, brushing his hand briefly over David's cock. David shivered as he looked into Taylor's eyes. The promise in them….

"Lunch time, you two!" Eric shattered the moment. They moved apart. Taylor's expression was a picture of disappointment.

"Come on." David nodded toward the boat. "I'm ready for some crab tart." *Among other things…* Taylor gazed at him for a moment and then gave a sharp nod. Time enough for other pursuits when they were back on dry land.

Taylor was feeling pleasantly buzzed. He'd had a couple of bottles of Wight Gold, Mark's favorite island beer and now he felt distinctly mellow. The food had gone down really well. Everyone had been appreciative of the tarts Andy had made fresh that morning, not to mention the huge tub of salad Taylor had put together. Luckily for him he'd gone overboard on the food—these guys all had extremely healthy appetites.

David had gone below to use the bathroom. Taylor couldn't believe how his friends had taken to him. He'd expected to get a lot of ribbing about David being older, but so far they'd said nothing.

Scratch that. Shane slid toward him across the bench seat. "He's nice."

Taylor didn't have to ask who. He gave a brief nod. "Glad you approve," he responded, a touch of sarcasm in his tone. Secretly he was pleased. These guys had always been so protective of him as they were growing up. They were a tight-knit group, had been since they were twelve years old, and their friendship had only gotten stronger with time. They were the first people Taylor came out to at the age of sixteen.

He'd been so nervous, unsure of their reaction to his declaration, and they hadn't let him down, not for a second. They had each hugged him tightly and told him it was fine if he was gay. Then Shane had stunned him by telling him they'd known for a while. Taylor's jaw had almost hit the pavement. So much for thinking his revelation was a surprise. He should have known, of course. These four knew him better than anyone, except for his mum.

"So, no lectures about him being too old for me?" Taylor watched for Shane's reaction. "Even if he *is* just a fuck buddy?"

Shane snorted. "I'm not surprised. I remember the way you used to look at Mr. MacNamara in our Year Eleven English class."

Taylor was horrified. "Oh God, tell me you're joking." He didn't think he'd been that obvious. He'd had a crush on the teacher for almost a year.

Shane snickered. "Taylor, how do you think we worked out that you were gay?" Taylor's eyes widened. "Not to mention we could tell you were lusting after Mr. Evans, the Biology teacher, in Year Twelve." He stared frankly at Taylor. "You obviously have a thing for older guys. So no, I'm not surprised about David at all."

Taylor was dumbfounded. And here he was thinking he'd been really discreet.

"So, what's he like?" Shane asked, eyes glinting. Taylor cocked his head. "In bed, stupid," Shane added, grinning.

Taylor stared at his friend open-mouthed. "Like I'm going to tell *you*," he managed to stammer out. "Allow me *some* secrets, for goodness' sake."

He took a drink from his beer bottle and glanced across at the others. Mark, Eric and Jason were stretched out on the deck on beach towels, sunning themselves, all decently attired once more in their shorts.

Shane pouted. "Aw, c'mon. Share." He winked. "I told *you* all about my first time with Annabel when I was fifteen."

Taylor almost spat a mouthful of beer all over Shane. "Yeah, and I *really* didn't need those pictures in my head, so thanks for that." Something crossed his mind. He gave Shane a sly look. "You sure you're not bi or something? Because first there was your reaction to us kissing, *now* the questions about my sex life…" He chuckled. Shane was as straight as they come.

Shane winked. "I'm confident enough in my sexuality to cope with hearing about your exploits. So…." He lowered his voice. "Is he a top or a bottom?" Taylor quirked his eyebrows and Shane reddened. "What? Of course I know the lingo. One of my best friends is gay. I had to do some research in case you ever wanted to, *you* know, discuss stuff."

Oh my God, he's being serious. Taylor was touched. He favored Shane with a warm smile and Shane's flush increased.

"Strictly a top, I think." If Shane had gone to all that trouble, the least Taylor could do was share. "And to answer your first question—he's great in bed." He kept his voice low. "And I'm hoping he gets to be great all over again tonight." His dick hardened at the thought of it.

Shane gave a low whistle. "You dirty boy. You two are going to be fucking like bunnies all the time he's here, aren't you?"

Taylor stared out at the horizon, his mind on David. "God, I hope so. It might go some way to making up for the sexual desert I've been crawling through since I came out. I'm going to make the most of it." And the fact that David was turning out to be a great guy was the icing on the cake.

"You two seem to be deep in conversation."

David had emerged from below and was looking over at the two of them with interest.

Hell. How much did he overhear? Taylor's cheeks heated up and David arched his eyebrows. He smirked. "Have I missed something interesting?"

"Nah, I was just subjecting Taylor to lurid details of my sex life," Shane replied easily. Taylor could have kissed him for the save. Shane winked at David. "I think you got here just in time. I don't think he could have taken much more."

"Oh hell no. No self-respecting gay guy needs to hear about het sex." David shuddered. "The mere thought." He gazed sympathetically at Taylor. "You poor boy." David chortled.

"Yeah, could have done with you appearing about five minutes ago," joked Taylor. "You have *no* idea what I've been through."

"Don't worry," David soothed. "I'll come round to your place tonight and help you get over it." And all of a sudden there was a predatory look in those blue eyes that sent shivers dancing up and down Taylor's spine. *As David would say, Hell yeah....*

"Sounds good," he managed to croak out. David's smiled widened. A sudden dig in the ribs from Shane brought him back down to Earth with a bump.

"And maybe it's time to head inland," Shane added with another grin.

Taylor could really get behind that idea.

Chapter Six

"Oh *fuck*, right there."

Taylor ground out the words as David thrust up into him, his cock deep inside him. Taylor's legs were splayed out over the arms of his armchair as he held on to David's shoulders. David gripped his hips as he fucked up into him, that long, fat dick pistoning into him with increasing speed.

"Oh God, Taylor. Can't last much longer. So fucking close." David gasped out as he slid even deeper into Taylor, nudging his gland continually now. God, how long had they been fucking? It felt like *hours*. David hadn't been through the door for ten seconds before Taylor had launched himself at him, leaping into his arms and wrapping his legs tightly around his waist. David hadn't even missed a beat. He'd carried Taylor into the living room and flopped him into the armchair, before dropping to his knees and pulling Taylor's shorts off in one swift movement. Taylor had cried out as David's mouth engulfed him—and had fought hard not to come on the spot when David deep throated him. David had chuckled around his shaft and swallowed. It was just too much. Taylor pumped come down David's throat, crying out his name as he shuddered through his orgasm. And David had swallowed every last drop.

David's chest was covered with a light sheen of perspiration. Taylor let go of David's shoulders and threw his arms around his neck, seizing David's mouth in a scorching kiss. David plunged his tongue into Taylor's mouth, mimicking the movement of that beautiful cock inside him.

Taylor's low moans were almost a constant soundtrack now, and he knew he was going to come for a second time that night. David shuddered and Taylor broke the kiss to throw back his head and cry out as David's heat filled him. It triggered his own climax and his body clamped down on David's cock as he continued to pump come into the condom. Taylor clutched David tightly, his dick pressed between their bodies as it jetted come over their damp skin. David stroked Taylor's back as he kissed his chest and neck, murmuring softly, no words but simply sounds that told of his pleasure.

"God, you feel so good inside me." Taylor shivered as David shifted his hips slightly, his shaft still deep within him. David said nothing but continued to kiss his neck, edging higher until at last their lips met. Taylor moaned, the sound lost as David devoured his mouth, his arms wrapping around Taylor to pull him closer. As David's cock began to slip from his body, Taylor let out a plaintive whimper. He didn't want it to end.

David released his mouth and pulled gently at Taylor's hair until he was looking into his eyes. "You feel damn good, too." One more tender kiss and then he pulled off the condom. Taylor got up from the armchair and stretched. He loved the way his body felt after sex. Too bad it wasn't something he got to enjoy often enough for his liking. But sex with David was another level entirely. If this was how it was going to be for the next three weeks…. Taylor was already anticipating David's departure with regret. He shook himself mentally. *Don't think like that. Just make the most of it while you have him.*

"Can I take a shower?"

Taylor smiled. "Sure. You don't need to ask. There are clean towels in the airing cupboard. Help yourself to my shampoo and body wash."

David cocked his head. "What's an airing cupboard?"

"It's where I keep all the clean bedding and towels, in a cupboard in the bathroom. The hot water tank is just underneath."

David's brow cleared. "Oh, you mean a linen closet. Why didn't you say so?" He winked and unfolded himself from the armchair. Taylor watched him amble out of the living room, admiring the view. David moved in such a self-assured manner, giving the impression of a man completely at ease with himself. Taylor envied him. He thought maybe that this was something that came with age. *Perhaps I'll seem as confident when I'm David's age.* Somehow Taylor doubted it. He listened to the sound of the shower running, and for one brief moment he was filled with the urge to go upstairs and slip into the shower with him. The thought of David, wet, glistening with soap, sliding his hands over that gorgeous body…

For God's sake, Taylor, it's like you're in heat! He chuckled to himself. Thoughts of David assailed him at all times of the day, and he seemed to be spending his days in a state of perpetual arousal. Not that he was complaining. It was like coming off a diet and finding himself in the middle of a cake shop, with an unlimited spending budget.

He looked out the window at the now darkened sky.

According to the weather forecast, the following day might be a good day for business. The only thing was Taylor was now torn. From their talks on the boat, he'd worked out that David had seen some of the island, but only a fraction of it. Taylor wanted to show off his home, but that meant taking time away from the water sports equipment hire business. It was at times like this that Taylor wished he wasn't working on his own.

Wait a minute... He grabbed his phone from the coffee table and scrolled through his contacts for Brian's number. Brian answered after several rings.

"You always did have rotten timing, little brother." Brian chuckled.

"I didn't interrupt anything important, did I?" Taylor wanted him to be in a good mood.

"Nah, I'm joking. It's not like I could get up to much with Mum and Dad hovering around, is it?"

Taylor laughed. Brian was currently residing in their parents' home while he looked for another place. Taylor was storing some of Brian's stuff in one of the spare bedrooms. "I bet that pissed Deb off." Deb was Brian's current girlfriend.

Brian groaned. "God, living with the parents is playing havoc with my sex life. Deb keeps telling me to get a move on and find somewhere to live bloody quick." He snickered. "Okay, what can I do for you?"

"I wanted to ask you a favor," Taylor began. "Are you working tomorrow?" Brian was a fireman and worked in shifts.

"Tomorrow's my day off."

Perfect. "How would you feel about spending what's predicted to be a warm, sunny day down here in the bay?" Taylor went for the hard sell. "Sunshine, plenty of beer in the fridge, lots of pretty girls on the beach to look at…"

Brian guffawed. "Ooh, you're really laying it on thick, aren't you? You want me to run the business tomorrow, I take it?"

Taylor smiled to himself. He was pretty sure Brian would be on board for it. "Yeah, if it's no trouble."

"Sure. Now tell me what you're up to."

Taylor hesitated. Brian was easy-going, like all his family, and none of them cared a damn that he was gay. They simply accepted it, which was a constant joy to him. Talk about being blessed. But Taylor had gotten into the habit of not talking about his personal life.

"Taylor? Is anything wrong?"

Taylor hastened to reassure his brother. "Nothing's wrong. It's just that there's this guy staying in the bay who's from the States, and I wanted to show him around the island."

There was that familiar chuckle again. "I take it said guy is worth the effort?"

Damn, Brian knew him far *too well.* "Definitely." Taylor opted for honesty.

"Then consider it done, little brother."

Taylor loved Brian's endearment, in spite of the fact that they were only two years apart. "Thanks, Bri. I owe you."

"Rubbish. You're already doing *me* a favor by storing all my shit. And speaking of which, I have a few places to look at this weekend. Hopefully one of them will suit."

Taylor hoped so. Being back at home was clearly a strain after living alone since he was twenty. Brian's landlord had sold up and given all his tenants a month's notice to find alternative accommodation. That had been six months ago. Brian must have been climbing the walls by now.

"Good luck," Taylor offered. "And I'll see you here about nine tomorrow morning, if that's okay." Brian reassured him that was fine, and they finished the conversation. Taylor sat back on the couch, smiling to himself. Now to decide where to take David. It suddenly occurred to him that he'd assumed David would be up for this. Maybe he should have spoken with him first. Taylor had always been impulsive.

David appeared in the doorway, his chest bare, a bath towel wrapped around his waist but riding low on his hips. His blond curls were still damp. Taylor couldn't help his body's reaction. His dick stiffened. And of course, in his still naked state, his arousal didn't go unnoticed. A smirk played about David's lips and his eyes gleamed with amusement.

He snorted. "God, the joys of being young. I swear you've got a permanent erection."

Taylor felt his cheeks heat up. "Well, what do you expect when you walk around the place looking so… so…" Words failed him. He wasn't about to tell David how much the man turned him on. Glancing down at his now fully erect cock, he realized he didn't need to. His traitorous body was doing all the talking. Taylor gave up. "Do you want to stay the night?" The thought of that hard, lean body curled around him all night long ….

David walked over to the couch and dropped the towel, revealing his own half-hard dick. He held out a hand to Taylor. "I thought you'd never ask. I'd love to. Let's go to bed. Now." He grinned.

Taylor wrapped his hand around David's and allowed himself to be pulled up from the couch, out through the door and up the stairs. *Someone* was certainly eager.

Who am I kidding? Taylor chuckled as David dragged him into his bedroom. He wanted this just as much as David.

David stood as close to the cliff edge as he could, peering down at the beach below. The sand revealed by the outgoing tide and the shingle at the highest point of the shore were a beautiful shade of orange. At the base of the cliff was an outcrop of land which had fallen in the past, and was now grown over with grass. David could make out a path which had been cut into the cliff, complete with steps leading down to the beach.

"Can we go down there?" he asked Taylor who stood next to him. It looked like a beautiful beach, and the view of the cliffs from down there would be stunning.

Taylor shook his head. "There used to be a set of wooden steps which went down about half way, but they collapsed some time ago. Up until then you could get down fairly easily, but without the steps it's impossible."

David sighed.

"Such a pity. It looks so pretty down there. I have to ask, why is this place called Whale Chine? And what in the hell is a *chine*, by the way?"

Taylor chuckled. "The story goes that a whale was found at the base of the cliff, a long time ago. And a chine is where water cut a ravine through the rock toward the sea." He beckoned with his finger. "Come over here and you can see what I mean." He led David over to where there was a sign declaring no beach access to Whale Chine. They stood at the cliff edge and David caught his breath as he looked down. The view was spectacular. He could see the base of the cliff, where the different layers of rock and sand rose up dramatically, their colors almost glowing in the afternoon sun. Rabbit holes dotted the top layer of ground on the opposite side of the chine. In fact, he could see rabbits sitting in the sunshine, munching away happily on grass. The faintest trickle of water could be heard below.

"Is that what I'm hearing? The water that cut through here?" David couldn't see it. The view of the base was obscured by rocks and shrubs.

"Yes, there's a stream that still flows into the sea. It's only a trickle, mind you, but you can see it at the bottom."

David was fascinated. Taylor's idea of showing him around the island had been a damn good one. They'd spent a wonderful morning driving along little country roads, stopping now and again to look at the view. David would have to download the photos from his camera's SD card before long—he'd taken so many pictures. Lunch had been in a little country pub in the tiny village of Shorwell.

They'd sat in the beer garden and David had been delighted to spot the stream which ran through it. He was even more amazed to see fish in there, their scales a glimmer of different colors. When Taylor told him he was looking at rainbow trout, David had stared in fascination.

"Where next, tour guide?" he asked with a wide grin.

Taylor scrubbed a hand across his cheek. "To be honest, it's getting a bit late for going somewhere else. But I took some trout from the freezer this morning. How do you fancy having a cookout on the beach this evening? We could light a fire and cook the fish, maybe bake some potatoes to go with them."

David loved the idea. "Could we stay out and look at the stars? I was so impressed that first night. The skies here are really clear." The thought of lying down on the beach, staring up at the night sky with its carpet of bright stars, was an attractive one.

Taylor smiled and David tried hard not to stare at him. The boy was simply beautiful when he did that. "Yeah, we can do that. I've got a couple of beach towels that we can lie on, and a disposable barbecue to cook on. Then we can make the fire and sit around it while we wait for it to get dark."

"Let's head back then." David couldn't wait. It sounded like an idyllic way to spend an evening. "And we can talk some more, too." Not that they hadn't spent a lot of time talking already. He'd talked about New York and Taylor had listened in rapt attention, asking lots of questions. It seemed the islander had a hankering for city life. It always amazed David how people from such differing backgrounds could connect on so many levels.

Talking with Taylor was always a delight. The young man talked about his life on the island, growing up in a close-knit community, something alien to David but appealing nonetheless. He loved to hear Taylor's stories about his family, but it made him wish his own life had been similar.

"So what was life like, growing up in New York?" Taylor wanted to know.

They lay on the sand, the remnants of their dinner tied up in a plastic bag, along with the paper plates they'd eaten from. The fish had been just delicious, the flavor superb. Taylor had cooked it in foil, with a sprinkling of fresh dill and sea salt, and it had pulled away easily from the skin and bones. David was fast becoming a big fan of fresh fish. The taste was nothing like what he was used to at home.

The beach was deserted, save for the two of them. There were a few lights showing in the windows of the houses along the bay, but not another sign of life. The blanket was soft beneath him and the air was still. Residual heat from the sand warmed David through the layer beneath him. Taylor had built a fire on the beach which burned away merrily, casting a warm glow over them. Taylor lay at his side, stretched out on his back, long legs crossed loosely at the ankles.

David folded his arms under his head and stared at the darkened sky with its dusting of stars. "Kinda lonely," he admitted. "Dad left when I was very little, and Mom never married again, so it was just her and me."

Not that there hadn't been lots of kids in the neighborhood, but his mom had always discouraged him from playing with them. "Mom was real keen for me to go to college, so she made sure my studies were my top priority."

"What did you study?"

"English." David had always loved what words could do. Words were powerful. "When I graduated I went into teaching. I thought it would be neat to inspire young minds, cultivate a love of language, maybe discover a future Pulitzer prize-winning novelist or three." He laughed inwardly now as he thought of how idealistic he'd been back then.

Taylor snorted. "And how did that work out?" Yeah, Taylor could obviously *see* how things had worked out.

David sighed. "Reality was a kick in the ass. The kids didn't wanna learn most of the time. Now and again there'd be one or two kids who showed an interest, sure, but they were in a minority." It was so far removed from his dreams that it had almost destroyed him. The daily grind of targets, report cards, more targets, meetings, bureaucracy... And always there was the pressure to do better, along with the constant criticism from the press that teachers weren't working hard enough.

Taylor's hand touched his arm. "If it makes you feel any better, life here for teachers isn't very different." David glanced at Taylor's face which glowed in the light from the fire. Taylor's expression was sympathetic.

David patted his hand.

"Doesn't surprise me," he said quietly. "But you'd think that people would value teachers. After all, we had the country's future in our hands."

Taylor's eyes widened. "That's a good way of putting it." He smiled. "I can tell you're going to be a good writer. You might be famous one day, you never know."

David fought hard not to laugh. *God, if he only knew….*

"So you quit teaching to write? That must have taken a lot of guts to walk away from your career like that." There was a note of awe in Taylor's voice. "I don't know if I could have done something so brave."

David wrapped his hand around Taylor's and squeezed it. "And deciding to run your own business isn't brave? Hell, that takes guts too." The boy clearly had balls.

He loved the shy smile that bloomed across Taylor's face. "Oh, I don't know about that," he said modestly.

David tightened his grip. "Don't you *ever* sell yourself short," he admonished. "You're doing something you love, and doing it well enough to enable you to do the things you enjoy, like traveling. And it means you get to live in this place." He flung out his arm in a wide sweep. "I really envy you having all this on your doorstep."

Taylor let out a contented sigh. "I love it here. I have to admit, when I go traveling, the hardest thing is leaving that sound."

David didn't need clarification. The constant soundtrack of the sea was fast becoming addictive. "Yeah, but you get to come home to it. It's always here, just waiting for you."

Taylor suddenly leaned across and kissed him lightly on the lips. "Thank you."

"For what?" The kiss was sweet and fleeting, the touch of his lips warm and soft.

"For reminding me of why I'm so lucky."

David smiled. "And I count myself lucky to get to share this beautiful place, even if it's only for a month." Yet the thought that he'd have to leave at the end of the month was already weighing heavily. How could this place get under his skin so goddamn fast?

"Hey, where are you?"

Taylor's voice pierced through the thoughts which swirled around in his head. David gave himself a mental shake and pulled Taylor closer, cupping his cheek. Taylor licked his lips and David couldn't resist. Hell, he didn't even *want* to resist. He threaded his fingers through the silky waves of Taylor's hair and brought their lips together in a soft, tender kiss. When Taylor flicked his tongue almost hesitantly along his lower lip, David gave a low moan and opened for him, pulling Taylor to lie on top on him, his weight pressing David into the sand below. He could feel Taylor's erection, full and heavy behind his zipper, and David pushed up with his hips, a gentle thrust, nothing more. It was enough to draw a groan from Taylor. At this rate, they'd be fucking right there on the beach within minutes.

It took a supreme effort, but David pushed Taylor gently back onto the towel. He leaned over him, noting the puzzled look in Taylor's eyes.

"Taylor... my God, boy, you turn me on. But this is not the place to be doing this, all right?" He pushed at his rigid cock with the heel of his hand. Fuck, he was so hard he ached. He watched Taylor's face as his words sank in.

Taylor shuddered and then took a deep breath. "Yeah, you're right." He sat up on the towel. "And for the record? You turn me on too." He inhaled sharply. "There was something I wanted to ask you."

David pulled himself upright and leaned back, his weight on his hands. "Go on."

"I already told you I go round to my parents' house a couple of Sundays every month for lunch, along with anyone else in the family who happens to be on the island at the time." David nodded. "I'm due to go have lunch next Sunday. Would you... would you like to come with me?"

David was stunned by the invitation. "Are you serious?"

Taylor nodded, his gaze fixed on David. "It's nothing big, honestly. I just thought you might enjoy it. And trust me, one more mouth to feed won't matter to Mum. She always prepares enough to feed a small army."

David chuckled at that. But he still wasn't convinced. "Won't your family think it strange if you bring along a perfect stranger to lunch?" And then something else occurred to him. "Do they know you're gay?"

Taylor laughed. "Oh, most definitely. They're probably the most supportive family on the planet. And in answer to your first question, they won't think it strange at all."

"They sound like great parents."

Taylor nodded. "One or more of us is always bringing along a guest to these shindigs, so there's a precedent." He paused for a moment. "Well, strictly speaking, I don't know what Grandma thinks. She's old school. I'm pretty sure she knows I'm gay, but she doesn't talk about it."

David had to admit he was intrigued. He'd loved hearing Taylor talk about his family. They sounded liked a great bunch of people. And if the truth be told, he was kind of flattered that Taylor had thought to ask him along in the first place.

"Yeah, okay," he said finally. It might be fun at that.

Taylor beamed. Then his eyes sparkled. "Oh, there *is* one thing I should warn you about, before you meet Mum."

David gave a slow nod. "Ah, *now* we're getting down to it." He grinned. "Hit me with it."

"Mum has this little habit of asking me if I'm seeing anyone, so be prepared." Taylor's grin matched his. "And seeing as you're going to be the first bloke I've ever brought home, she's going to have a field day with you." Those green eyes positively danced with amusement.

David groaned in mock horror. "You might have mentioned that before." He winked. "It's okay, Taylor. I'm a big boy now. I'm sure I can handle anything your mom throws at me."

And besides, it might be fun to see if he could make Taylor blush. He wondered how long it would take his mom to bring out Taylor's baby photos. Moms were the same the world over.

Yeah, if Taylor was foolhardy enough to invite him, David intended to have some fun—at Taylor's expense.

Chapter Seven

The sky outside his window was leaden—a perfect match to his mood.

David had awoken early with an aching back. He winced as he rolled over in bed. It was probably just a case of sleeping in an awkward position, because so far the bed had been supremely comfortable. Nevertheless, the pain didn't show any signs of disappearing real soon. David had hoped the hot shower would have eased things a little, but no such luck. He made his way carefully down the stairs, the constant twinges in his back now an annoyance.

The weather was the next thing to foul up his mood. There would be no sightseeing today. The heavy gray clouds threatened rain, and quite a lot of it, as far as David could tell. *Goddamn British climate.* He knew it was unreasonable to expect glorious sunshine every day, but clearly the last week or so had spoiled him. *Is it too much to ask, Big Guy, that I have some decent weather for what's sure to be my only trip over here?* He chuckled. He wasn't sure, but maybe God was having a few laughs at David's expense. He glanced down at his now empty coffee mug. He didn't even remember finishing it. Thank God, Vanessa had provided a coffee pot in the kitchen. He got up from the couch and winced as he walked over to the machine to pour another cup. At least the store in Ventnor sold decent coffee. That would have been beyond a joke to get here and have to put up with crap coffee.

God, just listen to yourself. Whining bitch. David couldn't help it.

His mood seemed as black as the clouds which appeared to press up against his windows. Yeah, a fanciful notion, but hell, it was pissing him off. He sipped his coffee and on impulse glanced at his phone. Yet another item on his shit list. He sure hoped no emergency came up at home, as there was no way anyone could contact him. The signal seemed to be intermittent, and he'd long since given up trying to call out. He switched it on, out of habit more than anything—and then stared in amazement.

There were five messages on his phone. And they were all from Clark.

For a moment David deliberated deleting them immediately. He didn't want to read anything from the little bastard. He held the phone loosely in his hand, unable to tear his gaze away from the screen. Why in the hell would Clark be texting him after all this time? Michael's comment about David maybe acting hastily prodded at him. *Had* he been too harsh? The messages sat there on the screen, almost taunting him. *Why didn't I delete his contact details?* He ignored the part of his brain that was telling him quietly that maybe he didn't want Clark out of his life completely. He snorted. Apparently some of his brain cells were demented.

You know *you won't get any peace until you find out what he wants.*

David hated that damn inner voice sometimes—especially when it was right.

He opened the first message.

David, I hope you're okay.

I know I'm the last person you want to hear from right now, but I just wanted you to know that I've been thinking a lot about what happened and I'm so, so sorry. I hope that one day you'll find it in your heart to forgive me.

That's all, babe. Take care.

David scowled. He'd had similar messages five months ago when he'd kicked the little shit's ass out of the apartment. He deleted the text and opened the next one.

David, I'm a little concerned about you. No one has seen you for a while. Is everything all right? Just let me know you're okay.

"Like I care if you're concerned," he addressed the phone. Delete, delete, delete…

David, I'm really starting to worry here. Where the hell are you?

David was getting bored now. He debated deleting the final messages without opening them, but couldn't bring himself to do it. *Only two more. Just get it over with.* He opened the fourth text and then realized it rolled over into the last text. Huh. Long message.

David, it's clear to me now that I made the biggest mistake of my life. Even if it was the one and only time I cheated on you, I shouldn't have done it, and I deserve everything you threw at me. But I still feel that we are meant to be together. We fit, babe. Ask yourself some questions: in your heart of hearts, do you miss me? Do you miss *us*? Cos I miss *you*. I miss your arms around me. I miss you inside me. God, I miss that. I miss hearing your laugh, seeing your smile.

Give us another chance, David. We can get over this. I love you. Clark

David felt as though he'd been punched in the gut. That lying, cheating, little sack of shit…He knew it was complete bullshit, but still there was that little niggle at the back of his mind. *Had* he thrown it all away too soon? And then his brain went into overdrive as he questioned his motives, second-guessed his reactions, analyzed every single event, until he thought he'd go mad.

"I don't *need* this crap!" he yelled up at the ceiling. "Fuck you, Clark, for putting me through this again!"

He held down the button on the phone, switching off completely, and then threw it across onto the couch. Enough.

The day didn't lend itself to sightseeing, thanks to the weather, but Taylor had a plan. And wonder of wonders, it didn't involve him getting David into his bed. He smiled to himself as he walked along the shingle path toward the Lighthouse. God, the man was addictive. Taylor had awoken with the idea of surfing. One look at the waves rolling into the bay and that was it. He was mentally reaching for his wetsuit. He had no idea if David had ever used a board, but he didn't mind teaching him. They could have a lot of fun.

He reached the deck and knocked on the patio door.

"Good morning!" he said cheerfully as the door slid back. Anything else he'd been about to say died in his throat when he got a good look at David. The man had a face like thunder. Taylor recoiled slightly.

"What do you want?" David's voice was a harsh rasp. He scowled at him, his body taut with tension.

"I just called round to see if you wanted to go surfing with me. The waves are perfect for it this morning." Taylor kept his tone light.

"Not today, okay?" David snapped out the words.

Taylor stepped back, hands held up. "All right, it was only a thought. If you change your mind, you—"

"Just leave me the hell alone, okay?" The words rang out loud and clear. Taylor flinched. David glared at him and then slid the door across. A few seconds later the blinds covered the window, obscuring Taylor's view.

Taylor stood for a moment and stared at the patio window, his brow furrowed. *What the fuck?* Okay, so he didn't know David all that well, but still, it stung. He fought to swallow as his throat tightened.

Well, standing here isn't going to accomplish anything. Taylor gave the door one last look and then turned on his heel and walked slowly back along the path to his house. He had no idea why his heart felt so heavy, but he knew of a cure. Something he always turned to when he needed to push aside the cares of the world. He got to the little shed which housed his boards and wetsuits and unlocked it. He went in and pulled the door shut behind him. Taylor squirmed out of his jeans and T-shirt and into the wetsuit. He grabbed a board, locked the shed and headed down the slipway to the beach. The waves were calling. A bit of time spent out in the water would wipe away the ache he felt inside. And as to why he was feeling like that in the first place? Taylor didn't have a clue.

For God's sake, it's just sex. It's not like you're best friends with the man, is it? He fucks you. End of story.

Except for some reason that Taylor couldn't quite work out, it wasn't.

He threw down his board and launched himself on top of it, sculling away from the shore, loving the feeling of being out in the water again. Taylor always felt at his most alive when he was out here, mastering the waves, pitting himself against the power of the sea. He lay prone on the board, watching for a good incoming wave, readying himself to feel the exhilaration that always surged through him as he rode the waves into the shore.

But when the waves came, the exhilaration didn't. Taylor couldn't get rid of the feelings that had plagued him ever since David had shut the door in his face. No matter how many times he got to his feet on the board, twisting his body as he balanced, arms outstretched, he couldn't shut out the cold sound of David's voice, still ringing in his ears. Taylor pushed his body to its limits in his determination to escape that voice, the emotions that surged through him, but it was to no avail. After a half hour and no release, Taylor had had enough. He sculled toward the shore, his thoughts gloomy. *Why the fuck am I letting David get to me like this?*

Good question. And one for which Taylor had no answer. Not one that made sense, anyway.

The sun was going down, the clouds having finally cleared by the end of the day, leaving a clear sky with pink tones at the horizon. *Typical*, Taylor thought. *A cloudy day and then it gets better when it's too late to enjoy it.* He sat on his porch on his recliner, a glass of beer on the deck beside him, his sketch book on his lap. It had taken most of the day but he'd finally managed to shuck off the thoughts and emotions that had tormented him throughout his surf. He took a long drink from his beer and then put down the glass and picked up his pencil. It had started as a meaningless doodle, but what had emerged from his pencil was a sketch of David's face. His expression bore no resemblance to the David of that morning. Taylor closed his eyes and pulled up his image in his mind. A smiling David, skin crinkling around his eyes, laughter lines around that beautiful mouth…

Taylor stilled. *Beautiful mouth?* He shook his head. David was becoming an obsession.

Movement in his peripheral vision had him looking up in time to see David walking stiffly toward him along the path. Taylor tensed—until he noticed how awkwardly David moved. Taylor closed his sketch book and put it down on the deck. He got to his feet and waited as David approached the ramp.

Before he could ask what was wrong, David beat him to it.

"Before you say a word, I have to apologize for this morning." David's blue eyes held pain. Taylor opened his mouth to reply but David held up his hand. "Just give me a minute, okay?"

Taylor snapped his mouth shut and waited.

David's gaze bored into him. "I had no goddamn right to speak to you the way I did. That was downright rude. And I am really sorry if I hurt your feelings. God knows, you'd be within your rights to kick me off your porch, but I'm hoping you won't." His eyes pleaded with Taylor.

Taylor felt the tension seep from his body. "It's okay," he replied quietly.

"The fuck it is," David retorted. "I treated you like shit. I can't apologize enough." He shifted on his feet and Taylor couldn't miss the crease which deepened between David's eyes, or the brief flash of pain across his face.

"David, what's wrong?" Concern filled him.

"It's nothing, just my stupid back which has decided to fuck up my day." David waved his hand dismissively. Taylor wasn't fooled.

"Has it been like this for long?"

David's expression was gloomy. "Ever since I woke up this morning. As far as I know, I haven't done anything to cause this. It just aches."

Taylor smiled. "Then you've come to the right place. Step this way, Mr. Hannon." He gestured toward the house. David tilted his head and Taylor winked. "I have something inside that might help."

David snorted. "Trust me, boy, your cock may be a thing of beauty, but I doubt it can cure my backache."

Taylor burst out laughing. "Well, that's the first time someone's paid my dick a compliment. Fortunately for you, that wasn't quite what I had in mind." He led David into the house and up the stairs into his bedroom. "Wait here a sec."

He went into the room which contained all Brian's stuff and pulled free the folded massage table. He dragged it into the bedroom and chuckled as he saw David's eyes widen. "This belongs to my brother. He's a fireman right now, but he also trained as a masseur. Come to think of it, he's had several occupations for someone who's only twenty-eight." He unfolded the table and set it up next to the bed. "I've learned a thing or two from him. In fact, Brian says I have magic hands." He flexed his fingers, wiggling them and David chortled. "Okay, out of those clothes and let's sort out your poor back."

While David undressed Taylor went into the bathroom and collected two large bath towels from the airing cupboard. He spread them over the table and then opened the drawer next to his bed, searching for the massage oil. He glanced at David who stood there naked next to the table, his dick flaccid. True to form, David didn't seem in the least bit perturbed to be nude.

Taylor got serious. "I need you to lie face-down on the table. I'm not going to bother with a towel over your arse, like real masseurs do. Heaven knows, I've seen it close up enough times by now." David snickered. He clambered onto the table, his usual fluidity lost as he moved awkwardly. He stretched out, head resting on his folded arms. Taylor opened the bottle of almond oil and poured a generous amount into his cupped palm. He began at David's shoulders, manipulating the muscles, kneading the flesh, really digging in with his fingers and the heels of his hands. David grunted, the sounds almost pushed out of him as Taylor went to work.

"God, you're good at this," David acknowledged as Taylor moved lower, thumbs pushing into his back, moving in slow, deliberate circles. Taylor smiled as he concentrated on his task. He knew he'd hit the spot when he moved to David's lower back and a loud groan burst from David's lips. "Hell, right there."

Taylor chuckled. *"Now* we're getting somewhere." He worked the area over, listening carefully for any sign that he was hurting David, but all he got were small grunts and the occasional low moan. Taylor applied himself diligently to his task, until he had worked up a sweat.

"That feels better already," David admitted. "Damn, boy, you're a marvel."

David's body looked awfully inviting, so much so that Taylor has a wicked idea. He bent low and spoke into David's ear. "And I'm not finished yet." He moved to the head of the table and leaned over David, sliding his hands down his spine until he reached the firm globes of David's arse. He squeezed the taut flesh, spreading those cheeks and slipping his hand into the crevice. When his fingers came into contact with David's hole, he felt the tremors which rippled through him.

"Yes." The single word was a whisper.

Hesitantly, Taylor stroked a finger over his pucker, and David shuddered. Stretched out above him, Taylor slowly pushed it into David's heat and gasped as David's body tightened around it.

"More," David demanded hoarsely.

Taylor pulled free of David's body and pulled off his T-shirt in one swift action.

He shoved his shorts down to his ankles and stepped out of them. David turned his head to one side and made as if to move. "Stay where you are." Taylor forced as much authority as he could muster into his voice. David stilled immediately and Taylor grinned. What a heady feeling.

He moved along the table until he was at the foot of it, looking along the length of David's body, his skin glistening with oil. Taylor climbed up onto the table and spread David's thighs. He couldn't miss the sharp intake of breath .

"I hope to God you like this," he breathed as he stretched out on his belly between David's legs, propped up on his elbows. He spread David's cheeks and licked over the hot little hole that glistened and convulsed invitingly.

"Oh *fuck*." David's body tensed and Taylor froze immediately, wondering if he'd gone too far—until David reached back to push Taylor's head insistently toward his crease. "Yeah, eat my ass."

Taylor grinned. "Yes sir." He licked over David's hole more boldly, pushing his tongue against it, feeling the muscle resist him. David's resultant groans echoed around the room and Taylor sucked and licked until he felt David start to loosen up. Only then did he slide two fingers into him, as he kissed those gorgeous mounds of flesh, occasionally biting softly. David panted as he pushed back, forcing Taylor's fingers deeper inside him until Taylor was fucking him with them.

Taylor was rock hard. All he wanted to do right now was sink his dick into that tight little hole. Wanted it with every fiber of his being.

Wanted it badly enough to lean close and whisper into David's ear.

"I want to fuck you."

There was no mistaking David's reaction this time. He froze.

"Taylor, I... I've never..." The words were stammered out.

Oh *hell*.

David's mind was in turmoil. Taylor's fingers inside him felt so fucking good, but clearly not good enough to override the emotions which surfaced. He'd never bottomed. Ever.

Taylor's damp chest pressed against his back, his cock sliding over his hole as Taylor moved to whisper in his ear.

"It's okay. We don't have to." But David had heard the need in his voice, the urgent wanting. Taylor moved to get up and David reacted without thinking.

"Wait." Taylor became still. "Let me turn over." Taylor lifted himself up and David rolled onto his back, no discomfort at all now. Damn, that felt so much better. He looked into Taylor's earnest face, his eyes half-hooded with desire. David pulled Taylor down onto him, wrapping one arm around him and cupping the back of his head with the other as he brought their lips together in a fierce kiss. Taylor groaned as David devoured his mouth hungrily. He could feel Taylor's hips bucking, his cock heavy against David's shaft which was already rigid.

When he broke the kiss, he looked into Taylor's eyes. Taylor regarded him intently.

David could see the need in those beautiful green eyes.

"You really want to do this, don't you?"

He watched Taylor blink, his mouth opening and closing, no words coming out. But then there was that dick, straining against him. *Guess that's a yes.* David took a deep breath. Just because he'd never, didn't mean it always had to be that way. And then he became aware of his body. His hard as steel cock. His hole which clenched at the thought of Taylor sliding into him. David took a deep breath and locked eyes with Taylor.

"Then fuck me."

Taylor's eyes grew large and round, and his breath escaped in short, quick bursts. "Really?"

David nodded, not trusting himself to speak. Taylor attacked his mouth in a relentless kiss that stole the breath from his body. When Taylor finally released him, he stared down at David, his pupils wide.

"How do you want to do this?"

David considered for a second or two. "I want to see your face."

Taylor nodded and then climbed off the table and went into the drawer where David knew the condoms and lube resided. Taylor dropped them onto the bed, came back to the table and held out his hand. "Your first time needs to be in a bed." He spoke so earnestly that David smiled. Talk about role reversal.

He grasped Taylor's hand and allowed the younger man to help him off the table. Taylor led him to the bed and lay down, holding his arms wide.

Without hesitation, David climbed onto the bed and moved to lie against Taylor, both men gasping as their bodies met. Taylor pushed him onto his back and began to kiss down his chest, tongue flicking at his nipples. David shivered. His cock pointed toward his navel, already leaking pre-come. He held his breath as Taylor inched his way lower, until he felt Taylor's warm breath on the head of his cock. Taylor's eyes met his and he smiled as he lapped at the clear liquid, before sucking David deep into that hot mouth. David arched up off the bed.

"I love that mouth of yours," David gasped as Taylor tightened his lips around David's length, cheeks hollowing as he sucked him deeper. God, the boy was relentless. All too soon he felt his orgasm begin to boil. "Taylor," he called out warningly. "Too much. I want to come with your cock in my ass." God, his voice sounded breathless. Taylor pulled back so rapidly that David had to laugh. "I gather you like that idea, too."

"Oh God, yes." Taylor knelt up between his thighs and tore open the foil square with his teeth.

"Let me." David took the condom from him and carefully rolled it over Taylor's length, noting the shudders which rippled through him. He opened the lube bottle one-handed and dribbled the viscous liquid over Taylor's dick which pointed straight up. David slicked it from head to root, watching the tremors which coursed through Taylor. David's hand stilled. "I have to ask. Have you ever topped?"

Taylor's gleeful smile gave him his answer before he opened his mouth. "Oh yes."

David took a calming breath. "Thank God for that."

Taylor surprised him by taking hold of his wrists and pinning them on the pillow above his head with one hand. David spread his legs wide and began to breathe faster as Taylor positioned himself, cock poised at David's hole. He stared at David, eyes impossibly wide.

"Do it." David was amazed at how hoarse his voice came out. He held his breath as Taylor pushed slowly into him, feeling his body open for him. Taylor's gaze was focused on the point where their bodies joined. Fuck, that cock felt huge inside him. David's breathing quickened and his body strained up from the bed, unable to move far because of that hand which held him trapped. Taylor pressed insistently into him until at last David could feel the prickle of his pubes against David's ass. Taylor became still and David felt impossibly full.

Taylor's gaze met his. "God, you're tight." He grinned. "And it feels so *good*." He began to move, slowly at first, but with increasing speed, his cock sliding into him with greater ease. David wanted to touch him. Hell, he *needed* to touch Taylor.

"Please, let me go."

Taylor didn't hesitate. He released David's hands and David reached up to pull Taylor down to him, Taylor's head dropping to his shoulder as he began to thrust into him. David's legs came up to tighten around Taylor's waist, his heels pushing against Taylor's ass, propelling him deeper into him.

"Oh God, David." Taylor's voice was husky. "Feels fantastic."

David's whole world had narrowed to the feeling of Taylor's body in his arms, Taylor balls-deep inside him. He started to move, hips rocking up, meeting Taylor's thrusts with equal measure. Taylor's body changed position subtly and suddenly a rocket went off inside him.

"Oh fuck, there. Right there."

Taylor was panting more rapidly now and David realized he was into the home stretch. He clung to Taylor's back, Taylor's breath loud in his ear as he slammed into him, balls slapping against his ass. All too soon David felt his balls ride up high, and he was there.

"Gonna come," he cried out, and then gasped as Taylor reached down to wrap his hand around David's cock which pulsed come between their bodies. David trembled as his orgasm shook him, his body tight around Taylor's dick. Taylor stiffened and David could feel the throb of his cock deep inside him as he emptied his balls into the latex. Taylor let out a howl and David felt the full body shudder which ran through him. Taylor's weight came to rest on him and David held him tightly, their bodies jolted by aftershocks which dissipated little by little until at last they lay in each other's arms, their breathing less erratic.

Taylor raised his head and before he could say a word David kissed him, their lips meeting in a sublimely sweet union, their bodies still connected. Taylor moaned softly. David loosened his grip on Taylor's body, both of them bathed in perspiration. David made a noise of disappointment as Taylor's cock slipped from his hole.

Taylor dealt with the condom, before moving back into David's arms. David held him closely, savoring the feel of Taylor's lean, hard body in his arms.

"Thank you," David whispered at last. "That… that was incredible."

Taylor craned his neck to look up at David. "Stay?" Those green eyes locked onto him.

David smiled. "Yeah, I'll stay." He loved the smile which stole over Taylor's face. David closed his eyes and relished the afterglow that only came from great sex.

As if he could move anyway.

Chapter Eight

"So are you going to tell me what else upset you yesterday morning?"

David rolled onto his side to look down at Taylor who lay beside him, the crisp white sheet just covering his groin. The sun had started its slow ascent into the sky and it looked like being a beautiful day. What day *was* it anyway? David was finding it difficult to keep track. He concentrated for a second and then worked out that it was Friday. God, he'd already been on the island for nearly two weeks. Where had the time gone?

Taylor was regarding him intently. David could smell him, the scent of bed-warmed skin, the sea and pure Taylor, a warm, earthy aroma that always fired up his dick. Taylor's tousled hair was adorable. Hell, the boy was always adorable when he woke up. As if to prove the validity of this statement, David's cock twitched as it lay there beneath the sheet. *Down, boy.* The thought of rolling Taylor onto his belly and plowing into that perfect little ass was already there in the forefront of his mind. Not that it took much to put it there.

"Not going to tell me?"

Taylor's words broke through, interrupting his hot little fantasy.

David sighed. "Let's just say I had a bad morning, and leave it at that."

Taylor stretched out a hand and ran it lightly over David's chest.

David shivered as Taylor tweaked gently at his nipple before moving lower to stroke his taut belly. David closed his eyes, surrendering to the memories of the previous night. Submitting to Taylor had been an unforgettable experience, one he'd never envisioned if he were honest, but God, Taylor's cock had felt so damn good in his ass. *What have I been missing out on all these years?* It wasn't that he'd never considered bottoming. It was more a case that his partners had wanted him to top them, which he was more than happy to do.

He knew he couldn't leave it at that, not when Taylor's eyes held that same look of concern that had been apparent on the porch last night. He held out his arm and Taylor snuggled up to him, his body warm and vital against David, his head resting on David's shoulder. David wrapped his arm around him and looked at the ceiling with its sculpted wallpaper and elaborate ceiling rose from which was suspended a large white paper lampshade. He took a deep breath.

"About five months ago, I had to kick out my boyfriend, Clark. I came home and found him fucking another guy in our bed."

He felt Taylor tense. "Oh God, David, that's awful. I'm so sorry."

David tightened his arm around the young man. "Yeah, well, it's over now. Or at least, I thought it was, until yesterday." He told Taylor about the messages, and then about his conversation with Michael. "So I guess I'm feeling confused right now. I know I did the right thing when I threw him out, but Michael had me thinking about it all over again."

His chest tightened. "And then Clark's messages just raked over everything." Leaving him feeling raw. Again.

"How long were you and Clark together?"

"Two years." And they had been two happy years. It was still something of a shock when the stories began to filter through to him after he and Clark had split. Stories about how Clark had been cheating on him constantly the whole time. Stories which labeled Clark as nothing but a little gold-digger. So many stories that David hadn't got a clue which way was up any more.

He couldn't share those with Taylor. Hell, if even *half* of them were true, David had been awfully blind, and that wasn't something he wanted to admit to. *Who wants to admit to being a fool, after all?* He lay there quietly, enjoying the feel of Taylor in his arms.

"I get it. You don't want to talk about it." Taylor pulled himself free and sat up, throwing off the sheet to reveal his morning wood. Christ, he had a beautiful body, tanned and lean.

"Where do you think *you're* going?" David joked, eyebrows arched. He pulled at his cock which was already reacting to the view. He made sure Taylor got an eyeful.

Taylor chuckled. "Getting you your morning coffee. Is that acceptable, *Master*?" Those green eyes twinkled with good humor.

David waved his hand imperiously, playing along. "Get on with it, slave, and be quick about it." He tried for an English accent, but came off sounding more like Dick Van Dyke in *Mary Poppins*.

Taylor stared at him for a second and then grinned. "I've learned a few things since you got here. Like how to do this." He flipped him the bird.

David burst into laughter. Taylor was still chuckling as he walked out of the bedroom naked, his cute little ass cheeks looking so inviting that David wanted to sink his teeth into them and leave marks. David folded his arms under his head and let out a sigh of contentment. There was no way he would let memories of Clark intrude into this place. Taylor's bed was a place of both peace and passion—and Clark had no place there.

"Oh my God, you're nervous."

David could hear the note of incredulity in Taylor's voice. They were sitting in the Nissan on the driveway of Taylor's parents' house, a large rambling edifice on the outskirts of Shanklin to the east of the island. The house sat in large grounds, surrounded by trees. A porch ran around the outside of the house, Chinese wisteria growing up over it, the tendrils now bare, all its flowers gone.

"Am not," David grumbled. God, he sounded like he was six.

Taylor giggled. "They won't eat you, you know. And there won't be many of them. Mum, Dad, my brother Brian and his girlfriend Deb, my sister Bev and her boyfriend Ciaran, maybe Auntie Pauline and Uncle Raymond…"

"You. Are. Not. Helping," David gritted out. He didn't have a clue why he was so nervous. He just knew that he felt like he was about to be checked out by prospective in-laws. "They're gonna ask me a load of questions, aren't they?"

Taylor grabbed his hand.

"David, as far as they know, you're a guy who's staying in Steephill Cove and I've been showing you around. I haven't told them any more than that."

David gave him a hopeful look. "They don't know that you and I are....?" He let the words trail off. Even *that* was out of character. It wasn't like him to be so coy.

Taylor's eyebrows shot up. "Certainly not. It's none of their business."

Well, that's something, I suppose. David took a deep breath. "Okay, I can do this. I'm a big boy."

Taylor snorted. "Oh, I'd say so. In fact, after what I saw in bed this morning? Definitely."

David pulled his hand free and glared at Taylor. "And no trying to embarrass the dumb American, right? Some of the things you say are downright weird. I know you *claim* to be speaking English, but I have yet to be convinced of that." Taylor chuckled. He knew David was only joking. "You *still* talk funny in my book." Christ, David felt jittery today. He knew he was probably being unreasonable, but he still had the notion that he'd walk into the house and every one of the people there would be able to read some invisible sign on his forehead that proclaimed him to be fucking Taylor. Quite *why* that should bother him, David wasn't sure. It just did.

Just then the front door opened and a tall, slim woman with long gray hair peered around it. Her face creased into a smile when she caught sight of Taylor.

"And I guess that's our cue to get out of the car."

David heaved a heavy sigh and opened the car door. He had to keep reminding himself—*this is supposed to be fun*. Because right now? It felt about as fun as root canal work.

"More roast potatoes, David?"

David grinned as he accepted the serving dish Taylor's dad—sorry, *Dennis*—handed him and helped himself to a few more of the crispy potatoes. He glanced quickly around the table. "I'm not hogging these, am I? Anyone else want some?"

Brian laughed. "No, help yourself. It's good to see a man with a healthy appetite. Little brother here doesn't exactly stuff himself when he comes to lunch." He winked at the others around the table. Everyone smiled.

Taylor whacked his brother on the arm. "Hey! That's 'cause trying to grab food with *you* around is like trying to eat when there's a whole shoal of piranhas just waiting to attack."

David tried not to laugh with his mouth full. He loved the way Taylor and his family interacted. It had taken him all of ten minutes after their arrival to fall in love with this energetic, funny, warm-natured and generous bunch of people. Valerie, Taylor's mom, was the sweetest woman David had ever had the good fortune to meet. She welcomed David warmly, and then introduced him to everyone. Dennis had a *really* firm handshake and David felt as if his arm was about to come off once everyone else had greeted him. It was great seeing how much they all adored Taylor, who, it turned out, was the baby of the family.

David took another forkful of roast beef and mopped up some of the delicious gravy. He closed his eyes as the taste burst upon his tongue. A snicker from across the table had him opening his eyes real quick, however. Taylor's sister Bev was watching him, her eyes bright with amusement. She turned her head to glance at Valerie. "Looks like you've got another fan, Mum."

David tried not to grin with a mouthful of food. He swallowed hurriedly. "Valerie, this is a wonderful meal."

Valerie's wrinkled cheeks were a pretty shade of pink. "Thank you, David. I'm pleased you like it so much. Have you had any opportunity to sample Taylor's cooking?" David felt Taylor stiffen in the seat next to him. "Taylor's a wonderful cook."

"*Muuuuuum!*" Taylor's face was bright red.

"Yeah, that should have been our first clue, eh Bri?" Dennis winked. "When Taylor was a teenager, every Sunday all the men would be in the lounge watching the sports, while *he* was in the kitchen with all the women, talking cooking."

Brian snorted. "Yeah, why didn't I think of that? You're right, Dad—all the signs were there." He took a sly glance at Taylor. David chuckled. They obviously liked to get a rise out of Taylor. David envied him this carefree, happy environment. Being part of a large family was something he'd always dreamed of, but as the years went by and his mom showed no signs of wanting to get married again, David had watched his dream dwindle away. Watching Taylor surrounded by so much love and acceptance was truly wonderful, not to mention inspiring.

When David thought of all the horror stories in the American press about kids who'd been abandoned by their families, simply because they were gay… Taylor was so lucky.

The point finally arrived where David couldn't eat another mouthful. He sat back in his chair and patted his belly with a satisfied smile on his face. "That was truly delicious."

Valerie's blush was really fetching. "Well, there *is* dessert"—a chorus of groans rang out around the table—"followed by coffee for those who want it."

David mentally assessed his pigged-out state. Dessert might be pushing it a little. He arched his eyebrows. "What's for dessert?" He could always say no.

Valerie beamed. "Taylor's favorite—lemon cheesecake."

Oh God. David had died and gone to heaven. And judging from the smirk on Bev's face, his facial expression was saying this loud and clear. "A tiny piece, maybe? Just a smidge?"

Valerie's eyes flashed with approval. "Okay, that's David sorted—Taylor? How about you?" There was a knowing look on her face that even David could read. Taylor was a goner.

"Yeah, okay, maybe a little piece, Mum, thank you."

David leaned toward him and spoke quietly into his ear. "I understand completely," he said, his tone serious. "You're only doing this to be polite."

Taylor gave him a grave nod. "Exactly. It would be rude to refuse, after all, when Mum's gone to the trouble of making it specially." They regarded each other for a moment, and then both cracked up simultaneously.

Valerie chuckled as she got up from the table to go into the kitchen. David was on his feet instantly, and was rewarded with another approving glance.

"Please, David, sit down. We don't stand on ceremony around here. And you can have your cheesecake in the lounge with your coffee." She smiled at him and then exited the room followed by Bev and Brian who carried the dishes. Dennis got up and after pushing his chair under the table, he headed for the French windows, a pack of cigars already in hand. He turned as he reached the window.

"David, do you smoke?" He held out the pack.

David waved his hand. "Thanks all the same, Dennis, but no, I don't smoke." Dennis nodded and went out into the garden, lighting up a cigar as he went. Soon the aroma drifted into the house.

Taylor leaned closer and whispered, "I wouldn't be so fond of kissing you if you did."

For some reason, this remark warmed David on the inside. During the last couple of days, he'd noticed a subtle difference when he and Taylor were together. Taylor had always been relaxed around him, but there was a new atmosphere when David spent the night. He couldn't put his finger on it, but it felt good. David gave Taylor a quick smile.

"Taylor?" Brian's voice wafted through from the kitchen. "David may be a guest, but *you*, however, are certainly not. How about giving us a hand with the washing-up?" David could hear the note of amusement in his voice. He nudged Taylor with his elbow.

"Go on out to the kitchen and do your chores."

Taylor's lower lip pushed out ever so slightly and David snickered. "Go on—I'll be fine in here. Your Dad is very civilized. He's not about to grill me."

"It's not Dad I'm worried about," Taylor muttered under his breath as he got up to leave the table. David smirked. He had no idea what on earth Taylor was concerned about. Taylor's parents were a lovely couple in their late fifties, early sixties at the most. He liked the way they acted around their kids, in a quiet, dignified manner. Only two of Taylor's siblings were present, but they'd each brought their partners. Bev was very similar in character to Brian: both had a nice line in sharply observed humor. Ciaran was a quiet soul who clearly adored his girlfriend. Taylor had told David a little of the family history. Bev and Ciaran had been together for about three years, and Valerie and Dennis were apparently very keen for the couple to make some kind of commitment. David estimated Bev to be in her early thirties. Deb was another quiet one, and she and Brian had been together for about a year. They were looking for a house together on the island.

The sound of laughter floated from the kitchen. David could hear Taylor's distinctive giggle. He smiled to himself. The easy-going young man was rarely without a smile or a laugh. It was a really endearing trait. David got up and walked through the bi-fold doors which separated the dining room from the lounge. The huge bay window overlooked a tranquil garden, its lawns neat and trim, the flower beds well stocked with shrubs. David loved the oak trees at the very edge of the garden. Their shade must've been very welcome in the height of summer.

He let out a sigh of contentment. Yet another place with a positive ambiance.

"Admiring our view?"

David turned to find Valerie approaching him, carrying a tray with coffee cups and saucers, a tall white coffee pot adorned with old fashioned roses, a sugar bowl and a jug of milk. He hastened to take it from her and set it down on the coffee table.

Valerie's smile increased. "I *do* like a man with manners." Her eyes, so reminiscent of Taylor's, gleamed with approval. David felt his cheeks heat up a little. Good manners were something his mother had instilled in him from an early age. It occurred to him for the first time that day that he was probably closer in age to Taylor's parents than to Taylor himself.

He walked to the window and looked out. Behind him he could hear the tell-tale sounds of Valerie pouring out the coffee.

"You have a beautiful home, Valerie." David loved the quiet setting. He tried to imagine a little Taylor growing up here, playing in the garden, maybe on the aged swing that hung from a branch of the biggest oak tree. He heard her come up behind him and turned to accept a coffee cup.

Valerie's expression was one of pride. "We love it here. We bought this place when Joseph, our oldest son, was only four." She indicated the photos which stood over the fireplace. David caught sight of a few photos of a tall, kindly-looking man, maybe in his mid-thirties. "Joseph works in Edinburgh. He gets down here about two, three times a year. You just missed meeting him, in fact."

She walked over to the fireplace, picked up a photo in a silver frame and handed it to David. "This is Mary, our other daughter. She and her husband Chris live in Llandudno in North Wales. They're overdue for a visit, to be honest." David couldn't miss the wistful tone of her voice.

David glanced at the pretty woman in the photo, her husband standing with his arm around her. He gave Valerie a knowing smile. "All the chicks have left the nest, huh?"

Valerie's expression was tinged with sadness. "Exactly. It's hard having Joseph and Mary living so far from us, but at least they stay in touch. It's been so nice having Brian living with us once more, these last few months." Her lips twisted into a half smile. "Though I doubt he's found it so pleasant, having to live with Mum and Dad again after all this time."

"I'm sure he's very grateful to you both for stepping in like this, in his hour of need so to speak," David said. There was that flash of approval again.

"I'm hoping his new place won't be too far away."

David snorted. "That's one thing I can't get over about the people who live on this island. Taylor mentioned the other day about going 'all the way to Newport.' I thought from the way he was talking, Newport had to be at the opposite end of the island." He shook his head. "You can imagine my surprise when I find out it's precisely twenty minutes away by car."

Valerie laughed. "I imagine distances are a little bigger where you come from, David. New York, I think Taylor said?"

David nodded. "Just a little." He snickered.

Valerie took Mary's photo from him and replaced it in its position. She stopped at the last photo, one of Taylor. Her look of love and pride was unmistakable as she stroked its frame.

"Your baby, right?"

Valerie jerked her head up and she smiled. "Yes, he's still my baby, though that's hardly an accurate description. He *is* twenty-six, after all."

David chuckled. "I hate to tell you this, Valerie, but no matter how old Taylor gets? He'll *always* be your baby."

Valerie regarded him with clear green eyes. "You like him." It wasn't a question.

"Yes." David decided to be frank. It wasn't as if it was a lie. Taylor was a lovely young man who made him smile—even when they weren't in bed together. He liked Taylor's sense of humor and his laid-back approach to life. Even after only two weeks of knowing him, David knew him to be honest and reliable, a sweet, earnest boy.

"Has he shown you his poetry?"

David stared at her in amazement. "Taylor writes *poetry*?"

Valerie nodded, walking toward the bookshelves to the left of the chimney breast. "He started writing about three or four years ago. He's never done anything with them, although his father and I are always telling him to send them to a publisher." She trailed a finger along a shelf, clearly searching for something.

David shook his head. "He never said a goddamn thing." He was stunned. Why hadn't Taylor said anything? He watched Valerie's face break into a smile as she pulled a slim volume from the shelf.

"Brian had his poems made into a little book for us last year. I don't know if Taylor's written anything recently." She held out the book to David. "You can borrow this, if you'd like."

David looked down at the small spiral-bound book, its cover simple, bearing the words 'Taylor Monroe - a poetry collection'. "Are you sure?"

Valerie nodded. "I wouldn't offer if I weren't sure. How much longer will you be on the island?"

"Another two weeks or so." He took the small volume and held it reverently. Taylor's writing.... wow. "Should I tell Taylor I have this?"

Valerie's cheeks pinked. "Best not to. Taylor tends to be easily embarrassed about things like this."

"Then how will I get it back to you?"

She smiled. "I'm sure we'll meet again, David, before you go. Besides, you haven't met my mother-in-law yet." Her eyes twinkled.

David tilted his head and then his brow cleared. "Ah yes, Taylor did mention her."

"She's gone to stay with my sister-in-law Pauline for a few months while Brian is here." She chuckled. "Brian is a sweet boy but he can be rather too exuberant around his grandmother. But apparently she's enjoying the change of scenery. Pauline lives in Yarmouth at the other side of the island."

David remembered Yarmouth, the quaint little boating town with its ferry and small harbor full of boats. "I'll have to tell Taylor I have an invite, then." He heard voices and hurriedly placed the book of poems into his jacket pocket. "Thanks for this, Valerie."

She winked. "Think nothing of it." She leaned closer. "Although it might make you see Taylor in a different light."

David grinned. "I'll take that chance." Truth be told, he couldn't wait to read it.

Who'd have thought it? That boy continually surprises me.

K.C. WELLS

Chapter Nine

"So how did Sunday lunch go?" Shane asked, sprawling in the seat opposite Taylor.

Taylor groaned and shook his head. "Oh *God*. At one point when David and I were in the garden, I'm sure I caught sight of Mum taking some sneaky photos of us on her phone." He sipped the creamy latte with its addition of vanilla. The café owner, Andy, had made little noises of disapproval, muttering something like 'why not have coffee that tastes of coffee, now *there's* an original idea.' Taylor had giggled. When Richard brought out their coffees, he'd winked. Richard knew Andy's ways.

It was a warm Monday morning. David had spent Sunday night at the Lighthouse, much to Taylor's surprise. The past week had seen him more *in* Taylor's bed than out of it. What surprised Taylor most was the disappointment he'd experienced when David had told him he'd be spending the night there. Taylor had gone to bed alone, his thoughts focused on the occupant of the Lighthouse, and not for the first time.

Shane raised his eyebrows. "Why would she be taking photos?"

Taylor shrugged. "Who knows *what* goes on in that head of hers sometimes?"

Shane snickered. "Was she doing the embarrassing mother bit?"

Taylor let loose another low groan.

"You have *no* idea. I swear, it was like she was trying to *sell* me. She kept telling David all this stuff about me. It was 'Taylor does this' and 'Taylor did that.' I didn't know where to look."

Shane snorted. "How did David take all this?"

Taylor laughed. "He thought it was hilarious. He knew *exactly* what she was doing." He took a drink of the latte, thinking about the situation. David had given him some understanding looks. Taylor guessed mothers were the same the world over. They'd joked about it all the way back to the bay.

"Oh boy."

Taylor looked up. Shane was staring at him, eyes wide. "What's up?"

"That look on your face, *that's* what's up." Shane quirked an eyebrow. "Got something you want to tell me?"

Taylor narrowed his eyes. "What are you talking about?"

Shane smirked. "The way you look when you talk about David."

Taylor frowned. "What look?" he persisted.

Shane's gentle smile transformed his face. "You care for him," he said softly.

Taylor was swift to react. "What?" The crease between his eyes deepened. "I don't have a clue what you're talking about, Shane."

Shane's face straightened. "Okay, then obviously I've got it wrong. My apologies." His eyes never left Taylor, however.

Taylor wasn't going to let him off that easily. "You think I have feelings for David, is that it?"

Shane merely lifted his eyebrows, saying nothing.

Taylor persisted. "Sure, he's a nice guy. He's fun to talk to, and he's great in bed. But that's as far as it goes." Still Shane said nothing. Taylor huffed. "Look, you're seeing things, all right?"

Shane held up his hands. "Okay, fine." Taylor quietened. Shane's eyes gleamed. "But methinks the gay boy doth protest too much." Taylor's mouth fell open. Shane chuckled. "Taylor, I *know* you. Maybe you haven't actually sat down and thought about it, but it's clear, to me at least, that you have feelings for David which go beyond the bedroom." Taylor stared at him, still open-mouthed. "Your face lights up when you talk about him. There's a change in your tone of voice. Maybe you're just too close to see it, but there's definitely something there, mate."

Taylor didn't know what to say. He didn't want to think too much about what Shane had said. Surely not....

Shane flicked him with the paper napkin. "Forget it. Okay?"

Taylor nodded absently. Inwardly, however, his thoughts raced. *Was* he falling for David? There was no doubt he liked the man's company. He loved waking up in his arms. It gave him a feeling of security. And he looked forward to spending time with him.

With a supreme effort, he shook off his present train of thought. He couldn't afford to think like that. David would be leaving in a few weeks' time. There was no way Taylor wanted to get emotionally involved with a man who would shortly be departing for the other side of the ocean. On that path lay only heartache.

David sat on the sofa where he'd woken up early that morning, Taylor's book of poetry open on his chest. The laptop sat open on the table before him.

Taylor's poetry…. David was still reeling. What a revelation. The depth of feeling caught in those little verses was incredible. Subtle nuances in one line, then straight into emotion so naked that it made David's heart ache. Taylor had talent—that was certain.

He picked up the book and leafed through it, searching for the one poem which had affected him most. He wasn't surprised Taylor hadn't made any attempt to get them published. Every word proclaimed its author as gay, and he wrote with an honesty that was breathtaking. Definitely not for mainstream publication, but David knew of a publishing house or two in the States that would certainly lap them up.

I see you, her hand clasped in yours.

Your gaze stutters away from my direction.

What is it you fear?

That if our eyes should meet, she would see the truth, the real you?

See you as you were last night, in all your naked glory,

Your hands restlessly caressing me,

Your lips against mine,

Soft at first, then devouring me with an intense hunger.

The curve of your form as you entered me,
So deep that you were all I knew, all I felt...
All I wanted.
She has you now.
Her hand tightens around yours possessively.
But last night?
Last night you were mine.

David ached when he glimpsed the raw feeling behind the lines. It must have hurt Taylor deeply not to be acknowledged by someone, after sharing both his bed and his body. The quiet yearning that leaped out at David, the desire to have someone possess him. The emotion contained within the covers of that little book was staggering. Valerie had been correct—it *had* made him see Taylor with very different eyes. And the more David saw, the more he liked this new Taylor. He'd read and re-read the poems, unable to put them down, until at last, exhausted, he'd fallen asleep on the sofa.

With the dawn had come something new. A voice in his head, clamoring to be heard. A couple of voices, actually. David knew from past experience not to ignore the voices. He did the only thing he could—he fired up the laptop and started writing.

The next thing he knew was the quiet knock on the patio door. David's head jerked up. Taylor was standing on the deck, dressed in his black shorts and black hoodie. *The air must have cooled out there*, David surmised. Taylor's arrival couldn't have been more opportune. He got up from the sofa and pulled the door open.

"Just the person I wanted to see."

David's heart was beating so fast, he could feel it like a jackhammer under his ribs. "I need you to do something for me."

"And good morning to you, too." Taylor gave him a wry smile.

That gave him pause. "God, I'm sorry. That's really rude of me." He gave Taylor an apologetic glance. "Good morning." Taylor favored him with a warm smile.

"Better," Taylor acknowledged. His eyes glittered. "Okay, so what do you need me to do?"

David pointed toward the laptop. "I woke up early this morning with a story in my head, that I just had to get down." He shook his head. "My God, Taylor—it just *poured* out of me. I couldn't stop it." It hadn't been like that since the first novel. A white-hot fever had possessed him, an all-consuming desire to get it all out of him before the muse abandoned him.

"Oh wow." Taylor's eyes were wide. David knew now that he probably had a fairly good idea of what that felt like. "What kind of story is it?"

"A gay romance," David confessed.

"Really?" Those expressive green eyes had widened further. "How far have you got with it?"

A good question. David went to the laptop and clicked open the document. The word count at the base of the screen read…. David froze.

"Fucking hell, I've written eight thousand words since dawn." The words crept out in an awed whisper. He faced Taylor, his heartbeat pounding in his ears. "Taylor, would you do something for me?"

Taylor nodded, his gaze fixed on David's face.

"Would...would you read it for me? Let me know what you think of it?"

Taylor's expression registered surprise—and pride. "Me? You want *my* opinion?"

"Of course," David declared earnestly. "I value your opinion."

He watched Taylor's face as the young man considered it. "Okay, then yes."

David beamed. He shifted out of the way and indicated the sofa. "Sit down."

Taylor's eyebrows arched. "What—now?"

David faltered. "Please," he begged. "I need to know." He had no idea why it was so important to have Taylor's approval—because it *was* his approval he was seeking—but he knew he couldn't wait. "Only, I can't be here while you read it. I'm too goddamn nervous. I'm gonna go for a walk on the beach. Give me a wave when you're through, all right?"

Shrugging, Taylor planted himself on the sofa in front of the laptop and began to read. David quickly exited the house by the patio door, and headed down the pebbled path and left onto the beach. He traversed the sand, his sandaled feet leaving indentations where the tide had retreated. He walked out toward the rocks near the café and hoisted himself up onto the sun-warmed concrete ledge below the café railings. He couldn't look at the Lighthouse, in case the mere action of looking in Taylor's direction would somehow jinx it.

What if it's total crap?

He tried not to think like that. The story had poured out of him at such a blistering rate that it had felt inspired. Surely something inspired couldn't be total crap.

Yeah, keep telling yourself that.

A voice pierced his meanderings. "David!"

David looked up to see Andy leaning over the railings. "Hi there."

Andy pointed toward the Lighthouse. "You're being waved at, mate." He grinned.

David turned. Taylor was standing on the deck, waving both arms energetically. Even from his vantage point David could see the huge grin on Taylor's face. His heart leaped. *Oh fuck.*

He got up, climbed up onto the concrete ledge below the café and dashed along the path. Taylor watched him approach, that shit-eating grin never once leaving his face. As David drew closer, he could see Taylor was almost bursting with excitement.

"David, it's brilliant!"

Oh, the *relief* that flooded through him on hearing those words. David came to a standstill in front of him. "Honestly? You really liked it?"

Taylor's face straightened immediately. "No, I'm lying. It was utter garbage." But he couldn't keep a straight face. That grin erupted once more. "David, it's fantastic. I can't believe how much you've written in such a short time. There's so much to it—the descriptions, the main characters. I didn't want to stop reading."

David couldn't help his reaction. He picked Taylor up in his arms and swung him around, laughing gleefully.

Taylor's joyful laughter mingled with his. At last David let him go, conscious of the spectacle he was making. "Let's go inside." He felt dizzy with excitement as he led Taylor into the house. *He likes it.*

Taylor went into the kitchen. "Can I put on some coffee?"

"Sure," David said with a wave of his hand. Taylor got the ground coffee from the fridge and proceeded to fill up the machine. David's thoughts were in a whirl. He couldn't wait to get back onto the laptop and write more. God, he'd missed this feeling. It was addictive.

"I'm not stupid, you know."

Taylor's words broke through. David turned to face him, his brow furrowed. "Excuse me?"

Taylor gestured toward the laptop. "Chris is me, isn't he? And Logan is you."

David's jaw dropped. "Oh Christ—is it *that* obvious?"

Taylor snickered. "Only to me, I suspect." His eyes met David's and a blush bloomed on his cheeks. "I'm flattered. Really."

Oh, thank God for that. David's heart started to beat normally again.

"There *is* something that has me puzzled, though." David tilted his head. "Why is this so important to you? I mean, you're a writer, you've had stuff published, haven't you? Why is *this* story so different?"

David let out a sigh. He walked over to the worktop and poured them both a mug of coffee. He returned to the sofa and sat down, Taylor right behind him.

David took a deep breath. Confession time. "This isn't what I usually write." Taylor blinked. "In fact, this is as far removed from my usual writing as it's possible to get."

Taylor's eyes widened. "Now I'm *really* intrigued."

David regarded him intently. It was now or never. He got up and walked over to his laptop bag and pulled out a copy of his latest book, *Secrets Kill*. He walked back slowly to where Taylor sat and handed it to him. Taylor took it, shaking his head slightly, his mouth opening but no sound coming out, his forehead creased. And then David watched as the penny dropped.

Taylor jerked his head up sharply. "You... *you're* James Blanchette?"

David nodded, unable to look away from that face, that expression of total surprise—and then watched as a whole new set of emotions revealed themselves.

Taylor swallowed hard. David watched the color drain from his face. His chin trembled.

"How could you do that?" The words were a whisper. "How could you lie to me these past weeks?"

David was stunned by his reaction. "I didn't lie to you—not exactly. It was more of a sin of omission." He knew he was being pedantic. Taylor's expression didn't change.

"Why wouldn't you tell me who you were?" Taylor demanded. He fixed David with an intense look.

David's gaze lowered. "I guess because I'd been burned once." He glanced at Taylor through his lashes. Taylor's face was burning. David sighed. "Remember I told you about my ex, Clark?"

He heard Taylor's small sound of acknowledgment. "Well, it turned out that Clark had only been with me because of who I was. I thought he was with me because he loved *me*, David Hannon—but as it turned out, the only person he was interested in was James Blanchette. I found out that he'd targeted me once he found out who I was. I never got to know this until we'd split up. My so-called friends decided to share all the stuff they'd been hearing since the start. God, if only they'd had the courage to speak up sooner... I keep thinking of all the pain I went through, and all of it needlessly."

David looked up at Taylor. That pained expression was still there.

"So Clark was a little gold-digging shit, I get that." Taylor ground out the words. "But you've known me for nearly three weeks now. I know that's not a great deal of time in the grand scheme of things, but surely it's enough for you to know that I'm no Clark." The words came out almost strangled. Taylor barked out a bitter laugh. "And here was me thinking we were becoming friends." He gave a slow, disbelieving shake of his head. "I guess I don't know you at all."

To David's horror, Taylor got to his feet and headed toward the patio door.

"Taylor, please.... Don't go." David scrubbed a hand across his face. There was a dullness in his chest that wouldn't quit, a knot in his belly that wouldn't go away. Fuck, why hadn't he been honest from the start?

Taylor paused at the threshold and turned to face him, his eyes dull. "Bye, David—or should I say, James?"

He opened his mouth as if to say more, but apparently thought better of it. He slid open the door, walked out onto the deck and closed the door behind him. The click as the lock engaged had a note of finality to it. David got to his feet and moved swiftly to the door, his hands pressed up against the glass. He watched Taylor's slow progress along the path, his feet seeming to drag.

Christ, look what I did to him. I stole the light right out of him.

He watched until Taylor reached his front door. Not once did he turn around to look back in David's direction. And still David stood there, palms flat against the glass, unable to believe what had just transpired.

David, you fucked up. But good.

Damn inner voice. Like he didn't *know* that already.

Taylor tried to get on with life. He busied himself with the business. He read—*anything* but James Blanchette. He avoided calls from his friends—first Shane, then Eric, then Mark—until finally he switched off his phone in sheer frustration. He told himself it was no big deal. It had just been sex, after all. He tried desperately not to look in the direction of the Lighthouse. *Yeah, I can do this.*

He lasted all of three days.

By Thursday night he was climbing the walls. He needed to talk to someone.

There was only one person he could think of, so he made the call.

Mum opened the door and held open her arms. "Come here," she said.

Taylor walked into her arms and buried his face in her soft hair. He stood like that for what seemed an eternity, until at last she disengaged herself and led him into the lounge. Taylor listened intently for any sign of who else was at home.

His mum gave him a knowing smile. "There's only me and your grandmother here today. Dad's out with his friend Peter. So we can talk in peace." She sat down on the comfy sofa and held out her arms once more. Taylor snuggled up to her. She said nothing but simply hugged him, placing soft kisses on his wavy hair. He drank in her reassuring presence. Never mind that he was twenty-six—at that moment he needed his mum. How long they sat like that, Taylor had no idea. After a while he shifted on the sofa, pulling his feet up and hugging his knees.

"Okay, now talk to me." She regarded him with a neutral expression. "What's upset you so much?"

Taylor stiffened. He wasn't sure how much he was prepared to share. He sat in silence, unsure of how to begin. To his surprise his mother reached down to the floor beside the sofa and brought up her laptop. He watched as she opened it and booted it up.

"I have something I want to show you. It might make things a little easier for you."

She clicked open a file and Taylor was suddenly confronted with images of himself and David. David laughing. David smiling. Himself looking so happy that it made him catch his breath. Oh fuck. *This* was what Shane had seen.

"*Now* talk to me."

To his surprise, Taylor found himself telling her. Everything. Her gaze never left his all the time he was talking. He watched anxiously for any sign of disgust or reproach, but her expression never altered. When he'd finished, she gave a slow nod of her head.

"I hate to break it to you, Taylor, but you're upset because David means something to you. If it was just sex, as you say, you'd shrug this off." She watched him intently. "You know I'm right, don't you?" Her gaze flicked to the screen. "You *do* make a lovely couple, you know."

Taylor stared at her aghast. "Mum, why are you doing this?"

She tilted her head. "I don't understand. Have I got it wrong?"

Taylor narrowed his lips. "It doesn't *matter* how I feel about David. He's going to be leaving at the end of September. So I repeat—why are you doing this? Why are you trying to put us together? It's only going to make it hurt all the more when he finally goes. And then I'll never see him again."

Her eyes gleamed. "One—life is too short, sweetheart. Right now you have David, and he makes you happy. So enjoy him while you can. Two—so what if you get hurt? *Life* hurts, and we can't go through it hoping to avoid pain, because, let's face it, that's not going to happen. So we make the most of every situation, and roll with the punches. And three—don't assume you'll never see him again. The universe has a way of working things out." She smiled sadly at him. "You and I should have had this conversation a long time ago."

Taylor frowned. "What do you mean?"

Mum took hold of his hands. "You and I never talked about sex, did we?"

Taylor felt the flush rise up his chest, neck and cheeks, until he was sure the tips of his ears were glowing. "*Mum.*"

"No, let me finish, please," she insisted. Taylor tried to ignore his burning face. "When you came out to us, I wasn't sure how to frame my thoughts. I wasn't unhappy that you were gay, but at the same time, I didn't know what advice to give you. I realize now I should have given you the same advice as the others, that sex is part of being in a loving, committed relationship."

Taylor became still. He couldn't look her in the eye. She pressed on.

"Taylor, I may be more than thirty years older than you, but that doesn't mean I don't know how the world works these days. I didn't imagine you were a virgin"—there went his cheeks again—"and when I got to read your poems—*all* your poems— I was left in no doubt." This time it was her cheeks that flushed.

Taylor stared at her in horror. "What do you mean—*all* my poems? The only one who's read them *all* is Brian and…" He put two and two together. "Oh God, he let you read them, didn't he?" Taylor had been careful how much of his poetry he'd shown to his parents. Brian had wanted to see everything, and because the two brothers were close, Taylor hadn't like to refuse him.

She nodded. "I'll be honest, darling. I cried when I read some of them. You were looking for love, but in all the wrong places." She looked down at their clasped hands.

"And yes, I liked David the moment I met him. I *had* hoped he'd be the one who would give you what you were looking for." Her gaze met his. "Because seeing you together? You complement each other."

Before he could say anything, she got to her feet. "I'm going to make some tea. Would you like some?" He nodded absently. Mum leaned down and kissed his cheek. "It will all work out, Taylor. Somehow." She straightened and left the lounge. Taylor sat back on the sofa and picked up the laptop from the coffee table. He flicked through the photos one more time. He had to admit it—his mother had a point. He and David looked really good together.

"He's a good looking boy."

Taylor gave a start. He hadn't heard his grandmother enter the room. He stood up to hug her gently. She was nearly half his size. Taylor chuckled. "He's hardly a boy, Grandma."

She let out a wry chuckle. "He is to me." She returned his hug and then pointed to the screen. "Is he the one, then?" Taylor widened his eyes and his grandmother chuckled. "I have ears and eyes, boy. I may be ninety, but I'm not dead. And just because I don't *talk* about things, doesn't mean I don't *know* about them." She arched her thin eyebrows and looked at him over the rim of her glasses. "And don't you forget it."

Taylor couldn't help the grin which spread across his face. His wonderful, remarkable family, who never ceased to surprise him. "Yes, Grandma," he said meekly.

His grandmother returned her gaze to the laptop screen. "Yes, indeed. A fine-looking boy."

She peered at Taylor. "You have good taste." And with that she exited the lounge, leaving Taylor to stare after her in wonder. He gazed at David, frozen on the screen as the pair of them laughed at something. His mother's words rang in his head.

Life is too short. Enjoy him while you can.

Before he could do that, he had some apologizing to do—if David was willing to listen.

K.C. WELLS

Chapter Ten

David stared at the laptop screen, reading the manuscript so far.

It was so ironic, it was untrue. Good sex got his creative juices flowing—but when it went wrong, his muse would disappear on him every time. He hadn't written a word since Taylor had walked out the door three days ago.

Of course, the lack of inspiration might also have had something to do with the amount of alcohol David had consumed since then. He knew he'd avoided looking in a mirror, that was for sure. Which got him thinking about the amount he'd been drinking since his arrival on the island. He was definitely drinking less. And he got the sneaking suspicion that Taylor had something to do with that.

Taylor.... The young man with his clear green eyes and wavy, dark brown hair had been on David's mind constantly these last few days. No mojo meant more time for reflection, and David had been forced to face facts. In a little under three weeks, that boy had got under his skin. And it wasn't just the sex anymore. Yeah, David had missed sharing Taylor's bed, but what kept coming to mind wasn't the fucking, but the holding, the caressing, the kissing... God, he missed kissing Taylor. He missed the light in Taylor's eyes when he laughed. The way he gestured with his hands when he talked. Those cute little faces he made when David said something unintentionally funny. David put his head in his hands. He missed Taylor, period.

He'd found himself looking toward West View, wondering what Taylor was doing at that moment. Was he thinking about David? A tiny part of him hoped Taylor was missing him, too. He'd stopped listening to that damn inner voice when it went all logical on him. So what if he was going back to the States within a couple of weeks? He allowed himself to fantasize about bringing Taylor to New York, showing him around his favorite haunts, going to the clubs, a thing David hadn't done since Clark. Spending days in bed, just…connecting.

He gave himself a mental shaking. *Ain't gonna happen—and it's your own stupid fault.* Yeah, the self-loathing jag hadn't quite finished with him yet. He scratched his chin, feeling the two days of stubble. Talk about letting himself go. He glared at the laptop. This was getting him nowhere.

Christ, enough of the hamster wheel already…

David got to his feet and mounted the stairs to his bedroom. He shucked off his sweatpants and walked into the bathroom where he flipped on the shower. Soon the hot water was cascading off his body, washing away soap and self-pity at the same time. He closed his eyes and stood still under the jets, concentrating on the feel of the water as it ran down his body in rivulets. It was a cleansing experience in more ways than one. When his mind was calmer and his body considerably cleaner, David switched off the shower and shook off the excess water from his body before reaching for the towel. Hair toweled dry, a close shave and David felt human again.

A fresh mug of coffee in hand, David sat down once more in front of the laptop.

He spent a good hour tweaking the manuscript until he was happy with the finished result. He glanced up and looked through the patio door at the landscape beyond. The afternoon sun shone down on a calm sea, the aftermath of the storm which had broken during the night. The sky looked as if it had been newly washed, not a cloud in sight. Talk about an Indian summer.

David slid open the door and stepped out onto the deck. The air temperature was pleasant and he decided to sit out on one of the deck chairs, facing out to sea. Sometimes when he was near the start of a book, it helped to sit quietly and let his mind focus on the characters. He had no idea where this story would take him—he would let the characters lead him. He closed his eyes and called to mind the youngest protagonist, Chris. Taylor had been correct, of course, and it was *his* face that David saw behind his eyelids. The gentle lapping of the waves on the rocks, the harsh cries of seagulls as they rose up on air currents, the warmth of the sun on his face— all these elements combined to lull him into an almost hypnotic state where he watched a scene unfold in his head. It was as if he were watching a film where everything flowed smoothly. He could see the location. He could hear the dialog.

He could hear footsteps on the pebbles as someone approached the deck.

David's eyes flew open. Taylor was standing beside the patio door.

"I'm not disturbing you, am I?" The hesitant tone in his voice was unmistakable.

David got to his feet. "No, of course not," he replied swiftly.

Taylor slipped his hands into the pockets of his shorts. He cleared his throat. David beckoned to him. "Come and sit down." Inside, his heart rejoiced. *Thank God. He's back.*

Taylor's gaze flicked to the chairs and then back to David. "If it's all right, I'll just say what I need to, and then I'll be out of your hair."

David felt the brief moment of elation slip from him. *Damn it. Maybe not.* "Okay." He fought hard to tamp down the overwhelming urge to pull Taylor into a fierce hug. There was an air of vulnerability about Taylor that called to David with an urgency that surprised him.

Taylor bit his lower lip. "Look, I'm sorry about the way I reacted the other day. Of course you didn't have to tell me about the books. That was your decision to make."

David shook his head. "No, you were right. I should have realized you were nothing like Clark. I should have trusted you. After all, you've never given me any cause to doubt you. You've always been straight with me." His lips twisted. "If you'll forgive the pun."

There was the faintest flicker of a smile. "Straight is the *last* word I'd use to describe me."

This time David let his smile break out fully. "Damn straight."

Taylor let loose a dry chuckle. When he took a step closer, David held his breath for a moment. "I'm so sorry," Taylor reiterated, his eyes focusing on David's.

David couldn't take it any longer.

He moved swiftly to where Taylor hovered indecisively and placed his hands on Taylor's upper arms. "Me too." His voice dropped to a whisper. "God, I've missed you."

Taylor's eyes grew wide. "Oh, yeah, me too." That look of yearning pulled at David.

They stared at each other for a second, until David seized his courage and leaned in closer, his lips brushing softly against Taylor's as he kissed him. Taylor's eyes closed and David deepened the kiss, savoring the warm, silky feel of Taylor's mouth against his. God, he'd missed this. Taylor let escape the tiniest moan as David brought his hand up to his jaw and held him firmly while he darted his tongue between Taylor's lips, tasting him. David snaked his arm around Taylor's waist, pulling him closer until he could feel heat radiating off him through the layers of clothing. And still they kissed, neither seemingly willing to break the connection. David's dick grew hard, his erection pushing against Taylor's hip. When Taylor rocked his hips slowly, grinding his own solid shaft against David's, it was David's turn to groan.

Taylor broke the kiss and locked eyes with David. "Take me to bed, David."

David's heart almost skipped a beat. "You sure?"

Taylor's face was one broad smile. "God, yes. I need to feel you inside me."

David didn't hesitate. He freed Taylor's jaw, grabbed his hand and all but dragged him into the house. Taylor grinned as David led him up the narrow winding staircase to where the sun spilled into the bright bedroom.

David moved to pull down the blinds but Taylor stopped him. "Leave them. The light is beautiful in here."

David smiled as he pulled Taylor to him once more, claiming his mouth in an urgent kiss. Taylor's breathing changed, becoming more shallow as he moved his hands over David's chest. David became caught up in the moment. He grabbed the hem of Taylor's dark blue sweater and pulled it up and off in one swift movement. Taylor's soft gasp was music to his ears. David pushed him back against the bed, Taylor falling onto the soft crumpled sheets with a low cry. David moved quickly to pull off his own sweater, loving the way Taylor's gaze traveled appreciatively over his body. He hooked his thumbs under the waistband of his sweatpants and eased them over his hips in a tantalizingly slow motion, his eyes never leaving Taylor's face.

"You are one sexy man, do you know that?" Taylor said. He licked his lips as David freed his dick. It pointed toward Taylor, bobbing gently.

David looked at the young man lying on his bed, his hand languidly stroking his thickening cock through his shorts, and he grinned. "You should see what *I'm* looking at." He moved onto the bed, crawling up Taylor's body until finally he reached his crotch. He batted Taylor's hand out of the way and then mouthed his erection through the fabric. He smiled against the heavy cock. Taylor had gone commando. Taylor shuddered as David unfastened his shorts and tugged at them impatiently. Taylor's thick, uncut cock rose up, a pearl of pre-come glistening invitingly at the slit.

David wasted no time. He licked at the head and then swallowed him to the root.

Taylor pushed up with his hips, crying out as David took him deep again and again. David held Taylor's cock steady while he pulled at his own, sliding it through his fist, its way eased by pre-come. Taylor's hands clutched convulsively at the sheet beneath him, his body trembling as he thrust into David.

"Please, David." Taylor's voice shook. "Please, don't make me wait."

David knew what he wanted. He pulled free of Taylor's glistening cock and reached into the drawer where he kept the lube and condoms. Fingers trembling, he gloved up and slicked himself, and then fixed his gaze on Taylor. "Hands and knees."

Taylor rolled onto his belly and then propped himself up, ass tilted. His hole twitched and David couldn't hold back his groan. "God, Taylor, don't think I've ever been this hard."

Taylor glanced back at him over his shoulder, his eyes pleading with David. "Now, please."

David hastily dribbled lube down his crease and pushed a couple of fingers inside that hot little hole. He watched a shudder run the length of Taylor's spine. Taylor dropped his head down toward the bed. David pulled his fingers free, pressed his cock against the tight pucker and pushed insistently, watching Taylor's body open up and take him in. Taylor let out a moan. David placed his hands on Taylor's hips. "Not sure how long I can last," he gasped out as he sank into gloriously tight heat.

Taylor pushed back suddenly, his hole swallowing David in one fluid motion. David cried out and gripped him tightly as he began to thrust, his shaft sliding in and out, balls slapping against Taylor's in an erotic soundtrack. Taylor pushed back to meet his thrusts, the two quickly establishing a rhythm which built in intensity.

David let go with one hand and gripped Taylor's shoulder, forcing himself even deeper inside him. He felt Taylor tighten around him and knew it wouldn't be long. He let go of Taylor's hip and pressed a hand flat between his shoulder blades, forcing his chest down to the bed, his ass higher. The subtle change of angle caused Taylor to cry out and David let loose a joyous peal of laughter.

"Oh God, Taylor, the way you feel."

Taylor turned his head to one side. "David, so close. Make me come."

David's hips snapped forward as he pushed Taylor closer to orgasm. He felt his balls tighten, that familiar tingle coiling inside him. He started to lose his rhythm as both of them edged closer to their mutual climax. He reached under Taylor and grabbed his cock. Taylor howled as his dick pulsed come onto the sheet, his body trembling. David's hoarse cry signaled his completion as he filled the latex, unable to contain the shudders which rippled through him.

"Oh *fuck*." Taylor's shout bounced off the walls. David lowered himself down to cover Taylor's body with his own, his chest pressed against the damp skin of Taylor's back, his cock buried deep within him.

He tilted Taylor's face toward him and kissed him, Taylor eagerly seeking his mouth. David broke the kiss to ease gently out of him, feeling Taylor shiver as his now softened cock slid from his body. He tied off the condom and dropped it to the floor before pulling Taylor into his arms, holding him close as they kissed, slow, sated kisses that seemed to go on and on. Taylor wrapped his arms around David and clung to him as David placed tender kisses on his cheeks, forehead, neck, slowly moving over him as he worshiped the young man's body with his lips and tongue.

Taylor stared up at David, eyelids half closed. "I missed you so much."

David broke off from his body worship to bestow a sweet kiss on his lips. "The longest three days of my life." And it was no lie. Taylor's absence left a void which he had been unable to fill. But it had taken their separation to bring home to David how much Taylor had come to mean to him. They had so little time left, and David intended to enjoy every single second of it.

"We have just over a week left. I want to spend as much time as possible with you. If that's okay?" Taylor's gaze flicked upward to meet David's.

David smiled. "You took the words right out of my mouth. Let's not waste a single day."

"Or night," Taylor added with his own shy smile.

David nodded in agreement. "Or night." Until it was time for him to leave the island, he wanted to fall asleep with Taylor in his arms every night. He wanted Taylor's sweet face to be the first thing he saw each morning.

David knew how quickly the time would fly. He would be doing his best to slow it down as much as was humanly possible. And now he knew Taylor would be doing the same.

David sank down onto the sand and pulled off his flippers. He flopped onto his back on the damp sand. "That was incredible!" Taylor had finally taken him snorkeling off the reef and they had spent a wonderful hour swimming together.

Taylor grinned at him as he rolled his wetsuit down to his waist. "I knew you'd love it." He took several deep breaths. "You're a really good swimmer, aren't you?"

David glowed with pride. This was praise indeed. "You think? I'm not as good as you and your friends, but I used to swim a lot at the Y. It was the only way to stay in shape. Spending too much time sitting at a desk is definitely *not* good for the waistline."

Taylor's eyes glittered appreciatively. "Oh, I don't know. I think you're in brilliant shape." There was suddenly a twinkle in his eye. "For a man your age."

David gave him a mock glare. "Oh, you're gonna pay for that one, brat." He clambered to his feet but Taylor was too fast for him. He was already off and running toward West View, his laughter floating back to David on the breeze. David gave chase, bounding across the sand, up the boat ramp and into the house. God, that boy could move. By the time David got into the hallway, Taylor had already squirmed out of his wetsuit and was on his way up the stairs, two at a time, heading to the bathroom.

"First one in the bathroom gets the shower!" he yelled.

"Ever thought of conserving water? Wanna share a shower?" David flung out at him as he pushed the door shut and tried to escape the clinging suit. He could hear Taylor's giggle above the sound of the shower.

"Better make it quick before I use up all the hot water, then!"

David shook his head as he climbed the stairs. The last three days had been idyllic. He and Taylor had been all over the island, sightseeing. Walks along quiet beaches, through secluded woodland, along the river Yar... David had never been so happy.

He grinned as he slipped into the bathroom. Steam rose from the shower cubicle, and he could make out enough of Taylor's form behind the glass to see that he was already fondling his cock. David laughed out loud.

"Oh, you're ready for me, aren't you?" He opened the shower door and his breath hitched at the sight of Taylor sliding a condom onto his cock and applying the silicone lube he'd bought that weekend. Taylor's eyes gleamed.

"Want you."

David swallowed. Oh *fuck*...

Taylor's grin was positively wicked. "I'll be gentle. To start with." He pointed to the tiled wall. "Assume the position."

David shivered. "Yes Sir."

Taylor lay on his back, looking up at the ceiling. The Lighthouse bedroom was bathed in a beautiful blue light. David lay beside him, snoring gently. Taylor gave him a fond glance and slipped carefully from the bed and padded over to the windows. The moon was set high in a cloudless night sky, its brilliant light reflected in the sea. Taylor leaned against the window frame and listened to the gentle waves which lapped the shore. He watched the moonlight sparkling on the calm sea which stretched out in all directions. He loved this place.

Taylor traveled to the mainland as little as possible. His main reason for leaving was to go to the airport to go off on one of his jaunts, but it was always the same. The island called him back. He hated that landlocked feeling he always got as he drove along the motorway to Heathrow airport, or even the short distance to Southampton airport. When he was on the island, he knew that if he went in *any* direction, there would be the sea. And that gave him peace.

"Come back to bed, babe."

Taylor turned his head. David was propped up on his elbow, staring up at him, a sleepy, gentle smile on his face. *Babe.* Taylor liked that. He walked to the foot of the bed, climbed onto it and slowly crawled across until he was once more lying at David's side. David pulled the sheets over him and curled up around his back, tucking his head in at Taylor's shoulder, Taylor lying in the protective curve of his strong arm.

"Can't sleep?" David's words were indistinct, sleep-heavy. Taylor craned his neck and kissed David softly.

"I'm fine," Taylor reassured him. "Close your eyes." He listened as David's breathing changed, becoming more regular as he slipped once more into sleep. For a while Taylor lay there, his thoughts far from tired. Following mum's advice was easy—Taylor's days and nights were filled with David. No, the difficult part was yet to come. Taylor didn't want to think about it, but the days were slipping by him so fast that it wouldn't be long before David would be driving out of Steephill and thereby Taylor's life forever. And taking Taylor's heart with him.

That part was no longer subject to speculation. Taylor had already lost his heart to David.

He thought on her words. *The universe has a way of working things out.*

Taylor closed his eyes. As if the universe cared about Taylor Monroe—or if Taylor's heart got broken. What was one more broken heart, after all?

Chapter Eleven

"Taylor, we need more coleslaw!"

Taylor gaped. "Where do you guys *put* it all?"

Eric grinned, patting his belly. "Growing boys here." His eyes narrowed. "So is there more coleslaw?"

Taylor was half way through getting to his feet when David reached out a hand to stop him.

"You stay here with the gang. I'll go fetch the slaw." He kissed the top of Taylor's head. "Anything else you want while I'm there?"

Taylor thought for a second. "There's another jar of mayo in the fridge—this pack of hyenas go through it like it's going out of style—and there are more Pringles in the cupboard, and—"

"Just leave it to me, all right?" David's lazy grin was doing things to Taylor's insides. David got to his feet and looked around at the little gathering of friends on the beach, not far from the Lighthouse. The sun had set an hour or so ago and the beach was empty apart from David, Taylor, and his friends. "You entertain your guests. I may be a while." He winked and started up the beach toward West View. Taylor watched him walk away, admiring the broad shoulders, the toned legs. God, David was good for the eyes.

A snicker broke his appreciation of David's fine form. Taylor glanced back to find all four friends staring at him. Taylor frowned. "What?"

Jason shook his head. "Well, I never thought I'd see *this* day." Mark murmured his agreement.

Taylor's frown deepened. "Huh?"

Jason's broad smile revealed white teeth. "Tay-lor's in lo-ove, Tay-lor's in lo-ove…" he sang. Eric laughed and Mark's giggles mingled with the happy sound.

Taylor glared accusingly at Shane. "Oh, *you've* been talking to them, haven't you?"

Shane held up his hands. "Hey, don't look at *me*. I haven't said a word. They are simply *observing*, my friend."

Taylor stared at him in surprise.

Mark leaned back on his hands, long legs stretched out on the blanket beneath him. "Taylor, the way he just kissed you, as if it was the most natural thing in the world."

Jason nodded. "Not to mention the way you two are around each other. There's this nice, intimate feel about you. I almost feel like I'm intruding on some private moment."

Eric shook his head. "No use denying it, mate. Time to 'fess up."

Shane watched the proceedings with a smug expression on his face. "See? It's not just me anymore. We *all* see it."

Taylor drew in a deep breath. "Oh God." He looked back toward the house, but there was no sign of David.

"You're in love with him, aren't you?" Eric watched Taylor's face carefully. The other three had suddenly become very still.

Taylor looked at the earnest faces of his best friends in all the world and smiled. *No point in hiding it, is there*? "Yes," he replied.

Shane was sitting next to him. He leaned across and threw an arm around Taylor's shoulders and pulled him into a tight hug. "See? That wasn't so bad, was it?"

Taylor chuckled. "You nut." He regarded the others. "It's really obvious? I suppose what I'm asking is… if you guys can see it, can David?" Maybe it was time to share what was going on inside his head. "The last thing I want to do is make David feel awkward. It's Tuesday, and by next Monday, David will be gone. No sense making his last days uncomfortable."

Mark stared at him. "Why would knowing you're in love with him make David feel uncomfortable?"

Taylor sighed. "Because I don't have a clue how he feels about me. Yeah, okay, so we're close. I'm sleeping with him every night. I'm spending every day with him. Being close is one thing. It's quite a leap from that to telling him I love him." Another quick glance toward the house. Taylor's shoulders sagged. "Especially if I'm never going to see him again." He darted a look at his friends. "Why aren't you all telling me I can't possibly be in love with him after only three weeks? Or at least telling me I must be crazy falling for a guy who's twenty years older than me?"

Eric let out a wry chuckle. "Taylor, I read this lovely line in a book a while back. 'The heart wants what it wants.' *Your* heart wants David." He got up on all fours, crawled across the blankets and kissed Taylor on top of his head. "And I for one think it's great." He retreated back to his spot by the fire.

"And so what if he's older than you?" Jason retorted. "God, the way you two just *fit* together…" His face took on a wistful expression. "I'd *love* to have that kind of connection with a girl." Mark hugged him and Jason smiled gratefully.

Shane's arm was still around Taylor's shoulders.

"I know it's going to hurt when he leaves. But at least you had this time together. You got to share four wonderful weeks with him." He winked. "And probably had the most sex you'll ever have for the rest of your life." There were snickers around the fire. Taylor's cheeks heated up.

"And when he's gone, we'll be here to pick up the pieces," said Eric, his eyes on Taylor. "We'll hold you up, dust you off and remind you that life goes on."

Taylor's chest tightened. He glanced around the fire at his friends, their faces glowing in the light from the flickering flames. He was *so* lucky to have them in his life.

"Heads up." Shane's voice lowered. "He's coming back." He got to his feet and went to help David whose arms were full. A chorus of appreciative noises greeted David as he reached the little group.

"David, you're a lifesaver!"

"More food! We demand more food!"

Taylor looked at the people around him and smiled. To be in his late twenties and still be friends with the boys he'd grown up with was phenomenal. He hoped they'd be part of his life for a long time to come. And part of him knew Eric was right. He was going to need them more than ever.

David sat down on the blanket next to him and cupped his cheek. "You okay?"

Taylor smiled. "I'm fine." He brushed his lips softly against David's, closing his eyes as he breathed deeply, taking in David's warm scent. "Just fine."

David came out of the bathroom after drying his hands to find Shane leaning against the newel post at the top of the stairs, arms folded. "You waiting for the bathroom? It's all yours."

Shane's brown eyes regarded him intently. "Actually, I was waiting to talk to you."

David clutched his chest. "Oh God—should I be worried here?" He grinned, but it faded as he watched Shane's expression. The red-haired young man looked grave. "Shane? What is it?"

Shane glanced down the stairs but the house was quiet. "Taylor's clearing up the stuff from the beach, so I'll make this quick." His eyes narrowed. "You're leaving next Monday." David nodded. "Well, what you choose to do after that is going to have consequences for Taylor—and some of those consequences have the potential to be more painful than others. I just want to make sure you're aware of your options."

David's heart beat that little bit faster. Shane was deadly serious. "I'm listening." David spoke quietly, focusing all his attention on him.

"When you leave, you might be tempted to tell him that you're going to stay in touch. You'll email. Skype. Phone. Whatever." Shane snapped out the words. "And if that's what happens? Great. Taylor would like that. You've come to mean a great deal to him, I hope you realize that." His eyes locked on David.

David became still. He knew he felt the same about Taylor—he just hadn't worked up the courage to tell him. And he'd intended doing exactly that. He didn't want to lose Taylor. "I do now." Knowing that Taylor might possibly feel the same was something that gladdened his heart.

"*But…* " Shane's voice hardened. "*If* you go down that road, you'd better be prepared for the long haul. I don't want to be on the other end of a phone consoling a miserable Taylor 'cause he hasn't heard from you in weeks, or God forbid, months." There was a dangerous glint in his eye. "If you're going to do that, or if you even *suspect* that this might happen—*you* know more than anyone if you're the sort of person who stays in touch—then you make a clean break of it when you leave. No more contact." Shane swallowed. "Better to hurt him all at once than drag out the pain."

In that moment David could have hugged him. Shane clearly cared deeply for Taylor. He'd only spoken out of concern for him.

"I will make you a promise, Shane." He fixed his gaze on Shane and didn't blink. "I will do everything in my power to make sure Taylor isn't hurt. I can't see into the future any more than you can, but I would never do *anything* to hurt him." His throat tightened. "I care for him too, all right?" He didn't look away.

Shane regarded him with that same intense gaze for a moment and then nodded. "Good enough." He held out his hand and David shook it. Before he could withdraw it, Shane gripped it tighter. "Because if you *do* hurt him? I will not be happy. *We* will not be happy—and we're an unforgiving bunch."

David clasped their joined hands with his.

"I hear you." He met Shane's gaze. "Taylor is a lucky man to have friends like you guys."

Shane's face finally creased into a smile. "We're the lucky ones."

The solemn moment was shattered by the sound of laughter as the others stumbled into the hallway, weighed down with the detritus from their beach picnic. Eric's voice floated up to them.

"Yeah, that's right, you two. Leave us to do *all* the work, why don't you?" The rich chuckle which followed his words belied any real complaint.

Shane cocked his head toward the noise. "And that's our cue." He gave David a brisk nod. "Glad we had this chat."

David returned his nod. "Likewise." He followed Shane downstairs. Damn it, he'd felt like he'd just been asked if his intentions were honorable.

Taylor opened the boot and grabbed his bags of shopping. The guys had gone through his fridge like a swarm of locusts the previous evening, and he'd been forced to make a trip into Ventnor. He'd intended to make the trip anyway: he had a special meal planned for tonight.

He shut the boot and worked his fingers through the handles of the plastic bags. There was no *way* he was making more than one trip down those steep steps. As he neared them he caught sight of a tall man with bleached blond hair and *very* tanned skin, immaculately dressed. The stranger looked a little lost.

"Can I help you?" Taylor offered.

The man's face morphed into a clear expression of relief. "Oh, thank *God*." He spoke with an American accent. "I haven't seen a single *soul* for the past twenty minutes. I'm trying to find Steephill Cove. Is it around here?"

Taylor smiled politely. "Yes, there are two paths that lead down here." He indicated the steps with his head. "I'm heading down there now, actually."

"Great!" The American picked up the overnight bag which was sitting at his feet and slung it over his shoulder. "I'll follow you." Taylor started down the steep path, his bags of shopping beginning to cut into his palms like cheese wire. He edged down carefully where the steps got steeper. Behind him he could hear the American puffing and muttering under his breath. Taylor couldn't catch everything he was saying. "…this had better be worth it… "

"Did you say something?" Taylor inquired. He glanced at the bag. "You staying in the bay?" He didn't think any of the properties were available for rent at the moment: they were either already occupied or shut up.

"I'm looking for the Lighthouse," the stranger huffed out, but added in an undertone, "not that it's any of your goddamn business."

Taylor stiffened. What a rude bastard. Then he realized what the American had said. The Lighthouse. He was looking for David. *Had* to be. The odds of there being *two* Americans in the bay was too great a coincidence. "I'll show you where it is," Taylor croaked.

He reached the bottom of the steps and waited until the guy emerged from the narrow path between the buildings.

Taylor flicked his head toward the Lighthouse. "That's it." The man pushed past him with a muttered thanks and headed in that direction. Taylor turned right and was immediately at West View. He clambered up the ramp and dropped his bags outside the front door. Taylor turned to watch the American's progress along the shingled path and up onto the deck. He rapped on the patio door.

Taylor's breath died in his throat when the door slid open and the American flung his arms around David and pushed him back into the house. Taylor stared at the Lighthouse with bated breath to see what, if anything happened next. Nothing. There was no sign of either man. Finally it dawned on him that he couldn't just stand around like that. Taylor opened his front door and lifted the shopping bags into the house, unable to resist looking back. Still nothing. Conscious of the chilled and frozen food in his bags, Taylor reluctantly went into the house and pushed the door closed behind him. The shopping couldn't wait. He'd have to come back later and see if there was anything going on. Then he remembered. He was cooking a meal for David.

Looks like that might be put on hold.

David disengaged himself from Clark's embrace and stepped back, mouth open in disbelief.

"What in the hell are you doing here?" Clark moved forward to put his arms around him but David held up his hands. "Just don't, okay?"

Clark's bottom lip popped right out.

"Aw, honey, is that any way to talk to me? After I've come all this way to find you?" David knew Clark thought his expression was cute. Right now, all David felt was shock.

"And *why* exactly are you here? How did you find me, if it comes to that?"

Clark's eyes widened. "I had to come find you. I sent you messages, emails, but you never answered. I was going frantic with worry." David's eyebrows shot up. He sincerely doubted *that*. "In the end I went to see Michael. He could see how upset I was, so he told me where I could find you." Clark opened his arms. "And here I am!" He beamed at David.

David groaned inwardly. Michael had neglected to mention *this* during their conversation. He felt sorry for him. He knew how convincing Clark could be. He stared at Clark, his expression neutral. "I repeat—why are you here?"

Clark's expression softened. "I've been going nuts since we parted, David. I haven't been sleeping. I've lost weight."

David let his gaze travel up and down Clark's frame. *Yeah, right.* "Well, forgive me for being skeptical, but you look fine to me." When Clark preened, David scowled. "And I didn't mean it like that." The hopeful look on Clark's face died.

"Babe, you gotta know how sorry I am for how I treated you. I shouldn't have let Miguel tempt me like that."

David squinted at him. "Oh, so all this was *Miguel's* fault, huh?"

Clark nodded unhappily. "Absolutely. You gotta believe me, David. I've been distraught since… since you threw me out."

His gaze dropped, but he glanced up at David through inky black lashes. David wasn't falling for it. Clark had used that coquettish look far too many times in the past. Seeing Clark here, trying to work his wiles on him… It made one thing abundantly clear. David knew he'd done the right thing all those months ago, just like he knew that every single goddamn word that came out of Clark's mouth was duplicitous.

"I haven't…*been* with anyone since then, you know." Clark's voice lowered, his tone coy. David fought hard not to snort. Clark should have quit when he had the chance. David knew Clark was the horniest little bastard on the planet. There was no *way* he'd gone for *five fucking months* without sex. And acting like some ill-treated little *virgin* was more than David was prepared to put up with.

"Okay, you can stop right there." Clark opened his mouth to say something, but David pressed ahead. "I'll call you a taxi to take you to the ferry and you can get the next one back to the mainland. I'll even order you a taxi to take you to the airport on the other side. You're not staying."

David had to admit it, the look of hurt that crossed Clark's face? That was damn good.

"But… but…" Clark's voice faltered. "I couldn't get a plane today. The earliest would be tomorrow now."

"Fine." David was losing patience. "Then you need to go look for a hotel for the night."

"Babe, be reasonable," Clark pleaded. "I have no money. I spent every cent I had just *getting* here." He glanced around at the interior of the Lighthouse.

"Surely there's enough space for me to stay here tonight?" His eyes grew large and round. "I won't be any bother, and I promise I'll leave, first thing in the morning." His chin trembled.

David didn't have it in him to be a complete and utter bastard. He closed his eyes, breathing deeply, and then opened them. "Fine," he said, his voice softer this time. He couldn't miss the triumphant gleam in Clark's eyes, which was gone as quickly as it had appeared. David gestured to the door behind him. "There's a spare bedroom that way. You can sleep there tonight." Clark's cocky expression faltered slightly. David wanted to laugh. It was obvious Clark hadn't been expecting *that*.

Right now David didn't give a *shit* what Clark had expected. The only thing on his mind was a certain young man across the bay who was expecting David to arrive for dinner—and who was going to be disappointed. One, there was no way David would be leaving Clark on his own in the house. And two—he didn't want Clark to know of Taylor's existence. He didn't trust Clark, not even an inch.

David looked toward West View and his chest tightened. He wanted Taylor.

Unfortunately, Taylor would have to wait. *Damn Clark. Damn him to hell.*

Taylor looked at the table, all set out with gleaming cutlery and sparkling wineglasses. And no David.

After an hour of waiting it became clear that David wasn't going to show.

There'd been no sign of life at the Lighthouse since the American guy had arrived, except that Taylor could make out the soft glow of the lamps in the living room. Taylor sat in his recliner, in his hand the opened bottle of wine, his eyes fixed on the house, its white boards still visible in the dim light. When the bedroom light shone out, spilling onto the sand, Taylor's heart had skipped a beat. He couldn't tear his eyes away. And when the light went out a little after midnight, his heart sank.

Oh well, at least I know now.

Taylor didn't have the slightest inclination to drag himself upstairs to bed. He grabbed a throw from the sofa and pulled it around his shoulders. Once outside, he sank onto the recliner and leaned back, letting his hand drift down as he sought the bottle once again. Taylor drank steadily until the bottle was empty and his eyes felt tired and sore. He kept the Lighthouse in his sights until finally he drifted off to sleep with a heavy heart.

K.C. WELLS

Chapter Twelve

The loud rap on the front door had Taylor rushing down the hall to fling it wide. Brian stood on the deck, hand raised, about to knock once more. Taylor's brief surge of hope faded.

"Hi, Bri. What are you doing here?" Taylor stood to one side to let his brother enter. He looked past him to the Lighthouse. *You have to stop this*, he told himself sternly. It was bad enough that he'd slept outside all night, waking in the dawn, light stiff and cold. Not to mention the fact that he'd woken up with a hangover.

Brian was staring at him with amusement. "You've not been reading your text messages, have you?" He smirked. "Oh, I forgot— crappy signal down here." He glanced around the living room. "I came to collect that box of DVDs I left here. I did text you to say I was coming."

Taylor gave him an apologetic look. "I'm sorry. I've not had my phone on. I'll get it for you." He exited the living room and went up to the rear bedroom where most of Brian's stuff was stored. After a minute or two he located the box and hoisted it up into his arms.

"You must be really excited by the news, eh?" Brian's voice reached him as he came down the stairs. Taylor came into the room and put the box down next to the coffee table. Brian gave him a happy smile. "Ooh, great, thanks for that." He opened the box and began rummaging through the plastic boxes, grinning.

Taylor's brow furrowed. "What news?"

Brian's face morphed into an expression of glee.

"Didn't you see the news last night? I thought you'd have been dancing with excitement by now." His eyes were bright.

Taylor gave as patient a sigh as he could muster. "You're not making sense, Bri."

Brian put down the DVD that he was looking at and gestured toward Taylor's bookshelves. "James Blanchette is your favorite author, isn't he?"

Taylor's heartbeat increased. "What?"

Brian grinned. "You don't know, do you? It was all over the Internet. Rumor has it some Hollywood producer is going to turn all the James Blanchette detective books into blockbuster movies. They were already discussing who could possibly play... oh, what's the detective's name?"

"Ed Manning," Taylor replied absently. His mind raced. Oh wow. David was about to be bigger than ever. Taylor's heart leaped. He was happy for him, he truly was. David was a nice guy.

Even if he *had* just broken Taylor's heart.

"You all right, little brother?"

Brian's words broke through his introspection. Taylor gave his brother a weak smile. "Yeah, I'm fine."

Brian quirked an eyebrow. "Bullshit."

Taylor should have known he couldn't hide anything from his big brother. "Okay, so I'm lying. I...I just can't talk about it right now. Understand?"

Brian nodded but his eyes were troubled. "If you want to talk about it, you know where I am." His eyes bored into Taylor. "Right?"

"Right," Taylor said with a nod.

Brian regarded him for a moment longer and then got to his feet. He pulled Taylor into a fierce hug, his cheek warm and scratchy against Taylor's. Brian released him and stepped back. "I'll leave you alone, then. I only came for this." He cupped Taylor's cheek. "You take care of yourself, Taylor." He picked up his box of DVDs.

Taylor dipped his chin toward his chest and led Brian to the front door. Brian paused at the threshold to give Taylor one last searching glance before disappearing down the boat ramp, holding tightly onto his box. He waved once before turning left to go to the path.

Taylor stood at the door, his eyes trained on the Lighthouse. In spite of the sadness which hung about him like a shroud, Taylor's heart rejoiced for David. And in that moment he decided to push aside the ache which hadn't left him all night, and go and congratulate David on his wonderful fortune. He locked up the house and walked slowly along the path to the Lighthouse. The morning sunlight sparkled on the sea and the sand was flat and as yet unblemished by footmarks. But for once the sight failed to lift his mood. Taylor walked onto the deck and lifted his hand to knock on the patio door.

Before his hand came into contact with the glass, the door slid open and David's guest appeared. His eyes widened in recognition.

"Oh, it's my little helper from yesterday." Taylor thought he detected the merest hint of a sneer in that voice. "What can I do for you?"

"I came to see David, to congratulate him on the news about Hollywood. I only just heard." Taylor tried to peer past him but there was no sign of David. Then he caught the sound of running water from the open window above his head. Ah. David was in the shower.

"Oh ho, so it's *David*, is it?" Those cool gray eyes widened further. "I did wonder who had been scratching his itch while he's been stuck out here in the back of beyond." His gaze traveled the length of Taylor's body. "My honey never could go *that* long without fucking *something*." Taylor squirmed. This guy gave him the creeps. "I'll be sure to pass on the message." He moved to close the door. Taylor reached out to stop him, earning himself a cool stare.

"Please, tell him he can come over later." Taylor was beginning to get a bad feeling. Sure enough, the man's next words sent his heart plummeting.

"I don't think that will be possible, seeing as we're flying back to the States tonight." His eyes gleamed. "I'm sure you were a good little fuck, but David won't be needing you any more—not now that he has *me*." There was no disguising the look of triumph on that face. "Nice meeting you... I didn't catch your name."

"It doesn't matter," Taylor mumbled as he turned to leave, stumbling off the step onto the pebbled path. He just wanted to get as far away from the Lighthouse as he could. He ran back to the house, not looking back once. He stripped off his shorts and sweater and wriggled into his wetsuit. The waves beckoned. Taylor was going to ride them until he was completely exhausted, 'til his mind and body were too tired to feel, to think.

He grabbed his surfboard and headed out the door and down onto the sand.

The sky was heavy and thick with cloud, but the waves were majestic, rolling into the bay and crashing against the rocks. Taylor watched them for a moment, marveling at the power and speed of them. He couldn't wait to get out there and shut off the thoughts that clamored inside his head. He tried to focus on his breathing, his stance—*anything* but the image of David's face which kept coming to the forefront of his mind.

Can't think about him. Not anymore. It hurts too much.

With a low cry that sounded like a sob to his ears, Taylor leaped into the surf and began to scull out to sea.

"You were fucking him, weren't you?" Clark sounded sullen. "The little twink out there that you can't keep your eyes off?"

David didn't even bother turning his head. "Not talking about him now—and besides, that's none of your business. Let's talk instead about you being on your way to the ferry. You have a plane to catch, right?" He stood at the patio door, his eyes trained on Taylor, watching him as he balanced on that board atop some pretty huge waves. To David's mind, there was something different about him. He'd lost count of how many times he'd watched Taylor do exactly this, and David had never failed to be impressed. Taylor's fluid movements, his ease in handling the board, his skill as he judged each wave...

Not today.

For a start, Taylor had been out there for what felt like *hours*. The boy had to be exhausted by now. And then there was the way he was riding the waves. His usual grace was gone, to be replaced by an air of…distraction, almost. Taylor didn't look as though he were in complete control.

"You could at least *look* at me when you're talking to me," Clark whined. "It was bad enough that you made me sleep downstairs last night."

David gave a small shake of his head, his focus still out in the bay. "I told you yesterday where you'd be sleeping."

"Yeah, but I thought you were gonna sleep *with* me." That plaintive note had crept back into Clark's voice. "It got real lonely, stuck down here last night."

David snorted. "So lonely that you thought you'd try coming up to my room." He caught Clark's quiet gasp. "Yeah, I heard you trying the door handle."

"What the fuck was all *that* about, by the way? You locking the door?" God, he sounded petulant. "I only wanted to—"

David ceased to hear him as he watched a huge wave roll in behind Taylor, crashing into him with such force that the young man was thrown forward—onto the rocks near the café.

"*Fuck!*" David wrenched open the patio door and vaulted over the picket fence, ignoring the pain in his hand as he landed awkwardly on it. He leaped over the railing and scrambled down onto the rocks, hardly noticing that he smashed his knee against the jagged corner of a particularly large rock, so intent was he on reaching Taylor.

The boy had surfaced, appearing to struggle weakly against the current, only to be hit again by another wave—and this time he disappeared from view.

"*Taylor!*" The name was torn from him in a scream. David raced across the frothing waves and dived into the churning water, striking out with a strong pull of his arms through the water to get to the inert figure being thrown about by the waves, desperate to get to him before he was driven dangerously close to the rocks yet again. The waves fought David with every stroke—as he tried valiantly to get closer, they flung him further away from Taylor. His eyes stung from the salt and he struggled to breathe against the rising tide of panic. The crashing waves drowned out all other sounds. He reached Taylor and grabbed hold of him, dragging him back toward the shore. Taylor's eyes were closed and there was a nasty cut on his forehead and cheekbone. David hooked his arm across Taylor's chest and under his arm, and began to swim as fast as he could, Taylor on his back, the water surging over his upturned face. David negotiated the narrow channel that he knew lay beneath the surface of the water. He wanted to avoid the rocks at all costs.

When his feet touched the bottom he struggled to stand, hoisting Taylor up into his arms. He could see figures running out to him across the sand, and he could make out Vanessa leading the way, her long blond hair trailing behind her, her face a mask of horror.

"Vanessa! Go call for a doctor!" He flung the words out as loud as he could to be heard above the surf. "I'll take him to the Lighthouse!"

He watched her nod and turn back toward the shore. He recognized Richard's tall form as he waded out toward him. "Help me!" Between them, they pulled Taylor onto the sand on his back. "I need to see if he's still breathing." David pressed an ear to his chest, relief flooding through him as he felt Taylor's heart beating. "Yes!" The shout of elation burst from his lips.

"We need to put him into the recovery position," Richard called out and proceeded to turn Taylor onto his side, bringing up his arm and leg. He turned Taylor's head to the side. To David's utter relief, the young man began to cough violently, spewing forth water onto the sand with retching sounds that wracked his body.

"That's it, baby, come back to me." David knelt beside Taylor on the sand. He wanted to take him in his arms so badly. The coughing eased off and Taylor rolled onto his back to stare up at David, his eyes focusing on David's face.

"Hi," he said weakly.

David couldn't hold back any longer. He leaned down and kissed Taylor's forehead tenderly. "Hi there yourself." Richard held Taylor's wrist as he took his pulse and looked at his watch. "Is he all right?"

Richard smiled reassuringly. "His heartbeat is steady, but he needs to get those cuts sorted out. Vanessa should have got hold of the doctor by now. He'll check him over." He glanced down at Taylor. "You're a lucky boy, Taylor." Richard's eyes flicked upward to David and then back to Taylor. He grinned. "You've been a busy boy too."

David felt his stomach roll as Taylor turned his face away, his expression suddenly sad. David slipped one arm under Taylor's shoulders and the other hooked under his knees, and then he staggered to his feet, hoisting Taylor up into his arms, holding him against his chest.

"David, what…" Taylor struggled for a moment.

"Hold on tight, babe. I'm taking you to the Lighthouse." David glanced briefly at the pale man. Taylor's arms reached up to lock around his neck and David cradled him as he carried him up the beach and onto the path which led to the Lighthouse, Richard following close behind.

"Thanks, Richard. I'll take it from here." Richard gave a brisk nod. "And thank you, for everything."

"No problem." Richard gave him his usual easy smile. "Glad to be of help. I'm going to get cleaned up, but please, pop over later and let me know how he's doing."

"Sure thing." David glanced down at the man in his arms. "I've got you," he murmured softly, trying to push down the feelings of panic which threatened to overwhelm him at any second. Taylor said nothing but buried his face in David's damp shirt. David made his way along the path to the Lighthouse, moving as smoothly as possible so as not to jar Taylor too much.

Clark hovered in the doorway and David made an impatient noise. "Out of my way, Clark." Clark stepped aside and David entered the house and headed for the spare room. It was easier than trying to negotiate that narrow staircase with his precious burden.

"Can you stand?" he asked Taylor. "We need to get you out of this wetsuit and into bed. The doc's on his way, hopefully."

Taylor started to protest. "I'm fine." He wobbled as he got to his feet, however and David shot out his hands to support him. He tugged at the zip and eased Taylor out of the neoprene suit. Taylor shivered. David grabbed the blanket from on top of the bed and wrapped it around him, pulling Taylor once more into his arms. He couldn't help but notice how Taylor stiffened. Before he could work out what was going on, there was a knock at the door.

Clark stuck his head around. "The doctor is here." That sullen tone was still in evidence.

"Fine," David snapped. He'd already had more than enough of Clark's petulance. Taylor's eyes widened. "Send him in, then." He had no time for Clark's theatrics right now. The door opened fully and the doctor entered, black bag in hand.

Taylor smiled, clearly recognizing him. "Hi, Dr. Hayward."

Dr. Hayward chuckled. "I haven't had to patch *you* up for a while, young man." He helped Taylor to the bed. "Let's have a look at you." David watched the elderly doctor check Taylor's pulse and blood pressure, and then look him over thoroughly. He opened his bag and got out some gauze, antiseptic cream and sterile strips. The doctor attended to the cuts on Taylor's face. David hovered in the background, saying nothing. His clothes were wringing wet but at that moment he couldn't give a damn. The rising panic which had threatened to consume him had all but disappeared. God, when he thought of what might have happened....

"David, you're bleeding."

Taylor's words broke through. David pulled himself together and looked down at his body. His left knee was a bloody mess, the skin scraped back, and his hand throbbed, the palm red and angry-looking. David tried to smile. "I'm fine." Taylor's brow furrowed. "No, really, I'm fine. Once you're tucked up in bed, I'll bathe my knee and put on some Band-aids."

Taylor grimaced. "Looks like you need more than that." Dr. Hayward nodded in agreement.

David let out a sigh. "Fine. You wanna check me over too, Doc?"

Dr. Hayward gave him a firm look. "Oh, I fully intend to," he replied dryly. David noticed Taylor's little smirk. Maybe the boy really was okay, after all. The doctor beckoned with his finger. "Sit here, please." He gestured toward the bed and David gave up, allowing the doctor to inspect his knee. He winced as the abraded flesh was prodded, albeit lightly. "Actually, you're right. It's not that bad. I'll clean this up with some wound wash and then I have some large sticking plaster that will do just fine."

David flashed Taylor a quick grin. Taylor's tight returning smile caused David's stomach to lurch. *What's going on here*? When the doc had finished and David was all patched up, he got to his feet and shook his hand.

"Thanks, Doc. Anything I need to be aware of?" He indicated Taylor with a flick of his head.

Dr. Hayward nodded.

"You need to keep an eye on him for the next few hours, to check for concussion. Don't let him sleep yet, not for a while anyway. Once he's eaten something, if everything is all right after that, *then* he can sleep."

"I *am* right here, y'know." Taylor's indignant tone had David snickering.

Dr. Hayward laughed. "Yes, and right now, *you* are the patient. And as the patient, you will do what you are told. Understood?" His eyes twinkled.

Taylor sighed. "Yes, doctor."

Dr. Hayward smiled. "Good boy." He winked at David. "I only get away with it because I've known Taylor since he was seven or eight years old." He chuckled. "He was stubborn back then, too."

David gave a half smile as he shook the doctor's hand. "Thanks for everything, Doc. The name's David Hannon, by the way."

Dr. Hayward dipped his chin in greeting and then released his hand. "Bye, Taylor. Look after yourself." He addressed David. "If you are at all concerned about him, don't hesitate to take him to St. Mary's hospital." David assured him he would. The doctor left and David sat down on the bed.

"You want to stay here or do you think you're strong enough to make it up the stairs to my room?"

Taylor's eyes grew large. "Can't I go home? I can look after myself, in spite of what Doc Hayward says."

David shook his head. "You're staying right here." To his dismay, Taylor looked distinctly uncomfortable. "What is it?"

"I don't want to get in the way," Taylor murmured.

David frowned. "What do you mean?"

Clark chose that moment to put his head around the door, a bored look on his face. "I'm hungry."

David had had enough. "Then find something to eat," he barked out. Clark retreated hastily. David noted how Taylor froze and all of a sudden, it became clear. "Let's get you up to my room and then we'll have a little chat." Taylor regarded him for a moment and then nodded. David helped him to his feet and pulled the blanket firmly around him. He led Taylor out of the room, his arm around his shoulders, and let him go first up the narrow staircase. He watched as Taylor glanced around the bedroom and David knew what he was looking for.

He pushed the door closed and then sat Taylor on the bed and went into the bathroom to flip on the shower. "Let's get all that salt water off of you," he called out. He'd gotten the water running hot when Taylor appeared in the doorway, dropping the blanket onto the floor. David stood to one side and let him get into the cubicle. When he saw how Taylor leaned against the tiled wall, that was it. David hurried stripped off his damp clothing and climbed into the shower with him.

Taylor jerked in surprise. "What are you…"

"You're in no state to be in here on your own. So I might as well shower with you." David poured shampoo into the palm of his hand and proceeded to wash Taylor's hair.

Taylor closed his eyes, still leaning against the cool tiles. "So that's Clark."

Aha. "Yeah, he turned up here yesterday. I'm sorry about dinner last night. I couldn't get away." Taylor stiffened. "And before you ask, Clark slept downstairs last night." David felt Taylor relax. Yeah, it was like he'd figured. Clark was the issue. He leaned close to whisper in Taylor's ear. "God, baby, I was so scared. I thought I'd lost you." A shiver rippled through him as he looked at the cut on his forehead and the patch of dressing on his cheek. It had been too close for comfort. He noticed Taylor's shudder.

David pulled Taylor under the jets and let the hot water sluice away all the lather, careful not to get the dressings too wet. He soaped up his hands and began to wash Taylor's body, running his hands gently over him. Taylor leaned into him, and then suddenly his arms wrapped around David, pulling him tight against him. Taylor tilted his face upward and David kissed those warm lips, his heart beating strongly as he tried not to think of just how badly things might have turned out. Taylor closed his eyes and opened for him, David sliding his tongue into that beautiful mouth, savoring the taste of him. He let the kiss continue for a while, until at last they parted.

"Let's get you into bed," he murmured as he flipped the shower off. David grabbed a thick towel from the rail and wrapped it around Taylor, rubbing him gently. Only when Taylor was dry did he grab a towel for himself. After wrapping it around his hips, he led Taylor toward the bed.

Taylor drew the sheets up over his chest and smiled as he snuggled into them. "The bed smells of you. It's nice."

David sat down beside him and stroked back the damp curls from his forehead, careful not to touch the tender skin where the strips held the cut tight. Taylor's eyes met David's. "Thank you. You saved my life." The words were uttered quietly but fervently.

David leaned over and kissed him. "When I think how this might have—"

Taylor laid a finger across his lips. "Don't." His chin trembled. "It was my fault. I wasn't paying attention. I shouldn't even have been out there in my state." David cocked his head and Taylor sighed. "I got drunk last night."

"Why?" David had never seen Taylor drink to excess. "And why did you go out surfing in that state?"

Taylor's expression was pained. "I don't want to talk about it. Besides, I should get out of your hair, if you're going to be packed up in time to catch your flight tonight."

David frowned. "Flight? What are you talking about? I'm not going anywhere tonight."

The crease between Taylor's eyes deepened. "But Clark said you and he were flying back to the States tonight."

David's jaw dropped. "Clark said... Wait a minute. When did you speak to Clark?"

"I met him yesterday when I showed him the way down to the bay. And then I spoke with him this morning when I came over here to congratulate you."

David froze. "You were here this morning? He never said a— Congratulate me about what?"

It was Taylor who froze. "The news about Hollywood wanting to make your books into movies." He frowned. "Surely your agent would have told you?"

David face-palmed. "Oh my God—I had my stupid phone switched off! I was so pissed off after getting those messages from Clark that I turned the goddamn thing off. Besides, I could never rely on getting a signal down here." He reached into the bedside drawer and pulled out his phone. "Not sure if this thing's still got power." He grabbed his power cable and plugged it into the socket, then attached it to the phone. He switched on the phone and watched impatiently as it fired up. He stared at the screen. "Oh fuck—there are at least ten messages on here from Juliet." Miracle of miracles—he had a signal. He speed-dialed Juliet immediately. He was surprised when she answered all right away. It had to be at least five in the morning over there.

"Where the hell have you been?" Juliet was almost shrieking down the phone. "Have you any *idea* how crazy I've been going over here?"

David did his best to calm her down and then got her to fill in the blanks. They spoke for about three minutes and then David hung up. Taylor watched him with wide eyes.

David shook his head in disbelief. "It's all true. The studio has been trying to get in contact with me for the last seven days. Juliet's been going frantic. Apparently news about this broke in the States four days ago." And then he started to put two and two together. "What exactly did Clark say to you this morning?" He listened as Taylor repeated their conversation.

David felt heat flush through his body, his muscles suddenly tense. *That fucking little....*

He got to his feet and pulled on his jeans and T-shirt which had been over the back of the chair. He smiled at Taylor. "You lie quiet, okay? There's something I have to do."

And it was going to be an absolute fucking pleasure.

Chapter Thirteen

Taylor lay snuggled in the soft sheets, trying to catch what was going on downstairs. David's face had been stony as he'd left the room. Taylor reached up to touch his forehead tentatively and winced. What an idiot. He knew better than to venture out with a hangover, but he hadn't exactly been thinking clearly.

You came off lucky, he told himself sternly. *If David hadn't seen you…* Taylor shuddered. He didn't want to think about that. He still couldn't believe that David had dived into the sea, fully clothed, to rescue him. The man was a hero. *My hero.* That got him chuckling. *Wait until Shane and the others get to hear this.* Then his face fell. Shane would most likely give him a good bollocking when he heard how utterly stupid Taylor had been. Oh well, he'd face that particular hurdle when he got there.

The sound of raised voices drifted up the stairs. Taylor shivered. He couldn't hear much of what was said, but David's angry tone was quite clear. Clark's voice was reduced to a petulant whine. Taylor couldn't give a shit. It was obvious now that Clark had lied to him, and even more obvious that David no longer had any feelings for him.

"You're a goddamn liar!"

The words were delivered with such vehemence that Taylor was startled. He caught the sound of movement. God, they weren't *fighting*, were they? Taylor couldn't stay put a moment longer, not when David might need him.

And how exactly *do you plan on helping him in* your *state?*

Taylor threw off the blanket and began to look around for some clothes to put on. No way was he walking downstairs wrapped in a blanket—or worse still, naked.

"And where do you think *you're* going?" David peered around the railing at the top of the stairs. Taylor froze in the middle of pulling David's long T-shirt over his head. He gazed at David. No signs of a struggle. David was regarding him with something akin to amusement. "You checking me out for bruises, or something?"

Taylor gave him a sheepish grin. "I got worried." He sagged back against the pillows in relief.

David came over and sat beside him on the bed. He took Taylor's hands in his and peered intently at him. "How are you feeling?"

Taylor gave him a half smile. "I'm okay. My head aches and my cheek feels like it's on fire, but I'll live." He raised his eyebrows, unsure how to phrase the question he was dying to ask.

David's expression was sad. "Clark's gone." Taylor's mouth fell open. "I shoved everything into that bag of his, threw it at him and told him to get lost." David scowled. "He denies it, but I know he only came out here when he heard about the movie rights deal. The timing is far too coincidental." His gaze dropped. "I suppose there was always a little part of me that hoped I'd got it wrong about him." He shook his head. "And yeah, it hurts to think I got it *so* wrong."

Taylor freed his hand and cupped David's cheek. "You only got it wrong because you're a good man." He took a deep breath and looked David in the eye.

"Trust me, I have standards. I only fall for good men." He let the words hang there, his pulse racing as he awaited David's reaction.

David's eyes widened. He said nothing for a moment and with each passing second of silence Taylor grew increasingly nervous. David studied his face with such care that Taylor felt his cheeks flush.

"Then it appears you and I have similar standards, because I seem to have fallen for a good man." David's breathing quickened.

Taylor found it hard to breathe. He focused on those soft lips that drew closer, closer, until at last they touched his own, a fleeting whisper of silk as David kissed him, edging nearer to pull Taylor into his arms. Taylor closed his eyes and surrendered to the moment—held in the protective circle of David's arms, their mouths meeting in a tender kiss that held the promise of so much more.

David broke the kiss to stretch out on the bed beside him, and Taylor placed his head carefully on David's chest, feeling the comforting, hypnotic thump of David's heart beneath his ribs. He reached up to stroke David's chest through the soft fabric.

"Are you still going on Monday?"

David nodded and Taylor's chest tightened. God, this was going to hurt so much.

David kissed his hair. "Juliet had been arranging meetings for me with the producers for next week. I fly out to the west coast on Tuesday, so let's hope the jet lag won't be kicking my ass *too* badly." He groaned. "God, this is gonna be a whole load of work."

Taylor chuckled against his chest.

"But it's going to be exciting, too. You might be asked for your input with the casting. You could end up working on the screenplay." He smiled. "David, it's going to be great." He tried not to think about the downside—David leaving him, just when they'd found each other.

"We have four days left," David murmured into his hair. "Can I ask you something? Can we spend those days together?" He kissed Taylor's forehead. "I don't want to lose a minute with you."

"Oh God, yes," Taylor responded fervently. "I feel the same way."

"Thank God for that." David tugged him closer. "I don't care where we sleep, by the way—this bed or yours—as long as you're in my arms every night."

Taylor craned his neck upward to demand a kiss and David seemed only too happy to oblige. Their lips met in a kiss which made Taylor's heart soar with its sweetness. Thoughts of their imminent parting set his heart beating faster.

Don't think about Monday. Live for now.

His mum would be *so* proud of him.

Time wasn't flying like an arrow—it moved along with all the speed of an Exocet missile.

David tried to hold on to each moment that they spent together, desperate to cement their time into his memories, but the passage of time was relentless.

They filled their days with long walks on the beach, holding hands, a thing David had never done in his entire life, but would always remember. Then there were intimate dinners at the Lighthouse. David didn't want to share Taylor with anyone and it filled his heart with joy to see his desires mirrored in Taylor. When Eric rang to invite them both to an afternoon on the boat, Taylor surprised him by refusing. After he'd hung up, Taylor confessed that he wanted David all to himself.

Thursday was a beautiful warm day, and they'd taken a picnic down to Compton Bay on the west coast of the island. The beach was fairly secluded, and David had been amazed—and aroused—when Taylor stripped off and lay nude next to him on their beach towels, David quickly following suit. And then surprisingly, despite his forty-six years, David had his first introduction to outdoor sex. The warmth of the sun on his back as he thrust slowly into Taylor, the soft moans Taylor made as David took his time, enjoying the feel of Taylor's firm body beneath him, thighs gripping his waist tightly… It was a magical time. And when they both came together, their hoarse cries mingled with the call of the red kites that soared over the cliffs above their heads on currents of air.

Friday and Saturday brought rain in abundance, but it didn't dampen their mood. They spent the two days in bed, talking, laughing, sharing stories. David sat with his laptop perched on his knee as he wrote more of his gay romance, Taylor beside him, listening to him read aloud, laughing and offering suggestions. They didn't bother with clothes, preferring to walk around the Lighthouse naked. Those two days were idyllic.

But the nights… Long nights of lying in each other's arms, bringing each other pleasure with lips, tongues, fingers and cocks. Nights that extended into the early hours of the morning with languid embraces and slow, deep penetration. They were no longer fucking—they were making love. And David didn't want it to end.

"I'll stay in touch." David spoke softly as they lay in bed together on Saturday night.

Taylor smiled at David's earnest expression. "I know you say that *now*, but you're going to be very busy." Taylor was a realist. David would be on the other side of the Atlantic. Once he returned home and immersed himself in his writing, not to mention the demands of Hollywood, he wouldn't have time to keep in touch. Okay, so Taylor knew it would hurt, but he wasn't about to make demands.

"I mean it." David rolled on top of him and stared down into his eyes. Taylor took a moment to savor the feeling of David's weight pressing him into the mattress, his shaft heavy and full against his hip. Taylor gave an experimental roll of his hips and watched as David's eyes rolled back. Oh yes—Taylor knew it wouldn't be long now. He reached up to hold David's head in his hands.

"David, honestly, it's okay. If we lose touch I *will* understand." He smiled. "I will always remember these weeks." As if he could forget. If they managed to stay in touch, all well and good. That would be a bonus.

If not, then a tiny piece of Taylor's heart would always be missing David.

"Do you know how wonderful you are?" That look on David's face was one of awe.

Taylor pulled his head down and kissed him, rocking his hips up from the bed in a slow, sensual motion. David groaned into his mouth as he reached down to grasp their dicks and slide them together through his fist.

Taylor's breathing quickened. "David, make love to me."

"God, yes." And David proceeded to do just that.

"Taylor, what's wrong?"

Taylor heard the concern in David's voice. He snuggled closer, enjoying the warmth of David's body as they sat together on the sofa. The day had been cool—the first touch of autumn—and Taylor had lit the fire. David seemed to be entranced by the flickering flames. He stared into them for long minutes at a time, his arm around Taylor. The clock quietly ticked away their last hours together. It was already ten in the evening. Sunday was disappearing fast.

There was nothing for it. Taylor had to say something. "I don't want to say goodbye."

He heard David's breath hitch. "Oh baby, I don't either. You've gotta know that."

Taylor shook his head. "You don't understand."

He sat up and turned to face David. "I've never felt this way about anyone. I keep asking myself why I had to lose my heart to someone who lived on the other side of the world to me."

David sighed. "It's hardly that. It's a seven hour flight from London. I'll pay for you to come see me. Whenever you want. Just say the word." He reached out to hold Taylor but Taylor leaned back out of his grasp.

"No, you need to listen," Taylor insisted. "I…I can't face saying goodbye to you in the morning." David's face fell and Taylor's heart sank. "I'm sorry, I'm a coward, I know that, but I can't stand the idea of watching you drive away from here. I hate goodbyes at the best of times but this is going to be sheer torture."

"So what are you saying?" David spoke quietly.

"Let's say goodbye now. Let's not drag it out 'til the morning." Taylor pushed the words out hurriedly, trying not to see the stunned expression on David's face.

"You mean it." He could hear the pain in David's voice.

Taylor groaned. "See, *this* is what I'm talking about. It's always going to hurt, no matter when we say it. At least this way, by the time I wake up, you'll be gone." He edged closer to David. "Let's just hold each other, and put as much feeling into it as we can. Then you can walk away back to the Lighthouse and get on with your life."

David stared at him incredulously. "You seriously think I can just walk away from you *that* easily? Do you have *any* idea how I feel about you? How much it's killing me inside to leave you?"

The iron band that had sat around Taylor's chest all day suddenly tightened. He struggled to breathe. The words wouldn't come.

David took Taylor's hands in his. "Okay. I'll do this. It's obviously what you want, so I'll do it. But Taylor,"—David's eyes bored into him—"I *will* be staying in touch."

Taylor swallowed. He wanted to believe David, he really did. "All right."

David pulled him into his arms and held him tightly. Taylor buried his head at the junction of neck and shoulder, breathing in the smell of David for the last time. He didn't want to let go.

They sat like that in silence, time ticking away their last minutes together. Taylor listened to the sound of David breathing, and felt his warm breath waft against his neck.

All too soon David broke away. "Then let's say goodbye." He got to his feet, taking Taylor with him. Their lips met in a slow, sweet kiss. When they parted, David stroked his cheek. "Thank you. For everything." He walked toward the front door, Taylor's hand still enclosed in his. The cool night air chilled Taylor's skin as the door opened, making him shiver.

David turned to face him, his eyes shining. "No matter what happens, I'll never forget you." He leaned in for one last kiss, his hand coming up to cup Taylor's cheek. Taylor leaned into the gentle touch and melted into the kiss, savoring the taste of David. Then they broke apart and David let go of his face, finally relinquishing his hold on Taylor's hand.

He turned away, but not quickly enough that Taylor didn't catch sight of a tear glistening on his cheek. He watched David walk down the boat ramp and along the pebbled path toward the Lighthouse. As he reached the picket fence, David turned back toward him and waved. Taylor raised his hand and waved back until David had entered the door and was no longer in sight.

He stood there, eyes still trained on the Lighthouse, desperate for one last glimpse of David that he knew in his heart was not going to come. Finally he forced himself to move. He stepped back into the house and closed the door, shutting out the cold night air and the sight of the Lighthouse, its white boards gleaming in the moonlight.

And that's that, he thought, his heart feeling heavier than it had ever felt in his whole life. All he wanted to do was sleep. *'Cause when I wake up? He'll be gone. And then I can get on with living without him.*

What in the hell had awoken him?

Taylor opened his eyes and stared blearily at the LED clock beside his bed. It was three in the morning. He listened, trying to ascertain what had disturbed his sleep.

There it was again. This time Taylor caught it. The sound of stones rattling against his bedroom window. He climbed out of bed and went over to the large window which overlooked the bay. The moon hung low in the sky, casting its silvery light over the sea.

Taylor jumped suddenly as more stones rattled against the glass. He unfastened the catch and pulled up the window.

He leaned out cautiously, not wanting to be hit in the face by yet more pebbles. To his surprise, David stood below the window, arm poised to fling another handful of tiny pebbles.

"David, what are you doing?" Taylor whispered.

David's upturned face was plainly visible in the moonlight. "Let me in, Taylor!" There was a note of agitation in his voice. Taylor closed the window and hurried naked down the stairs. When he opened the front door David pushed inside and closed it behind him. He caught Taylor up in his arms and kissed him. Taylor let escape a startled low cry. He broke away and pushed David off.

"What are you doing here?"

David grinned. "I had to see you. I haven't stopped thinking about you since I walked out of the door."

Taylor groaned. This really wasn't helping. "David," he began helplessly, "you have to—"

"Now *you* need to listen," David interjected, laying a single finger on Taylor's lips. "I've been thinking. Leaving you tonight really made me look at my life. More importantly, it made me look at what I was willing to let go. And I came to a conclusion." He locked eyes with Taylor. "I don't want to lose you."

Taylor's head was spinning. "What are you saying?"

There was that joyous smile again. "Babe, I'm a writer. All I need is a laptop, a power source and a plentiful supply of good coffee." He winked. "So as long as I have those things? I can write anywhere—even here." He paused, his eyes still fixed on Taylor's face.

Taylor didn't dare breathe.

He's not saying what I think he's saying—is he?

"But... what about the movie deal?"

David laughed. "What about it? If we need to go to New York, we go to New York. Hollywood? Then sure, we'll go to Hollywood. I have the apartment in Manhattan. When we're not there I can sublet it. As least we'd have somewhere to live if we have to go to the States." He grinned. "You told me how much you love big cities. Well, baby, they don't come much bigger than New York." His expression softened. "But I want to live here—with you."

Taylor was trying desperately to be practical. "But where would you live?"

David shrugged. "I'll buy a house. As long as you live in it with me."

Taylor stilled. "You're serious."

David caught him up in his arms once more and swung him round. "Damn straight I'm serious!" He kissed Taylor exuberantly on the lips and then leaned back to look him in the eye. "Where you wanna live, Taylor? Just name the place."

Taylor had only one thing on his mind. "It would have to be near the sea." He couldn't be without that sound.

"Hell, yes." David's joy was infectious. "What about this place? Would your parents sell it to me?" Taylor's jaw dropped and David laughed in delight. "Well, you told me they hardly ever rent it out. So they're not making an income from it. I could buy it—for us." His eyes met Taylor's. "Taylor, I'm asking you to live with me. I love it here." David cupped Taylor's cheek tenderly. "I love you."

Taylor's heart soared. "I love you, too."

And then he was in David's arms and David was kissing him, long kisses that were growing more heated with every passing second.

David broke the kiss, panting. "Let's go to bed. I've got a flight to catch in a few hours." His voice became husky. "And I know how I want to spend my last hours with you." He gripped Taylor's arse and ground his dick against Taylor's. He winked. "I can always sleep on the plane."

Taylor knew the feeling. He was suddenly too excited to sleep. "You're still going home?"

David finally quietened. "Yes, baby, but I'll be back. There are things I need to do, but I'll get them done just as fast as I can, and then I'll be back here, in your arms." He kissed the tip of Taylor's nose. "I know immigration will probably be a real ball-ache, but we'll get through it." He smiled at Taylor. "Because when it's all over? We'll be together."

Taylor's face creased into a smile. "Together."

He could live with that.

Epilogue

"Taylor! Stop staring at your phone!"

With a supreme effort Taylor dragged his attention away from his phone and glanced up. Shane was grinning at him. "Sorry," Taylor apologized. "I was expecting a text from—"

"From David, yes, we know," cut in Jason with a cheeky grin. Beside him, Mark and Eric were chuckling. Taylor's cheeks heated up.

"Hasn't he given you an idea yet of how much longer it will be before he can come back here?" Eric wanted to know. "How long has it been now since he left?"

"Four weeks, three days and"—Taylor gave his watch a quick glance—"twelve hours."

"What—no minutes and seconds?" joked Mark. All four friends were laughing now.

Taylor gave a sheepish grin. "Have I been a real pain since he's been gone?"

"Yes," came the prompt chorus of four voices. Taylor stared in frank astonishment, until they all collapsed in giggles.

"To tell the truth, it's been rather sweet," Shane said, his eyes twinkling. He pulled his fleece jacket tightly around him. "Does David know what he's letting himself in for with our British weather? Personally, I think you're both mad for wanting to live here. You could buy a house in LA, for goodness' sake!" He shivered. The breeze which blew through the open air section of the Beach Shack was a chilling reminder that winter wasn't far away.

The next day would be the first of November.

Taylor glanced around at his friends who had braved the chill wind to have a coffee at the café. It wouldn't be long before it would shut its doors for the winter. Richard stepped out of the warm kitchen to check if they needed anything. Taylor gave him a grateful nod. He had a lot of time for the man since that awful day.

"So what's the plan?" Shane asked. "How long can David stay here before you have to put the immigration wheels in motion?"

"He's got a visa," Taylor told them. "To be honest, I wasn't paying a lot of attention to that part." He'd been more concerned to hear when David would be able to get back to the UK. "He says he's a lot closer to being able to give me a date. It took them forever to sort out the details of the deal with Hollywood." David's publishers had sold the movie rights and David's financial future was looking very secure. *Their* future, he corrected himself. There were days when Taylor still found it difficult to believe that David was really going to be living with him.

"Is your mum planning anything for when he gets here?" Jason asked, a gleam in his eye.

Taylor chuckled. "Oh God. She and Dad have this huge family party planned out. David won't know what hit him." He couldn't resist peeking at his phone once more. Nothing. He sighed and brought his attention back to his friends. "You should have seen David and Dad talking via Skype the other week." David had called his dad to have a chat, and it had ended up being a rather serious discussion. "I think Dad was doing the whole 'what are your intentions toward my son' routine."

Shane coughed suddenly, his cheeks bright red.

Taylor regarded him intently. "Yeah, you may well cough, Shane Richmond. I heard all about your little chat with my boyfriend." He arched his eyebrows and Shane bit his lower lip.

"Has David finished his manuscript yet?" asked Mark.

Taylor grinned. "Which one? He's half way through the latest James Blanchette masterpiece, but he finally finished the gay romance and he's submitted it to a publishing company in the States, under his real name." He snickered. "David figured the world wasn't ready to find out that James Blanchette is really gay. It will be interesting to see if he's as successful writing as David Hannon."

"Of course he will be," Mark said with a smile. "He's a damn good writer." Taylor favored him with a grateful glance. When he'd finally shared David's secret with them—once David had given him the go-ahead to do so—Mark had asked to borrow one of Taylor's books. Mark had quickly become a fan.

"And of course, he's not the only writer in the family, is he?" Shane teased.

Taylor felt his cheeks heating up. David had finally persuaded him to send his poetry to a publisher in New York. They were still waiting to hear if he'd been successful. Taylor was trying not to chew his nails down to the quick. He knew it could be quite a while before he heard anything, and David had already given him a list of alternative publishers in anticipation of the rejection slip. Taylor still couldn't believe he'd actually had the nerve to submit his poems.

Taylor's phone warbled and he pounced on it.

Eric laughed. "So keen. Wonder if they'll still be like this after ten years together."

Jason's expression was suddenly wistful. "Knowing these two? They'll still be like this when they're pensioners."

Taylor looked up in surprise. "That's a lovely thing to say, Jase." Jason blushed. Taylor opened the message and smiled. "Aw."

"What does lover boy say this time?" Eric demanded. "Come on, you *know* you're going to tell us anyway."

Taylor smiled. "It says, 'Miss you babe.'" His friends smiled. Taylor's fingers flew over the buttons. *When can you be here?* He awaited David's reply eagerly. Surely it couldn't be long now.

Seconds later he had a reply. *Sooner than you think.*

Taylor's heart beat faster. It looked as though they were finally getting somewhere.

Can't wait to see you, he typed. He hugged the phone to his chest. Although they talked every night via Skype, it wasn't the same. He longed to hold David in his arms, not to mention all the time he was planning to spend in bed with him. It had been a *very* long four weeks, three days, eleven hours and… fifty minutes. He smiled to himself. **Really* can't wait to see you.*

Then turn around came back the cryptic reply. Taylor stared at the message, his brow furrowed. It didn't make sense. His phone warbled again. *Taylor. Behind you.*

Taylor's heart hammered. Slowly he turned around and the breath died in his throat. David was standing by the gate at the end of the café, dressed in a warm jacket and jeans.

"Oh my God."

Taylor was up on his feet and flying through the café to where David stood with outstretched arms. Taylor launched himself at his lover, leaping into his arms and seizing his mouth in a passionate kiss, David's arms wrapped tightly around him.

"Oh God, it's so good to see you," David gasped out between kisses, clutching Taylor to him as if he were afraid to let him out of his sight. Taylor kissed David's cheeks, eyelids, forehead and neck. David was really there. "Love you so much, babe."

Taylor's heart rejoiced to hear those words from his lover's lips. "Love you, too." They kissed, oblivious to everyone and everything—until Shane's wry chuckle broke through.

David released Taylor and slipped an arm around his waist. He raised his hand in greeting to the others who had walked up behind Taylor. "Hi guys." Taylor leaned against him, unwilling to break their connection. Eric and Shane nodded toward him, and Mark and Jason waved back.

Taylor looked around. "Where's all your stuff?"

David groaned. "You think I was about to *cripple* myself trying to lug three suitcases down those steps? They're in the rental car at the top." He winked. "I was hoping to find some big, strong guys to give me a hand."

Eric burst into laughter. "And that's our cue to leave." Everyone joined in. He grinned at David and held out his hand. "C'mon, give me your keys. We'll go up and fetch down your suitcases."

David shook his head. "I was joking, Eric."

Eric chuckled.

"But I wasn't. Besides, the way *you're* going, you won't be able to let go of Taylor long enough to fetch them, so we'll save you the trouble." He winked at the others. "You can owe us a pint—provided you can tear yourself away from your boyfriend for long enough."

David laughed and threw him a set of keys. "The registration number is on the keyring."

Eric gestured to the others. "Come on, guys, let's help out the newlyweds." Amid chuckles the four friends made their way out of the café, each patting David on the arm as they passed by.

David and Taylor walked slowly along the path to West View, David's arm still around Taylor's waist.

David was chuckling and shaking his head. "Newlyweds."

"Why didn't you tell me you were coming?" Taylor demanded.

David smiled. "I wanted to surprise you." His eyes gleamed. "Did it work?"

Taylor beamed. "The best surprise ever." He leaned his head against David's shoulder. "So how long are you here for this time?"

David sighed. "Until they throw me out of the country, I guess." He kissed the top of Taylor's head. "God, I missed you." He stared up at the house. "I missed this place too."

Taylor reached down and took his hand. "I missed you, too. I made a startling discovery while you were away."

"Oh yeah?" inquired David. "And what was that?"

"That pop group The Police had it nailed all those years ago. In the words of their song, 'a bed's too big without you.'"

David smiled.

"Once the guys have brought down my cases, and we've chatted for a while, I'm gonna have you in that bed about two minutes after they've gone out the door."

"It'll take you that long?" joked Taylor, although his cock was already hardening at the thought.

David pulled Taylor to him, molding him to his lean, firm body. "And about two minutes after *that*, I'm gonna be inside you, making love to you."

Taylor tried not to moan at the idea. "Oh God, yes," he whispered. He led David up the boat ramp and under the porch.

David stood looking around at the bay as Taylor fumbled with his keys. He smiled. "You're not the only one who made a discovery or two. I had an epiphany of my own."

Taylor pushed open the front door. "And what was that?" he said, turning to face David, unable to keep the sappy grin from his face.

"That old saying is so true. Home is where the heart is."

Taylor held out his hand and David took it. Taylor stepped across the threshold and gave David a warm, loving smile as he led him into the house.

"Then welcome home."

The End

About the author

Born and raised in the north-west of England, K.C.Wells always loved writing. Words were important. Full stop. However, when childhood gave way to adulthood, the writing ceased, as life got in the way.

K.C. discovered erotic fiction in 2009, where the purchase of a ménage storyline led to the startling discovery that reading about men in love was damn hot. In 2012, arriving at a really low point in life led to the desperate need to do something creative. An even bigger discovery waited in the wings – *writing* about men in love was even hotter...

K.C. now writes full-time and is loving every minute of her new career.

The laptop still has no idea of what hit it... it only knows that it wants a rest, please. And it now has to get used to the idea that where K.C goes, it goes.

K.C. can be reached via email (**k.c.wells@btinternet.com**), on Facebook (**http://www.facebook.com/KCWellsWorld**) or through comments at the K.C.Wells website (**www.kcwellsworld.com**) K.C. loves to hear from readers.

Printed in Great Britain
by Amazon

56906216R00219